"THE PEDESTRIAN" by Ray Bradbury
When walking becomes a thing of the past, is anyone safe
on the streets?

"THE MOON IS GREEN" by Fritz Leiber
After the bombs, they clung to the safety of the dark world
within . . . till a stranger showed one woman the way to
the light.

"WHAT HAVE I DONE?" by Mark Clifton
When the aliens chose him as a mentor, would he prove
the betrayer of humanity—or its savior?

"COST OF LIVING" by Robert Sheckley
Was modernization a boon to mankind, or was the price of
the future too high to pay?

These are just four of the special tours into the many realms
of science fiction which await you when—

**ISAAC ASIMOV
PRESENTS
THE GREAT SF STORIES
14**

Isaac Asimov Presents The Great SF Stories #14 (1952)

Edited by Isaac Asimov
and Martin H. Greenberg

DAW BOOKS, INC.
DONALD A. WOLLHEIM, PUBLISHER

1633 Broadway, New York, NY 10019

DAW Collectors Book No. 660.

First DAW Printing, January 1986

1 2 3 4 5 6 7 8 9

Acknowledgments

CONTENTS

1952 INTRODUCTION

In the world outside reality it was another violent year, marked by war and revolution. On February 6 King George VI of Great Britain died and his daughter Elizabeth became Queen Elizabeth II. Late that month Great Britain announced it had manufactured its own atomic weapon; on March 30, President Harry S. Truman confirmed that he would not run for office in the upcoming election, and later announced that the United States had tested the first hydrogen bomb in the Pacific.

On April 28 Matthew Ridgway became Supreme Allied Commander of NATO foces, replacing General Dwight D. Eisenhower, who had his eye on politics. Egypt experienced its first and so far only military coup in July as the "Free Officers" under Mohammed Neguib and Gamal Abdul Nasser overthrew the monarchy; King Farouk sailed into the sunset on the royal yacht, taking with him what was believed to be the world's largest pornography collection. Also in the Middle East, Prince Hussain became King of Jordan when his older brother, Talal, was declared insane. On September 11, Ethiopia officially acquired the coastal strip known as Eritrea, the scene of a major civil war and tragedy as these words are written.

October saw the declaration of a "State of Emergency" in Kenya, as members of the Kikuyu tribe, organized as the "Mau Mau" launched attacks against British citizens and property. November 4 saw an enormous Republican victory in the Presidential contest, as Eisenhower defeated Adlai Stevenson of Illinois 442 electoral votes to 89.

The year ended with a show trial of Czech Communist Party leaders, including Rudolf Slansky, for treason, and the visit of President-elect Eisenhower to Korea, fulfilling a campaign pledge. Fighting in that war-torn land continued throughout 1952.

During 1952 Ernest Hemingway published *The Old Man and the Sea*, Felix Bloch and Edward M. Purcell of the United States won the Nobel Prize for Physics for their investigations into the nature of magnetic fields, and Eddie Arcaro aboard Hill Gail won the Kentucky Derby. Jacob Epstein sculpted *Madonna and Child*, Ralph Ellison published *The Invisible Man*, and radioactive carbon tests for dating artifacts were first used in a systematic fashion. Popular song hits included "Your Cheating Heart," "Jambalaya," "Wheel of Fortune," and "I Saw Mommy Kissing Santa Claus."

The first contraceptive pills were made in 1952. Rocky Marciano beat Jersey Joe Walcott for the heavyweight boxing title, Selman A. Waksman was rewarded for his discovery of streptomycin with the Nobel prize for Medicine and Physiology, and Chagall painted "The Green Night," Marianne Moore won a Pulitzer Prize for her *Collected Poems*. The United States won the most gold medals at the 1952 summer Olympic Games, but the star was the Czech distance runner Emil Zatopek. Popular films of the year, and some that were just good and not popular, were "High Noon," with Gary Cooper in his greatest role, "The Greatest Show on Earth," "Limelight," "Othello," and "This Is Cinerama," an attempt by Hollywood to stem the seemingly irresistible tide of television and its effects on the habits of the American people.

In 1952 Samuel Beckett published *Waiting for Godot*, Albert Schweitzer won the Nobel Peace Prize, the great Julius Boros won the U.S. Open Gold Championship, the Brooklyn Dodgers would have to wait till next year as they dropped the World Series to the Yankees four games to three. *East of Eden* by John Steinbeck, *The Silver Chalice* by Thomas B. Costain, and *Giant* by Edna Ferber were best sellers, while Norman Vincent Peale published *The Power of Positive Thinking*.

Death took Eva Peron, George Santayana, Alfred Einstein (the musicologist), John Dewey, and Chaim Weizmann.

Mel Brooks may still have been Melvin Kaminsky, but we are beginning to doubt it.

In the real world it was another excellent year as science fiction prepared for the paperback explosion that was about to occur, and Donald Day contributed some fine fan scholarship to the field with his pioneering *The Index to the Science Fiction Magazines*, 1926-1950.

Notable books published in 1952 included *Limbo* by Bernard

Wolfe, *The Legion of Time* by Jack Williamson (serialized much earlier), *Murder in Millennium VI* by Curme Gray, the magnificent *City* by Clifford D. Simak, *You Shall Know Them* by Vercors, *Player Piano* by Kurt Vonnegut, Jr., *Jack of Eagles* by James Blish, and *The Sound of His Horn* by Sarban. Three major novels were serialized in 1952: *Gravy Planet* (later renamed *The Space Merchants*) by Frederik Pohl and C. M. Kornbluth, *The Demolished Man* by Alfred Bester, and *The Currents of Space* by Isaac Asimov. Length considerations prevent us from including three wonderful novellas in this book—"Surface Tension" by James Blish, "Bring the Jubilee" by Ward Moore, and "Baby Is Three" by Theodore Sturgeon.

New sf magazines rolled off the presses in increasing numbers in 1952, highlighted by the appearance of *If*, under the editorship of the underrated Paul Fairman and *Fantastic*, a companion to *Amazing Stories*. Lester del Rey was in the editor's chair of two other ventures, *Space Science Fiction* and *Science Fiction Adventures*. British readers got another homegrown product as *Nebula Science Fiction* was born, while *Space Stories*, *Dynamic Science Fiction*, and *Fantastic Science Fiction* (not the *Fantastic* mentioned above) helped fill newsstands in the United States, although the last-named magazine folded the same year, as did the slightly longer established *Marvel Science Fiction*.

In the real world, more important people made their maiden voyages into reality: in March—Daniel F. Galouye with "Rebirth"; in April—Frank Herbert with "Looking for Something" and Ron Goulart with "Letters to the Editor"; in May (a really great month)—Daniel Keyes with "Precedent," Robert Sheckley with "Final Examination," and Mark Clifton with "What Have I Done?" (included in this volume); in June—"The Spectre General" by Theodore Cogswell; in July—"Beyond Lies the Wub" by Philip K. Dick; in August—the revolutionary "The Lovers" by Philip José Farmer; in November—"Walk to the World" by Algis Budrys; and in December—"The Reluctant Weapon" by Howard L. Myers.

Fantastic films (in terms of category, not quality) included *Captive Women*, *Invasion U.S.A.*, *Red Planet Mars*, the ever in our hearts *Bela Lugosi Meets A Brooklyn Gorilla*, the delightful *Monkey Business*, and the best of the year, the wonderful *The Man in the White Suit*, starring Alec Guinness.

The Family gathered in Chicago for the Tenth World Science Fiction Convention.

Distant Wings were beating as Douglas Adams and Lisa Tuttle were born.

Let us travel back to that honored year of 1952 and enjoy the best stories that the real world bequeathed to us.

THE PEDESTRIAN

Ray Bradbury (1920–)

It has become somewhat fashionable to take cheap shots at Ray Bradbury and downplay his position in the history of modern science fiction. I don't agree with those critics who often point out the lack of accurate science in his stories. Bradbury, like Harlan Ellison, is a fantasist, a writer who grabs you by the throat or the heart and hangs on. Besides, his social philosophy happens to agree with mine.

The early 1950s were good years for him professionally, with deserved awards and critical acclaim. His *The Illustrated Man* (1951) and *The Golden Apples of the Sun* (1953) contain much of his best work from these years, and should be on the shelf of everyone who cares about this field.

"The Pedestrian" is one of his most famous stories, a textbook example of the kind of social extrapolation at which science fiction excells, and, with the advent of cable television and VCRs, a haunting reminder of what yet might be. (MHG)

Ray was once stopped by a policeman for the crime of being a pedestrian and, therefore, a suspicious character, so the story has the mark of personal bitterness on it.

Ray and I are of an age and share memories. We both remember how it was before World War II, when cars were much fewer and air-conditioning, except in movie theaters, was nonexistent. The streets were full of walking people at all times in our cities (day and night in New York). What's more, on summer evenings, the population was sitting out in front of the houses in full force, for it was unbearably hot inside.

The result? One could walk anywhere in safety for one was always surrounded by crowds.

As automobiles increased in number and air-conditioning became common, the sidewalks thinned out and became depopulated. Crime on the streets was easier and the sidewalks grew even more depopulated in consequence. Now, outside working hours, the streets of the city are cavernous and echoing.

My recipe for controlling urban crime, then. Easy! Bring back the pedestrian! Turn off the air-conditioners! (IA)

To enter out into that silence that was the city at eight o'clock of a misty evening in November, to put your feet upon that buckling concrete walk, to step over grassy seams and make your way, hands in pockets, through the silences, that was what Mr. Leonard Mead most dearly loved to do. He would stand upon the corner of an intersection and peer down long moonlit avenues of sidewalk in four directions, deciding which way to go, but it really made no difference; he was alone in this world of A.D. 2053, or as good as alone, and with a final decision made, a path selected, he would stride off, sending patterns of frosty air before him like the smoke of a cigar.

Sometimes he would walk for hours and miles and return only at midnight to his house. And on his way he would see the cottages and homes with their dark windows, and it was not unequal to walking through a graveyard where only the faintest glimmers of firefly light appeared in flickers behind the windows. Suddenly gray phantoms seemed to manifest upon inner room walls where a curtain was still undrawn against the night, or there were whisperings and murmurs where a window in a tomblike building was still open.

Mr. Leonard Mead would pause, cock his head, listen, look, and march on, his feet making no noise on the lumpy walk. For long ago he had wisely changed to sneakers when strolling at night, because the dogs in intermittent squads would parallel his journey with barkings if he wore hard heels, and lights might click on and faces appear and an entire street be startled by the passing of a lone figure, himself, in the early November evening.

On this particular evening he began his journey in a westerly direction, toward the hidden sea. There was a good crystal frost in the air; it cut the nose and made the lungs blaze like a Christmas tree inside; you could feel the cold light going on and off, all the branches filled with invisible snow. He listened to the faint push of his soft shoes through autumn leaves with satisfaction, and whistled a cold quiet whistle between his teeth, occasionally picking up a leaf as he passed, examining its skeletal pattern in the infrequent lamplights as he went on, smelling its rusty smell.

"Hello, in there," he whispered to every house on every side as he moved. "What's up tonight on Channel 4, Channel 7, Channel 9? Where are the cowboys rushing, and do I see the United States Cavalry over the next hill to the rescue?"

The street was silent and long and empty, with only his shadow moving like the shadow of a hawk in midcountry. If he closed his eyes and stood very still, frozen, he could imagine himself upon the center of a plain, wintry, windless American desert with no house in a thousand miles, and only dry river beds, the streets, for company.

"What is it now?" he asked the houses, noticing his wrist watch. "Eight-thirty P.M.? Time for a dozen assorted murders? A quiz? A revue? A comedian falling off the stage?"

Was that a murmur of laughter from within a moon-white house? He hesitated, but went on when nothing more happened. He stumbled over a particularly uneven section of sidewalk. The cement was vanishing under flowers and grass. In ten years of walking by night or day, for thousands of miles, he had never met another person walking, not once in all that time.

He came to a cloverleaf intersection which stood silent where two main highways crossed the town. During the day it was a thunderous surge of cars, the gas stations open, a great insect rustling and a ceaseless jockeying for position as the scarab-beetles, a faint incense puttering from their exhausts, skimmed homeward to the far directions. But now these highways, too, were like streams in a dry season, all stone and bed and moon radiance.

He turned back on a side street, cricling around toward his home. He was within a block of his destination when the lone car turned a corner quite suddenly and flashed a fierce white cone of light upon him. He stood entranced, not unlike a night moth, stunned by the illumination, and then drawn toward it.

A metallic voice called to him:

"Stand still. Stay where you are! Don't move!"

He halted.

"Put up your hands!"

"But—" he said.

"Your hands up! Or we'll shoot!"

The police, of course, but what a rare, incredible thing; in a city of three million, there was only *one* police car left, wasn't that correct? Ever since a year ago, 2052, the election year, the force had been cut down from three cars to one. Crime was ebbing; there was no need now for the police, save for this one lone car wandering and wandering the empty streets.

"Your name?" said the police car in a metallic whisper. He couldn't see the men in it for the bright light in his eyes.

"Leonard Mead," he said.

"Speak up!"

"Leonard Mead!"

"Business or profession?"

"I guess you'd call me a writer."

"No profession," said the police car, as if talking to itself. The light held him fixed, like a museum specimen, needle thrust through chest.

"You might say that," said Mr. Mead. He hadn't written in years. Magazines and books didn't sell anymore. Everything went on in the tomblike houses at night now, he thought, continuing his fancy. The tombs, ill-lit by television light, where the people sat like the dead, the gray or multicolored lights touching their faces, but never really touching *them*."

"No profession," said the phonograph voice, hissing. "What are you doing out?"

"Walking," said Leonard Mead.

"Walking!"

"Just walking," he said simply, but his face felt cold.

"Walking, just walking, walking?"

"Yes, sir."

"Walking where? For what?"

"Walking for air. Walking to see."

"Your address!"

"Eleven South Saint James Street."

"And there is air *in* your house, you have an *air-conditioner*, Mr. Mead?"

"Yes."

"And you have a viewing screen in your house to see with?"

"No."

"No?" There was a crackling quiet that in itself was an accusation.

"Are you married, Mr. Mead?"

"No."

"Not married," said the police voice behind the fiery beam. The moon was high and clear among the stars and the houses were gray and silent.

"Nobody wanted me," said Leonard Mead with a smile.

"Don't speak unless you're spoken to!"

Leonard Mead waited in the cold night.

"Just *walking*, Mr. Mead?"

"Yes."

"But you haven't explained for what purpose."

"I explained; for air, and to see, and just to walk."

"Have you done this often?"

"Every night for years."

The police car sat in the center of the street with its radio throat faintly humming.

"Well, Mr. Mead," it said.

"Is that all?" he asked politely.

"Yes," said the voice. "Here." There was a sigh, a pop. The back door of the police car sprang wide. "Get in."

"Wait a minute, I haven't done anything!"

"Get in."

"I protest!"

"Mr. Mead."

He walked like a man suddenly drunk. As he passed the front window of the car he looked in. As he had expected there was no one in the front seat, no one in the car at all.

"Get in."

He put his hand to the door and peered into the back seat, which was a little cell, a little black jail with bars. It smelled of riveted steel. It smelled of harsh antiseptic; it smelled too clean and hard and metallic. There was nothing soft there.

"Now if you have a wife to give you an alibi," said the iron voice. "But—"

"Where are you taking me?"

The car hesitated, or rather gave a faint whirring click, as if information, somewhere, was dropping card by punch-slotted card under electric eyes. "To the Psychiatric Center for Research on Regressive Tendencies."

He got in. The door shut with a soft thud. The police car rolled through the night avenues, flashing its dim lights ahead.

They passed one house on one street a moment later, one house in an entire city of houses that were dark, but this one particular house had all of its electric lights brightly lit, every window a loud yellow illumination, square and warm in the cool darkness.

"That's *my* house," said Leonard Mead.

No one answered him.

The car moved down the empty river-bed streets and off away, leaving the empty streets with the empty sidewalks, and no sound and no motion all the rest of the chill November night.

THE MOON IS GREEN

Fritz Leiber (1911–)

I'd like to take a moment to pay my respects and offer thanks to Everett F. Bleiler and T. E. Dikty, two gentlemen who pioneered the "Year's Best" concept in science fiction. Their very good series lasted for nine years (the last three volumes were edited by Dikty alone), 1949-1957, and they also included interesting notes, introductions, and guest essays. Everett F. Bleiler is still one of the field's most distinguished critics and editors.

It is interesting to note that of the nineteen stories in this book only four were among the fifteen in their fine *The Best Science Fiction Stories: 1953* (which covers 1952): "Command Performance" by Walter M. Miller, Jr., "Game for Blondes" by John D. MacDonald, "Fast Falls the Eventide" by Eric Frank Russell, and Fritz Leiber's "The Moon Is Green," which you are about to read, and which, for some puzzling reason, has been rarely reprinted. (MHG)

My own feeling as to why "The Moon Is Green" is rarely reprinted is that people don't want to know the danger. In 1952 the danger was still new and it seemed the very stuff of science fiction, but that didn't mean people wanted to hear it.

A third of a century has passed since Fritz wrote the story and the danger is far greater. We have bigger and better nuclear bombs, missiles that can carry them anywhere, and consequences that are worse than anything Fritz could have imagined.

There is good reason to think that even a moderate nuclear exchange will send so much dust into the stratosphere as to cut off sunlight for a dangerously long time and kill most or all of life on Earth.

19

There is, however, a solution to this "nuclear winter." For me, and others who think as I do, there is only one solution—no nuclear war under any circumstances. Even an overwhelming first strike is likely to kill not only the stricken, but the striker, and all the neutrals, too.

To those belligerent people who favor a "strong" defense, the solution is to deny the nuclear winter will take place and to call those who say it will happen harsh names. It is so much easier to deny, rather than to face even the possibility of an unpleasant truth, that "The Moon Is Green" is not likely to be much in demand except to those old-fashioned enough to believe that facing an unpleasant truth may be the key to survival. (IA)

"Effie! What the devil are you up to?"

Her husband's voice, chopping through her mood of terrified rapture, made her heart jump like a startled cat, yet by some miracle of feminine self-control her body did not show a tremor.

Dear God, she thought, *he mustn't see it. It's so beautiful, and he always kills beauty.*

"I'm just looking at the Moon," she said listlessly. "It's green."

Mustn't, mustn't see it. And now, with luck, he wouldn't. For the face, as if it also heard and sensed the menace in the voice, was moving back from the window's glow into the outside dark, but slowly, reluctantly, and still faunlike, pleading, cajoling, tempting, and incredibly beautiful.

"Close the shutters at once, you little fool, and come away from the window!"

"Green as a beer bottle," she went on dreamily, "green as emeralds, green as leaves with sunshine striking through them and green grass to lie on." She couldn't help saying those last words. They were her token to the face, even though it couldn't hear.

"Effie!"

She knew what that last tone meant. Wearily she swung shut the ponderous lead inner shutters and drove home the heavy bolts. That hurt her fingers; it always did, but he mustn't know that.

"You know that those shutters are not to be touched! Not for five more years at least!"

"I only wanted to look at the Moon," she said, turning around, and then it was all gone—the face, the night, the Moon, the magic—and she was back in the grubby, stale little hole, facing an angry, stale little man. It was then that the eternal thud of the air-conditioning fans and the crackle of the electrostatic precipitators that sieved out the dust reached her consciousness again like the bite of a dentist's drill.

"Only wanted to look at the Moon!" he mimicked her in falsetto. "Only wanted to die like a little fool and make me that much more ashamed of you!" Then his voice went gruff and professional. "Here, count yourself."

She silently took the Geiger counter he held at arm's length, waited until it settled down to a steady ticking slower than a clock—due only to cosmic rays and indicating nothing dangerous—and then began to comb her body with the instrument. First her head and shoulders, then out along her arms and back along their under side. There was something oddly voluptuous about her movements, although her features were gray and sagging.

The ticking did not change its tempo until she came to her waist. Then it suddenly spurted, clicking faster and faster. Her husband gave an excited grunt, took a quick step forward, froze. She goggled for a moment in fear, then grinned foolishly, dug in the pocket of her grimy apron and guiltily pulled out a wristwatch.

He grabbed it as it dangled from her fingers, saw that it had a radium dial, cursed, heaved it up as if to smash it on the floor, but instead put it carefully on the table.

"You imbecile, you incredible imbecile," he softly chanted to himself through clenched teeth, with eyes half closed.

She shrugged faintly, put the Geiger counter on the table, and stood there slumped.

He waited until the chanting had soothed his anger before speaking again. He said quietly, "I do suppose you still realize the sort of world you're living in?"

*   *   *

She nodded slowly, staring at nothingness. Oh, she realized all right, realized only too well. It was the world that hadn't realized. The world that had gone on stockpiling hydrogen bombs. The world that had put those bombs in cobalt shells, although it had promised it wouldn't, because the cobalt made them much more terrible and cost no more. The world that had started throwing those bombs, always telling itself that it hadn't thrown enough of them yet to make the air really dangerous with the deadly radioactive dust that came from the cobalt. Thrown them and kept on throwing until the danger point, where air and ground would become fatal to all human life, was approached.

Then, for about a month, the two great enemy groups had hesitated. And then each, unknown to the other, had decided it could risk one last gigantic and decisive attack without exceeding the danger point. It had been planned to strip off the cobalt cases, but someone forgot and then there wasn't time. Besides, the military scientists of each group were confident that the lands of the other had got the most dust. The two attacks came within an hour of each other.

After that, the Fury. The Fury of doomed men who think only of taking with them as many as possible of the enemy, and in this case—they hoped—all. The Fury of suicides who know they have botched up life for good. The Fury of cocksure men who realized they have been outsmarted by fate, the enemy, and themselves, and know that they will never be able to improvise a defense when arraigned before the high court of history—and whose unadmitted hope is that there will be no high court of history left to arraign them. More cobalt bombs were dropped during the Fury than in all the preceding years of the war.

After the Fury, the Terror. Men and women with death sifting into their bones through their nostrils and skin, fighting for bare survival under a dust-hazed sky that played fantastic tricks with the light of Sun and Moon, like the dust from Krakatoa that drifted around the world for years. Cities, countryside, and air were alike poisoned, alive with deadly radiation.

The only realistic chance for continued existence was to retire, for the five or ten years the radiation would remain deadly, to some well-sealed and radiation-shielded place that must also be copiously supplied with food, water, power, and a means of air-conditioning.

Such places were prepared by the far-seeing, seized by the

stronger, defended by them in turn against the desperate hordes of the dying . . . until there were no more of those.

After that, only the waiting, the enduring. A mole's existence, without beauty or tenderness, but with fear and guilt as constant companions. Never to see the sun, to walk among the trees—or even know if there were still trees.

Oh, yes, she realized what the world was like.

"You understand, too, I suppose, that we were allowed to reclaim this ground-level apartment only because the Committee believed us to be responsible people, and because I've been making a damn good showing lately?"

"Yes, Hank."

"I thought you were eager for privacy. You want to go back to the basement tenements?"

God, no! Anything rather than that fetid huddling, that shameless communal sprawl. And yet, was this so much better? The nearness to the surface was meaningless; it only tantalized. And the privacy magnified Hank.

She shook her head dutifully and said, "No, Hank."

"Then why aren't you careful? I've told you a million times, Effie, that glass is no protection against the dust that's outside that window. The lead shutter must never be touched! If you make one single slip like that and it gets around, the Committee will send us back to the lower levels without blinking an eye. And they'll think twice before trusting me with any important jobs."

"I'm sorry, Hank."

"Sorry? What's the good of being sorry? The only thing that counts is never to make a slip! Why the devil do you do such things, Effie? What drives you to it?"

She swallowed. "It's just that it's so dreadful being cooped up like this," she said hesitatingly, "shut away from the sky and the sun. I'm just hungry for a little beauty."

"And do you suppose I'm not?" he demanded. "Don't you suppose I want to get outside, too, and be carefree and have a good time? But I'm not so damn selfish about it. I want my children to enjoy the sun, and my children's children. Don't you see that that's the all-important thing and that we have to behave like mature adults and make sacrifices for it?"

"Yes, Hank."

He surveyed her slumped figure, her lined and listless face. "You're a fine one to talk about hunger for beauty," he told her.

Then his voice grew softer, more deliberate. "You haven't forgotten, have you, Effie, that until last month the Committee was so concerned about sterility? That they were about to enter my name on the list of those waiting to be allotted a free woman? Very high on the list, too!"

She could nod even at that one, but not while looking at him. She turned away. She knew very well that the Committee was justified in worrying about the birth rate. When the community finally moved back to the surface again, each additional healthy young person would be an asset, not only in the struggle for bare survival, but in the resumed war against Communism which some of the Committee members still counted on.

It was natural that they should view a sterile woman with disfavor, and not only because of the waste of her husband's germplasm, but because sterility might indicate that she had suffered more than the average from radiation. In that case, if she did bear children later on, they would be more apt to carry a defective heredity, producing an undue number of monsters and freaks in future generations, and so contaminating the race.

Of course she understood it. She could hardly remember the time when she didn't. Years ago? Centuries? There wasn't much difference in a place where time was endless.

His lecture finished, her husband smiled and grew almost cheerful.

"Now that you're going to have a child, that's all in the background again. Do you know, Effie, that when I first came in, I had some very good news for you? I'm to become a member of the Junior Committee and the announcement will be made at the banquet tonight." He cut short her mumbled congratulations. "So brighten yourself up and put on your best dress. I want the other Juniors to see what a handsome wife the new member has got." He paused. "Well, get a move on!"

She spoke with difficulty, still not looking at him. "I'm terribly sorry, Hank, but you'll have to go alone. I'm not well."

He straightened up with an indignant jerk. "There you go again! First that infantile, inexcusable business of the shutters,and now this! No feeling for my reputation at all. Don't be ridiculous, Effie. You're coming!"

"Terribly sorry," she repeated blindly, "but I really can't. I'd just be sick. I wouldn't make you proud of me at all."

"Of course you won't," he retorted sharply. "As it is, I have to spend half my energy running around making excuses for you—why you're so odd, why you always seem to be ailing, why you're always stupid and snobbish and say the wrong thing. But tonight's really important, Effie. It will cause a lot of bad comment if the new member's wife isn't present. You know how just a hint of sickness starts the old radiation-disease rumor going. You've *got* to come, Effie."

She shook her head helplessly.

"Oh, for heaven's sake, come on!" he shouted, advancing on her. "This is just a silly mood. As soon as you get going, you'll snap out of it. There's nothing really wrong with you at all."

He put his hand on her shoulder to touch her around, and at his touch her face suddenly grew so desperate and gray that for a moment he was alarmed in spite of himself.

"Really?" he asked, almost with a note of concern.

She nodded miserably.

"Hmm!" He stepped back and strode about irresolutely. "Well, of course, if that's the way it is . . ." He checked himself and a sad smile crossed his face. "So you don't care enough about your old husband's success to make one supreme effort in spite of feeling bad?"

Again the helpless headshake. "I just can't go out tonight, under any circumstances." And her gaze stole toward the lead shutters.

He was about to say something when he caught the direction of her gaze. His eyebrows jumped. For seconds he stared at her incredulously, as if some completely new and almost unbelievable possibility had popped into his mind. The look of incredulity slowly faded, to be replaced by a harder, more calculating expression. But when he spoke again, his voice was shockingly bright and kind.

"Well, it can't be helped, naturally, and I certainly wouldn't want you to go if you weren't able to enjoy it. So you hop right into bed and get a good rest. I'll run over to the men's dorm to freshen up. No, really, I don't want you to have to make any effort at all. Incidentally, Jim Barnes isn't going to be able to come to the banquet either—touch of the old 'flu, he tells me, of all things."

He watched her closely as he mentioned the other man's name, but she didn't react noticeably. In fact, she hardly seemed to be hearing his chatter.

"I got a bit sharp with you, I'm afraid, Effie," he continued contritely. "I'm sorry about that. I was excited about my new job and I guess that was why things upset me. Made me feel let down when I found you weren't feeling as good as I was. Selfish of me. Now you get into bed right away and get well. Don't worry about me a bit. I know you'd come if you possibly could. And I know you'll be thinking about me. Well, I must be off now."

He started toward her, as if to embrace her, then seemed to think better of it. He turned back at the doorway and said, emphasizing the words, "You'll be completely alone for the next four hours." He waited for her nod, then bounced out.

She stood still until his footsteps died away. Then she straightened up, walked over to where he'd put down the wristwatch, picked it up and smashed it hard on the floor. The crystal shattered, the case flew apart, and something went *zing!*

She stood there breathing heavily. Slowly her sagged features lifted, formed themselves into the beginning of a smile. She stole another look at the shutters. The smile became more definite. She felt her hair, wet her fingers and ran them along her hairline and back over her ears. After wiping her hands on her apron, she took it off. She straightened her dress, lifted her head with a little flourish, and stepped smartly toward the window.

Then her face went miserable again and her steps slowed.

No, it couldn't be, and it won't be, she told herself. It had been just an illusion, a silly romantic dream that she had somehow projected out of her beauty-starved mind and given a moment's false reality. There couldn't be anything alive outside. There hadn't been for two whole years.

And if there conceivably were, it would be something altogether horrible. She remembered some of the pariahs—hairless, witless creatures, with radiation welts crawling over their bodies like worms, who had come begging for succor during the last months of the Terror—and been shot down. How they must have hated the people in refuges!

But even as she was thinking these things, her fingers were caressing the bolts, gingerly drawing them, and she was opening the shutters gently, apprehensively.

No, there couldn't be anything outside, she assured herself wryly, peering out into the green night. Even her fears had been groundless.

But the face came floating up toward the window. She started back in terror, then checked herself.

For the face wasn't horrible at all, only very thin, with full lips and large eyes and a thin proud nose like the jutting beak of a bird. And no radiation welts or scars marred the skin, olive in the tempered moonlight. It looked, in fact, just as it had when she had seen it the first time.

For a long moment the face stared deep, deep into her brain. Then the full lips smiled and a half-clenched, thin-fingered hand materialized itself from the green darkness and rapped twice on the grimy pane.

Her heart pounding, she furiously worked the little crank that opened the window. It came unstuck from the frame with a tiny explosion of dust and a *zing* like that of the watch, only louder. A moment later it swung open wide and a puff of incredibly fresh air caressed her face and the inside of her nostrils, stinging her eyes with unanticipated tears.

The man outside balanced on the sill, crouching like a faun, head high, one elbow on knee. He was dressed in scarred, snug trousers and an old sweater.

"Is it tears I get for a welcome?" he mocked her gently in a musical voice. "Or are those only to greet God's own breath, the air?"

He swung down inside and now she could see he was tall. Turning, he snapped his fingers and called, "Come, puss."

A black cat with a twisted stump of a tail and feet like small boxing gloves and ears almost as big as rabbits' hopped clumsily in view. He lifted it down, gave it a pat. Then, nodding familiarly to Effie, he unstrapped a little pack from his back and laid it on the table.

She couldn't move. She even found it hard to breathe.

"The window," she finally managed to get out.

He looked at her inquiringly, caught the direction of her stabbing finger. Moving without haste, he went over and closed it carelessly.

"The shutters, too," she told him, but he ignored that, looking around.

"It's a snug enough place you and your man have," he commented. "Or is it that this is a free-love town or a harem spot, or just a military post?" He checked her before she could answer. "But let's not be talking about such things now. Soon enough I'll be scared to death for both of us. Best enjoy the kick of meeting, which is always good for twenty minutes at the least." He smiled at her rather shyly. "Have you food? Good, then bring it."

She set cold meat and some precious canned bread before him and had water heating for coffee. Before he fell to, she shredded a chunk of meat and put it on the floor for the cat, which left off its sniffing inspection of the walls and ran up eagerly mewing. Then the man began to eat, chewing each mouthful slowly and appreciatively.

From across the table Effie watched him, drinking in his every deft movement, his every cryptic quirk of expression. She attended to making the coffee, but that took only a moment. Finally she could contain herself no longer.

"What's it like up there?" she asked breathlessly. "Outside, I mean."

He looked at her oddly for quite a space. Finally, he said flatly, "Oh, it's a wonderland for sure, more amazing than you tombed folk could ever imagine. A veritable fairyland." And he quickly went on eating.

"No, but really," she pressed.

Noting her eagerness, he smiled and his eyes filled with playful tenderness. "I mean it, on my oath," he assured her. "You think the bombs and the dust made only death and ugliness. That was true at first. But then, just as the doctors foretold, they changed the life in the seeds and loins that were brave enough to stay. Wonders bloomed and walked." He broke off suddenly and asked, "Do any of you ever venture outside?"

"A few of the men are allowed to," she told him, "for short trips in special protective suits, to hunt for canned food and fuels and batteries and things like that."

"Aye, and those blind-souled slugs would never see anything but what they're looking for," he said, nodding bitterly. "They'd never see the garden where a dozen buds blossom where one did before, and the flowers have petals a yard across, with stingless bees big as sparrows gently supping their nectar. Housecats grown spotted and huge as leopards (not little runts like Joe Louis here) stalk through those gardens. But they're gentle beasts, no more harmful than the rainbow-scaled snakes that glide around their paws, for the dust burned all the murder out of them, as it burned itself out.

"I've even made up a little poem about that. It starts, 'Fire can hurt me, or water, or the weight of Earth. But the dust is my friend.' Oh, yes, and then the robins like cockatoos and squirrels like a princess's ermine! All under a treasure chest of Sun and Moon and stars that the dust's magic powder changes from ruby to emerald and sapphire and amethyst and back again. Oh, and then the new children—''

"You're telling the truth?" she interrupted him, her eyes brimming with tears. "You're not making it up?"

"I am not," he assured her solemnly. "And if you could catch a glimpse of one of the new children, you'd never doubt me again. They have long limbs as brown as this coffee would be if it had lots of fresh cream in it, and smiling delicate faces and the whitest teeth and the finest hair. They're so nimble that I—a sprightly man and somewhat enlivened by the dust—feel like a cripple beside them. And their thoughts dance like flames and make me feel a very imbecile.

"Of course, they have seven fingers on each hand and eight toes on each foot, but they're the more beautiful for that. They have large pointed ears that the Sun shines through. They play in the garden, all day long, slipping among the great leaves and blooms, but they're so swift that you can hardly see them, unless one chooses to stand still and look at you. For that matter, you have to look a bit hard for all these things I'm telling you."

"But it is true?" she pleaded.

"Every word of it," he said, looking straight into her eyes. He put down his knife and fork. "What's your name?" he asked softly. "Mine's Patrick."

"Effie," she told him.

He shook his head. "That can't be," he said. Then his face brightened. "Euphemia," he exclaimed. "That's what Effie is short for. Your name is Euphemia." As he said that, looking at her, she suddenly felt beautiful. He got up and came around the table and stretched out his hand toward her.

"Euphemia—" he began.

"Yes?" she answered huskily, shrinking from him a little, but looking up sideways, and very flushed.

"Don't either of you move," Hank said.

The voice was flat and nasal because Hank was wearing a nose respirator that was just long enough to suggest an elephant's trunk. In his right hand was a large blue-black automatic pistol.

They turned their faces to him. Patrick's was abruptly alert, shifty. But Effie's was still smiling tenderly, as if Hank could not break the spell of the magic garden and should be pitied for not knowing about it.

"You little—" Hank began with an almost gleeful fury, calling her several shameful names. He spoke in short phrases,
closing tight his unmasked mouth between them while he sucked
in breath through the respirator. His voice rose in a crescendo.
"And not with a man of the community, but a pariah! A
pariah!"

"I hardly know what you're thinking, man, but you're quite
wrong," Patrick took the opportunity to put in hurriedly,
conciliatingly. "I just happened to be coming by hungry tonight,
a lonely tramp, and knocked at the window. Your wife was a bit
foolish and let kindheartedness get the better of prudence—"

"Don't think you've pulled the wool over my eyes, Effie,"
Hank went on with a screechy laugh, disregarding the other man
completely. "Don't think I don't know why you're suddenly
going to have a child after four long years."

At that moment the cat came nosing up to his feet. Patrick
watched him narrowly, shifting his weight forward a little, but
Hank only kicked the animal aside without taking his eyes off
them.

"Even that business of carrying the wristwatch in your pocket
instead of on your arm," he went on with channeled hysteria.
"A neat bit of camouflage, Effie. Very neat. And telling me it
was my child, when all the while you've been seeing him for
months!"

"Man, you're mad; I've not touched her!" Patrick denied
hotly though still calculatingly, and risked a step forward, stopping when the gun instantly swung his way.

"Pretending you were going to give me a healthy child,"
Hank raved on, "when all the while you knew it would be—
either in body or germ plasm—a thing like *that*!"

He waved his gun at the malformed cat, which had leaped to
the top of the table and was eating the remains of Patrick's food,
though its watchful green eyes were fixed on Hank.

"I should shoot him down!" Hank yelled, between sobbing,
chest-racking inhalations through the mask. "I should kill him
this instant for the contaminated pariah he is!"

All this while Effie had not ceased to smile compassionately.
Now she stood up without haste and went to Patrick's side.
Disregarding his warning, apprehensive glance, she put her arm
lightly around him and faced her husband.

"Then you'd be killing the bringer of the best news we've
ever had," she said, and her voice was like a flood of some

warm sweet liquor in that musty, hate-charged room. "Oh, Hank, forget your silly, wrong jealousy and listen to me. Patrick here has something wonderful to tell us."

Hank stared at her. For once he screamed no reply. It was obvious that he was seeing for the first time how beautiful she had become, and that the realization jolted him terribly.

"What do you mean?" he finally asked unevenly, almost fearfully.

"I mean that we no longer need to fear the dust," she said, and now her smile was radiant. "It never really did hurt people the way the doctors said it would. Remember how it was with me, Hank, the exposure I had and recovered from, although the doctors said I wouldn't at first—and without even losing my hair? Hank, those who were brave enough to stay outside, and who weren't killed by terror and suggestion and panic—they adapted to the dust. They changed, but they changed for the better. Everything—"

"Effie, he told you lies!" Hank interrupted, but still in that same agitated, broken voice, cowed by her beauty.

"Everything that grew or moved was purified," she went on ringingly. "You men going outside have never seen it, because you've never had eyes for it. You've been blinded to beauty, to life itself. And now all the power in the dust has gone and faded, anyway, burned itself out. That's true, isn't it?"

She smiled at Patrick for confirmation. His face was strangely veiled, as if he were calculating obscure changes. He might have given a little nod; at any rate, Effie assumed that he did, for she turned back to her husband.

"You see, Hank? We can all go out now. We need never fear the dust again. Patrick is a living proof of that," she continued triumphantly, standing straighter, holding him a little tighter. "Look at him. Not a scar or a sign, and he's been out in the dust for years. How could he be this way, if the dust hurt the brave? Oh, believe me, Hank! Believe what you see. Test it if you want. Test Patrick here."

"Effie, you're all mixed up. You don't know—" Hank faltered, but without conviction of any sort.

"Just test him," Effie repeated with utter confidence, ignoring—not even noticing—Patrick's warning nudge.

"All right," Hank mumbled. He looked at the stranger dully. "Can you count?" he asked.

Patrick's face was a complete enigma. Then he suddenly

spoke, and his voice was like a fencer's foil—light, bright, alert, constantly playing, yet utterly on guard.

"Can I count? Do you take me for a complete simpleton, man? Of course I can count!"

"Then count yourself," Hank said, barely indicating the table.

"Count myself, should I?" the other retorted with a quick facetious laugh. "Is this a kindergarten? But if you want me to, I'll willing." His voice was rapid. "I've two arms, and two legs, that's four. And ten fingers and ten toes—you'll take my word for them?—that's twenty-four. A head, twenty-five. And two eyes and a nose and a mouth—"

"With this, I mean," Hank said heavily, advanced to the table, picked up the Geiger counter, switched it on, and handed it across the table to the other man.

But while it was still an arm's length from Patrick, the clicks began to mount furiously, until they were like the chatter of a pigmy machine gun. Abruptly the clicks slowed, but that was only the counter shifting to a new scaling circuit, in which each click stood for 512 of the old ones.

With those horrid, rattling little volleys, fear cascaded into the room and filled it, smashing like so much colored glass all the bright barriers of words Effie had raised against it. For no dreams can stand against the Geiger counter, the twentieth century's mouthpiece of ultimate truth. It was as if the dust and all the terrors of the dust had incarnated themselves in one dread invading shape that said in words stronger than audible speech, "Those were illusions, whistles in the dark. This is reality, the dreary, pitiless reality of the Burrowing Years."

Hank scuttled back to the wall. Through chattering teeth he babbled, ". . . enough radioactives . . . kill a thousand men . . . freak . . . a freak . . ." In his agitation he forgot for a moment to inhale through the respirator.

Even Effie—taken off guard, all the fears that had been drilled into her twanging like piano wires—shrank from the skeletal-seeming shape beside her, held herself to it only by desperation.

Patrick did it for her. He disengaged her arm and stepped briskly away. Then he whirled on them, smiling sardonically, and started to speak, but instead looked with distaste at the chattering Geiger counter he held between fingers and thumb.

"Have we listened to this racket long enough?" he asked.

Without waiting for an answer, he put down the instrument on the table. The cat hurried over to it curiously and the clicks began again to mount in a minor crescendo. Effie lunged for it frantically, switched it off, darted back.

"That's right," Patrick said with another chilling smile. "You do well to cringe, for I'm death itself. Even in death I could kill you, like a snake." And with that his voice took on the tones of a circus barker. "Yes, I'm a freak, as the gentleman so wisely said. That's what one doctor who dared talk with me for a minute told me before he kicked me out. He couldn't tell me why, but somehow the dust doesn't kill me. Because I'm a freak, you see, just like the men who ate nails and walked on fire and ate arsenic and stuck themselves through with pins. Step right up, ladies and gentlemen—only not too close!—and examine the man the dust can't harm. Rappaccini's child, brought up to date; his embrace, death!

"And now," he said, breathing heavily, "I'll get out and leave you in your damned lead cave."

He started toward the window. Hank's gun followed him shakingly.

"Wait!" Effie called in an agonized voice. He obeyed. She continued falteringly, "When we were together earlier, you didn't act as if . . ."

"When we were together earlier, I wanted what I wanted," he snarled at her. "You don't suppose I'm a bloody saint, do you?"

"And all the beautiful things you told me?"

"That," he said cruelly, "is just a line I've found that women fall for. They're all so bored and so starved for beauty—as *they* generally put it."

"Even the garden?" Her question was barely audible through the sobs that threatened to suffocate her.

He looked at her and perhaps his expression softened just a trifle.

"What's outside," he said flatly, "is just a little worse than either of you can imagine." He tapped his temple. "The garden's all here."

"You've killed it," she wept. "You've killed it in me. You've both killed everything that's beautiful. But you're worse," she screamed at Patrick, "because he only killed beauty once, but you brought it to life just so you could kill it again. Oh, I can't stand it! I won't stand it!" And she began to scream.

Patrick started toward her, but she broke off and whirled away from him to the window, her eyes crazy.

"You've been lying to us," she cried. "The garden's there. I know it is. But you don't want to share it with anyone."

"No, no, Euphemia," Patrick protested anxiously. "It's hell out there, believe me. I wouldn't lie to you about it."

"Wouldn't lie to me!" she mocked. "Are you afraid, too?"

With a sudden pull, she jerked open the window and stood before the blank green-tinged oblong of darkness that seemed to press into the room like a menacing, heavy, wind-urged curtain.

At that Hank cried out a shocked, pleading "Effie!"

She ignored him. "I can't be cooped up here any longer," she said. "And I won't, now that I know. I'm going to the garden."

Both men sprang at her, but they were too late. She leaped lightly to the sill, and by the time they had flung themselves against it, her footsteps were already hurrying off into the darkness.

"Effie, come back! Come back!" Hank shouted after her desperately, no longer thinking to cringe from the man beside him, or how the gun was pointed. "I love you, Effie. Come back!"

Patrick added his voice. "Come back, Euphemia. You'll be safe if you come back right away. Come back to your home."

No answer to that at all.

They both strained their eyes through the greenish murk. They could barely make out a shadowy figure about half a block down the near-black canyon of the dismal, dust-blown street, into which the greenish moonlight hardly reached. It seemed to them that the figure was scooping something up from the pavement and letting it sift down along its arms and over its bosom.

"Go out and get her, man," Patrick urged the other. "For if I go out for her, I warn you I won't bring her back. She said something about having stood the dust better than most, and that's enough for me."

But Hank, chained by his painfully learned habits and by something else, could not move.

And then a ghostly voice came whispering down the street, chanting, "Fire can hurt me, or water, or the weight of the Earth. But the dust is my friend."

Patrick spared the other man one more look. Then, without a word, he vaulted up and ran off.

Hank stood there. After perhaps a half minute he remembered to close his mouth when he inhaled. Finally he was sure the street was empty. As he started to close the window, there was a little *mew*.

He picked up the cat and gently put it outside. Then he did close the window, and the shutters, and bolted them, and took up the Geiger counter, and mechanically began to count himself.

LOST MEMORY

Peter Phillips (1921–)

British newspaperman Peter Phillips returns to this series (see his wonderful "Dreams Are Sacred" in Volume 10) with what most people consider his finest story. If only the urge to write could be controlled by the reader! Phillips is one writer that I really wish would resume his career.

"Lost Memory" is an excellent example of the use of point-of-view, an approach for which science fiction is tailor-made. Sf writers have a variety of possibilities to work with—aliens observing humans; humans observing aliens (who frequently turn out to be bigger-than-life imitations of humans); humans from the past or present observing humans of the future via time travel; and humans from the future commenting on humans of "today." Here Phillips offers us a truly alien viewpoint—that of intelligent machines. The story also contains a last line that I have remembered since I first read it in Groff Conklin's *Science Fiction Terror Tales* almost thirty years ago. (MHG)

Sometimes I have a vague feeling that all robot stories belong to me. Intellectually, I know that's not so, of course, but I'm talking about an emotional force within me.

I get upset when robots do not behave as I have dictated they ought to behave. I disapprove not only of robots that are evil, violent, disloyal, or undutiful, but of the stories in which they appear, and of the authors who write them.

Thus, the movie *2001: A Space Odyssey* was ruined for me by the episode where Hal, the computer, kills some of the crew and is itself dismantled in consequence.

Contrariwise, and in reverse, I am interested in the paradox of robots that are essentially good, virtuous and caring, but

35

who, through circumstances beyond their understanding, achieve results that we ourselves can only see as cruel.

Think of the damage that the best of us can do, and *do* do, because we are thoughtless, or, more frustrating yet, because there are things we just don't know—and perhaps can't know.

Read the story and you'll see what I'm muttering about. (IA)

I collapsed joints and hung up to talk with Dak-whirr. He blinked his eyes in some discomfort.

"What do you want, Palil?" he asked complainingly.

"As if you didn't know."

"I can't give you permission to examine it. The thing is being saved for inspection by the board. What guarantee do I have that you won't spoil it for them?"

I thrust confidentially at one of his body-plates. "You owe me a favor," I said. "Remember?"

"That was a long time in the past."

"Only two thousand revolutions and a reassembly ago. If it wasn't for me, you'd be eroding in a pit. All I want is a quick look at its thinking part. I'll vrull the consciousness without laying a single pair of pliers on it."

He went into a feedback twitch, an indication of the conflict between his debt to me and his self-conceived duty.

Finally he said, "Very well, but keep tuned to me. If I warn that a board member is coming, remove yourself quickly. Anyway how do you know it has consciousness? It may be mere primal metal."

"In that form? Don't be foolish. It's obviously a manufacture. And I'm not conceited enough to believe that we are the only form of intelligent manufacture in the Universe."

"Tautologous phrasing, Palil," Dak-whirr said pedantically. "There could not conceivably be 'unintelligent manufacture.' There can be no consciousness without manufacture, and no manufacture without intelligence. Therefore there can be no consciousness without intelligence. Now if you should wish to dispute—"

I tuned off his frequency abruptly and hurried away. Dak-whirr is a fool and a bore. Everyone knows there's a fault in his logic circuit, but he refuses to have it traced down and repaired. Very unintelligent of him.

The things had been taken into one of the museum sheds by the carriers. I gazed at it in admiration for some moments. It was quite beautiful, having suffered only slight exterior damage, and it was obviously no mere conglomeration of sky metal.

In fact, I immediately thought of it as "he" and endowed it with the attributes of self-knowing, although, of course, his consciousness could not be functioning or he would have attempted communication with us.

I fervently hoped that the board, after his careful disassembly and study, could restore his awareness so that he could tell us himself which solar system he came from.

Imagine it! He had achieved our dream of many thousands of revolutions—space flight—only to be fused, or worse, in his moment of triumph.

I felt a surge of sympathy for the lonely traveler as he lay there, still, silent, non-emitting. Anyway, I mused, even if we couldn't restore him to self-knowing, an analysis of his construction might give us the secret of the power he had used to achieve the velocity to escape his planet's gravity.

In shape and size he was not unlike Swen—or Swen Two, as he called himself after his conversion—who failed so disastrously to reach our satellite, using chemical fuels. But where Swen Two had placed his tubes, the stranger had a curious helical construction studded at irregular intervals with small crystals.

He was thirty-five feet tall, a gracefully tapering cylinder. Standing at his head, I could find no sign of exterior vision cells, so I assumed he had some kind of vrulling sense. There seemed to be no exterior markings at all, except the long, shallow grooves dented in his skin by scraping to a stop along the hard surface of our planet.

I am a reporter with warm current in my wires, not a cold-thinking scientist, so I hesitated before using my own vrulling sense. Even though the stranger was non-aware—perhaps permanently—I felt it would be a presumption, an invasion of privacy. There was nothing else I could do, though, of course.

I started to vrull, gently at first, then harder, until I was positively glowing with effort. It was incredible; his skin seemed absolutely impermeable.

The sudden realization that metal could be so alien nearly fused something inside me. I found myself backing away in horror, my self-preservation relay working overtime.

Imagine watching one of the beautiful cone-rod-and-cylinder assemblies performing the Dance of the Seven Spanners, as he's conditioned to do, and then suddenly refusing to do anything except stump around unattractively, or even becoming obstinately motionless, unresponsive. That might give you an idea of how I felt in that dreadful moment.

Then I remembered Dak-whirr's words—there could be no such thing as an "unintelligent manufacture." And a product so beautiful could surely not be evil. I overcame my repugnance and approached again.

I halted as an open transmission came from someone near at hand.

"Who gave that squeaking reporter permission to snoop around here?"

I had forgotten the museum board. Five of them were standing in the doorway of the shed, radiating anger. I recognized Chirik, the chairman, and addressed myself to him. I explained that I'd interfered with nothing and pleaded for permission on behalf of my subscribers to watch their investigation of the stranger. After some argument, they allowed me to stay.

I watched in silence and some amusement as one by one they tried to vrull the silent being from space. Each showed the same reaction as I had when they failed to penetrate the skin.

Chirik, who is wheeled—and inordinately vain about his suspension system—flung himself back on his supports and pretended to be thinking.

"Fetch Fiff-fiff," he said at last. "The creature may still be aware, but unable to communicate on our standard frequencies."

Fiff-fiff can detect anything in any spectrum. Fortunately he was at work in the museum that day and soon arrived in answer to the call. He stood silently near the stranger for some moments, testing and adjusting himself, then slid up the electromagnetic band.

"He's emitting," he said.

"Why can't we get him?" asked Chirik.

"It's a curious signal on an unusual band."

"Well, what does he say?"

"Sounds like utter nonsense to me. Wait, I'll relay and convert it to standard."

I made a direct recording naturally, like any good reporter.

"—after planetfall," the stranger was saying. "Last dribble of power. If you don't pick this up, my name is Entropy. Other instruments knocked to hell, airlock jammed and I'm too weak to open it manually. Becoming delirious, too, I guess. Getting strong undirectional ultra-wave reception in Inglish, craziest stuff you ever heard, like goblins muttering, and I know we were the only ship in this sector. If you pick this up, but can't get a fix in time, give my love to the boys in the mess. Signing off for another couple of hours, but keeping this channel open and hoping . . ."

"The fall must have deranged him," said Chirik, gazing at the stranger. "Can't he see us or hear us?"

"He couldn't hear you properly before, but he can now, through me," Fiff-fiff pointed out. "Say something to him, Chirik."

"Hello," said Chirik doubtfully. "Er—welcome to our planet. We are sorry you were hurt by your fall. We offer you the hospitality of our assembly shops. You will feel better when you are repaired and repowered. If you will indicate how we can assist you—"

"What the hell! What ship is that? Where are you?"

"We're here," said Chirik. "Can't you see us or vrull us? Your vision circuit is impaired, perhaps? Or do you depend entirely on vrulling? We can't find your eyes and assumed either that you protected them in some way during flight, or dispensed with vision cells altogether in your conversion."

Chirik hesitated, continued apologetically: "But we cannot understand how you vrull, either. While we thought that you were unaware, or even completely fused, we tried to vrull you. Your skin is quite impervious to us, however."

The stranger said: "I don't know if you're batty or I am. What distance are you from me?"

Chirik measured quickly. "One meter, two-point-five centimeters from my eyes to your nearest point. Within touching distance, in fact." Chirik tentatively put out his hand. "Can you not feel me, or has your contact sense also been affected?"

It became obvious that the stranger had been pitifully deranged. I reproduce his words phonetically from my record, although some of them make little sense. Emphasis, punctuative pauses and spelling of unknown terms are mere guesswork, of course.

He said: "For godsakeman stop talking nonsense, whoever you are. If you're outside, can't you see the airlock is jammed? Can't shift it myself. I'm badly hurt. Get me out of here, please."

"Get you out of where?" Chirik looked around, puzzled. "We brought you into an open shed near our museum for a preliminary examination. Now that we know you're intelligent, we shall immediately take you to our assembly shops for healing and recuperation. Rest assured that you'll have the best possible attention."

There was a lengthy pause before the stranger spoke again, and his words were slow and deliberate. His bewilderment is understandable, I believe, if we remember that he could not see, vrull or feel.

He asked: "What manner of creature are you? Describe yourself."

Chirik turned to us and made a significant gesture toward his thinking part, indicating gently that the injured stranger had to be humored.

"Certainly," he replied. "I am an unspecialized bipedal manufacture of standard proportions, lately self-converted to wheeled traction, with a hydraulic suspension system of my own devising which I'm sure will interest you when we restore your sense circuits."

There was an even longer silence.

"You are robots," the stranger said at last. "Crise knows how you got here or why you speak Inglish, but you must try to understand me. I am mann. I am a friend of your master, your maker. You must fetch him to me at once."

"You are not well," said Chirik firmly. "Your speech is incoherent and without meaning. Your fall has obviously caused several serious feedbacks of a very serious nature. Please lower your voltage. We are taking you to our shops immediately. Reserve your strength to assist our specialists as best you can in diagnosing your troubles."

"Wait. You must understand. You are—ogodno that's no good. Have you no memory of mann? The words you use—what meaning have they for you? *Manufacture*—made by hand hand

hand damyou. *Healing*. Metal is not healed. *Skin*. Skin is not metal. *Eyes*. Eyes are not scanning cells. Eyes grow. Eyes are soft. My eyes are soft. Mine eyes have seen the glory—steady on, sun. Get a grip. Take it easy. You out there listen.''

''Out where?'' asked Prr-chuk, deputy chairman of the museum board.

I shook my head sorrowfully. This was nonsense, but, like any good reporter, I kept my recorder running.

The mad words flowed on. ''You call me he. Why? You have no seks. You are knewter. You are *it it it!* I am he, he who made you, sprung from shee, born of wumman. What is wumman, who is silv-ya what is shee that all her swains commend her ogod the bluds flowing again. Remember. Think back, you out there. These words were made by mann, for mann. Hurt, healing, hospitality, horror, deth by loss of blud. *Deth. Blud.* Do you understand these words? Do you remember the soft things that made you? Soft little mann who konkurred the Galaxy and made sentient slaves of his machines and saw the wonders of a million worlds, only this miserable representative has to die in lonely desperation on a far planet, hearing goblin voices in the darkness.''

Here my recorder reproduces a most curious sound, as though the stranger were using an ancient type of vibratory molecular vocalizer in a gaseous medium to reproduce his words before transmission, and the insulation on his diaphragm had come adrift.

It was a jerky, high-pitched, strangely disturbing sound; but in a moment the fault was corrected and the stranger resumed transmission.

''Does blud mean anything to you?''

''No,'' Chirik replied simply.

''Or deth?''

''No.''

''Or wor?''

''Quite meaningless.''

''What is your origin? How did you come into being?''

''There are several theories,'' Chirik said. ''The most popular one—which is no more than a grossly unscientific legend, in my opinion—is that our manufacturer fell from the skies, imbedded in a mass of primal metal on which He drew to erect the first assembly shop. How He came into being is left to conjecture. My own theory, however—''

"Does legend mention the shape of this primal metal?"

"In vague terms, yes. It was cylindrical, of vast dimensions."

"An interstellar vessel," said the stranger.

"That is my view also," said Chirik complacently. "And—"

"What was the supposed appearance of your—manufacturer?"

"He is said to have been of magnificent proportions, based harmoniously on a cubical plan, static in Himself, but equipped with a vast array of senses."

"An automatic computer," said the stranger.

He made more curious noises, less jerky and at a lower pitch than the previous sounds.

He corrected the fault and went on: "God that's funny. A ship falls, menn are no more, and an automatic computer has pupps. Oh, yes, it fits in. A self-setting computer and navigator, operating on verbal orders. It learns to listen for itself and know itself for what it is, and to absorb knowledge. It comes to hate menn—or at least their bad qualities—so it deliberately crashes the ship and pulps their puny bodies with a calculated nicety of shock. Then it propagates and does a dam fine job of selective erasure on whatever it gave its pupps to use for a memory. It passes on only the good it found in menn, and purges the memory of him completely. Even purges all of his vocabulary except scientific terminology. Oil is thicker than blud. So may they live without the burden of knowing that they are—ogod they must know, they must understand. You outside, what happened to this manufacturer?"

Chirik, despite his professed disbelief in the supernormal aspects of the ancient story, automatically made a visual sign of sorrow.

"Legend has it," he said, "that after completing His task, He fused himself beyond possibility of healing."

Abrupt, low-pitched noises came again from the stranger. "Yes. He would. Just in case any of His pupps should give themselves forbidden knowledge and an infeeryorrity komplecks by probing his mnemonic circuits. The perfect self-sacrificing muther. What sort of environment did He give you? Describe your planet."

Chirik looked around at us again in bewilderment, but he replied courteously, giving the stranger a description of our world.

"Of course," said the stranger. "Of course. Sterile rock and metal suitable only for you. But there must be some way. . . ."

He was silent for a while.

"Do you know what growth means?" he asked finally. "Do you have anything that grows?"

"Certainly," Chirik said helpfully. "If we should suspend a crystal of some substance in a saturated solution of the same element or compound—"

"No, no," the stranger interrupted. "Have you nothing that grows of itself, that fruktiffies and gives increase without your intervention?"

"How could such a thing be?"

"Crisellmytee I should have guessed. If you had one blade of gras, just one tiny blade of growing gras, you could extrapolate from that to me. Green things, things that feed on the rich brest of erth, cells that divide and multiply, a cool grove of treez in a hot summer, with tiny warmbludded burds preening their fethers among the leeves; a feeld of spring weet with newbawn mise timidly threading the dangerous jungul of stroks; a stream of living water where silver fish dart and pry and feed and procreate; a farm yard where things grunt and cluck and greet the new day with the stirring pulse of life, with a surge of blud. Blud—"

For some inexplicable reason, although the strength of his carrier wave remained almost constant, the stranger's transmission seemed to be growing fainter.

"His circuits are failing," Chirik said. "Call the carriers. We must take him to an assembly shop immediately. I wish he would reserve his power."

My presence with the museum board was accepted without question now. I hurried along with them as the stranger was carried to the nearest shop.

I now noticed a circular marking in that part of his skin on which he had been resting, and guessed that it was some kind of orifice through which he would have extended his planetary traction mechanism if he had not been injured.

He was gently placed on a disassembly cradle. The doctor in charge that day was Chur-chur, an old friend of mine. He had been listening to the two-way transmissions and was already acquainted with the case.

Chur-chur walked thoughtfully around the stranger.

"We shall have to cut," he said. "It won't pain him, since his intra-molecular pressure and contact senses have failed. But since we can't vrull him, it'll be necessary for him to tell us where his main brain is housed or we might damage it.''

Fiff-fiff was still relaying, but no amount of power boost would make the stranger's voice any clearer. It was quite faint now, and there are places on my recorder tape from which I cannot make even the roughest phonetic transliteration.

''. . . strength going. Can't get into my zoot . . . done for if they bust through lock, done for if they don't . . . must tell them I need oxygen . . .''

''He's in bad shape, desirous of extinction,'' I remarked to Chur-chur, who was adjusting his arc-cutter. ''He wants to poison himself with oxidation now.''

I shuddered at the thought of that vile, corrosive gas he had mentioned, which causes that almost unmentionable condition we all fear—rust.

Chirik spoke firmly through Fiff-fiff. ''Where is your thinking part, stranger? Your central brain?''

''In my head,'' the stranger replied. ''In my head ogod my head . . . eyes blurring everything going dim . . . luv to mairee . . . kids . . . a carry me home to the lone prayree . . . get this bluddy airlock open then they'll see me die . . . but they'll see me . . . some kind of atmosphere with this gravity . . . see me die . . . extrapolate from body what I was . . . what they are damthem damthem damthem . . . mann . . . master . . . I AM YOUR MAKER!''

For a few seconds the voice rose strong and clear, then faded away again and dwindled into a combination of those two curious noises I mentioned earlier. For some reason that I cannot explain, I found the combined sound very disturbing despite its faintness. It may be that it induced some kind of sympathetic oscillation.

Then came words, largely incoherent and punctuated by a kind of surge like the sonic vibrations produced by variations of pressure in a leaking gas-filled vessel.

''. . . done it . . . crawling into chamber, closing inner . . . must be mad . . . they'd find me anyway . . . but finished . . . want see them before I die . . . want see them see me . . . liv few seconds, watch them . . . get outer one open . . .''

Chur-chur had adjusted his arc to a broad, clean, blue-white glare. I trembled a little as he brought it near the edge of the circular marking in the stranger's skin. I could almost feel the disruption of the intra-molecular sense currents in my own skin.

"Don't be squeamish, Palil," Chur-chur said kindly. "He can't feel it now that his contact sense has gone. And you heard him say that his central brain is in his head." He brought the cutter firmly up to the skin. "I should have guessed that. He's the same shape as Swen Two, and Swen very logically concentrated his main thinking part as far away from his explosion chambers as possible."

Rivulets of metal ran down into a tray which a calm assistant had placed on the ground for that purpose. I averted my eyes quickly. I could never steel myself enough to be a surgical engineer or assembly technician.

But I had to look again, fascinated. The whole area circumscribed by the marking was beginning to glow.

Abruptly the stranger's voice returned, quite strongly, each word clipped, emphasized, high-pitched.

"Ar no no no . . . god my hands . . . they're burning through the lock and I can't get back I can't get away . . . stop it you feens stop it can't you hear . . . I'll be burned to deth I'm here in the airlock . . . the air's getting hot you're burning me alive. . ."

Although the words made little sense, I could guess what had happened and I was horrified.

"Stop, Chur-chur," I pleaded. "The heat has somehow brought back his skin currents. It's hurting him."

Chur-chur said reassuringly: "Sorry, Palil. It occasionally happens during an operation—probably a local thermo-electric effect. But even if his contact senses have started working again and he can't switch them off, he won't have to bear this very long."

Chirik shared my unease, however. He put out his hand and awkwardly patted the stranger's skin.

"Easy there," he said. "Cut out your senses if you can. If you can't, well, the operation is nearly finished. Then we'll repower you, and you'll soon be fit and happy again, healed and fitted and reassembled."

I decided that I liked Chirik very much just then. He exhibited almost as much self-induced empathy as any reporter; he might even come to like my favorite blue stars, despite his cold scientific exactitude in most respects.

My recorder tape shows, in its reproduction of certain sounds, how I was torn away from this strained reverie.

During the one-and-a-half seconds since I had recorded the distinct vocables "burning me alive," the stranger's words had become quite blurred, running together and rising even higher in pitch until they reached a sustained note—around E-flat in the standard sonic scale.

It was not like a voice at all.

This high, whining noise was suddenly modulated by apparent words, but without changing its pitch. Transcribing what seem to be words is almost impossible, as you can see for yourself—this is the closest I can come phonetically:

"Eeee ahahmbeeeing baked aliive in an uvennn ahdeeer-jee-sussunmuuutherrr!"

The note swooped higher and higher until it must have neared supersonic range, almost beyond either my direct or recorded hearing.

Then it stopped as quickly as a contact break.

And although the soft hiss of the stranger's carrier wave carried on without perceptible diminution, indicating that some degree of awareness still existed, I experienced at that moment one of those quirks of intuition given only to reporters.

I felt that I would never greet the beautiful stranger from the sky in his full senses.

Chur-chur was muttering to himself about the extreme toughness and thickness of the stranger's skin. He had to make four complete cutting revolutions before the circular mass of nearly white-hot metal could be pulled away by a magnetic-grapple.

A billow of smoke puffed out of the orifice. Despite my repugnance, I thought of my duty as a reporter and forced myself to look over Chur-chur's shoulder.

The fumes came from a soft, charred, curiously shaped mass of something which lay just inside the opening.

"Undoubtedly a kind of insulating material," Churh-chur explained.

He drew out the crumpled blackish heap and placed it carefully on a tray. A small portion broke away, showing a red, viscid substance.

"It looks complex," Chur-chur said, "but I expect the stranger will be able to tell us how to reconstitute it or make a substitute."

His assistant gently cleaned the wound of the remainder of the material, which he placed with the rest; and Chur-chur resumed his inspection of the orifice.

You can, if you want, read the technical accounts of Chur-chur's discovery of the stranger's double skin at the point where the cut was made; of the incredible complexity of his driving mechanism, involving principles which are still not understood to this day; of the museum's failure to analyze the exact nature and function of the insulating material found in only that one portion of his body; and of the other scientific mysteries connected with him.

But this is my personal, non-scientific account. I shall never forget hearing about the greatest mystery of all, for which not even the most tentative explanation has been advanced, nor the utter bewilderment with which Chur-chur announced his initial findings that day.

He had hurriedly converted himself to a convenient size to permit actual entry into the stranger's body.

When he emerged, he stood in silence for several minutes. Then, very slowly, he said:

"I have examined the 'central brain' in the forepart of his body. It is no more than a simple auxiliary computer mechanism. It does not possess the slightest trace of consciousness. And there is no other conceivable center of intelligence in the remainder of his body."

There is something I wish I could forget. I can't explain why it should upset me so much. But I always stop the tape before it reaches the point where the voice of the stranger rises in pitch, going higher and higher until it cuts out.

There's a quality about that noise that makes me tremble and think of rust.

WHAT HAVE I DONE?

by Mark Clifton (1906–1963)

Mark Clifton became a science fiction writer in his late forties, after a career as an industrial psychologist, a profession which served him well in his writing. It's not exactly accurate to say that he burst upon the sf scene like a nova, (he certainly didn't make the impression on the readership that Philip José Farmer did in 1952, for example) but he was noticed, particularly by other writers, who knew a unique talent when they saw one. His total contribution to the field was not great, twenty odd stories and three novels—including *They'd Rather Be Right* (with Frank Riley, in hardcover in 1957), which is surely the least known and most neglected novel ever to win a Hugo Award; *Eight Keys to Eden* (1960); and *When They Came From Space* (1962).

But it was those shorter works, full of cynicism, irony, compassion, and urbanity that caught the eye of critics like Judith Merrill.

Clifton had conducted over 200,000 interviews in a career that lasted a quarter of a century, and he had seen virtually every type of American. His job was to see through facades and find the real person, and this shows in his stories. And what stories they were—space permits only mention of a few here—"Clerical Error," "What Now Little Man?" and "Hang Head, Vandel!" this last published shortly before his untimely death. Most of his best stories can be found in *The Science Fiction of Mark Clifton,* 1980.

He did not die a happy man, for he was disillusioned with the science fiction field, which seemed to him to be unwilling to take chances—yet where else would he have been welcome at all in the decade 1952 to 1962?

"What Have I Done?" was his first published science fiction. (MHG)

I suppose I know as much about the intellectual workings of John Campbell's mind as anyone and I can usually tell a "Campbell story," one which has a thesis that Campbell is fond of. This is a Campbell story. However, it's not a thesis we ought to accept without questioning.

Is it typical behavior to have crucified Jesus, for instance? I wonder. It seems to me as I listen to Christian theology that Jesus joined humanity in order to redeem it, and for this re- demption to take place, he *had* to be be crucified, thus taking the sins of humanity on his own shoulders and expiating them. If that is so, then Judas, Caiaphas, and Pontius Pilate had essential parts to play in this drama of redemption, and had they refused those parts, all of humanity would still be resting under original sin. That should make those men heroes, shouldn't it, as they accepted the weary load of eternal obloquy in order to make redemption possible? Can it be Judas that we have unfairly destroyed rather than Jesus? Just a thought—but that would have made a Campbell story, too.

Is it typical human behavior to have poisoned Socrates? Every time I read one of Plato's dialogues and find myself immersed in Socratic irony, I wish myself on that Athenian jury so I could vote for the hemlock. Maybe it *is* typical, then, but one might argue he deserved it. Write a story about a person who is ideally virtuous and deserved poisoning and that would be a Campbell story, too.

But what is the *truth* of it? I don't know, except that I consider it safe to say that human beings are too complex to make easy generalizations either fair or convincing. (IA)

It had to be. It would be stupid to say that the burden should have fallen to a great statesman, a world leader, a renowned scientist. With all modesty, I think I am one of the few who could have caught the problem early enough to avert disaster. I have a peculiar skill. The whole thing hinged on that. I have learned to know human beings.

The first time I saw the fellow, I was at the drugstore counter buying cigarettes. He was standing at the magazine rack. One might have thought from the expression on his face that he had never seen magazines before. Still, quite a number of people get that rapt and vacant look when they can't make up their minds to a choice.

The thing which bothered me in that casual glance was that I couldn't recognize him.

There are others who can match my record in taking case histories. I happened to be the one who came in contact with this fellow. For thirty years I have been listening to, talking with, counseling people—over two hundred thousand of them. They have not been routine interviews. I have brought intelligence, sensitivity and concern to each of them.

Mine has been a driving, burning desire to know people. Not from the western scientific point of view of devising tools and rules to measure animated robots and ignoring the man beneath. Nor from the eastern metaphysical approach to painting a picture of the soul by blowing one's breath upon a fog to be blurred and dispersed by the next breath.

Mine was the aim to know the man by making use of both. And there was some success.

A competent geographer can look at a crude sketch of a map and instantly orient himself to it anywhere in the world—the bend of a river, the angle of a lake, the twist of a mountain range. And he can mystify by telling in finest detail what is to be found there.

After about fifty thousand studies where I could predict and then observe and check, with me it became the lift of a brow, the curve of a mouth, the gesture of a hand, the slope of a shoulder. One of the universities became interested, and over a long controlled period they rated me 92 percent accurate. That was fifteen years ago. I may have improved some since.

Yet standing there at the cigarette counter and glancing at the young fellow at the magazine rack, I could read nothing. Nothing at all.

If this had been an ordinary face, I would have catalogued it and forgotten it automatically. I see them by the thousands. But this face would not be catalogued nor forgotten, because there was nothing in it.

I started to write that it wasn't even a face, but of course it was. Every human being has a face—of one sort or another.

In build he was short, muscular, rather well proportioned. The hair was crew cut and blond, the eyes were blue, the skin fair. All nice and standard Teutonic—only it wasn't.

I finished paying for my cigarettes and gave him one more glance, hoping to surprise an expression which had some meaning. There was none. I left him standing there and walked out on the street and around the corner. The street, the store fronts, the traffic cop on the corner, the warm sunshine were all so familiar I didn't see them. I climbed the stairs to my office in the building over the drugstore. My employment agency waiting room was empty. I don't cater to much of a crowd because it cuts down my opportunity to talk with people and further my study.

Margie, my receptionist, was busy making out some kind of a report and merely nodded as I passed her desk to my own office. She is a good conscientious girl who can't understand why I spend so much time working with bums and drunks and other psychos who obviously won't bring fees into the sometimes too small bank account.

I sat down at my desk and said aloud to myself, "The guy is a fake! As obvious as a high school boy's drafting of a dollar bill."

I heard myself say that and wondered if I was going nuts, myself. What did I mean by fake? I shrugged. So I happened to see a bird I couldn't read, that was all.

Then it struck me. But that would be unique. I hadn't had that experience for twenty years. Imagine the delight, after all these years, of exploring an unreadable!

I rushed out of my office and back down the stairs to the street. Hallahan, the traffic cop, saw me running up the street and looked at me curiously. I signaled to him with a wave of a hand that everything was all right. He lifted his cap and scratched his head. He shook his head slowly and settled his cap back down. He blew a whistle at a woman driver and went back to directing traffic.

I ran into the drugstore. Of course the guy wasn't there. I looked all around, hoping he was hiding behind the pots and pans counter, or something. No guy.

I walked quickly back out on the street and down to the next corner. I looked up and down the side streets. No guy.

I dragged my feet reluctantly back toward the office. I called up the face again to study it. It did no good. The first mental glimpse of it told me there was nothing to find. Logic told me there was nothing to find. If there had been, I wouldn't be in such a stew. The face was empty—completely void of human feelings or character.

No, those weren't the right words. Completely void of human—being!

I walked on past the drugstore again and looked in curiously, hoping I would see him. Hallahan was facing my direction again, and he grinned crookedly at me. I expect around the neighborhood I am known as a character. I ask the queerest questions of people, from a layman's point of view. Still, applicants sometimes tell me that when they asked a cop where was an employment agent they could trust they were sent to me.

I climbed the stairs again, and walked into my waiting room. Margie looked at me curiously, but she only said, "There's an applicant. I had him wait in your office." She looked like she wanted to say more, and then shrugged. Or maybe she shivered. I knew there was something wrong with the bird, or she would have kept him in the waiting room.

I opened the door to my office, and experienced an overwhelming sense of relief, fulfillment. It was he. Still, it was logical that he should be there. I run an employment agency. People come to me to get help in finding work. If others, why not he?

My skill includes the control of my outward reactions. That fellow could have no idea of the delight I felt at the opportunity to get a full history. If I had found him on the street, the best I might have done was a stock question about what time is it, or have you got a match, or where is the city hall. Here I could question him to my heart's content.

I took his history without comment, and stuck to routine questions. It was all exactly right.

He was ex-G.I., just completed college, major in astronomy, no experience, no skills, no faintest idea of what he wanted to do, nothing to offer an employer—all perfectly normal for a young grad.

No feeling or expression either. Not so normal. Usually they're petulantly resentful that business doesn't swoon at the chance of hiring them. I resigned myself to the old one-two of attempting to steer him toward something practical.

"Astronomy?" I asked. "That means you're heavy in math. Frequently we can place a strong math skill in statistical work." I was hopeful I could get a spark of something.

It turned out he wasn't very good at math. "I haven't yet reconciled my math to—" he stopped. For the first time he showed a reaction—hesitancy. Prior to that he had been a statue from Greece—the rounded expressionless eyes, the too perfect features undisturbed by thought.

He caught his remark and finished, "I'm just not very good at math, that's all."

I sighed to myself. I'm used to that, too. They give degrees nowadays to get rid of guys, I suppose. Sometimes I'll go for days without uncovering any usable knowledge. So in a way, that was normal.

The only abnormal part of it was he seemed to think it didn't sound right. Usually the lads don't even realize they should know something. He seemed to think he'd pulled a boner by admitting that a man can take a degree in astronomy without learning math. Well, I wouldn't be surprised to see them take their degree without knowing how many planets there are.

He began to fidget a bit. That was strange, also. I thought I knew every possible combination of muscular contractions and expansions. This fidget had all the reality of a puppet activated by an amateur. And the eyes—still completely blank.

I led him up one mental street and down the next. And of all the false-fronted stores and cardboard houses and paper lawns, I never saw the like. I get something of that once in a while from a fellow who has spent a long term in prison and comes in with a manufactured past—but never anything as phony as this one was.

Interesting aspect to it. Most guys, when they realize you've spotted them for a phony, get out as soon as they can. He didn't. It was almost as though he were—well, testing; to see if his answers would stand up.

I tried talking astronomy, of which I thought I knew a little. I found I didn't know anything, or he didn't. This bird's astronomy and mine had no point of reconciliation.

And then he had a slip of the tongue—yes he did. He was talking, and said, "The ten planets—"

He caught himself, "Oh that's right. There's only nine."

Could be ignorance, but I didn't think so. Could be he knew of the existence of a planet we hadn't yet discovered.

I smiled. I opened a desk drawer and pulled out a couple science-fiction magazines. "Ever read any of these?" I asked.

"I looked through several of them at the newsstand awhile ago," he answered.

"They've enlarged my vision," I said. "Even to the point where I could believe that some other star system might hold intelligence." I lit a cigarette and waited. If I was wrong, he would merely think I was talking at random.

His blank eyes changed. They were no longer Greek statue eyes. They were no longer blue. They were black, deep bottomless black, as deep and cold as space itself.

"Where did I fail in my test?" he asked. His lips formed a smile which was not a smile—a carefully painted-on-canvas sort of smile.

Well, I'd had my answer. I'd explored something unique, all right. Sitting there before me, I had no way of determining whether he was benign or evil. No way of knowing his motive. No way of judging—anything. When it takes a lifetime of learning how to judge even our own kind, what standards have we for judging an entity from another star system?

At that moment I would like to have been one of those space-opera heroes who, in similar circumstances, laugh casually and say, "What ho! So you're from Arcturus. Well, well. It's a small universe after all, isn't it?" And then with linked arms they head for the nearest bar, bosom pals.

I had the almost hysterical thought, but carefully suppressed, that I didn't know if this fellow would like beer or not. I will not go through the intermuscular and visceral reactions I experienced. I kept my seat and maintained a polite expression. Even with humans, I know when to walk carefully.

"I couldn't feel anything about you," I answered his question. "I couldn't feel anything but blankness."

He looked blank. His eyes were nice blue marble again. I liked them better that way.

There should be a million questions to be asked, but I must have been bothered by the feeling that I held a loaded bomb in my hands. And not knowing what might set it off, or how, or when. I could think of only the most trivial.

"How long have you been on Earth?" I asked. Sort of a when did you get back in town, Joe, kind of triviality.

"For several of your weeks," he was answering. "But this is my first time out among humans."

"Where have you been in the meantime?" I asked.

"Training." His answers were getting short and his muscles began to fidget again.

"And where do you train?" I kept boring in.

As an answer he stood up and held out his hand, all quite correctly. "I must go now," he said. "Naturally you can cancel my application for employment. Obviously we have more to learn."

I raised an eyebrow. "And I'm supposed to just pass over the whole thing? A thing like this?"

He smiled again. The contrived smile which was a symbol to indicate courtesy. "I believe your custom on this planet is to turn your problems over to your police. You might try that." I could not tell whether it was irony or logic.

At that moment I could think of nothing else to say. He walked out of my door while I stood beside my desk and watched him go.

Well, what was I supposed to do? Follow him?

I followed him.

Now I'm no private eye, but I've read my share of mystery stories. I knew enough to keep out of sight. I followed him about a dozen blocks into a quiet residential section of small homes. I was standing behind a palm tree, lighting a cigarette, when he went up the walk of one of these small houses. I saw him twiddle with the door, open it, and walk in. The door closed.

I hung around a while and then went up to the door. I punched the doorbell. A motherly gray-haired woman came to the door, drying her hands on her apron. As she opened the door she said, "I'm not buying anything today."

Just the same, her eyes looked curious as to what I might have.

I grinned my best grin for elderly ladies. "I'm not selling anything, either," I answered. I handed her my agency card. She looked at it curiously and then looked a question at me.

"I'd like to see Joseph Hoffman," I said politely.

She looked puzzled. "I'm afraid you've got the wrong address, sir," she answered.

I got prepared to stick my foot in the door, but it wasn't necessary. "He was in my office just a few minutes ago," I said. "He gave that name and this address. A job came in right after he left the office, and since I was going to be in this neighborhood anyway, I thought I'd drop by and tell him in person. It's sort of rush," I finished. It had happened many times before, but this time it sounded lame.

"Nobody lives here but me and my husband," she insisted. "He's retired."

I didn't care if he hung by his toes from trees. I wanted a young fellow.

"But I saw the young fellow come in here," I argued. "I was just coming around the corner, trying to catch him. I saw him."

She looked at me suspiciously. "I don't know what your racket is," she said through thin lips, "but I'm not buying anything. I'm not signing anything. I don't even want to talk to you." She was stubborn about it.

I apologized and mumbled something about maybe making a mistake.

"I should say you have," she rapped out tartly and shut the door in righteous indignation. Sincere, too. I could tell.

An employment agent who gets the reputation of being a right guy makes all kinds of friends. That poor old lady must have thought a plague of locusts had swept in on her for the next few days.

First the telephone repair man had to investigate an alleged complaint. Then a gas service man had to check the plumbing. An electrician complained there was a power short in the block and he had to trace their house wiring. We kept our fingers crossed hoping the old geezer had never been a construction man. There was a mistake in the last census, and a guy asked her a million questions.

That house was gone over rafter by rafter and sill by sill, attic and basement. It was precisely as she said. She and her husband lived there; nobody else.

In frustration, I waited three months. I wore out the sidewalks haunting the neighborhood. Nothing.

Then one day my office door opened and Margie ushered a young man in. Behind his back she was radiating heart throbs and fluttering her eyes.

He was the traditionally tall, dark and handsome young fellow, with a ready grin and sparkling dark eyes. His personality hit me like a sledge hammer. A guy like that never needs to go to an employment agency. An employer will hire him at the drop of a hat, and wonder later why he did it.

His name was Einar Johnson. Extraction, Norwegian. The

dark Norse strain, I judged. I took a chance on him thinking he had walked into a booby hatch.

"The last time I talked with you," I said, "your name was Joseph Hoffman. You were Teutonic then. Not Norse."

The sparkle went out of his eyes. His face showed exasperation and there was plenty of it. It looked real, too, not painted on.

"All right. Where did I flunk this time?" he asked impatiently.

"It would take me too long to tell you," I answered. "Suppose you start talking." Strangely, I was at ease. I knew that underneath he was the same incomprehensible entity, but his surface was so good that I was lulled.

He looked at me levelly for a long moment. Then he said, "I didn't think there was a chance in a million of being recognized. I'll admit that other character we created was crude. We've learned considerable since then, and we've concentrated everything on this personality I'm wearing."

He paused and flashed his teeth at me. I felt like hiring him myself. "I've been all over Southern California in this one," he said. "I've had a short job as a salesman. I've been to dances and parties. I've got drunk and sober again. Nobody, I say nobody, has shown even the slightest suspicion."

"Not very observing, were they?" I taunted.

"But you are," he answered. "That's why I came back here for the final test. I'd like to know where I failed." He was firm.

"We get quite a few phonies." I answered. "The guy drawing unemployment and stalling until it is run out. The geezik whose wife drives him out and threatens to quit her job if he doesn't go to work. The plainclothes detail smelling around to see if maybe we aren't a cover for a bookie joint or something. Dozens of phonies."

He looked curious. I said in disgust, "We know in the first two minutes they're phony. You were phony also, but not of any class I've seen before. And," I finished dryly, "I've been waiting for you."

"Why was I phony?" he persisted.

"Too much personality force," I answered. "Human beings just don't have that much force. I felt like I'd been knocked flat on my . . . well . . . back."

He sighed. "I've been afraid you would recognize me one way or another. I communicated with home. I was advised that if you spotted me, I was to instruct you to assist us."

I lifted a brow. I wasn't sure how much authority they had to instruct me to do anything.

"I was to instruct you to take over the supervision of our final training, so that no one could ever spot us. If we are going to carry out our original plan that is necessary. If not, then we will have to use the alternate." He was almost didactic in his manner, but his charm of personality still radiated like an infrared lamp.

"You're going to have to tell me a great deal more than that," I said.

He glanced at my closed door.

"We won't be interrupted," I said. "A personnel history is private."

"I come from one of the planets of Arcturus," he said.

I must have allowed a smile of amusement to show on my face, for he asked, "You find that amusing?"

"No," I answered soberly, and my pulses leaped because the question confirmed my conclusion that he could not read my thoughts. Apparently we were as alien to him as he to us. "I was amused," I explained, "because the first time I saw you I said to myself that as far as recognizing you, you might have come from Arcturus. Now it turns out that accidentally I was correct. I'm better than I thought."

He gave a fleeting polite smile in acknowledgment. "My home planet," he went on, "is similar to yours. Except that we have grown overpopulated."

I felt a twinge of fear.

"We have made a study of this planet and have decided to colonize it." It was a flat statement, without any doubt behind it.

I flashed him a look of incredulity. "And you expect me to help you with that?"

He gave me a worldly wise look—almost an ancient look. "Why not?" he asked.

"There is the matter of loyalty to my own kind, for one thing," I said. "Not too many generations away and we'll be overpopulated also. There would hardly be room for both your people and ours on Earth."

"Oh that's all right," he answered easily. "There'll be plenty of room for us for quite some time. We multiply slowly."

"We don't," I said shortly. I felt this conversation should be taking place between him and some great statesman—not me.

"You don't seem to understand," he said patiently. "Your

race won't be here. We have found no reason why your race should be preserved. You will die away as we absorb."

"Now just a moment," I interrupted. "I don't want our race to die off." The way he looked at me I felt like a spoiled brat who didn't want to go beddie time.

"Why not?" he asked.

I was stumped. That's a good question when it is put logically. Just try to think of a logical reason why the human race should survive. I gave him at least something.

"Mankind," I said, "has had a hard struggle. We've paid a tremendous price in pain and death for our growth. Not to have a future to look forward to, would be like paying for something and never getting the use of it."

It was the best I could think of, honest. To base argument on humanity and right and justice and mercy would leave me wide open. Because it is obvious that man doesn't practice any of these. There is no assurance he ever will.

But he was ready for me, even with that one. "But if we are never suspected, and if we absorb and replace gradually, who is to know there is no future for humans?"

And as abruptly as the last time, he stood up suddenly. "Of course," he said coldly, "we could use our alternative plan: Destroy the human race without further negotiation. It is not our way to cause needless pain to any life form. But we can.

"If you do not assist us, then it is obvious that we will eventually be discovered. You are aware of the difficulty of even blending from one country on Earth to another. How much more difficult it is where there is no point of contact at all. And if we are discovered, destruction would be the only step left."

He smiled and all the force of his charm hit me again. "I know you will want to think it over for a time. I'll return."

He walked to the door, then smiled back at me. "And don't bother to trouble that poor little woman in that house again. Her doorway is only one of many entrances we have opened. She doesn't see us at all, and merely wonders why her latch doesn't work sometimes. And we can open another, anywhere, anytime. Like this—"

He was gone.

I walked over and opened the door. Margie was all prettied up and looking expectant and radiant. When she didn't see him come out she got up and peeked into my office. "But where did he go?" she asked with wide eyes.

"Get hold of yourself girl," I answered. "You're so dazed you didn't even see him walk right by you."

"There's something fishy going on here," she said.

Well, I had a problem. A first rate, genuine, dyed in the wool dilemma.

What was I to do? I could have gone to the local authorities and got locked up for being a psycho. I could have gone to the college professors and got locked up for being a psycho. I could have gone to maybe the FBI and got locked up for being a psycho. That line of thinking began to get monotonous.

I did the one thing which I thought might bring help. I wrote up the happenings and sent it to my favorite science-fiction magazine. I asked for help and sage counsel from the one place I felt awareness and comprehension might be reached.

The manuscript bounced back so fast it might have had rubber bands attached to it, stretched California to New York. I looked the little rejection slip over, front and back, and I did not find upon it those sage words of counsel I needed. There wasn't even a printed invitation to try again some time.

And for the first time in my life I knew what it was to be alone—genuinely and irrevocably alone.

Still, I could not blame the editor. I could see him cast the manuscript from him in disgust, saying, "Bah! So another evil race comes to conquer Earth. If I give the fans one more of those, I'd be run out of my office." And like the deacon who saw the naughty words written on the fence, saying, "And misspelled, too."

The fable of the boy who cried "Wolf! Wolf!" once too often came home to me now. I was alone with my problem. The dilemma was my own. On one hand was immediate extermination. I did not doubt it. A race which can open doors from one star system to another, without even visible means of mechanism, would also know how to—disinfect.

On the other hand was extinction, gradual, but equally certain, and none the less effective in that it would not be perceived. If I refused to assist, then acting as one lone judge of all the race, I condemned it. If I did assist, I would be arch traitor, with an equal final result.

For days I sweltered in my miasma of indecision. Like many a man before me, uncertain of what to do, I temporized. I decided to play for time. To play the role of traitor in the hopes I might learn a way of defeating them.

Once I had made up my mind, my thoughts raced wildly through the possibilities. If I were to be their instructor on how to walk unsuspected among men, then I would have them wholly in my grasp. If I could build traits into them, common ordinary traits which they could see in men all about them, yet which would make men turn and destroy them, then I would have my solution.

And I knew human beings. Perhaps it was right, after all, that it became my problem. Mine alone.

I shuddered now to think what might have happened had this being fallen into less skilled hands and told his story. Perhaps by now there would be no man left upon Earth.

Yes, the old and worn-out plot of the one little unknown guy who saved Earth from outer evil might yet run its course in reality.

I was ready for the Arcturan when he returned. And he did return.

Einar Johnson and I walked out of my office after I had sent a tearful Margie on a long vacation with fancy pay. Einar had plenty of money, and was liberal with it. When a fellow can open some sort of fourth-dimensional door into a bank vault and help himself, money is no problem.

I had visions of the poor bank clerks trying to explain things to the examiners, but that wasn't my worry right now.

We walked out of the office and I snapped the lock shut behind me. Always conscious of the cares of people looking for work, I hung a sign on the door saying I was ill and didn't know when I would be back.

We walked down the stairs and into the parking lot. We got into my car, my own car, please note, and I found myself sitting in a sheltered patio in Beverly Hills. Just like that. No awful wrenching and turning my insides out. No worrisome nausea and emptiness of space. Nothing to dramatize it at all. Car—patio, like that.

I would like to be able to describe the Arcturans as having long snaky appendages and evil slobbering maws, and stuff like that. But I can't describe the Arcturans, because I didn't see any.

I saw a gathering of people, roughly about thirty of them, wandering around the patio, swimming in the pool, going in and out of the side doors of the house. It was a perfect spot. No one bothers the big Beverly Hills home without invitation.

The natives wouldn't be caught dead looking toward a star's house. The tourists see the winding drive, the trees and grass, and perhaps a glimpse of a gabled roof. If they can get any thrill out of that then bless their little spending money hearts, they're welcome to it.

Yet if it should become known that a crowd of strange acting people are wandering around in the grounds, no one would think a thing about it. They don't come any more zany than the Hollywood crowd.

Only these were. These people could have made a fortune as life-size puppets. I could see now why it was judged that the lifeless Teutonic I had first interviewed was thought adequate to mingle with human beings. By comparison with these, he was a snappy song and dance man.

But that is all I saw. Vacant bodies wandering around, going through human motions, without human emotions. The job looked bigger than I had thought. And yet, if this was their idea of how to win friends and influence people, I might be successful after all.

There are dozens of questions the curious might want answered—such as how did they get hold of the house and how did they get their human bodies and where did they learn to speak English, and stuff. I wasn't too curious. I had important things to think about. I supposed they were able to do it, because here it was.

I'll cut the following weeks short. I cannot conceive of what life and civilization on their planet might be like. Yardsticks of scientific psychology are used to measure a man, and yet they give no indication at all of the inner spirit of him, likewise, the descriptive measurements of their civilization are empty and meaningless. Knowing about a man, and knowing a man are two entirely different things.

For example, all those thalamic urges and urgencies which we call emotion were completely unknown to them, except as they saw them in antics on TV. The ideals of man were also unknown—truth, honor, justice, perfection—all unknown. They had not even a division of sexes, and the emotion we call love was beyond their understanding. The TV stories they saw must have been like watching a parade of ants.

What purpose can be gained by describing such a civilization to man? Man cannot conceive accomplishment without first having the dream. Yet it was obvious what they accomplished, for they were here.

When I finally realized there was no point of contact between man and these, I knew relief and joy once more. My job was easy. I knew how to destroy them. And I suspected they could not avoid my trap.

They could not avoid my trap because they had human bodies. Perhaps they conceived them out of thin air, but the veins bled, the flesh felt pain and heat and pressure, the glands secreted.

Ah yes, the glands secreted. They would learn what emotion could be. And I was a master at wielding emotion. The dream of man has been to strive toward the great and immortal ideals. His literature is filled with admonishments to that end. In comparison with the volume of work which tells us what we should be, there is very little which reveals us as we are.

As part of my training course, I chose the world's great literature, and painting, and sculpture, and music—those mediums which best portray man lifting to the stars. I gave them first of all, the dream.

And with the dream, and with the pressure of the glands as kicker, they began to know emotion. I had respect for the superb acting of Einar when I realized that he, also, had still known no emotion.

They moved from the puppet to the newborn babe—a newborn babe in training, with an adult body, and its matured glandular equation.

I saw emotions, all right. Emotions without restraint, emotions unfettered by taboos, emotions uncontrolled by ideals. Sometimes I became frightened and all my skill in manipulating emotions was needed. At other times they became perhaps a little too Hollywood, even for Hollywood. I trained them into more ideal patterns.

I will say this for the Arcturans, they learned—fast. The crowd of puppets to the newborn babes, to the boisterous boys and girls to the moody and unpredictable youths, to the matured and balanced men and women. I watched the metamorphosis take place over the period of weeks.

I did more.

All that human beings had ever hoped to be, the brilliant, the idealistic, the great in heart, I made of these. My little 145 I.Q. became a moron's level. The dreams of the greatness of man which I had known became the vaguest wisps of fog before the reality which these achieved.

My plan was working.

Full formed, they were almost like gods. And training these things into them, I trained their own traits out. One point I found we had in common. They were activated by logic, logic carried to heights of which I had never dreamed. Yet my poor and halting logic found point of contact.

They realized at last that if they let their own life force and motivation remain active they would carry the aura of strangeness to defeat their purpose. I worried, when they accepted this. I felt perhaps they were laying a trap for me, as I did for them. Then I realized that I had not taught them deceit.

And it was logical, to them, that they follow my training completely. Reversing the position, placing myself upon their planet, trying to become like them, I must of necessity follow my instructor without question. What else could they do?

At first they saw no strangeness that I should assist them to destroy my race. In their logic the Arcturan was most fit to survive, therefore he should survive. The human was less fit, therefore he should perish.

I taught them the emotion of compassion. And when they began to mature their human thought and emotion, and their intellect was blended and shaded by such emotion, at last they understood my dilemma.

There was irony in that. From my own kind I could expect no understanding. From the invaders I received sympathy and compassion. They understand at last my traitorous action to buy a few more years for Man.

Yet their Arcturan logic still prevailed. They wept with me, but there could be no change of plan. The plan was fixed, they were merely instruments by which it was to be carried out.

Yet, through their compassion, I did get the plan modified.

This was the conversation which revealed that modification. Einar Johnson, who as the most fully developed had been my constant companion, said to me one day, "To all intents and purposes we have become human beings." He looked at me and smiled with fondness, "You have said it is so, and it must be so. For we begin to realize what a great and glorious thing a human is."

The light of nobility shone from him like an aura as he told me this, "Without human bodies, and without the emotion-intelligence equation which you call soul, our home planet cannot begin to grasp the growth we have achieved. We know now that we will never return to our own form, for by doing that we would lose what we have gained.

"Our people are logical, and they must of necessity accept our recommendation, as long as it does not abandon the plan entirely. We have reported what we have learned, and it is conceived that both our races can inhabit the Universe side by side.

"There will be no more migration from our planet to yours. We will remain, and we will multiply, and we will live in honor, such as you have taught us, among you. In time perhaps we may achieve the greatness which all humans now have.

"And we will assist the human kind to find their destiny among the stars as we have done."

I bowed my head and wept. For I knew that I had won.

Four months had gone. I returned to my own neighborhood. On the corner Hallahan left the traffic to shift for itself while he came over to me with the question, "Where have you been?"

"I've been sick," I said.

"You look it," he said frankly. "Take care of yourself, man. Hey—Lookit that fool messing up traffic." He was gone, blowing his whistle in a temper.

I climbed the stairs. They still needed repainting as much as ever. From time to time I had been able to mail money to Margie, and she had kept the rent and telephone paid. The sign was still on my door. My key opened the lock.

The waiting room had that musty, they've-gone-away look about it. The janitor had kept the windows tightly closed and there was no freshness in the air. I half hoped to see Margie sitting at her desk, but I knew there was no purpose to it. When a girl is being paid for her time and has nothing to do, the beach is a nice place to spend it.

There was dust on my chair, and I sank down into it without bothering about the seat of my pants. I buried my head in my arms and I looked into the human soul.

Now the whole thing hinged on that skill. I know human beings. I know them as well as anyone in the world, and far better than most.

I looked into the past and I saw a review of the great and fine and noble and divine torn and burned and crucified by man.

Yet my only hope of saving my race was to build these qualities, the fine, the noble, the splendid, into these thirty beings. To creat the illusion that all men were likewise great. No less power could have gained the boom of equality for man with them.

I look into the future. I see them, one by one, destroyed. I gave them no defense. They are totally unprepared to meet man as he genuinely is—and they are incapable of understanding.

For these things which man purports to admire the most—the noble, the brilliant, the splendid—these are the very things he cannot tolerate when he finds them.

Defenseless, because they cannot comprehend, these thirty will go down beneath the ravening fury of rending and destroying man always displays whenever he meets his ideal face to face.

I bury my head in my hands.

What have I done?

FAST FALLS THE EVENTIDE

Eric Frank Russell (1905–1978)

We have discussed the career and life of the tall, British Eric Frank Russell several times in this series, but it is worth repeating that he was a man who recognized that all life is in the last analysis interconnected, that compassion is a virtue, and that cooperation is better than division. These feelings and ideas were expressed in more than sixteen books in the science fiction/fantasy field, not a large number by the standards of the genre. It is sobering to realize that he wrote practically nothing between from 1960 until his death. It is also interesting to me that John W. Campbell, Jr., the great editor of *Astounding/Analog,* considered him his favorite writer.

"Fast Falls the Eventide" is a wonderful example of Russel's philosophy. (MHG)

I did not know that John Campbell considered Russell his favorite writer. At various times I thought Heinlein, van Vogt, Sturgeon, del Rey, or even I was. As I think of it, however, Russell is a good choice. It was his novella, "Sinister Barrier," which inspired Campbell to introduce his never-to-be-sufficiently-admired-and-lamented *Unknown*.

Then, too, Russell's writing was absolutely reliable. He never wrote a story that was not workmanlike, not easy reading, not interesting, not good.

Finally, he shared Campbell's belief that somehow Earthmen would always win out; that there was something special about Earthmen. So this is a "Campbell story," too, and though I sometimes find Campbell stories hard to take when I disagree with the premise, Russell makes even the strangest Campbellisms palatable. (IA)

It was an old world, incredibly old, with a pitted moon and a dying sun and a sky too thin to hold a summer cloud. There were trees upon it but not the trees of yore, for these were the result of eons of gradual accommodation. They inhaled and exhaled far less than did their distant forebears and they sucked more persistently at the aged soul.

So did the herbs.

And the flowers.

But the petal-lacking, rootless children of this sphere, the ones able to move around of their own volition, these could not compensate by sitting in one place and drawing from the ground. So slowly, ever so slowly they had dispensed with what once had been a basic need. They could manage quite well on the bare minimum of oxygen. Or at a pinch without any at all, experiencing no more than mild discomfort, a certain lassitude. All could do this without exception.

The children of this world were bugs.

And birds.

And bipeds.

Moth, magpie and man, all were related. All had the same mother: an ancient sphere rolling around a weakly glowing orange ball that some day would flicker and go out. Their preparation for this end had been long and arduous, partly involuntary, partly deliberate. This was their time: the age of fulfillment, shared between all, belonging to all.

Thus it was in no way odd that Melisande should talk to a small beetle. It sat attentively on the back of her pale, long-fingered hand, a tiny creature, black with crimson spots, clean and shiny as if subjected to hours of patient polishing. A lady-bird. An amusingly toylike entity that seemed to lack a miniature handle in its side with which to wind it up.

Of course the ladybird could not understand a word of what was being said. It was not *that* intelligent. Time had run so far and the atmosphere become so thin that the insect's wings had adapted accordingly and now were twice the size of those owned by ladybirds of long ago. And with the physical alteration there had been mental alteration; its pin-sized brain was different too. By the standard of its own humble kind it had climbed several rungs up the ladder of life. Though it could not determine meanings, it knew when it was being addressed, sought human company, derived comfort from the sound of a human voice.

And so with the others.

The birds.

The latter-day bees.

All the timid things that once had run for a hiding place or sought shelter in the dark.

Those who had survived—and many species had not—were shy no more. Regardless of whether or not they could understand the mouth-noises made, they liked to be spoken to, their existence acknowledged. They could and did listen for hours, extracting strange pleasure from the intimacy of sound. Or was the pleasure strange?

Perhaps not, for there were times when the sonic relationship was reversed and men stood fascinated while, in lilting language peculiarly its own, a blackbird or nightingale poured forth its very soul.

It was the same indefinable ecstasy.

You see?

So Melisande talked as she walked and Little Redspots listened with his own insectual pleasure until finally she gently flipped her hand and laughed, "Ladybird, ladybird, fly away home."

It raised colorful wing-cases, spread gauzy wings and fluttered from sight. Melisande paused to look at the stars. In these times they could be seen with briliance and clarity by day as well as by night, a phenomenon that would have made her air-loving ancestors become filled with fear lest the breath of life soon depart.

No such sensation was within her as she studied the stars. There was only curiosity and speculation coming from a purely personal source. To her, the five-miles-high atmosphere, the dim sun, the sparkling stars were all normal. Often she looked at the stars, sorting them out, identifying them, asking herself the same question again and again.

"Which one?"

And the heavens answered only, "Ah, which?"

Ceasing her speculation, she tripped lightly onward along the narrow woodland path that led into the valley. Far to her left, on the verge of the horizon, something long, slender and metallic arrowed down from the sky and vanished beyond the curve of the earth. A little later a much muted thundering came to her ears.

Neither the sight nor the sound captured her attention. They were too ordinary. The ships of space came often to this ancient world, sometimes once in a month, sometimes twice in a day. Rarely were any two alike. Rarely did the people of one vessel resemble the crew of another.

They had no common language, these visitors from the glittering dark. They spoke a multitude of tongues. Some could talk only mentally, in powerfully projected thought-forms. Some were nonvocal and nontelepathic, could not speak at all, and communicated by means of dexterous finger-motions, ultra-rapid vibration of cilia or other gesticulatory devices.

Once, not so long ago, she had been briefly entertained by the slate-colored, armor-skinned personnel of a ship from Khva, a world unthinkable distances beyond Andromeda. They had been completely blind and totally dumb, making superfast limb-signals at each other and registering them through sensitive esp-organs. They had talked to her without voice and admired her without eyes.

All this was what made learning so hard. At seven hundred years of age she had just finished her final examinations and gained the status of an adult. Long, long ago one might have absorbed the wisdom of an era in a mere century. In the dimmer days still farther back one might have done it in ten years. But not today. Not today.

Now in these solemn times of the final centuries the knowledge to be imbibed was in quantity far too great for swift assimilation. It was an immense pile of data created by the impact of a mighty cosmos composed of worlds without end. Each new ship added a few modest grains to the mass, and the mountain already so built was as nothing to the titanic quantities yet to come—if this world lived long enough to receive them.

If!

There was the rub. Creation was conquered and made the slave of the shapes it had brought forth. The atom and the power within the atom were tools in the hands or pseudo-hands of matter forms able to think and move. Macrocosm and microcosm were equally the playthings of those whose ships roamed endlessly through the tremendous void.

But there were none who knew how to revive an expiring sun. It could not be done in theory, much less in fact.

It was impossible.

So here and there, at great intervals, a senile sun would flare up awhile, collapse into itself, flare again like a feeble thing making its last frantic snatch at life and then become extinguished for all time. A tiny spark in the dark suddenly blown out, unnoticed and unmissed from the limitless host that still blazed on.

Almost each vanishing marked tragedy, perhaps immediate in one case and delayed in another. Some life forms could resist cold longer than others but eventually succumbed just the same. By their superior techniques some could warm themselves and their worlds until the raw material sources of their heat were exhausted. Then they, too, became as if they had never been.

Any system whose primary reverted to an enormous cinder thereby became the property of a great, white, greedy idiot bearing the same of Supernal Frost. He would share his dreary estates with none but the dead.

Melisande thought of all these things as she reached the valley. But the thoughts were not morbid; they held nothing of sadness or resentment. She was of her own kind and it was a life form old in experience and remarkably astute. It had faced the inevitable a thousand times before and had learned the futility of battering against it head-on. It knew what to do with an immovable object: one climbs over it or burrows under it or sneaks around it. One uses one's brains because they are there to be used.

Inevitability was not to be feared.

That which cannot be stayed must be avoided with skill and ingenuity.

A great marble palace sprawled across the end of the valley. Its farther side faced a long series of shrub-dotted and flower-carpeted terraces with narrow lawns and feathery fountains. Its nearer side was the back looking upon nothing but the valley. Melisande always approached it from the rear because the path through the woods was the shortcut to home.

Mounting the steps she experienced a thrill of excitement as she entered the huge edifice. Wide, mosaic-floored corridors with walls bearing colorful murals led her to the east wing whence came a steady murmur of voices and occasionally the penetrating sound of a caller-trumpet.

Bright-eyed with anticipation, she went into a large hall whose seats rose in semicircular tiers to considerable height. It was a place originally designed to hold four thousand. The number of people now seated therein came to no more than two hundred— almost a score of empty seats for every one occupied. The place looked bare. The voices of the few floated hollowly around the emptiness, were echoed by the curved walls and reflected by the overhead cupola.

All the world was like this: facilities for thousands available to mere dozens. Cities with small-town populations; towns numbering no more citizens than a one-time village; and villages holding only three or four families. Whole streets of houses of which half a dozen were homes while the others, empty, silent and glassy-eyed, stared at the lowering sky.

There were just over one million people on this world. Once upon a time they had numbered four thousand millions. The vanished numbers had long since taken to the star-trails, not like rats leaving a sinking ship but boldly, confidently as those whose destiny has become magnified until too great for the confines of one planet.

The small remainder were to follow as soon as they were ready. And that was why the two hundred were here, waiting in the hall, fidgety, chattering, a little on edge as they listened for the fateful blare of the caller-trumpet.

"Eight-two-eight Hubert," it suddenly gave forth. "Room Six."

A blond giant came up from his seat, stalked down the aisle watched by almost two hundred pairs of eyes. Voices were temporarily silent. He went past Melisande who smiled and murmured low.

"Good luck!"

"Thanks!"

Then he was gone through the distant door. The chatterers resumed. Melisande sat herself at the end of a row next to a thin, swarthy youth of some seven and a half centuries, little older than herself.

"I'm a minute late," she whispered. "Have they been calling long?"

"No," he assured. "That last name was the fourth." He stretched out his legs, pulled them in, stretched them out again, surveyed his fingernails, shifted in his seat, registered vague discomfort. "I wish they'd hurry up with this. The strain is rather—"

"Nine-nine-one José-Pietro," boomed the trumpet. "Room Twenty."

He heard it with his mouth open, his eyes startled. The way he came to his feet was slow, uncertain. He licked thin lips suddenly gone dry, cast an appealing glance at Melisande.

"That's me!"

"They must have heard you," she laughed. "Well, don't you want to go?"

"Yes, of course." He edged past her, his gaze on the door through which the blond Hubert had gone. "But when it comes to the point I sort of go weak in the knees."

She made a negligent gesture. "Nobody's going to amputate your legs. They're simply waiting to give you a document—and maybe it'll be one with a gold seal."

Throwing her a look of silent gratitude, he speeded up, exited with a mite more self-assurance.

"Seven-seven Jocelyn—Room Twelve."

And immediately after, "Two-four-oh Betsibelle—Room Nineteen."

Two girls went out, one dark and plump and smiling, one tall, slender, red-haired and serious.

Came a series of names in quick succession: Lurton, Irene, George, Teresa-Maria, Robert and Elena. Then, after a short interval, the summons for which she was waiting.

"Four-four Melisande—Room Two!"

The man in Room Two had light gray eyes, snowy hair and smooth, unlined features. He might have been middle-aged—or old, extremely old. There was no way of telling at a time when a person can retain a seamless face and snowy locks for more than a thousand years.

Waiting for her to be seated, he said: "Well, Melisande, I am happy to say you have passed."

"Thank you, my tutor.

"I felt sure you would pass. I viewed it as almost a foregone conclusion." He smiled across at her, went on, "and now you want to know where you are weak, where you are strong. Those are the essential details, aren't they?"

"Yes, my tutor." She uttered it in low tones, her hands folded demurely in her lap.

"In general knowledge you are excellent," he informed. "That is something of which to be proud—that one should hold the immense storehouse of wisdom described by the inadequate

name of general knowledge. You are also most satisfactory in
sociology, mass-psychology, ancient and modern philosophies
and transcosmic ethics.'' He leaned forward, looking at her.
''But you are rather poor in general communications.''

''I am sorry, my tutor.'' She bit her lower lip, vexed with
herself.

''You are nontelepathic and seem quite unable to develop even
rudimentary receptivity. When it comes to visual signaling you
are somewhat better but still not good enough. Your communication rate is sluggish, your mistakes numerous, and you appear to
be handicapped by a form of tactile uncertainty.''

She was now looking at the floor, her face wearing a blush of
shame. ''I regret it, my tutor.''

''There is nothing to regret,'' he contradicted sharply. ''One
cannot excel in everything, much as one might like to do so.''
He waited for her eyes to come up, then proceeded, ''as for
purely vocal forms of communication, you are no more than fair
in the guttural languages.'' A pause, then: ''But you are superb
in the liquid ones.''

''Ah!'' Her features brightened.

''Your oral and written tests for liquid languages were taken in
the speech-patterns of the Valreans of Sirius. Your errors were
exactly none. Your vocal rate was three hundred twenty words
per minute. The average for the Valreans is three hundred fourteen. That means you can speak their language a little better than
they can themselves.'' He smiled to himself, deriving much
satisfaction from the thought that his pupil could outshine the
very originators of a linguistic mode. ''So now, Melisande, the
time has come to make serious decisions.''

''I am ready, my tutor.'' Her gaze forward was steady, level
and unswerving.

''First I must give you this.'' He handed her a thin scroll from
which dangled a crimson cord terminating in a gold seal. ''I
congratulate you.''

''Thank you!'' Her fingers took it, held it, fondled it like
something infinitely precious.

''Melisande,'' he asked, gently, ''do you desire children?''

Her answer came evenly, undisturbed, quite without trace of
embarrassment. ''Not yet, my tutor.''

''Then you consider yourself free to go out?'' He gestured
toward the window beyond which a multimillion lights gleamed
and beckoned.

"Yes."

His face became solemn. "But you will not abandon all thoughts of children of your own? You will not plunge so deeply and become so absorbed as to be forgetful of your own shape and kind?"

"I think not," she promised.

"I am glad of that, Melisande. We are scattered afar, in little groups and numbers over an immensity of places. There is no need to increase our count within the cosmos, no need at all. But we should not reduce that count. We should maintain it. That way lies immortality as a species."

"Yes, I know. I have thought of it often." She studied her scroll without really seeing it. "I shall play my little part when the right moment comes."

"You have plenty of time, anyway. You are very young." He sighed as if he wished he could say the same of himself. Crossing the room to where a machine stood by the wall, he opened a cabinet at its side, took out a thick wad of cards. "We'll sort the applications and narrow them down to those most suitable."

He fed the cards one by one into the machine. They were no more than rectangles of thin, white plastic each bearing a reference number at the head, the rest being perforated with many circular or square-shaped holes. When the lot had been inserted he opened a cover revealing a small keyboard. On this he typed, "Nonvocals," and pulled a lever at one side.

The machine clicked, whirred, expelled cards in rapid succession. When it had finished, he glanced at its retention-counter.

"Eighty-four left."

Again resorting to the keyboard, he picked out the word, "Gutturals." The machine responded by throwing out another spray of cards. "Supersonics." More cards. "Staccatos." Out shot a little bunch. "Whistlers." No result.

"Twenty-one." He glanced at his pupil. "They are all liquid speakers now but I think it would be as well if we eliminated the slow ones, don't you?" Getting her nod, he reset the keyboard, "300-max." Several cards emerged. Extracting the remainder, he shuffled them in sensitive fingers, eyed the stars through the window. "There are eleven, Melisande. You have eleven worlds from which to choose."

Filing the first card into a different part of the machine, he set a pair of dials and pressed a stud. The apparatus emitted a faint hum while it warmed up, then a voice came from its hidden speaker.

It said: "Application Number 109,747. Valrea, a union of four planets located in—"

Abruptly it cut off as he jabbed another stud in response to a wave of Melisande's hand.

"You are not interested?"

"No, my tutor. Perhaps I ought to be because I already know their language and that would save a lot of bother. But they have some of us already, haven't they?"

"Yes. They applied for four hundred. We sent them thirty-six and, much later on, another twenty." He regarded her with almost paternal solicitude. "You would have company there, Melisande. You would have others of your own kind, few as they are."

"That may be," she admitted. "But is it fair that people like the Valreans, who have gained some of what they want, should be given still more while others who have none should continue to be denied?"

"No, it is not." He fed in a second card.

"Application 118,451," said the machine. "Brank, a single planet located in the Horse's Head Nebula, Section A71, Subsection D19. Mass 1.2. Civilization type-F. The dominant life form is a bipedal vertebrate as shown."

A screen above the apparatus glowed in full colors, depicted several gaunt, greenish-skinned creatures with long, spindly arms and legs, seven-fingered hands, hairless skulls and enormous yellow eyes.

For another ten minutes the voice poured forth a flood of data concerning Brank and its emaciated inhabitants. Then it ceased and the machine went quiescent.

"Thirty years ago they asked for a hundred of us," he told Melisande. "We sent ten. They have now been allocated another six of which you may be one if you so desire."

Seeing that she was noncommittal, he slid another card into the apparatus.

"Application 120,776. Nildeen, a planet with one large satellite, heavily populated, located in the Maelstrom, Section L7, Subsection CC3."

It went on and on. The appropriate life form displayed itself on the screen, a tentacular, eyeless type of being with esp-organs protruding from its head like an insect's antennae. The Nildeens already had had forty of Melisande's kind, still wanted more. She turned them down.

The eleventh and last card aroused her greatest interest, caused her to lean forward with ears alert and eyes alight.

"Application 141,048. Zelam, a single planet located on the fringe of the known, reference numbers and coordinates not yet filed. Recent contact. Mass I. Civilization type-J. Dominant life form is reptilian as shown."

They had a faint resemblance to erect alligators, though Melisande did not know it. All of her own planet's lizardlike species had vanished a million years ago. There were now no local forms to which she could liken these horny-skinned, long-jawed and toothy Zelamites. By the standards of the dim past they were appallingly ugly; but by the standards of her especial planet and her especial era they were not ugly. They were merely an individualistic aspect of the same universal thing which is named Intelligence.

True, the varying forms might also vary in the accuracy with which they reflected this elusive but cosmos-wide thing, yet, taking the long view, it was nothing but a variation in time. Some had more centuries to catch up than did others. Some had come early on the scene and that was their good fortune. Others had come late and that was their hard luck. They were like differently handicapped runners in the same field, spread out, panting, some in front, some behind, but all heading the same way, all destined to pass the finish line. The Zelamites were held-back runners.

"I will go to those," she said, making it an irrevocable decision.

Spreading the eleven cards across his desk, he surveyed them with a bothered frown. "They asked for sixty. Everyone asks for far too many, especially the newcomers. We've none to spare just yet. But we don't like to refuse anyone."

"So?"

"It has been suggested that we send them one, just one, as a beginning. It would show willingness if nothing else."

"I am one," she pointed out.

"Yes, yes, I know." He had the resigned air of a person about to be cornered without hope of escape. "We would rather that one were masculine."

"Why?"

The query defeated him completely. "There is no reason at all except that we would prefer it."

"Surely, my tutor, it would be a retrograde step and quite unworthy of us to insist upon something without any reason?"

"Not if it does no harm," he countered. "There is the true test—whether it does harm or good."

"Does it do the Zelamites good to refuse them a suitable volunteer?"

"We are not refusing them, Melisande. There are others besides yourself. Someone else may also have chosen Zelam. A dozen may wish to go there. At this stage, with so many applications, we just can't send all of them. Only one can go now. Others may follow later."

"Find out for me, please," she begged.

A mite unwillingly he flicked the switch on his desk and spoke into the silver instrument beside it.

"How many have selected Zelam, Reference 141,048?"

There was quite a long wait before the answer came, "None."

Switching off, he leaned back, eyed her thoughtfully. "You will be lonely."

"All first arrivals are lonely."

"There may arise perils beyond imagining."

"Which will remain the same whether borne by one or shared by a hundred," she gave back, undismayed.

Searching around for one last item of discouragement, he told her, "The Zelamites are nocturnal. They will expect you to work at night and sleep by day."

"Those of us on Brank have been doing the same for years, and many more elsewhere. My tutor, should it be harder for me than for them?"

"No, it should not." He came across to her. "I see that you are determined in your choice. If it be your destiny, it is not for me to thwart it." Taking her hand, he raised it gently, impressed a light kiss upon her fingers in the conventional farewell. "Good luck, Melisande. I am glad to have had you as a pupil of mine."

"Thank you, my tutor." Holding her scroll tightly to her breast, she paused in the doorway as she went out, gave him a final bright-eyed smile. "And I am proud to have had you!"

Long after she had gone he sat and gazed absently at the door. They came and they went, one after another. Each arrived as an utter stranger, departed like a child of his very own taking some of his essential essence with them.

And each one that went forever among the vast concourse of stars made his dying world a fraction smaller, barer, less possessed of life. It is not easy to remain with a long-loved sphere which is nearing its end, to watch the flame die down, watch the shadows creep and grow.

Even at the terrific velocities of this age the journey to Zelam was long and tedious, stretching through days and weeks into many months. It involved several changes, first from a huge hyperspatial mainliner to a smaller branchliner, then to a light blue sphere crewed by dumb Xanthians, then to a battered old rocketship manned by a weirdly mixed mob among whom were two bipeds of Melisande's own kind. Finally to a strange, wedge-shaped and mysteriously powered contraption which sinuous and scintillant Haldisians employed for trading around a small group of systems in one of which was the planet called Zelam.

Beyond this point was a great sprawl of darkness in which reposed a coil of brilliant mist that eventually would be reached by bigger and better ships. Another island universe. Another mighty host of living shapes and forms the highest of which would share one thing in common—and therefore prove willing to share it yet again.

But the length of the trip had been useful. With the aid of a phonetic dictionary and a rudimentary tape recorder provided by Zelam, plus her own natural aptitude, she had become an accomplished speaker of the language by the time the planet rolled into view.

Lacking ladder, ramps or anything of that nature, the Haldisians got rid of her by the simple expedient of throwing her through the outer door of the air lock. A power exerted by them personally or perhaps by some unseen apparatus within the vessel—she did not know which—took hold of her, lowered her gently the forty feet to earth. Her luggage followed the same way. So did two of the crew. Another two came out but floated upward, gained the ship's flat topside, commenced opening cargo hatches.

There was a small Zelamite deputation to meet her, the news of her coming having been received a few days before. They were bigger than she had expected for the screen on which she had first seen them had given no indication of relative size. The shortest of them towered head and shoulders above her, had sharp-toothed jaws the length of her arm and looked as if he could cut her in half at one savage snap.

The largest and oldest of the group, a heavily built and warty-faced individual, came forward to meet her as the others hastened to pick up her bags.

"You are the one named Melisande?"

"That's me," she admitted, smiling at him.

He responded with what looked remarkably like a threatening snarl. It did not mislead her in the least. Her kind had learned a thousand centuries ago that those with different facial contours and bony structure perforce must have different ranges of expressions. She knew that the alarming grimace was nothing but an answering smile.

The tone of his voice proved it as he went on, "We are pleased to have you." His orange-colored eyes with their slot-shaped pupils studied her a moment before he added in mild complaint, "We asked for a hundred and hoped to get ten, perhaps twenty."

"More will come in due course."

"It is to be hoped so." He threw a significant glance toward the ship from which items of cargo were floating down. "The Haldisians have twenty. We are tired of hearing them boast about it. We think we are entitled to at least as many."

"They started with two of us," she pointed out. "The others came later—as yours will do. We have no choice but to deal with applications in strict rotation."

"Oh, well—" He spread the long fingers of one hand in the Zelamite equivalent of a shrug, conducted her to a six-wheeled vehicle standing nearby, superintended the loading of her luggage, then got in beside her. "I must compliment you on your fluency. It is remarkable."

"Thank you."

She concentrated on the blue-moss coated and yellow-flowered landscape as he drove to town at a fast pace. His body exuded a faintly pungent odor which her nostrils noted but her brain ignored. That was another very ancient lesson: that different metabolisms produce different manifestations. How boring would the universe be if all its creatures were identically the same!

They drew up before a long, low stone-built edifice with high-tilted roofs and plastic windows. The place was imposing mostly because of its lengthy façade. It stretched at least half a mile, had a blue-moss carpet along its front and a railed yard at each end.

"This is your college." He pointed to the nearer end. "And there is your home." Observing her expression he added by way of explanation. "Of course, we cannot expect more than one person can do. We built apartments for ten, with space for extensions if we were lucky enough to get more of you."

"I see." Getting out, she watched her bags being taken inside. Despite centuries of training, free choice of destination and months of anticipatory journeying, some adjustment still was necessary. "And there is your home," he had said. It would take her at least a week and perhaps a month to get used to thinking of it as home. Probably even more because domestic routine would be topsy-turvy so long as she slept daytimes and worked nights.

"Before you go in," he suggested, "what about something to eat?"

"Good heavens, no!" She gave a tinkling laugh. "The Haldisians insisted on providing a farewell dinner. They didn't know when to stop. I don't feel like looking at any more food for days."

"*Armph!*" The twist on his reptilian face suggested that he'd have liked it better if the Haldisians had left well alone. "In that case, all I can offer you is the rest and relaxation you must need. Do you think you might be ready to start work tomorrow evening?"

"Most certainly."

"You can have longer if you wish."

"Tomorrow evening will do," she assured.

"Good—I will tell Nathame. He is our chief cultural supervisor and high in governmental affairs. He will call to see you shortly before you begin."

Giving her another wide-jawed and toothy smile, he drove away. She watched him go, then went and inspected her front door which the luggage-bearers had left invitingly open. It was a simple vertical shutter affair wound up and down by a side handle and could be fastened from the inside only by means of a small bolt.

Beyond it lay the passage, solid, motionless, solely to be walked upon and not for automatic transport. And lights that had to be switched because they knew nothing of perpetual illumination. But it was home-to-be.

She stepped inside.

Nathame came with the twilight on the next day. A sharp-eyed, alert specimen of Zelamite life, he wore glittering insignia on his shoulder-straps, bore himself with authoritative self-assurance. For a while he chatted inconsequentially, his keen gaze never shifting from her face, then added a grumble to the effect that if one person were another world's idea of a hundred it might be better to ask for ten thousand and thus obtain the number really required.

He fell silent for a bit, occupied by his own thoughts, then said: "Before we made contact with other people we had no history but our own. Now we've had to learn the lore of a whole galaxy. It is a record voluminous enough to absorb a lifetime. Nevertheless, I have specialized in it and have learned one thing: that your own particular kind of life is supremely clever."

"Do you think so?" She watched him curiously.

"I do not *think* it. I *know* it." He warmed to his subject. "History records that between sixty and seventy life forms have disappeared from the universal scene. Some warred together and exploded each other's worlds. Some were the victims of cosmic collisions that could be neither foreseen nor avoided. They vanished—*pouf!*—like that! The large majority died when their suns died and warmth went away from them and supernal cold took over." His orange-colored orbs still stared at her unblinking. "It proves one thing: that an entire species can be exterminated and become as though it had never been."

"Not necessarily," she contradicted, "because—"

"Ah!" He held up a hand to halt her. "Of a verity it is for *your* kind to deny the possibility. What or who can wipe out a life form scattered over a hundred million worlds? Nothing! Nobody!"

"I don't think anyone would wish to try."

"Not unless they were completely crazy," he agreed. "You have made yourselves invincible. You have preserved yourselves for eternity. I call that cleverness of the highest order." He pulled a face. "And how have you done it?"

"How do you imagine?" she invited.

"By using your great experience and immense wealth of wisdom to exploit the snobbery of lesser races."

"I don't see it that way."

Ignoring her, he went determinedly on, "Your people anticipated disaster. They foresaw that when your sun collapsed no other planet and no other system could or would accept a sudden influx of refugees numbering thousands of millions. But nobody minds a few dozen or hundreds, especially if they add to their hosts' prestige. Comes the master stroke: you persuade them to scramble for self-esteem like children clamoring for gifts. You made them *want* you.''

"But surely—"

He silenced her again, clasped his hands together in a peculiarly artificial manner, minced across the room and spoke in high-pitched, long-drawn vowels, manifestly imitating a type of character with which she was not yet familiar.

"*Really*, Thasalmie, we wouldn't *dream* of sending *our* children to a *state* school. We've shipped them to the central college at Hei. *Terribly* expensive, of course. They have *Terran* tutors there and it makes *such* a difference in later life when one can say that one has been educated by *Terrans*.''

Relaxing into a normal pose, he said, "You see? Since the first Haldisian ships discovered us we've had visits from about twenty life forms. Every one of them took up a patronizing attitude. What, you have no Terrans? By the stars, you must be backward! Why, we have twenty on our world—or forty, or fifty as the case may be.'' His nostrils twitched as he emitted a loud snort. "They boast and they brag and act so superior that everyone on this world develops a severe inferiority complex and starts screaming for an army of Terrans without delay.''

"Braggarts and boasters are not Terran educated,'' she informed. "We don't produce that kind.''

"Maybe you don't, but that's the effect of your presence among those you've not yet taught. They shine in reflected glory. So I say again that you are supremely clever, and on three counts. You are making use of the fact that the more intelligent a people the less they enjoy being thought stupid. Secondly, you have thus insured your own survival for all time. Thirdly, by being content merely to maintain your numbers and not increase them you are also maintaining the confidence of your various hosts. Nobody views with alarm an alien colony that never grows.''

She smiled at him and remarked, "All along you've been inviting me to say, 'Look who's talking!' Haven't you?''

"Yes, but you were too diplomatic.'' Moving nearer and speaking with greater seriousness, he continued, "We asked for a hundred of your kind. Had we got them we would have asked for more. And more again. Not for prestige, but for other and better reasons.''

"Such as?''

"We look far ahead. The Haldisians, who know more about it than we, say that ours is a short-term sun. That means an end similar to the end of your world. We must seek the same way out because we can conceive no other. The path your kind has made our kind can tread also. The demand for Terrans is greater than the supply—and there aren't many more of you, are there?"

"Not many," she admitted. "About a million. The old world hasn't long to go."

"Some day we shall be compelled to say that, too. It would be nice if by that time the Zelamites had become an acceptable substitute for Terrans." He made an imperative gesture. "So there is your job as far as one can take it. It's a hard job. Starting with our brightest children you must make us clever enough to share your salvation."

"We'll do our best," she promised, deliberately using the plural.

It did not escape him. Even his face could register gratification. Saluting her, he took his departure. Re-angling her mind and directing it exclusively to the task in hand, she hurried along the main corridor, reached the room from which was coming a shrill uproar.

Silence dropped like a heavy curtain as she entered. Taking her place by the desk, she surveyed the hundred small, thin-snouted, slot-eyed faces that in turn were examining her with youthful candidness.

"We shall commence tonight with the basic subject of transcosmic ethics," she informed. Turning around, she faced the dark rectangle that had no counterpart on Terra, picked up the white stick at its base and wrote upon the blackboard in a firm, clear hand.

"Lesson One. Intelligence is like candy. It comes in an endless variety of shapes, sizes and colors, no one of which is less delectable than the others."

She glanced over her shoulder to insure that they were giving attention, found them copying it down, orange eyes intent. One had his tongue out, its purple tip laboriously following the movements of his writing instrument.

Involuntarily her gaze shifted to the transparent roof through which the galactic host looked down. Somewhere within that gleaming swarm was a little red light, weak and dimming. Somewhere near to it was another, silvery blue, shining to the very last.

The ancient fountain.

The guiding star.

Old Mother Earth.

THE BUSINESS, AS USUAL

by Mack Reynolds (1917–1983)

The science fiction of the 1950s was in many ways a subversive activity. Not only did it poke fun at the materialism and foibles of the American people—it also attacked some of the most revered institutions in American life like advertising, banking, insurance companies—in short, capitalism, which it (and I'm here talking mainly of the group of writers associated with *Galaxy*) attacked rather ruthlessly when you think about it, but almost never from a Marxist perspective and almost never proposing alternatives of a socialist or related type. Rugged individualism was the preferred response to corporate greed.

Mack Reynolds was the son of radical parents and he possessed a commitment to social justice that was tempered by a clear head and vast experience. He traveled all over the world, including to numerous Eastern European and socialist countries, and he knew what a Potemkin Village was. He was as critical of phony social justice as he was of its absence. As a science fiction writer, he loved to test social ideas in fictional settings, and he was one of the very few writers of his time to set his stories in Eastern Europe and to a lesser extent, the Third World. He discussed every "ism" that he could, and he didn't miss many.

He wasn't a particularly good writer in a stylistic sense, but he had a strong flair for adventure, and for a man of ideas, he excelled at depicting all forms of violence and combat. A prolific writer, he published nearly fifty novels, which have tended to overshadow his tighter, and I think better, short fiction. His popularity declined dramatically toward the end of his life, and he left a large body of unpublished work, some of which is now beginning to appear. (MHG)

I always find time-travel paradox stories entertaining. My novel *The End of Eternity*, is one long collection of time-travel paradoxes (though I did my best to make self-consistent sense out of them) and, of course, the master at that, as at everything else, was Bob Heinlein (see his immortal "By His Bootstraps," for instance).

Actually, I've always thought that the mere existence, in such quantity, of time-travel paradoxes is *a priori* evidence that time travel, at least backward in time, is impossible. You can go forward in time by moving at near the speed of light, thanks to the relativistic slowing of time under such conditions, but you can't come back again. You are marooned forever in the future and, under those conditions, no paradoxes arise.

Just the same, time-travel is so useful and dramatic a situation for science fiction, that even I, who am so rigid about my notions as to what is and is not possible in science would refuse to consider abandoning it. (Faster-than-light travel is another probably impossible phenomenon that I refuse to abandon.) (IA)

"Listen," the time traveler said to the first pedestrian who came by, "I'm from the twentieth century. I've only got fifteen minutes and then I'll go back. I guess it's too much to expect you to understand me, eh?"

"Certainly, I understand you."

"Hey! You talk English fine. How come?"

"We call it Amer-English. I happen to be a student of dead languages."

"Swell! But, listen, I only got a few minutes. Let's get going."

"Get going?"

"Yeah, yeah. Look, don't you get it? I'm a time traveler. They picked me to send to the future. I'm important."

"Ummm. But you must realize that we have time travelers turning up continuously these days."

"Listen, that rocks me, but I just don't have time to go into it, see? Let's get to the point."

"Very well. What have you got?"

"What d'ya mean, what've I got?"

The other sighed. "Don't you think you should attempt to acquire some evidence that you have been in the future? I can warn you now, the paradoxes involved in time travel prevent you from taking back any knowledge which might alter the past. On your return, your mind will be blank in regard to what happened here."

The time traveler blinked. "Oh?"

"Definitely. However, I shall be glad to make a trade with you."

"Listen, I get the feeling I came into this conversation half a dozen sentences too late. What'd'ya mean, a trade?"

"I am willing to barter something of your century for something of mine, although, frankly, there is little in your period that is of other than historical interest to us." The pedestrian's eyes held a gleam now. He cleared his throat. "However, I have here an atomic pocket knife. I hesitate to even tell you of the advantages it has over the knives of your period."

"Okay. I got only ten minutes left, but I can see you're right. I've got to get something to prove I was here."

"My knife would do it," the pedestrian nodded.

"Yeah, yeah. Listen, I'm a little confused, like. They picked me for this job the last minute—didn't want to risk any of these professor guys, see? That's the screwiest knife I ever saw, let me have it for my evidence."

"Just a minute, friend. Why should I give you my knife? What can you offer in exchange?"

"But I'm from the twentieth century."

"Ummm. And I'm from the thirtieth."

The time traveler looked at him for a long moment. Finally, "Listen, pal, I don't have a lot of time. Now, for instance, my watch—"

"Ummm. And what else?"

"Well, my money, here."

"Of interest only to a numismatist."

"Listen, I *gotta* have some evidence I been in the thirtieth century!"

"Of course. But business is business as the proverb goes."

"I wish the hell I had a gun."

"I have no use for a gun in this age," the other said primly.

"No, but I have," the time traveler muttered. "Look, fella, my time is running out by the second. What d'ya want? You see what I got, clothes, my wallet, a little money, a key ring, a pair of shoes."

"I'm willing to trade, but your possessions are of small value. Now some art object—an original Al Capp or something."

The time traveler was plaintive. "Do I look like I'd be carrying around art objects? Listen, I'll give you everything I got but my pants for that screwy knife."

"Oh, you want to keep your pants, eh? What're you trying to do, Anglo me down?—Or does your period antedate the term?"

"Anglo . . . what? I don't get it."

"Well, I'm quite an etymologist—"

"That's too bad, but—"

"Not at all, a fascinating hobby," the pedestrian said. "Now as to the phrase *Anglo me down*. The term Anglo first came into popular use during the 1850—1950 period. It designated persons from the eastern United States, English descent principally, who came into New Mexico and Arizona shortly after the area was liberated—I believe that was the term used at the time—from Mexico. The Spanish and Indians came to know the easterners as Anglos."

The time traveler said desperately, "Listen, *pal*, we get further and further from—"

"Tracing back the derivation of the phrase takes us along two more side trails. It goes back to the fact that these Anglos became the wealthiest businessmen of the twentieth century. So much so that they soon dominated the world with their dollars."

"Okay, okay. I know all about that. Personally I never had enough dollars to dominate anybody, but—"

"Very well, the point is that the Anglos became the financial wizards of the world, the most clever dealers, the sharpest bargainers, the most competent businessmen."

The time traveler shot a quick despairing look at his watch. "Only three—"

"The third factor is one taken from still further in the past. At one time there was a racial minority, which many of the Anglos held in disregard, called the Joos. For many years the term had been used, to *Joo you down*—meaning to make the price lower. As the Anglos assumed their monetary dominance, the term evolved from *Joo you down* to *Anglo you down;* and thus it has come down to our own day, although neither Anglo nor Joo still exists as a separate people."

The time traveler stared at him. "And I won't be able to take the memory of this story back with me, eh? And me a guy named Levy." He darted another look at his watch and groaned. "Quick!" he said, "Let's make this trade; everything I got for that atomic knife!"

The deal was consummated. The citizen of the thirtieth century stood back, his loot in his arms, and watched as the citizen of the twentieth, nude but with the knife grasped tightly and happily in hand, faded slowly from view.

The knife poised momentarily in empty air, then dropped to the ground as the time traveler completely disappeared.

The other stooped, retrieved it, and stuck it back in his pocket. "Even more naive than usual," he muttered. "Must have been one of the very first. I suppose they'll never reconcile themselves to the paradoxes. Obviously, you can carry things *forward* in time, since that's the natural flow of the dimension; but you just can't carry anything, not even memory, *backward* against the current."

He resumed his journey homeward.

Marget, hands on hips, met him at the door. "Where in *kert* have you been?" she snapped.

"You mustn't swear, darling," he said. "I met another time traveler on the way home."

"You didn't—"

"Certainly, why not? If I didn't somebody else would."

"But you've already got the closet overflowing with—"

"Now Marget, don't look that way. One of these days some museum or collector—"

She grunted skeptically and turned back into the house.

A SOUND OF THUNDER

by Ray Bradbury

The second of Ray Bradbury's contributions to the best of 1952 is this wonderful time-paradox story, a tale which has exerted tremendous influence on other writers in a variety of media. Time travel to prehistoric eras has become common-place in sf, and can be found in theme anthologies like *The Science Fictional Dinosaur* (1982) and *Dawn of Time* (1979).

"A Sound of Thunder" is a deeply felt plea for the importance of all life and the interrelatedness of all things. (MHG)

Having just talked about time-travel paradox stories in con-nection with the previous item, here we are again. Going back in time, in and of itself, threatens paradox, and nobody has ever described it as well, or as forcefully, as Ray Bradbury does in this story.

I might as well tell you that this is my favorite Ray Bradbury story of all those he's written that I've read. Had Marty not put it on the list of his own accord, I would have insisted on his doing so. Had he objected, we might very nearly have had to fight over it.

However, it didn't come to that and it couldn't. Our tastes are very much alike and that is one reason why we can be co-anthologists even in a matter as delicate as choosing the best stories of a year, without any friction at all. (IA)

The sign on the wall seemed to quaver under a film of sliding warm water. Eckels felt his eyelids blink over his stare, and the sign burned in this momentary darkness:

TIME SAFARI, INC.

SAFARIS TO ANY YEAR IN THE PAST.

YOU NAME THE ANIMAL.

WE TAKE YOU THERE.

YOU SHOOT IT.

A warm phlegm gathered in Eckels' throat; he swallowed and pushed it down. The muscles around his mouth formed a smile as he put his hand slowly out upon the air, and in that hand waved a check for ten thousand dollars to the man behind the desk.

"Does this safari guarantee I come back alive?"

"We guarantee nothing," said the official, "except the dinosaurs." He turned. "This is Mr. Travis, your Safari Guide in the Past. He'll tell you what and where to shoot. If he says no shooting, no shooting. If you disobey instructions, there's a stiff penalty of another ten thousand dollars, plus possible government action, on your return."

Eckels glanced across the vast office at a mass and tangle, a snaking and humming of wires and stell boxes, at an aurora that flickered now orange, now silver, now blue. There was a sound like a gigantic bonfire burning all of Time, all the years and all the parchment calendars, all the hours piled high and set aflame.

A touch of the hand and this burning would, on the instant, beautifully reverse itself. Eckels remembered the wording in the advertisements to the letter. Out of chars and ashes, out of dust and coals, like golden salamanders, the old years, the green years, might leap; roses sweeten the air, white hair turn Irish-black, wrinkles vanish; all, everything fly back to seed, flee death, rush down to their beginnings, suns rise in western skies and set in glorious easts, moons eat themselves opposite to the custom, all and everything cupping one in another like Chinese boxes, rabbits into hats, all and everything returning to the fresh death, the seed death, the green death, to the time before the beginning. A touch of a hand might do it, the merest touch of a hand.

"Unbelievable." Eckels breathed, the light of the Machine on his thin face. "A real Time Machine." He shook his head. "Makes you think. If the election had gone badly yesterday, I might be here now running away from the results. Thank God Keith won. He'll make a fine President of the United States.''

''Yes,'' said the man behind the desk. ''We're lucky. If Deutscher had gotten in, we'd have the worst kind of dictatorship. There's an anti-everything man for you, a militarist, anti-Christ, anti-human, anti-intellectual. People called us up, you know, joking but not joking. Said if Deutscher became President they wanted to go live in 1492. Of course it's not our business to conduct Escapes, but to form Safaris. Anyway, Keith's President now. All you got to worry about is—''

''Shooting my dinosaur,'' Eckels finished it for him.

''A *Tyrannosaurus rex*. The Tyrant Lizard, the most incredible monster in history. Sign this release. Anything happens to you, we're not responsible. Those dinosaurs are hungry.''

Eckels flushed angrily. ''Trying to scare me!''

''Frankly, yes. We don't want anyone going who'll panic at the first shot. Six Safari leaders were killed last year, and a dozen hunters. We're here to give you the severest thrill a *real* hunter ever asked for. Traveling you back sixty million years to bag the biggest game in all of Time. Your personal check's still there. Tear it up.''

Mr. Eckels looked at the check. His fingers twitched.

''Good luck,'' said the man behind the desk. ''Mr. Travis, he's all yours.''

They moved silently across the room, taking their guns with them, toward the Machine, toward the silver metal and the roaring light.

First a day and then a night and then a day and then a night, then it was day-night-day-night-day. A week, a month, a year, a decade! A.D. 2055. A.D. 2019. 1999! 1957! Gone! The Machine roared.

They put on their oxygen helmets and tested the intercoms.

Eckels swayed on the padded seat, his face pale, his jaw stiff. He felt the trembling in his arms and he looked down and found his hands tight on the new rifle. There were four other men in the Machine. Travis, the Safari Leader, his assistant, Lesperance, and two other hunters, Billings and Kramer. They sat looking at each other, and the years blazed around them.

''Can these guns get a dinosaur cold?'' Eckels felt his mouth saying.

''If you hit them right,'' said Travis on the helmet radio.

"Some dinosaurs have two brains, one in the head, another far down the spinal column. We stay away from those. That's stretching luck. Put your first two shots into the eyes, if you can, blind them, and go back into the brain."

The Machine howled. Time was a film run backward. Suns fled and ten million moons fled after them. "Think," said Eckels. "Every hunter that ever lived would envy us today. This makes Africa seem like Illinois."

The Machine slowed; its scream fell to a murmur. The Machine stopped.

The sun stopped in the sky.

The fog that had enveloped the Machine blew away and they were in an old time, a very old time indeed, three hunters and two Safari Heads with their blue metal guns across their knees.

"Christ isn't born yet," said Travis. "Moses has not gone to the mountain to talk with God. The Pyramids are still in the earth, waiting to be cut out and put up. *Remember* that. Alexander, Caesar, Napoleon, Hitler—none of them exists."

The man nodded.

"That"—Mr. Travis pointed—"is the jungle of sixty million two thousand and fifty-five years before President Keith."

He indicated a metal path that struck off into green wilderness, over streaming swamp, among giant ferns and palms.

"And that," he said, "is the Path, laid by Time Safari for your use. It floats six inches above the earth. Doesn't touch so much as one grass blade, flower, or tree. It's an anti-gravity metal. Its purpose is to keep you from touching this world of the past in any way. Stay on the Path. Don't go off it. I repeat. *Don't go off*. For *any* reason! If you fall off, there's a penalty. And don't shoot any animal we don't okay."

"Why?" asked Eckels.

They sat in the ancient wilderness. Far birds' cries blew on a wind, and the smell of tar and an old salt sea, moist grasses, and flowers the color of blood.

"We don't want to change the Future. We don't belong here in the Past. The government doesn't *like* us here. We have to pay big graft to keep our franchise. A Time Machine is a finicky business. Not knowing it, we might kill an important animal, a small bird, a roach, a flower even, thus destroying an important link in a growing species."

"That's not clear," said Eckels.

"All right," Travis continued, "say we accidentally kill one

mouse here. That means all the future families of this one
particular mouse are destroyed, right?''

"Right.''

"And all the families of the families of the families of that one
mouse! With a stamp of your foot you annihilate first one, then a
dozen, then a thousand, a million, a *billion* possible mice!''

"So they're dead," said Eckels. "So what?''

"So what?'' Travis snorted quietly. "Well, what about the
foxes that'll need those mice to survive? For want of ten mice, a
fox dies. For want of ten foxes, a lion starves. For want of a
lion, all manner of insects, vultures, infinite billions of life
forms are thrown into chaos and destruction. Eventually it all
boils down to this: fifty-nine million years later, a caveman, one
of a dozen on the *entire world*, goes hunting wild boar or
saber-toothed tiger for food. But you, friend, have *stepped* on all
the tigers in that region. By stepping on *one* single mouse. So
the caveman starves. And the caveman, please note, is not just
any expendable man, no! He is an *entire future nation*. From his
loins would have sprung ten sons. From *their* loins one hundred
sons, and thus onward to a civilization. Destroy this one man,
and you destroy a race, a people, an entire history of life. It is
comparable to slaying some of Adam's grandchildren. The stomp
of your foot, on one mouse, could start and earthquake, the
effects of which could shake our earth and destinies down through
Time, to their very foundations. With the death of that one
caveman, a billion others yet unborn are throttled in the womb.
Perhaps Rome never rises on its seven hills. Perhaps Europe is
forever a dark forest, and only Asia waxes healthy and teeming.
Step on a mouse and you crush the Pyramids. Step on a mouse
and you leave your print, like a Grand Canyon, across Eternity.
Queen Elizabeth might never be born, Washington might not
cross the Delaware, there might never be a United States at all.
So be careful. Stay on the Path. *Never* step off!''

"I see,'' said Eckels. "Then it wouldn't pay for us even to
touch the *grass?*''

"Correct. Crushing certain plants could add up infinitesi-
mally. A little error here would multiply in sixty million years,
all out of proportion. Of course maybe our theory is wrong.
Maybe Time *can't* be changed by us. Or maybe it can be
changed only in little subtle ways. A dead mouse here makes an
insect imbalance there, a population disproportion later, a bad
harvest further on, a depression, mass starvation, and, finally, a

change in *social* temperament in far-flung countries. Something much more subtle, like that. Perhaps only a soft breath, a whisper, a hair, pollen on the air, such a slight, slight change that unless you looked close you wouldn't see it. Who knows? Who really can say he knows? We don't know. We're guessing. But until we do know for certain whether our messing around in Time *can* make a big roar or a little rustle in history, we're being careful. This Machine, this Path, your clothing and bodies, were sterilized, as you know, before the journey. We wear these oxygen helmets so we can't introduce our bacteria into an ancient atmosphere."

"How do we know which animals to shoot?"

"They're marked with red paint," said Travis. "Today, before our journey, we sent Lesperance here back with the Machine. He came to this particular era and followed certain animals."

"Studying them?"

"Right," said Lesperance. "I track them through their entire existence, noting which of them lives longest. Very few. How many times they mate. Not often. Life's short. When I find one that's going to die when a tree falls on him, or one that drowns in a tar pit, I note the exact hour, minute, and second. I shoot a paint bomb. It leaves a red patch on his side. We can't miss it. Then I correlate our arrival in the Past so that we meet the Monster not more than two minutes before he would have died anyway. This way, we kill only animals with no future, that are never going to mate again. You see how *careful* we are?"

"But if you came back this morning in Time," said Eckels eagerly, "you must've bumped into *us*, our Safari! How did it turn out? Was it successful? Did all of us get through—alive?"

Travis and Lesperance gave each other a look.

"That'd be be a paradox," said the latter. "Time doesn't permit that sort of mess—a man meeting himself. When such occasions threaten, Time steps aside. Like an airplane hitting an air pocket. You felt the Machine jump just before we stopped? That was us passing ourselves on the way back to the Future. We saw nothing. There's no way of telling *if* this expedition was a success, *if we* got our monster, or whether all of us—meaning *you*, Mr. Eckels—got out alive."

Eckels smiled palely.

"Cut that," said Travis sharply. "Everyone on his feet!"

They were ready to leave the Machine.

The jungle was high and the jungle was broad and the jungle

was the entire world forever and forever. Sounds like music and sounds like flying tents filled the sky, and those were pterodactyls soaring with cavernous gray wings, gigantic bats of delirium and night fever. Eckels, balanced on the narrow Path, aimed his rifle playfully.

"Stop that!" said Travis. "Don't even aim for fun, blast you! If your guns should go off—"

Eckels flushed. 'Where's our *Tyrannosaurus?*"

Lesperance checked his wristwatch. "Up ahead. We'll bisect his trail in sixty seconds. Look for the red paint! Don't shoot till we give the word. Stay on the path. *Stay on the Path!*"

They moved forward in the wind of morning.

"Strange," murmured Eckels. "Up ahead, sixty million years, Election Day over. Keith made President. Everyone celebrating. And here we are, a million years lost, and they don't exist. The things we worried about for months, a life-time, not even born or thought of yet."

"Safety catches off, everyone!" ordered Travis. "You, first shot, Eckels. Second, Billings. Third, Kramer."

"I've hunted tiger, wild boar, buffalo, elephant, but now, this is *it*," said Eckels. "I'm shaking like a kid."

"Ah," said Travis.

Everyone stopped.

Travis raised his hand. "Ahead," he whispered. "In the mist. There he is. There's His Royal Majesty now."

The jungle was wide and full of twitterings, rustlings, murmurs, and sighs.

Suddenly it all ceased, as if someone had shut a door.

Silence.

A sound of thunder.

Out of the mist, one hundred yards away, came *Tyrannosaurus rex.*

"It," whispered Eckels. "It . . ."

"Sh!"

It came on great oiled, resilient, striding legs. It towered thirty feet above half of the trees, a great evil god, folding its delicate watchmaker's claws close to its oily reptilian chest. Each lower leg was a piston, a thousand pounds of white bone, sunk in thick ropes of music, sheathed over in a gleam of pebbled skin like the mail of a terrible warrior. Each thigh was a ton of meat, ivory, and steel mesh. And from the great breathing cage of the upper body those two delicate arms dangled out front, arms with hands which might pick up and examine men like toys, while the snake neck coiled. And the head itself, a ton of sculptured stone, lifted easily upon the sky. Its mouth gaped, exposing a fence of teeth like daggers. Its eyes rolled, ostrich eggs, empty of all expression save hunger. It closed its mouth in a death grin. It ran, its pelvic bones crushing aside trees and bushes, its taloned feet clawing damp earth, leaving prints six inches deep wherever it settled its weight. It ran with a gliding ballet step, far too poised and balanced for its ten tons. It moved into a sunlit arena warily, its beautifully reptilian hands feeling the air.

"Why, why," Eckels twitched his mouth. "It could reach up and grab the moon."

"Sh!" Travis jerked angrily. "He hasn't seen us yet."

"It can't be killed." Eckels pronounced this verdict quietly, as if there could be no argument. He had weighed the evidence and this was his considered opinion. The rifle in his hands seemed a cap gun. "We were fools to come. This is impossible."

"Shut up!" hissed Travis.

"Nightmare."

"Turn around," commanded Travis. "Walk quietly to the Machine. We'll remit one half your fee."

"I didn't realize it would be this *big*," said Eckels. "I miscalculated, that's all. And now I want out."

"It *sees* us!"

"There's the red paint on its chest!"

The Tyrant Lizard raised itself. Its armored flesh glittered like a thousand green coins. The coins, crusted with slime, streamed. In the slime, tiny insects wriggled, so that the entire body seemed to twitch and undulate, even while the monster itself did not move. It exhaled. The stink of raw flesh flew down the wilderness.

"Get me out of here," said Eckels. "It was never like this before. I was always sure I'd come through alive. I had good guides, good safaris, and safety. This time, I figured wrong. I've met my match and admit it. This is too much for me to get hold of."

"Don't run," said Lesperance. "Turn around. Hide in the Machine."

"Yes." Eckels seemed to be numb. He looked at his feet as if trying to make them move. He gave a grunt of helplessness.

"Eckels!"

He took a few steps, blinking, shuffling.

"Not *that* way!"

The Monster, at the first motion, lunged forward with a terrible scream. It covered one hundred yards in six seconds. The rifles jerked up and blazed fire. A windstorm from the beast's mouth engulfed them in the stench of slime and old blood. The Monster roared, teeth glittering with sun.

Eckels, not looking back, walked blindly to the edge of the Path, his gun limp in his arms, stepped off the Path, and walked, not knowing it, in the jungle. His feet sank into green moss. His legs moved him, and he felt alone and remote from the events behind.

The rifles cracked again. Their sound was lost in shriek and lizard thunder. The great level of the reptile's tail swung up, lashed sideways. Trees exploded in clouds of leaf and branch. The Monster twitched its jeweler's hands down to fondle at the men, to twist them in half, to crush them like berries, to cram them into its teeth and its screaming throat. Its boulder-stone eyes leveled with the men. They saw themselves mirrored. They fired at the metallic eyelids and the blazing black iris.

Like a stone idol, like a mountain avalanche, *Tyrannosaurus* fell. Thundering, it clutched trees, pulled them with it. It wrenched and tore the metal Path. The men flung themselves back and away. The body hit, ten tons of cold flesh and stone. The guns fired. The Monster lashed its armored tail, twitched its snake jaws, and lay still. A fount of blood spurted from its throat. Somewhere inside, a sac of fluids burst. Sickening gushes drenched the hunters. They stood, red and glistening.

The thunder faded.

The jungle was silent. After the avalanche, a green peace. After the nightmare, morning.

Billings and Kramer sat on the pathway and threw up. Travis and Lesperance stood with smoking rifles, cursing steadily.

In the Time Machine, on his face, Eckels lay shivering. He had found his way back to the Path, climbed into the Machine.

Travis came walking, glanced at Eckels, took cotton gauze from a metal box, and returned to the others, who were sitting on the Path.

"Clean up."

They wiped the blood from their helmets. They began to curse too. The Monster lay, a hill of solid flesh. Within, you could hear the sighs and murmurs as the farthest chambers of it died, the organs malfunctioning, liquids running a final instant from pocket to sac to spleen, everything shutting off, closing up forever. It was like standing by a wrecked locomotive or a steam shovel at quitting time, all valves being released or levered tight. Bones cracked; the tonnage of its own flesh, off balance, dead weight, snapped the delicate forearms, caught underneath. The meat settled, quivering.

Another cracking sound. Overhead, a gigantic tree branch broke from its heavy mooring, fell. It crashed upon the dead beast with finality.

"There." Lesperance checked his watch. "Right on time. That's the giant tree that was scheduled to fall and kill this animal originally." He glanced at the two hunters. "You want the trophy picture?"

"What?"

"We can't take a trophy back to the Future. The body has to stay right here where it would have died originally, so the insects, birds, and bacteria can get at it, as they were intended to. Everything in balance. The body stays. But we *can* take a picture of you standing near it."

The two men tried to think, but gave up, shaking their heads.

They let themselves be led along the metal Path. They sank wearily into the Machine cushions. They gazed back at the ruined Monster, the stagnating mound, where already strange reptilian birds and golden insects were busy at the steaming armor.

A sound on the floor of the Time Machine stiffened them. Eckels sat there, shivering.

"I'm sorry," he said at last.

"Get up!" cried Travis.

Eckels got up.

"Go out on that Path alone," said Travis. He had his rifle pointed. "You're not coming back in the Machine. We're leaving you here!"

Lesperance seized Travis's arm. "Wait—"

"Stay out of this!" Travis shook his hand away. "This fool nearly killed us. But it isn't *that* so much, no. It's his *shoes!* Look at them! He ran off the Path. That *ruins* us! We'll forfeit! Thousands of dollars of insurance! We guarantee no one leaves the Path. He left it. Oh, the fool! I'll have to report to the government. They might revoke our license to travel. Who knows *what* he's done to Time, to History!"

"Take it easy, all he did was kick up some dirt."

"How do we *know?*" cried Travis. "We don't know anything! It's all a mystery! Get out here, Eckels!"

Eckels fumbled his shirt. "I'll pay anything. A hundred thousand dollars!"

Travis glared at Eckels' cheekbook and spat. "Go out there. The Monster's next to the Path. Stick your arms up to your elbows in his mouth. Then you can come back with us."

"That's unreasonable!"

"The Monster's dead, you idiot. The bullets! The bullets can't be left behind. They don't belong in the Past; they might change anything. Here's my knife. Dig them out!"

The jungle was alive again, full of the old tremorings and bird cries. Eckels turned slowly to regard the primeval garbage dump, that hill of nightmares and terror. After a long time, like a sleepwalker he shuffled out along the Path.

He returned, shuddering, five minutes later, his arms soaked and red to the elbows. He held out his hands. Each held a number of steel bullets. Then he fell. He lay where he fell, not moving.

"You didn't have to make him do that," said Lesperance.

"Didn't I? It's too early to tell." Travis nudged the still body. "He'll live. Next time he won't go hunting game like this. Okay." He jerked his thumb wearily at Lesperance. "Switch on. Let's go home."

1492. 1776. 1812.

They cleaned their hands and faces. They changed their caking shirts and pants. Eckels was up and around again, not speaking. Travis glared at him for a full ten minutes.

"Don't look at me," cried Eckels. "I haven't done anything."

"Who can tell?"

"Just ran off the Path, that's all, a little mud on my shoes—what do you want me to do—get down and pray?"

"We might need it. I'm warning you, Eckels, I might kill you yet. I've got my gun ready."

"I'm innocent. I've done nothing!"

1999. 2000. 2055.

The Machine stopped.

"Get out," said Travis.

The room was there as they had left it. But not the same as they had left it. The same man sat behind the same desk. But the same man did not quite sit behind the same desk.

Travis looked around swiftly. "Everything okay here?" he snapped.

"Fine. Welcome home!"

Travis did not relax. He seemed to be looking at the very atoms of the air itself, at the way the sun poured through the one high window.

"Okay, Eckels, get out. Don't ever come back."

Eckels could not move.

"You heard me," said Travis. "What're you *staring* at?"

Eckels stood smelling of the air, and there was a thing to the air, a chemical taint so subtle, so slight, that only a faint cry of his sublimal senses warned him it was there. The colors, white, gray, blue, orange, in the wall, in the furniture, in the sky beyond the window, were . . . were . . . And there was a *feel*. His flesh twitched. His hands twitched. He stood drinking the oddness with the pores of his body. Somewhere, someone must have been screaming one of those whistles that only a dog can hear. His body screamed silence in return. Beyond this room, beyond this wall, beyond this man who was not quite the same man seated at his desk that was not quite the same desk . . . lay an entire world of streets and people. What sort of world it was now, there was no telling. He could feel them moving there, beyond the walls, almost, like so many chess pieces blown in a dry wind. . . .

But the immediate thing was the sign painted on the office wall, the same sign he had read earlier today on first entering.

Somehow, the sign had changed:

> TYME SEFARI INC.
>
> SEFARIS TU ANY YEER EN THE PAST.
>
> YU NAIM THE ANIMALL.
>
> WEE TAEKYUTHAR.
>
> YU SHOOT ITT.

Eckels felt himself fall into a chair. He fumbled crazily at the thick slime on his boots. He held up a clod of dirt, trembling. "No, it *can't* be. Not a *little* thing like that. No!"

Embedded in the mud, glistening green and gold and black, was a butterfly, very beautiful and very dead.

"Not a little thing like *that!* Not a butterfly!" cried Eckels.

It fell to the floor, an exquisite thing, a small thing that could upset balances and knock down a line of small dominoes and then big dominoes and then gigantic dominoes, all down the years across Time. Eckels' mind whirled. It *couldn't* change things. Killing one butterfly couldn't be *that* important! Could it?

His face was cold. His mouth trembled, asking: "Who—Who won the presidential election yesterday?"

The man behind the desk laughed. "You joking? You know very well. Deutscher, of course! Who else? Not that fool weakling Keith. We got an iron man now, a man with guts!" The official stopped. "What's wrong?"

Eckels moaned. He dropped to his knees. He scrabbled at the golden butterfly with shaking fingers. "Can't we," he pleaded to the world, to himself, to the officials, to the Machine, "can't we take it *back*, can't we *make* it alive again? Can't we start over? Can't we—"

He did not move. Eyes shut, he waited, shivering. He heard Travis breathe loud in the room; he heard Travis shift his rifle, click the safety catch, and raise the weapon.

There was a sound of thunder.

HOBSON'S CHOICE

by Alfred Bester (1913–)

Alfred Bester last appeared in this series with "Oddy and Id" in Volume 3 (1941). His career in science fiction has been marked by long periods of inactivity, but in the 1950s he shone like a star. His two novels of the decade, *The Demolished Man* (1953) and *The Stars My Destination* (1957 in the U.S.) were notable for their stylistic courage and for Bester's skillful use of modern psychoanalytic theory. They remain classics and were highly influential on later writers. Two collections, *Starburst* (1958) and *The Dark Side of the Earth* (1964) contain the bulk of his best short fiction, much of which is as innovative and exciting as those two great novels. He returned to it in the mid-seventies with interesting novels and several short stories, but his own earlier act was a very tough one to follow.

"Hobson's Choice" is a marvelous combination of humor and alienation. (MHG)

Once upon a time there was a man who rented out horses. His name was Thomas Hobson, he had his livery stable in Cambridge, England, and he lived in the time of Shakespeare.

He found that when his customers had their choice of horses, they invariably chose the best (naturally). The result was that his good horses were worked to death, while his poorer ones stood idle. This struck him as a bad deal.

He therefore arranged his horses in line and insisted that each customer take the horse at the head of the line regardless of its appearance, quality, or the customer's own taste. Every returning horse went to the end of the line and in this way, every horse was used in strict rotation.

Any customer who asked if he might have his choice of a

103

horse, was answered firmly, "You *have* a choice, sir. That one, right there, at the head of the line is your choice."

And so "Hobson's choice" came to mean "no choice at all."

I tell you all this because I think that the title of a story is an integral part of the story, and, ideally, should shed light upon it. Therefore, the more you understand about the significance of a title, the more you understand about the significance of the story to which it is attached. (IA)

This is a warning to accomplices like you, me, and Addyer.

> *Can you spare price of one cup coffee, honorable sir? I am indigent organism which are hungering.*

By day, Addyer was a statistician. He concerned himself with such matters as statistical tables, averages and dispersions, groups that are not homogeneous and random sampling. At night, Addyer plunged into an elaborate escape fantasy divided into two parts. Either he imagined himself moved back in time a hundred years with a double armful of the *Encyclopaedia Britannica*, best-sellers, hit plays and gamblings records, or else he imagined himself transported forward in time a thousand years to the Golden Age of perfection.

There were other fantasies which Addyer entertained on odd Thursdays, such as (by a fluke) becoming the only man left on earth with a world of passionate beauties to fecundate; such as acquiring the power of invisibility which would enable him to rob banks and right wrongs with impunity, such as possessing the mysterious power of working miracles.

Up to this point you and I and Addyer are identical. Where we part company is in the fact that Addyer was a statistician.

> *Can you spare cost of one cup coffee, honorable miss? For blessed charitability? I am beholden.*

On Monday, Addyer rushed into his chief's office, waving a sheaf of papers. "Look here, Mr. Grande," Addyer sputtered.

"I've found something fishy. Extremely fishy . . . In the statistical sense, that is."

"Oh, hell," Grande answered. "You're not supposed to be finding anything. We're in between statistics until the war's over."

"I was leafing through the Interior Department's reports. D'you know our population's up?"

"Not after the atom bomb it isn't," said Grande. "We've lost double what our birthrate can replace." He pointed out the window to the twenty-five-foot stub of the Washington Monument. "There's your documentation."

"But our population's up 3.0915 percent." Addyer displayed his figures. "What about that, Mr. Grande?"

"Must be a mistake somewhere," Grande muttered after a moment's inspection. "You'd better check."

"Yes, sir," said Addyer scurrying out of the office. "I knew you'd be interested, sir. You're the ideal statistician, sir." He was gone.

"Poop," said Grande and once again began computing the quantity of bored respirations left to him. It was his personalized anesthesia.

On Tuesday, Addyer discovered that there was no correlation between the mortality/birthrate ratio and the population increase. The war was multiplying mortality and reducing births; yet the population was minutely increasing. Addyer displayed his discovery to Grande, received a pat on the back and went home to a new fantasy in which he woke up a million years in the future, learned the answer to the enigma and decided to remain amid snow-capped mountains and snow-capped bosoms, safe under the aegis of a culture saner than Aureomycin.

On Wednesday, Addyer requisitioned the comptometer and file and ran a test check on Washington, D.C. To his dismay he discovered that the population of the former capital was down 0.0029 percent. This was distressing, and Addyer went home to escape into a dream about Queen Victoria's Golden Age where he amazed and confounded the world with his brilliant output of novels, plays and poetry, all cribbed from Shaw, Galsworthy and Wilde.

Can you spare price of one coffee, honorable sir? I am distressed individual needful of chariting.

On Thursday, Addyer tried another check, this time on the city of Philadelphia. He discovered that Philadelphia's population was up 0.0959 percent. Very encouraging. He tried a rundown on Little Rock. Population up 1.1329 percent. He tested St. Louis. Population up 2.0924 percent . . . and this despite the complete extinction of Jefferson County owing to one of those military mistakes of an excessive nature.

"My God!" Addyer exclaimed, trembling with excitement. "The closer I get to the center of the country, the greater the increase. But it was the center of the country that took the heaviest punishment in the buz-raid. What's the answer?"

That night he shuttled back and forth between the future and the past in his ferment, and he was down at the shop by 7 A.M. He put a twenty-four-hour claim on the compo and files. He followed up his hunch and he came up with a fantastic discovery which he graphed in approved form. On the map of the remains of the United States he drew concentric circles in colors illustrating the areas of population increase. The red, orange, yellow, green and blue circles formed a perfect target around Finney County, Kansas.

"Mr. Grande," Addyer shouted in a high statistical passion, "Finney County has got to explain this."

"You go out there and get that explanation," Grande replied, and Addyer departed.

"Poop," muttered Grande and began integrating his pulse rate with his eye-blink.

Can you spare price of one coffee, dearly madam? I am starveling organism requiring nutritiousment.

Now, travel in those days was hazardous. Addyer took ship to Charleston (there were no rail connections remaining in the North Atlantic states) and was wrecked off Hatteras by a rogue mine. He drifted in the icy waters for seventeen hours, muttering through his teeth: "Oh, Christ! If only I'd been born a hundred years ago."

Apparently this form of prayer was potent. He was picked up by a navy sweeper and shipped to Charleston where he arrived just in time to acquire a subcritical radiation burn from a raid which fortunately left the railroad unharmed. He was treated for the burn from Charleston to Macon (change) from Birmingham to Memphis (bubonic plague) to Little Rock (polluted water) to

Tulsa (fallout quarantine) to Kansas City (the O.K. Bus Co. Accepts No Liability for Lives Lost through Acts of War) to Lyonesse, Finney County, Kansas.

And there he was in Finney County with its great magma pits and scars and radiation streaks; whole farms blackened and razed; whole highways so blasted they looked like dotted lines; whole population 4-F. Clouds of soot and fallout neutralizers hung over Finney County by day, turning it. into a Pittsburgh on a still afternoon. Auras of radiation glowed at night, highlighted by the blinking red warning beacons, turning the county into one of those overexposed night photographs, all blurred and cross-hatched by deadly slashes of light.

After a restless night in thé Lyonesse Hotel, Addyer went over to the county seat for a check on their birth records. He was armed with the proper credentials, but the county seat was not armed with the statistics. That excessive military mistake again. It had extinguished the seat.

A little annoyed, Addyer marched off to the County Medical Association office. His idea was to poll the local doctors on births. There was an office and one attendant who had been a practical nurse. He informed Addyer that Finney County had lost its last doctor to the army eight months previous. Midwives might be the answer to the birth enigma but there was no record of midwives. Addyer would simply have to canvass from door to door, asking if any lady within practiced that ancient profession.

Further piqued, Addyer returned to the Lyonesse Hotel and wrote on a slip of tissue paper: HAVING DATA DIFFICULTIES. WILL REPORT AS SOON AS INFORMATION AVAILABLE. He slipped the message into an aluminum capsule, attached it to his sole surviving carrier pigeon and dispatched it to Washington with a prayer. Then he sat down at his window and brooded.

He was aroused by a curious sight. In the street below, the O.K. Bus Co. had just arrived from Kansas City. The old coach wheezed to a stop, opened its door with some difficulty and permitted a one-legged farmer to emerge. His burned face was freshly bandaged. Evidently this was a well-to-do burgess who could afford to travel for medical treatment. The bus backed up for the return trip to Kansas City and honked a warning horn. That was when the curious sight began.

From nowhere . . . absolutely nowhere . . . a horde of people appeared. They skipped from back alleys, from behind rubble piles; they popped out of stores, they filled the street. They were all jolly, healthy, brisk, happy. They laughed and chatted as they climbed into the bus. They looked like hikers and tourists, carrying knapsacks, carpetbags, box lunches and even babies. In two minutes the bus was filled. It lurched off down the road, and as it disappeared Addyer heard happy singing break out and echo from the walls of rubble.

"I'll be damned," he said.

He hadn't heard spontaneous singing in over two years. He hadn't seen a carefree smile in over three years. He felt like a color-blind man who was seeing the full spectrum for the first time. It was uncanny. It was also a little blasphemous.

"Don't those people know there's a war on?" he asked himself. And a little later: "They looked too healthy. Why aren't they in uniform?"

And last of all: "Who *were* they anyway?"

That night Addyer's fantasy was confused.

Can you spare price of one cup coffee, kindly sir? I am estrangered and faintly from hungering.

The next morning Addyer arose early, hired a car at an exorbitant fee, found he could not buy any fuel at any price and ultimately settled for a lame horse. He was allergic to horse dander and suffered asthmatic tortures as he began his house-to-house canvass. He was discouraged when he returned to the Lyonesse Hotel that afternoon. He was just in time to witness the departure of the O.K. Bus Co.

Once again a horde of happy people appeared and boarded the bus. Once again the bus hirpled off down the broken road. Once again the joyous singing broke out.

"I *will* be damned," Addyer wheezed.

He dropped into the county surveyor's office for a large-scale map of Finney County. It was his intent to plot the midwife coverage in accepted statistical manner. There was a little difficulty with the surveyor who was deaf, blind in one eye and spectacleless in the other. He could not read Addyer's credentials with any faculty or facility. As Addyer finally departed with the map, he said to himself, "I think the old idiot thought I was a spy."

And later he muttered, "Spies?"

And just before bedtime: "Holy Moses! Maybe *that's* the answer to *them.*"

That night he was Lincoln's secret agent, anticipating Lee's every move, outwitting Jackson, Johnston and Beauregard, foiling John Wilkes Booth, and being elected President of the United States by 1968.

The next day the O.K. Bus Co. carried off yet another load of happy people.

And the next.

And the next.

"Four hundred tourists in five days," Addyer computed. "The country's filled with espionage."

He began loafing around the streets trying to investigate these joyous travelers. It was difficult. They were elusive before the bus arrived. They had a friendly way of refusing to pass the time. The locals of Lyonesse knew nothing about them and were not interested. Nobody was interested in much more than painful survival these days. That was what made the singing obscene.

After seven days of cloak-and-dagger and seven days of counting, Addyer suddenly did the big take. "It adds up," he said. "Eighty people a day leaving Lyonesse. Five hundred a week. Twenty-five thousand a year. Maybe that's the answer to the population increase." He spent fifty-five dollars on a telegram to Grande with no more than a hope of delivery. The telegram read: "EUREKA. I HAVE FOUND (IT)."

Can you spare price of lone cup coffee, honorable madam? I am not tramp-handler but destitute life form.

Addyer's opportunity came the next day. The O.K. Bus Co. pulled in as usual. Another crowd assembled to board the bus, but this time there were too many. Three people were refused passage. They weren't in the least annoyed. They stepped back, waved energetically as the bus started, shouted instructions for future reunions and then quietly turned and started off down the street.

Addyer was out of his hotel room like a shot. He followed the trio down the main street, turned left after them onto Fourth Avenue, passed the ruined schoolhouse, and passed the demolished telephone building, passed the gutted library, railroad station, Protestant church, Catholic church . . . and finally reached the outskirts of Lyonesse and then open country.

Here he had to be more cautious. It was difficult stalking the spies with so much of the dusky road illuminated by warning lights. He wasn't suicidal enough to think of hiding in radiation pits. He hung back in an agony of indecision and was at last relieved to see them turn off the broken road and enter the old Baker farmhouse.

"Ah-ha!" said Addyer.

He sat down at the edge of the road on the remnants of a missile and asked himself. "Ah-ha what?" He could not answer, but he knew where to find the answer. He waited until dusk deepened to darkness and then slowly wormed his way forward toward the farmhouse.

It was while he was creeping between the deadly radiation glows and only occasionally butting his head against grave markers that he first became aware of two figures in the night. They were in the barnyard of the Baker place and were performing most peculiarly. One was tall and thin. A man. He stood stock-still, like a lighthouse. Upon occasion he took a slow, stately step with infinite caution and waved an arm in slow motion to the other figure. The second was also a man. He was stocky and trotted jerkily back and forth.

As Addyer approached, he heard the tall man say: "Rooo booo fooo mooo hwaaa looo fooo."

Whereupon the trotter chattered, "Wd-nk-kd-ik-md-pd-ld-nk."

Then they both laughed: the tall man like a locomotive, the trotter like a chipmunk. They turned. The trotter rocketed into the house. The tall man drifted in. And that was amazingly that.

"Oh-ho," said Addyer.

At that moment a pair of hands seized him and lifted him from the ground. Addyer's heart constricted. He had time for one convulsive spasm before something vague was pressed against his face. As he lost consciousness his last idiotic thought was of telescopes.

Can you spare price of solitary coffee for no-loafing unfortunate, honorable sir? Charity will blessings.

When Addyer awoke he was lying on a couch in a small whitewashed room. A gray-haired gentleman with heavy features was seated at a desk alongside the couch, busily ciphering on bits of paper. The desk was cluttered with what appeared to be intricate timetables. There was a small radio perched on one side.

"L-Listen . . ." Addyer began faintly.

"Just a minute, Mr. Addyer," the gentleman said pleasantly. He fiddled with the radio. A glow germinated in the middle of the room over a circular copper plate and coalesced into a girl. She was extremely nude and extremely attractive. She scurried to the desk, patted the gentleman's head with the speed of a pneumatic hammer. She laughed and chattered, "Wd-nk-tk-ik-lt-nk."

The gray-haired man smiled and pointed to the door. "Go outside and walk it off," he said. She turned and streaked through the door.

"It has something to do with temporal rates," the gentleman said to Addyer. "I don't understand it. When they come forward they've got accumulated momentum." He began ciphering again. "Why in the world did you have to come snooping, Mr. Addyer?"

"You're spies," Addyer said. "She was talking Chinese."

"Hardly. I'd say it was French. Early French. Middle fifteenth century."

"Middle fifteenth century!" Addyer exclaimed.

"That's what I'd say. You begin to acquire an ear for those stepped-up tempos. Just a minute, please."

He switched the radio on again. Another glow appeared and solidified into a nude man. He was stout, hairy and lugubrious. With exasperating slowness he said, "Mooo fooo blooo wawww hawww pooo."

The gray-haired man pointed to the door. The stout man departed in slow motion.

"The way I see it," the gray-haired man continued conversationally, "when they come back they're swimming against the time current. That slows 'em down. When they come forward, they're swimming with the current. That speeds 'em up. Of course, in any case it doesn't last longer than a few minutes. It wears off."

"What?" Addyer said. "Time travel?"

"Yes. Of course."

"That thing . . ." Addyer pointed to the radio. "A time machine?"

"That's the idea. Roughly."

"But it's too small."

The gray-haired man laughed.

"What is this place anyway? What are you up to?"

"It's a funny thing," the gray-haired man said. "Everybody used to speculate about time travel. How it would be used for exploration, archaeology, historical and social research and so on. Nobody ever guessed what the real use would be. . . . Therapy.''

"Therapy? You mean medical therapy?''

"That's right. Psychological therapy for the misfits who won't respond to any other cure. We let them emigrate. Escape. We've set up stations every quarter century. Stations like this.''

"I don't understand.''

"This is an immigration office.''

"Oh, my God!'' Addyer shot up from the couch. "Then you're the answer to the population increase. Yes? That's how I happened to notice it. Mortality's up so high and birth's down so low these days that your time-addition becomes significant. Yes?''

"Yes, Mr. Addyer.''

"Thousands of you coming here. From where?''

"From the future, of course. Time travel wasn't developed until C/H 127. That's . . . oh, say, A.D. 2505 your chronology. We didn't set up our chain of stations until D/H 189.''

"But those fast-moving ones. You said they came forward from the past.''

"Oh, yes, but they're all from the future originally. They just decided they went too far back.''

"Too far?''

The gray-haired man nodded and reflected. "It's amusing, the mistakes people will make. They become unrealistic when they read history. Lose contact with facts. Chap I knew . . . wouldn't be satisfied with anything less than Elizabethan times 'Shakespeare,' he said. 'Good Queen Bess. Spanish Armada. Drake and Hawkins and Raleigh. Most virile period in history. The Golden Age. That's for me.' I couldn't talk sense into him, so we sent him back. Too bad.''

"Well?'' Addyer asked.

"Oh, he died in three weeks. Drank a glass of water. Typhoid.''

"You didn't inoculate him? I mean, the army when it sends men overseas always . . .''

"Of course we did. Gave him all the immunization we could. But diseases evolve and change too. New strains develop. Old strains disappear. That's what causes pandemics. Evidently our shots wouldn't take against the Elizabethan typhoid. Excuse me. . .''

Again the glow appeared. Another nude man appeared, chattered briefly and then whipped through the door. He almost collided with the nude girl who poked her head in, smiled and called in a curious accent, 'Ie vous prie de me pardonner. Quy estoit cette gentilhomme?''

"I was right," the gray-haired man said. "That's Medieval French. They haven't spoken like that since Rabelais." To the girl he said, "Middle English, please. The American dialect."

"Oh, I'm sorry, Mr. Jelling. I get so damned fouled up with my linguistics. Fouled? Is that right? Or do they say . . ."

"Hey!" Addyer cried in anguish.

"They say it, but only in private these years. Not before strangers."

"Oh, yes. I remember. Who was that gentleman who just left?"

"Peters."

"From Athens?"

"That's right."

"Didn't like it, eh?"

"Not much. Seems the Peripatetics didn't have plumbing."

"Yes. You begin to hanker for a modern bathroom after a while. Where do I get some clothes . . . or don't they wear clothes this century?"

"No, that's a hundred years forward. Go see my wife. She's in the outfitting room in the barn. That's the big red building."

The tall lighthouse-man Addyer had first seen in the farmyard suddenly manifested himself behind the girl. He was now dressed and moving at normal speed. He stared at the girl; she stared at him. "Splem!" they both cried. They embraced and kissed shoulders.

"St'u my rock-ribbering rib-rockery to heart the hearts two," the man said.

"Heart's too, argal, too heart." The girl laughed.

"Eh? Then you st'u too."

They embraced again and left.

"What was that? Future talk?" Addyer asked. "Shorthand?"

"Shorthand?" Jelling exclaimed in a surprised tone. "Don't you know rhetoric when you hear it? That was thirtieth-century rhetoric, man. We don't talk anything else up there. Prosthesis, Diastole, Epergesis, Metabasis, Hendiadys . . . And we're all born scanning."

"You don't have to sound so stuck-up," Addyer muttered enviously. "I could scan too if I tried."

"You'd find it damned inconvenient trying at your time of life."

"What difference would that make?"

"It would make a big difference," Jelling said, "because you'd find that living is the sum of conveniences. You might think plumbing is pretty unimportant compared to ancient Greek philosophers. Lots of people do. But the fact is, we already know the philosophy. After a while you get tired of seeing the great men and listening to them expound the material you already know. You begin to miss the conveniences and familiar patterns you used to take for granted."

"That," said Addyer, "is a superficial attitude."

"You think so? Try living in the past by candlelight, without central heating, without refrigeration, canned foods, elementary drugs. . . . Or, futurewise, try living with Berganlicks, the Twenty-Two Commandments, duodecimal calendars and currency, or try speaking in meter, planning and scanning each sentence before you talk . . . and damned for a contemptible illiterate if you forget yourself and speak spontaneously in your own tongue."

"You're exaggerating," Addyer said. "I'll bet there are times where I could be very happy. I've thought about it for years, and I . . ."

"Tcha!" Jelling snorted. "The great illusion. Name one."

"The American Revolution."

"Pfui! No sanitation. No medicine. Cholera in Philadelphia. Malaria in New York. No anesthesia. The death penalty for hundreds of small crimes and petty infractions. None of the books and music you like best. None of the jobs or professions for which you've been trained. Try again."

"The Victorian Age."

"How are your teeth and eyes? In good shape? They'd better be. We can't send your inlays and spectacles back with you. How are your ethics? In bad shape? They'd better be or you'd starve in that cutthroat era. How do you feel about class distinctions? They were pretty strong in those days. What's your religion? You'd better not be a Jew or Catholic or Quaker or Moravian or any minority. What's your politics? If you're a reactionary today the same opinions would make you a dangerous radical a hundred years ago. I don't think you'd be happy."

"I'd be safe."

"Not unless you were rich; and we can't send money back. Only the flesh. No, Addyer, the poor died at the average age of forty in those days . . . worked out, worn out. Only the privileged survived, and you wouldn't be one of the privileged."

"Not with my superior knowledge?"

Jelling nodded wearily. "I knew *that* would come up sooner or later. What superior knowledge? Your hazy recollection of science and invention? Don't be a damned fool, Addyer. You enjoy your technology without the faintest idea of how it works."

"It wouldn't have to be hazy recollection. I could prepare."

"What, for instance?"

"Oh . . . say, the radio. I could make a fortune inventing the radio."

Jelling smiled. "You couldn't invent radio until you'd first invented the hundred allied technical discoveries that went into it. You'd have to create an entire new industrial world. You'd have to discover the vacuum rectifier and create an industry to manufacture it, the self-heterodyne circuit, the non-radiating neutrodyne receiver and so forth. You'd have to develop electric power production and transmission and alternating current. You'd have to—but why belabor the obvious? Could you invent internal combustion before the development of fuel oils?"

"My God!" Addyer groaned.

"And another thing," Jelling went on grimly. "I've been talking about technological tools, but language is a tool too; the tool of communication. Did you ever realize that all the studying you might do could never teach you how a language was really used centuries ago? Do you know how the Romans pronounced Latin? Do you know the Greek dialects? Could you learn to speak and think in Gaelic, seventeenth-century Flemish, Old Low German? Never. You'd be a deaf-mute."

"I never thought about it that way," Addyer said slowly.

"Escapists never do. All they're looking for is a vague excuse to run away."

"What about books? I could memorize a great book and . . ."

"And what? Go back far enough into the past to anticipate the real author? You'd be anticipating the public too. A book doesn't become great until the public's ready to understand it. It doesn't become profitable until the public's ready to buy it."

"What about going forward into the future?" Addyer asked.

"I've already told you. It's the same problem only in reverse. Could a medieval man survive in the twentieth century? Could he stay alive in street traffic? Drive cars? Speak the language? Think in the language? Adapt to the tempo, ideas and coordinations you take for granted? Never. Could someone from the twenty-fifth century adapt to the thirtieth? Never."

"Well, then," Addyer said angrily, "if the past and future are so uncomfortable, what are those people traveling around for?"

"They're not traveling," Jelling said. "They're running."

"From what?"

"Their own time."

"Why?"

"They don't like it."

"Why not?"

"Do you like yours? Does any neurotic?"

"Where are they going?"

"Any place but where they belong. They keep looking for the Golden Age. Tramps! Time stiffs! Never satisfied. Always searching, shifting . . . bumming through the centuries. Pfui! Half the panhandlers you meet are probably time bums stuck in the wrong century."

"And those people coming here . . . they think *this* is a Golden Age?"

"They do."

"They're crazy," Addyer protested. "Have they seen the ruins? The radiation? The war? The anxiety? The hysteria?"

"Sure. That's what appeals to them. Don't ask me why. Think of it this way: you like the American Colonial period, yes?"

"Among others."

"Well, if you told Mr. George Washington the reasons why you liked his time, you'd probably be naming everything he hated about it."

"But that's not a fair comparison. This is the worst age in all history."

Jelling waved his hand. "That's how it looks to you. Everybody says that in every generation; but take my word for it, no matter when you live and how you live, there's always somebody else somewhere else who thinks you live in the Golden Age."

"Well, I'll be damned," Addyer said.

Jelling looked at him steadily for a moment. "You will be," he said sorrowfully. "I've got bad news for you, Addyer. We can't let you remain. You'll talk and make trouble, and our secret's got to be kept. We'll have to send you out one-way."

"I can talk wherever I go."

"But nobody'll pay attention to you outside your own time.

You won't make sense. You'll be an eccentric . . . a lunatic . . . a foreigner . . . safe.''

"What if I come back?"

"You won't be able to get back without a visa, and I'm not tattooing any visa on you. You won't be the first we've had to transport if that's any consolation to you. There was a Japanese, I remember . . .''

"Then you're going to send me somewhere in time? Permanently?"

"That's right. I'm really very sorry."

"To the future or the past?''

"You can take your choice. Think it over while you're getting undressed.''

"You don't have to act so mournful," Addyer said. "It's a great adventure. A high adventure. It's something I've always dreamed.''

"That's right. It's going to be wonderful.''

"I could refuse," Addyer said nervously.

Jelling shook his head. "We'd only drug you and send you anyway. It might as well be your choice.''

"It's a choice I'm delighted to make.''

"Sure. That's the spirit, Addyer.''

"Everybody says I was born a hundred years too soon.''

"Everybody generally says that . . . unless they say you were born a hundred years too late.''

"Some people say that too.''

"Well, think it over. It's a permanent move. Which would you prefer . . . the phonetic future or the poetic past?''

Very slowly Addyer began to undress as he undressed each night when he began the prelude to his customary fantasy. But now his dreams were faced with fulfillment and the moment of decision terrified him. He was a little blue and rather unsteady on his legs when he stepped to the copper disk in the center of the floor. In answer to Jelling's inquiry he muttered his choice. Then he turned argent in the aura of an incandescent glow and disappeared from his time forever.

Where did he go? You know. I know. Addyer knows. Addyer traveled to the land of our pet fantasy. He escaped into the refuge that is our refuge, to the time of our dreams; and in practically no time at all he realized that he had in truth departed from the only time for himself.

Through the vistas of the years every age but our own seems

glamorous and golden. We yearn for the yesterdays and tomorrows, never realizing that we are faced with Hobson's choice . . . that today, bitter or sweet, anxious or calm, is the only day for us. The dream of time is the traitor, and we are all accomplices to the betrayal of ourselves.

Can you spare price of one coffee, honorable sir? No, sir, I am not panhandling organism. I am starveling Japanese transient stranded in this somiserable year. Honorable sir! I beg in tears for holy charity. Will you donate to this destitute person one ticket to township of Lyonesse? I want to beg on knees for visa. I want to go back to year 1945 again. I want to be in Hiroshima again. I want to go home.

YESTERDAY HOUSE

by Fritz Leiber

The always welcome Fritz Leiber returns again with this interesting and historically important story. "Yesterday House" is arguably the *first* story ever published that comes reasonably close to describing the process we now refer to as *cloning*. The theme underlying the story is one of the oldest in science fiction and one of the oldest ideas in folklore—the attempt to create artificial life.

If Brian W. Aldiss is right in his claim that Mary Shelley's *Frankenstein* (1818) is the first true science fiction novel, then the theme is *the* oldest. Writers since Shelley have speculated about how life might be created in the laboratory and what effect this might have on themselves and on society in a variety of ways, ranging from genetic engineering to simply duplicating people. The theme is indeed a powerful one—what if not only God could make a tree? Or a human being? (MHG)

In earlier days when the death rate was high and life expectancy low, the death of children and of young lovers and of blooming young wives was a common-place, and literature reflected that. It filled the works of people like Edgar Allan Poe and Charles Dickens, and one could not help reacting to their longing even when one had not one's self suffered such a loss.

I have been fortunate in this respect and have thus far suffered little from circumstance, but I react powerfully when the proper buttons are pushed.

There's a very old-fashioned poem, "The Barrel-Organ" by Alfred Noyes, which must be a very bad poem because a) I understand everything it says, and b) it tears at my heart-strings every time I read it. Noyes describes the effect of the barrel-organ's music on various people and there is one verse, which, of all the verses, I've never been able to get through intact. In it, a laborer stands listening to the "voices of the dead," while the organ player pipes. The listener's hands tremble; his face smoulders. Finally he is so overcome by the music that he can only stare into the sunset where the love of his youth has gone—"For he hears her softly singing and his lonely soul is led/ Through the land where the dead dreams go." It got to me this time, as well, just remembering it, but I thought of when I was reading "Yesterday House." (IA)

The narrow cove was quiet as the face of an expectant child, yet so near the ruffled Atlantic that the last push of wind carried the *Annie O.* its full length. The man in gray flannels and sweatshirt let the sail come crumping down and hurried past its white folds at a gait made comically awkward by his cramped muscles. Slowly the rocky ledge came nearer. Slowly the blue V inscribed on the cove's surface by the sloop's prow died. Sloop and ledge kissed so gently that he hardly had to reach out his hand.

He scrambled ashore, dipping a sneaker in the icy water, and threw the line around a boulder. Unkinking himself, he looked back through the cove's high and rocky mouth at the gray-green scattering of islands and the faint dark line that was the coast of Maine. He almost laughed in satisfaction at having disregarded vague warnings and done the thing every man yearns to do once in his lifetime—gone to the farthest island out.

He must have looked longer than he realized, because by the time he dropped his gaze the cove was again as glassy as if the *Annie O.* had always been there. And the splotches made by his sneaker on the rock had faded in the hot sun. There was something very unusual about the quietness of this place. As if time, elsewhere hurrying frantically, paused here to rest. As if all changes were erased on this one bit of Earth.

The man's lean, melancholy face crinkled into a grin at the banal fancy. He turned his back on his new friend, the little green sloop, without one thought for his nets and specimen bottles, and set out to explore. The ground rose steeply at first and the oaks were close, but after a little way things went downhill and the leaves thinned and he came out on more rocks—and realized that he hadn't quite gone to the farthest one out.

Joined to this island by a rocky spine, which at the present low tide would have been dry but for the spray, was another green, high island that the first had masked from him all the while he had been sailing. He felt a thrill of discovery, just as he'd wondered back in the woods whether his might not be the first human feet to kick through the underbrush. After all, there were thousands of these islands.

Then he was dropping down the rocks, his lanky limbs now moving smoothly enough.

To the landing side of the spine, the water was fairly still. It even began with another deep cove, in which he glimpsed the spiny spheres of sea urchins. But from seaward the waves chopped in, sprinkling his trousers to the knees and making him wince pleasurably at the thought of what vast wings of spray and towers of solid water must crash up from here in a storm.

He crossed the rocks at a trot, ran up a short grassy slope, raced through a fringe of trees—and came straight up against an eight-foot fence of heavy mesh topped with barbed wire and backed at a short distance with high, heavy shrubbery.

Without pausing for surprise—in fact, in his holiday mood, using surprise as a goad—he jumped for the branch of an oak whose trunk touched the fence, scorning the easier lower branch on the other side of the tree. Then he drew himself up, worked his way to some higher branches that crossed the fence, and dropped down inside.

Suddenly cautious, he gently parted the shrubbery and, before the first surprise could really sink in, had another.

A closely mown lawn dotted with more shrubbery ran up to a snug white Cape Cod cottage. The single strand of a radio aerial stretched the length of the roof. Parked on a neat gravel driveway that crossed just in front of the cottage was a short, square-lined, touring car that he recognized from remembered pictures as an ancient Essex. The whole scene had about it the same odd quietness as the cove.

Then, with the air of a clockwork toy coming to life, the white door opened and an elderly woman came out, dressed in a long, lace-edged dress and wide, lacy hat. She climbed into the driver's seat of the Essex, sitting there very stiff and tall. The motor began to chug bravely, gravel skittered, and the car rolled off between the trees.

The door of the house opened again and a slim girl emerged. She wore a white silk dress that fell straight from square neckline to hip-height waistline, making the skirt seem very short. Her dark hair was bound with a white bandeau so that it curved close to her cheeks. A dark necklace dangled against the white of the dress. A newspaper was tucked under her arm.

She crossed the driveway and tossed the paper down on a rattan table between three rattan chairs and stood watching a squirrel zigzag across the lawn.

The man stepped through the wall of shrubbery, called "Hello!" and walked toward her.

She whirled around and stared at him as still as if her heart had stopped beating. Then she darted behind the table and waited for him there. Granting the surprise of his appearance, her alarm seemed not so much excessive as eerie. As if, the man thought, he were not an ordinary stranger, but a visitor from another planet.

Approaching closer, he saw that she was trembling and that her breath was coming in rapid, irregular gasps. Yet the slim, sweet, patrician face that stared into his had an underlying expression of expectancy that reminded him of the cove. She couldn't have been more than eighteen.

He stopped short of the table. Before he could speak, she stammered out, "Are you he?"

"What do you mean?" he asked, smiling puzzledly.

"The one who sends me the little boxes."

"I was out sailing and I happened to land in the far cove. I didn't dream that anyone lived on this island, or even came here."

"No one ever does come here," she replied. Her manner had changed, becoming at once more wary and less agitated, though still eerily curious.

"It startled me tremendously to find this place," he blundered on. "Especially the road and the car. Why, this island can't be more than a quarter of a mile wide."

"The road goes down to the wharf," she explained, "and up to the top of the island, where my aunts have a treehouse."

He tore his mind away from the picture of a woman dressed

like Queen Mary clambering up a tree. "Was that your aunt I saw driving off?"

"One of them. The other's taken the motorboat in for supplies." She looked at him doubtfully. "I'm not sure they'll like it if they find someone here."

"There are just the three of you?" he cut in quickly, looking down the empty road that vanished among the oaks.

She nodded.

"I suppose you go in to the mainland with your aunts quite often?"

She shook her head.

"It must get pretty dull for you."

"Not very," she said, smiling. "My aunts bring me the papers and other things. Even movies. We've got a projector. My favorite stars are Antonio Morino and Alice Terry. I like her better even than Clara Bow."

He looked at her hard for a moment. "I suppose you read a lot?"

She nodded. "Fitzgerald's my favorite author." She started around the table, hesitated, suddenly grew shy. "Would you like some lemonade?"

He'd noticed the dewed silver pitcher, but only now realized his thirst. Yet when she handed him a glass, he held it untasted and said awkwardly, "I haven't introduced myself. I'm Jack Barr."

She stared at his outstretched right hand, slowly extended her own toward it, shook it up and down exactly once, then quickly dropped it.

He chuckled and gulped some lemonade. "I'm a biology student. Been working at Wood's Hole the first part of the summer. But now I'm here to do research in marine ecology— that's sort of sea-life patterns—of the inshore islands. Under the direction of Professor Kesserich. You know about him, of course?"

She shook her head.

"Probably the greatest living biologist," he was proud to inform her. "Human physiology as well. Tremendous geneticist. In a class with Carlson and Jacques Loeb. Martin Kesserich—he lives over there at town. I'm staying with him. You ought to have heard of him." He grinned. "Matter of fact, I'd never have met you if it hadn't been for Mrs. Kesserich."

The girl looked puzzled.

Jack explained, "The old boy's been off to Europe on some

conferences, won't be back for a couple days more. But I was to get started anyhow. When I went out this morning Mrs. Kesserich—she's a drab sort of person—said to me, 'Don't try to sail to the farther islands.' So, of course, I had to. By the way, you still haven't told me your name.''

"Mary Alice Pope," she said, speaking slowly and with an odd wonder, as if she were saying it for the first time.

"You're pretty shy, aren't you?"

"How would I know?"

The question stopped Jack. He couldn't think of anything to say to this strangely attractive girl dressed almost like a "flapper."

"Will you sit down?" she asked him gravely.

The rattan chair sighed under his weight. He made another effort to talk. "I'll bet you'll be glad when summer's over."

"Why?"

"So you'll be able to go back to the mainland."

"But I never go to the mainland."

"You mean you stay out here all winter?" he asked incredulously, his mind filled with a vision of snow and frozen spray and great gray waves.

"Oh, yes. We get all our supplies on hand before winter. My aunts are very capable. They don't always wear long lace dresses. And now I help them."

"But that's impossible!" he said with sudden sympathetic anger. "You can't be shut off this way from people your own age!"

"You're the first one I ever met." She hesitated. "I never saw a boy or a man before, except in movies."

"You're joking!"

"No, it's true."

"But why are they doing it to you?" he demanded, leaning forward. "Why are they inflicting this loneliness on you, Mary?"

She seemed to have gained poise from his loss of it. "I don't know why. I'm to find out soon. But actually I'm not lonely. May I tell you a secret?" She touched his hand, this time with only the faintest trembling. "Every night the loneliness gathers in around me—you're right about that. But then every morning new life comes to me in a little box."

"What's that?" he said sharply.

"Sometimes there's a poem in the box, sometimes a book, or pictures, or flowers, or a ring, but always a note. Next to the notes I like the poems best. My favorite is the one by Matthew Arnold that ends:

"Ah, love, let us be true
To one another! for the world
     which seems
To lie before us like a land of
     dreams,
So various, so beautiful, so new,
Hath really neither joy, nor love,
     nor light,
Nor certitude—"

"Wait a minute," he interrupted. "Who sends you these boxes?"

"I don't know."

"But how are the notes signed?"

"They're wonderful notes," she said. "So wise, so gay, so tender, you'd imagine them being written by John Barrymore or Lindbergh."

"Yes, but how are they signed?"

She hesitated. "Never anything but 'Your Lover.' "

"And so when you first saw me, you thought—" He began, then stopped because she was blushing.

"How long have you been getting them?"

"Ever since I can remember. I have two closets of the boxes. The new ones are either by my bed when I wake or at my place at breakfast."

"But how does this—person get these boxes to you out here? Does he give them to your aunts and do they put them there?"

"I'm not sure."

"But how can they get them in winter?"

"I don't know."

"Look here," he said, pouring himself more lemonade, "how long is it since you've been to the mainland?"

"Almost eighteen years. My aunts tell me I was born there in the middle of the war."

"What war?" he asked startledly, spilling some lemonade.

"The World War, of course. What's the matter?"

Jack Barr was staring down at the spilled lemonade and feeling a kind of terror he'd never experienced in his waking life. Nothing around him had changed. He could still feel the same hot sun on his shoulders, the same icy glass in his hand, scent the same lemon-acid odor in his nostrils. He could still hear the faint *chop-chop* of the waves.

And yet everything had changed, gone dark and dizzy like a landscape glimpsed just before a faint. All the little false notes had come to a sudden focus. For the lemonade had spilled on the headline of the newspaper the girl had tossed down, and the headline read:

HITLER IN NEW DEFIANCE

Under the big black banner of that head swam smaller ones:

**Foes of Machado Riot in Havana
Big NRA Parade Planned
Balbo Speaks in New York**

Suddenly he felt a surge of relief. He had noticed that the paper was yellow and brittle-edged.

"Why are you so interested in old newspapers?" he asked.

"I wouldn't call day-before-yesterday's paper old," the girl objected, pointing at the dateline: July 20, 1933.

"You're trying to joke," Jack told her.

"No, I'm not."

"But it's 1951."

"Now it's you who are joking."

"But the paper's yellow."

"The paper's always yellow."

He laughed uneasily. "Well, if you actually think it's 1933, perhaps you're to be envied," he said, with a sardonic humor he didn't quite feel. "Then you can't know anything about the Second World War, or television, or the V-2s, or bikini bathing suits, or the atomic bomb, or—"

"Stop!" She had sprung up and retreated around her chair, white-faced. "I don't like what you're saying."

"But—"

"No, please! Jokes that may be quite harmless on the mainland sound different here."

"I'm really not joking," he said after a moment.

She grew quite frantic at that. "I can show you all last week's papers! I can show you magazines and other things. I can prove it!"

She started toward the house. He followed. He felt his heart begin to pound.

At the white door she paused, looking worriedly down the road. Jack thought he could hear the faint *chug* of a motorboat. She pushed open the door and he followed her inside. The small-windowed room was dark after the sunlight. Jack got an impression of solid old furniture, a fireplace with brass andirons.

"Flash!" croaked a gritty voice. "After their disastrous break day before yesterday, stocks are recovering. Leading issues . . ."

Jack realized that he had started and had involuntarily put his arm around the girl's shoulders. At the same time he noticed that the voice was coming from the curved brown trumpet of an old-fashioned radio loudspeaker.

The girl didn't pull away from him. He turned toward her. Although her gray eyes were on him, her attention had gone elsewhere.

"I can hear the car. They're coming back. They won't like it that you're here."

"All right, they won't like it."

Her agitation grew. "No, you must go."

"I'll come back tomorrow," he heard himself saying.

"Flash! It looks as if the World Economic Conference may soon adjourn, mouthing jeers at old Uncle Sam who is generally referred to as Uncle Shylock."

Jack felt a numbness on his neck. The room seemed to be darkening, the girl growing stranger still.

"You must go before they see you."

"Flash! Wiley Post has just completed his solo circuit of the Globe after a record-breaking flight of seven days, eighteen hours and forty-five minutes. Asked how he felt after the energy-draining feat, Post quipped . . ."

He was halfway across the lawn before he realized the terror into which the grating radio voice had thrown him.

He leaped for the branch overhanging the fence, vaulted up with the risky help of a foot on the barbed top. A surprised squirrel, lacking time to make its escape up the trunk, sprang to the ground ahead of him. With terrible suddenness, two steel-jawed semicircles clanked together just over the squirrel's head. Jack landed with one foot to either side of the sprung trap, while the squirrel darted off with a squeak.

Jack plunged down the slope to the rocky spine and ran across it, spray from the rising waves spattering him to the waist. Panting now, he stumbled up into the oaks and undergrowth of the first island, fought his way through it, finally reached the silent cove. He loosed the line of the *Annie O.*, dragged it as near to the cove's mouth as he could, plunged knee-deep in freezing water to give it a final shove, scrambled aboard, snatched up the boathook, and punched at the rocks.

As soon as the *Annie O.* was nosing out of the cove into the cross waves, he yanked up the sail. The freshening wind filled it and sent the sloop heeling over, with inches of white water over the lee rail, and plunging ahead.

For a long while, Jack was satisfied to think of nothing but the wind and the waves and the sail and speed and danger, to have all his attention taken up balancing one against the other, so that he wouldn't have to ask himself what year it was, and whether time was an illusion, and wonder about flappers and hidden traps.

When he finally looked back to the island, he was amazed to see how tiny it had grown, as distant as the mainland.

Then he saw a gray motorboat astern. He watched it as it slowly overtook him. It was built like a lifeboat, with a sturdy low cabin in the bow and wheel amidship. Whoever was at the wheel had long gray hair that whipped in the wind. The longer he looked, the surer he was that it was a woman wearing a lace dress. Something that stuck up inches over the cabin flashed darkly beside her. Only when she lifted it to the roof of the cabin did it occur to him that it might be a rifle.

But just then the motorboat swung around in a turn that sent waves drenching over it, and headed back toward the island. He watched it for a minute in wonder, then his attention was jolted by an angry hail.

Three fishing smacks, also headed toward town, were about to cross his bow. He came around into the wind and waited with shaking sail, watching a man in a lumpy sweater shake a fist at him. Then he turned and gratefully followed the dark, wide, fanlike sterns and age-yellowed sails.

II

The exterior of Martin Kesserich's home—a weathered white cube with narrow, sharp-paned windows, topped by a cupola— was nothing like its lavish interior.

In much the same way, Mrs. Kesserich clashed with the darkly gleaming furniture, Persian rugs and bronze vases around her. Her shapeless black form, poised awkwardly on the edge of a huge sofa, made Jack think of a cow that had strayed into the drawing room. He wondered again how a man like Kesserich had come to marry such a creature.

Yet when she lifted up her little eyes from the shadows, he had the uneasy feeling that she knew a great deal about him. The eyes were still those of a domestic animal, but of a wise one that has been watching the house a long, long while from the barnyard.

He asked abruptly, "Do you know anything of a girl around here named Mary Alice Pope?"

The silence lasted so long that he began to think she'd gone into a bovine trance. Then she looked him up and down and nodded, but he felt that the nod was not so much an answer to his question as an answer to him. Without a word she got up and went to a tall cabinet. Feeling on a ledge behind it for a key, she opened a panel, opened a cardboard box inside, and took something from it.

"Mr. Barr," she said, "I am going to show you something. Then I am going to tell you something."

She handed him a photograph. He held it up to the failing light and sucked in his breath with surprise.

It was a picture of the girl he'd met that afternoon. Same flat-bosomed dress—flowered rather than white—no bandeau, same beads. Same proud, demure expression, perhaps a bit happier.

"That is Mary Alice Pope," Mrs. Kesserich said in a strangely flat voice. "She was Martin's fiancée. She was killed in a railway accident in 1933."

The small sound of the cabinet door closing brought Jack back to reality. He realized that he no longer had the photograph. Against the gloom by the cabinet, Mrs. Kesserich's white face looked at him with what seemed a controlled, almost placid eagerness.

"Sit down," she said. "Now is the part I tell you."

Without a thought as to why she hadn't asked him a single question—he was much too dazed for that—he obeyed. Mrs. Kesserich resumed her position on the edge of the sofa.

"You must understand, Mr. Barr, that Mary Alice Pope was the one love of Martin's life. He is a man of very deep and strong feelings, yet as you probably know, anything but kindly or demonstrative. Even when he first came here from Hungary with his older sisters Hani and Hilda, there was a cloak of loneliness about him—or rather about the three of them.

"Hani and Hilda were athletic outdoor women, yet fiercely proud—I don't imagine they ever spoke to anyone in America except as to a servant—and with a seething distaste for all men except Martin. They showered all their devotion on him. So of course, though Martin didn't realize it, they were consumed with jealousy when he fell in love with Mary Alice Pope. They'd thought that since he'd reached forty without marrying, he was safe.

"Mary Alice came from a purebred, or as a biologist would say, inbred British stock. She was very young, but very sweet, and up to a point very wise. She sensed Hani's and Hilda's feelings right away and did everything she could to win them over. For instance, though she was afraid of horses, she took up horseback riding, because that was Hani's and Hilda's favorite pastime. Naturally, Martin knew nothing of her fear, and naturally his sisters knew about it from the first. But—and here is where Mary's wisdom fell short—her brave gesture did not pacify them: it only increased their hatred.

"Except for his research, Martin was blind to everything but his love. It was a beautiful and yet frightening passion, an insane cherishing as narrow and intense as his sisters' hatred."

With a start, Jack remembered that it was Mrs. Kesserich telling him all this.

She went on, "Martin's love directed his every move. He was building a home for himself and Mary, and in his mind he was building a wonderful future for them as well—not vaguely, if you know Martin, but year by year, month by month. This winter, he'd plan, they would visit Buenos Aires, next summer they would sail down the inland passage and he would teach Mary Hungarian for their trip to Budapest the year after, where he would occupy a chair at the university for a few months . . . and so on. Finally the time for their marriage drew near. Martin had been away. His research was keeping him very busy—"

Jack broke in with, "Wasn't that about the time he did his definitive work on growth and fertilization?"

Mrs. Kesserich nodded with solemn appreciation in the gathering darkness. "But now he was coming home, his work done. It was early evening, very chilly, but Hani and Hilda felt they had to ride down to the station to meet their brother. And although she dreaded it, Mary rode with them, for she knew how delighted he would be at her cantering to the puffing train and his running up to lift her down from the saddle to welcome him home.

"Of course there was Martin's luggage to be considered, so the station wagon had to be sent down for that." She looked defiantly at Jack. "I drove the station wagon. I was Martin's laboratory assistant."

She paused. "It was almost dark, but there was still a white cold line of sky to the west. Hani and Hilda, with Mary between them, were waiting on their horses at the top of the hill that led down to the station. The train had whistled and its headlight was graying the gravel of the crossing.

"Suddenly Mary's horse squealed and plunged down the hill. Hani and Hilda followed—to try to catch her, they said, but they didn't manage that, only kept her horse from veering off. Mary never screamed, but as her horse reared on the tracks, I saw her face in the headlight's glare.

"Martin must have guessed, or at least feared what had happened, for he was out of the train and running along the track before it stopped. In fact, he was the first to kneel down beside Mary—I mean, what had been Mary—and was holding her all bloody and shattered in his arms."

A door slammed. There were steps in the hall. Mrs. Kesserich stiffened and was silent. Jack turned.

The blur of a face hung in the doorway to the hall—a seemingly young, sensitive, suavely handsome face with aristocratic jaw. Then there was a click and the lights flared up and Jack saw the close-cropped gray hair and the lines around the eyes and nostrils while the sensitive mouth grew sardonic. Yet the handsomeness stayed, and somehow the youth, too, or at least a tremendous inner vibrancy.

"Hello, Barr," Martin Kesserich said, ignoring his wife.

The great biologist had come home.

III

"Oh, yes, and Jamieson had a feeble paper on what he called individualization in marine worms. Barr, have you ever thought much about the larger aspects of the problem of individuality?"

Jack jumped slightly. He had let his thoughts wander very far.

"Not especially, sir," he mumbled.

The house was still. A few minutes after the professor's arrival, Mrs. Kesserich had gone off with an anxious glance at Jack. He knew why and wished he could reassure her that he would not mention their conversation to the professor.

Kesserich had spent perhaps a half hour briefing him on the more important papers delivered at the conferences. Then, almost as if it were a teacher's trick to show up a pupil's inattention, he had suddenly posed this question about individuality.

"You know what I mean, of course," Kesserich pressed. "The factors that make you you, and me me."

"Heredity and environment," Jack parroted like a freshman.

Kesserich nodded. "Suppose—this is just speculation—that we could control heredity and environment. Then we could recreate the same individual at will."

Jack felt a shiver go through him. "To get exactly the same pattern of hereditary traits. That'd be far beyond us."

"What about identical twins?" Kesserich pointed out. "And then there's parthenogenesis to be considered. One might produce a duplicate of the mother without the intervention of the male." Although his voice had grown more idly speculative, Kesserich seemed to Jack to be smiling secretly. "There are many examples in the lower animal forms, to say nothing of the technique by which Loeb caused a sea urchin to reproduce with no more stimulus than a salt solution."

Jack felt the hair rising on his neck. "Even then you wouldn't get exactly the same pattern of hereditary traits."

"Not if the parent were of very pure stock? Not if there were some special technique for selecting ova that would reproduce all the mother's traits?"

"But environment would change things," Jack objected. "The duplicate would be bound to develop differently."

"Is environment so important? Newman tells about a pair of identical twins separated from birth, unaware of each other's existence. They met by accident when they were twenty-one. Each was a telephone repairman. Each had a wife the same age. Each had a baby son. And each had a fox terrier called 'Trixie.' That's without trying to make environments similar. But suppose you did try. Suppose you saw to it that each of them had exactly the same experiences at the same times . . ."

For a moment it seemed to Jack that the room was dimming and wavering, becoming a dark pool in which the only motionless thing was Kesserich's sphinxlike face.

"Well, we've escaped quite far enough from Jamieson's marine worms," the biologist said, all brisk again. He said it as if Jack were the one who had led the conversation down wild and unprofitable channels. "Let's get on to your project. I want to talk it over now, because I won't have any time for it tomorrow."

Jack looked at him blankly.

"Tomorrow I must attend to a very important matter," the biologist explained.

Jack felt sudden unanticipated hate twist his heart.

IV

Morning sunlight brightened the colors of the wax flowers under glass on the high bureau that always seemed to emit the faint odor of old hair combings. Jack pulled back the diamond-patterned quilt and blinked the sleep from his eyes. He expected his mind to be busy wondering about Kesserich and his wife—things said and half said last night—but found instead that his thoughts swung instantly to Mary Alice Pope, as if to a farthest island in a world of people.

Downstairs, the house was empty. After a long look at the cabinet—he felt behind it, but the key was gone—he hurried down to the waterfront. He stopped only for a bowl of chowder and, as an afterthought, to buy half a dozen newspapers.

The sea was bright, the brisk wind just right for the *Annie O*. There was eagerness in the way it smacked the sail and in the creak of the mast. And when he reached the cove, it was no longer still, but nervous with faint ripples, as if time had finally begun to stir.

After the same struggle with the underbrush, he came out on the rocky spine and passed the cove of the sea urchins. The spiny creatures struck an uncomfortable chord in his memory.

This time he climbed the second island cautiously, scrapping the innocent-seeming ground ahead of him intently with the boathook he'd brought along for the purpose. He was only a few yards from the fence when he saw Mary Alice Pope standing behind it.

He hadn't realized that his heart would begin to pound or that, at the same time, a shiver of almost supernatural dread would go through him.

He hadn't realized until this moment that he loved her.

The girl eyed him with an uneasy hostility and immediately began to speak in a hushed, hurried voice. "You must go away at once and never come back. You're a wicked man, but I don't want you to be hurt. I've been watching for you all morning."

He tossed the newspapers over the fence. "You don't have to read them now," he told her. "Just look at the datelines and a few of the headlines."

When she finally lifted her eyes to his again, she was trembling. She tried unsuccessfully to speak.

"Listen to me," he said. "You've been the victim of a scheme to make you believe you were born around 1916 instead of 1933, and that it's 1933 now instead of 1951. I'm not sure why it's been done, though I think I know who you really are."

"But"—the girl faltered—"my aunts tell me it's 1933."

"They would."

"And there are the papers . . . the magazines . . . the radio."

"The papers are old ones. The radio's faked—some sort of recording. I could show you if I could get at it."

"*These* papers might be faked," she said, pointing to where she'd let them drop on the ground.

"They're new," he said. "Only old papers get yellow."

"But why would they do it to me? *Why?*"

"Come with me to the mainland, Mary. That'll set you straight quicker than anything."

"I couldn't," she said, drawing back. "He's coming tonight."

"He?"

"The man who sends me the boxes . . . and my life."

Jack shivered. When he spoke, his voice was rough and quick. "A life that's completely a lie, that's cut you off from the world. Come with me, Mary."

She looked up at him wondering. For perhaps ten seconds the silence held and the spell of her eerie sweetness deepened.

"I love you, Mary," Jack said softly.

She took a step back.

"Really, Mary, I do."

She shook her head. "I don't know what's true. Go away."

"Mary," he pleaded, "read the papers I've given you. Think things through. I'll wait for you here."

"You can't. My aunts would find you."

"Then I'll go away and come back. About sunset. Will you give me an answer?"

She looked at him. Suddenly she whirled around. He, too, heard the *chuff* of the Essex. "They'll find us," she said. "And if they find you, I don't know what they'll do. Quick, run!" And she darted off herself, only to turn back to scramble for the papers.

"But will you give me an answer?" he pressed.

She looked frantically up from the papers. "I don't know. You mustn't risk coming back."

"I will, no matter what you say."

"I can't promise. Please go."

"Just one question," he begged. "What are your aunts names?"

"Hani and Hilda," she told him, and then she was gone. The hedge shook where she'd darted through.

Jack hesitated, then started for the cove. He thought for a moment of staying on the island, but decided against it. He could probably conceal himself suc cessfully, but whoever found his boat would have him at a disadvantage. Besides, there were things he must try to find out on the mainland.

As he entered the oaks, his spine tightened for a moment, as if someone were watching him. He hurried to the rippling cove, wasted no time getting the *Annie O.* underway. With the wind still in the west, he knew it would be a hard sail. He'd need half a dozen tacks to reach the mainland.

When he was about a quarter of a mile out from the cove, there was a sharp *smack* beside him. He jerked around, heard a distant *crack* and saw a foot-long splinter of fresh wood dangling from the edge of the sloop's cockpit, about a foot from his head.

He felt his skin tighten. He was the bull's-eye of a great watery target. All the air between him and the island was tainted with menace.

Water splashed a yard from the side. There was another distant *crack.* He lay on his back in the cockpit, steering by the sail, taking advantage of what little cover there was.

There were several more *cracks.* After the second, there was a hole in the sail.

Finally Jack looked back. The island was more than a mile astern. He anxiously scanned the sea ahead for craft. There were none. Then he settled down to nurse more speed from the sloop and wait for the motorboat.

But it didn't come out to follow him.

V

Same as yesterday, Mrs. Kesserich was sitting on the edge of the couch in the living room, yet from the first Jack was aware of a great change. Something had filled the domestic animal with grief and fury.

"Where's Dr. Kesserich?" he asked.

"Not here!"

"Mrs. Kesserich," he said, dropping down beside her, "you were telling me something yesterday when we were interrupted."

She looked at him. "You *have* found the girl?" she almost shouted.

"Yes," Jack was surprised into answering.

A look of slyness came into Mrs. Kesserich's bovine face. "Then I'll tell you everything, I can now.

"When Martin found Mary dying, he didn't go to pieces. You know how controlled he can be when he chooses. He lifted Mary's body as if the crowd and the railway men weren't there, and carried it to the station wagon. Hani and Hilda were sitting on their horses nearby. He gave them one look. It was as if he had said, 'Murderers!'

"He told me to drive home as fast as I dared, but when I got there, he stayed sitting by Mary in the back. I knew he must have given up what hope he had for her life, or else she was dead already. I looked at him. In the domelight, his face had the most deadly and proud expression I've ever seen on a man. I worshiped him, you know, though he had never shown me one ounce of feeling. So I was completely unprepared for the naked appeal in his voice.

"Yet all he said at first was, 'Will you do something for me?' I told him, 'Surely,' and as we carried Mary in, he told me the rest. He wanted me to be the mother of Mary's child."

Jack stared at her blankly.

Mrs. Kesserich nodded. "He wanted to remove an ovum from Mary's body and nurture it in mine, so that Mary, in a way, could live on."

"But that's impossible!" Jack objected. "The technique is being tried now on cattle, I know, so that a prize heifer can have several calves a year, all nurtured in 'scrub heifers,' as they're called. But no one's ever dreamed of trying it on human beings!"

Mrs. Kesserich looked at him contemptuously. "Martin had mastered the technique twenty years ago. He was willing to take the chance. And so was I—partly because he fired my scientific imagination and reverence, but mostly because he said he would marry me. He barred the doors. We worked swiftly. As far as anyone was concerned, Martin, in a wild fit of grief, had locked himself up for several hours to mourn over the body of his fiancée.

"Within a month we were married, and I finally gave birth to Mary's child."

Jack shook his head. "You gave birth to your own child."

She smiled bitterly. "No, it was Mary's. Martin did not keep his whole bargain with me—I was nothing more than his 'scrub wife' in every way."

"You *think* you gave birth to Mary's child."

Mrs. Kesserich turned on Jack in anger. "I've been wounded by him, day in and day out, for years, but I've never failed to recognize his genius. Besides, you've seen the girl, haven't you?"

Jack had to nod. What confounded him most was that, granting the near-impossible physiological feat Mrs. Kesserich had described, the girl should look so much like the mother. Mothers and daughters don't look that much alike; only identical twins do. With a thrill of fear, he remembered Kesserich's casual words: ". . . parthenogenesis . . . pure stock . . . special techniques . . ."

"Very well," he forced himself to say, "granting that the child was Mary's and Martin's—"

"No! Mary's alone!"

Jack suppressed a shudder. He continued quickly. "What became of the child?"

Mrs. Kesserich lowered her head. "The day it was born, it was taken away from me. After that, I never saw Hilda and Hani, either."

"You mean," Jack asked, "that Martin sent them away to bring up the child?"

Mrs. Kesserich turned away. "Yes."

Jack asked incredulously, "He trusted the child with the two people he suspected of having caused the mother's death?"

"Once when I was his assistant," Mrs. Kesserich said softly, "I carelessly broke some laboratory glassware. He kept me up all night building a new setup, though I'm rather poor at working with glass and usually get burned. Bringing up the child was his sisters' punishment."

"And they went to that house on the farthest island? I suppose it was the house he'd been building for Mary and himself."

"Yes."

"And they were to bring up the child as his daughter?"

Mrs. Kesserich started up, but when she spoke it was as if she had to force out each word. "As his wife—as soon as she was grown."

"How can you know that?" Jack asked shakily.

The rising wind rattled the windowpane.

"Because today—eighteen years after—Martin broke all of his promises to me. He told me he was leaving me."

VI

White waves shooting up like dancing ghosts in the moon-sketched, spray-swept dark were Jack's first beacon of the island and brought a sense of physical danger, breaking the trancelike yet frantic mood he had felt ever since he had spoken with Mrs. Kesserich.

Coming around farther into the wind, he scudded past the end of the island into the choppy sea on the landward side. A little later he let down the reefed sail in the cove of the sea urchins, where the water was barely moving, although the air was shaken by the pounding of the surf on the spine between the two islands.

After making fast, he paused a moment for a scrap of cloud to pass the moon. The thought of the spiny creatures in the black fathoms under the *Annie O.* sent an odd quiver of terror through him.

The moon came out and he started across the glistening rocks of the spine. But he had forgotten the rising tide. Midway, a wave clamped around his ankles, tried to carry him off, almost made him drop the heavy object he was carrying. Sprawling and drenched, he clung to the rough rock until the surge was past.

Making it finally up to the fence, he snipped a wide gate with the wire-cutters.

The windows of the house were alight. Hardly aware of his shivering, he crossed the lawn, slipping from one clump of shrubbery to another, until he reached one just across the drive from the doorway. At that moment he heard the approaching *chuff* of the Essex, the door of the cottage opened, and Mary Alice Pope stepped out, closely followed by Hani or Hilda.

Jack shrank close to the shrubbery. Mary looked pale and blank-faced, as if she had retreated within herself. He was acutely conscious of the inadequacy of his screen as the ghostly headlights of the Essex began to probe through the leaves.

But then he sensed that something more was about to happen than just the car arriving. It was a change in the expression of the face behind Mary that gave him the cue—a widening and sidewise flickering of the cold eyes, the puckered lips thinning into a cruel smile.

The Essex shifted into second and, without any warning, accelerated. Simultaneously, the woman behind Mary gave her a violent shove. But at almost exactly the same instant, Jack ran. He caught Mary as she sprawled toward the gravel, and lunged ahead without checking. The Essex bore down upon them, a square-snouted, roaring monster. It swerved viciously, missed them by inches, threw up gravel in a skid, and rocked to a stop, stalled.

The first, incredulous voice that broke the pulsing silence, Jack recognized as Martin Kesserich's. It came from the car, which was slewed around so that it almost faced Jack and Mary.

"Hani, you tried to kill her! You and Hilda tried to kill her again!"

The woman slumped over the wheel slowly lifted her head. In the indistinct light, she looked the twin of the woman behind Jack and Mary.

"Did you really think we wouldn't?" she asked in a voice that spat with passion. "Did you actually believe that Hilda and I would serve this eighteen years' penance just to watch you go off with her?" She began to laugh wildly. "You've never understood your sisters at all!"

Suddenly she broke off, stiffly stepped down from the car. Lifting her skirts a little, she strode past Jack and Mary.

Martin Kesserich followed her. In passing, he said, "Thanks, Barr." It occurred to Jack that Kesserich made no more question of his appearance on the island than of his presence in the laboratory. Like Mrs. Kesserich, the great biologist took him for granted.

Kesserich stopped a few feet short of Hani and Hilda. Without shrinking from him, the sisters drew closer together. They looked like two gaunt hawks.

"But you waited eighteen years," he said. "You could have killed her at any time, yet you chose to throw away so much of your lives just to have this moment."

"How do you know we didn't like waiting eighteen years?" Hani answered him. "Why shouldn't we want to make as strong an impression on you as anyone? And as for throwing our lives away, that was your doing. Oh, Martin, you'll never know anything about how your sisters feel!''

He raised his hands in bafflement. ''Even assuming that you hate me''—at the word ''hate'' both Hani and Hilda laughed softly—''and that you were prepared to strike at both my love and my work, still, that you should have waited . . .''

Hani and Hilda said nothing.

Kesserich shrugged. ''Very well,'' he said in a voice that had lost all its tension. ''You've wasted a third of a lifetime looking forward to an irrational revenge. And you've failed. That should be sufficient punishment.''

Very slowly, he turned around and for the first time looked at Mary. His face was clearly revealed by the twin beams from the stalled car.

Jack grew cold. He fought against accepting the feelings of wonder, of poignant triumph, of love, of renewed youth he saw entering the face in the headlights. But most of all he fought against the sense that Martin Kesserich was successfully drawing them all back into the past, to 1933 and another accident. There was a distant hoot and Jack shook. For a moment he had thought it a railway whistle and not a ship's horn,

The biologist said tenderly, ''Come, Mary.''

Jack's trembling arm tightened a trifle on Mary's waist. He could feel *her* trembling.

''Come, Mary,'' Kesserich repeated.

Still she didn't reply.

Jack wet his lips. ''Mary isn't going with you, Professor,'' he said.

''Quiet, Barr,'' Kesserich ordered absently. ''Mary, it is necessary that you and I leave the island at once. Please come.''

''But Mary isn't coming,'' Jack repeated.

Kesserich looked at him for the first time. ''I'm grateful to you for the unusual sense of loyalty—or whatever motive it may have been—that led you to follow me out here tonight. And of course I'm profoundly grateful to you for saving Mary's life. But I must ask you not to interfere further in a matter which you can't possibly understand.''

He turned to Mary. ''I know how shocked and frightened you must feel. Living two lives and then having to face two deaths—it must be more terrible than anyone can realize. I expected this meeting to take place under very different circumstances. I wanted to explain everything to you very naturally and gently, like the messages I've sent you every day of your second life. Unfortunately, that can't be.

"You and I must leave the island right now."

Mary stared at him, then turned wonderingly toward Jack, who felt his heart begin to pound warmly.

"You still don't understand what I'm trying to tell you, Professor," he said, boldly now. "Mary is not going with you. You've deceived her all her life. You've taken a fantastic amount of pains to bring her up under the delusion that she is Mary Alice Pope, who died in—"

"She *is* Mary Alice Pope," Kesserich thundered at him. He advanced toward them swiftly. "Mary darling, you're confused, but you must realize who you are and who I am and the relationship between us."

"Keep away," Jack warned, swinging Mary half behind him. "Mary doesn't love you. She can't marry you, at any rate. How could she, when you're her father?"

"Barr!"

"Keep off!" Jack shot out the flat of his hand and Kesserich went staggering backward. "I've talked with your wife—your wife on the mainland. She told me the whole thing."

Kesserich seemed about to rush forward again, then controlled himself. "You've got everything wrong. You hardly deserve to be told, but under the circumstances I have no choice. Mary is not my daughter. To be precise, she has no father at all. Do you remember the work that Jacques Loeb did with sea urchins?"

Jack frowned angrily. "You mean what we were talking about last night?"

"Exactly. Loeb was able to cause the egg of a sea urchin to develop normally without union with a male germ cell. I have done the same thing with a human being. This girl is Mary Alice Pope. She has exactly the same heredity. She has had exactly the same life, so far as it could be reconstructed. She's heard and read the same things at exactly the same times. There have been the old newspapers, the books, even the old recorded radio programs. Hani and Hilda have had their daily instructions, to the letter. She's retraced the same time-trail."

"Rot!" Jack interrupted. "I don't for a moment believe what you say about her birth. She's Mary daughter—or the daughter of your wife on the mainland. And as for retracing the same time-trail, that's senile self-delusion. Mary Alice Pope had a normal life. This girl has been brought up in cruel imprisonment by two insane, vindictive old women. In your own frustrated desire, you've pretended to yourself that you've recreated the girl you lost. You haven't. You couldn't. Nobody could—the great Martin Kesserich or anyone else!"

Kesserich, his features working, shifted his point of attack. "Who are you, Mary?"

"Don't answer him," Jack said. "He's trying to confuse you."

"Who are you?" Kesserich insisted.

"Mary Alice Pope," she said rapidly in a breathy whisper before Jack could speak again.

"And when were you born?" Kesserich pressed on.

"You've been tricked all your life about that," Jack warned.

But already the girl was saying, "In 1916."

"And who am I then?" Kesserich demanded eagerly. "Who am I?"

The girl swayed. She brushed her head with her hand.

"It's so strange," she said, with a dreamy, almost laughing throb in her voice that turned Jack's heart cold. "I'm sure I've never seen you before in my life, and yet it's as if I'd known you forever. As if you were closer to me than—"

"Stop it!" Jack shouted at Kesserich. "Mary loves me. She loves me because I've shown her the lie her life has been, and because she's coming away with me now. Aren't you, Mary?"

He swung her around so that her blank face was inches from his own. "It's me you love, isn't it, Mary?"

She blinked doubtfully.

At that moment Kesserich charged at them, went sprawling as Jack's fist shot out. Jack swept up Mary and ran with her across the lawn. Behind him he heard an agonized cry—Kesserich's— and cruel, mounting laughter from Hani and Hilda.

Once through the ragged doorway in the fence, he made his way more slowly, gasping. Out of the shelter of the trees, the wind tore at them and the ocean roared. Moonlight glistened, now on the spine of black wet rocks, now on the foaming surf.

Jack realized that the girl in his arms was speaking rapidly, disjointedly, but he couldn't quite make out the sense of the words and then they were lost in the crash of the surf. She struggled, but he told himself that it was only because she was afraid of the menacing waters.

He pushed recklessly into the breaking surf, raced gasping across the middle of the spine as the rocks uncovered, sprang to the higher ones as the next wave crashed behind, showering them with spray. His chest burning with exertion, he carried the girl the few remaining yards to where the *Annie O.* was tossing. A sudden great gust of wind almost did what the waves had failed to do, but he kept his footing and lowered the girl into the boat, then jumped in after.

She stared at him wildly. "What's that?"

He, too, had caught the faint shout. Looking back along the spine just as the moon came clear again, he saw white spray rise and fall—and then the figure of Kesserich stumbling through it.

"Mary, wait for me!"

The figure was halfway across when it lurched, started forward again, then was jerked back as if something had caught its ankle. Out of the darkness, the next wave sent a line of white at it, neck-high, crashed.

Jack hesitated, but another great gust of wind tore at the half-raised sail, and it was all he could do to keep the sloop from capsizing and head her into the wind again.

Mary was tugging at his shoulder. "You must help him," she was saying. "He's caught in the rocks."

He heard a voice crying, screaming crazily above the surf:

"Ah, love, let us be true
To one another! for the world—"

The sloop rocked. Jack had it finally headed into the wind. He looked around for Mary.

She had jumped out and was hurrying back, scrambling across the rocks toward the dark, struggling figure that even as he watched was once more engulfed in the surf.

Letting go the lines, Jack sprang toward the stern of the sloop.

But just then another giant blow came, struck the sail like a great fist of air, and sent the boom slashing at the back of his head.

His last recollection was being toppled out onto the rocks and wondering how he could cling to them while unconscious.

VII

The little cove was once again as quiet as time's heart. Once again the *Annie O.* was a sloop embedded in a mirror. Once again the rocks were warm underfoot.

Jack Barr lifted his fiercely aching head and looked at the distant line of the mainland, as tiny and yet as clear as something viewed through the wrong end of a telescope. He was very tired. Searching the island, in his present shaky condition, had taken all the strength out of him.

He looked at the peacefully rippling sea outside the cove and thought of what a churning pot it had been during the storm. He thought wonderingly of his escape—somehow in his unconsciousness he had struggled up to the shelter of the oaks, for that was where he had awakened.

He thought of Mrs. Kesserich sitting alone in her house, scanning the newspapers that would have nothing to tell.

He thought of the empty island behind him and the motorboat gone from the wharf.

He thought of the vanished Essex and the freshly smashed rail at the end of the wharf and the carlike shape he'd thought he'd seen deep beneath the green water there.

He wondered if the sea had pulled down Martin Kesserich and Mary Alice Pope. He wondered if only Hani and Hilda had gone away in the motorboat.

Or were Hani and Hilda down in the Essex? In that case . . .

He winced, remembering what he had done to Martin and Mary by his blundering infatuation. In his way, he told himself, he had been as bad as the two old women.

His love for Mary was not gone, but he could see it in its tinied perspective. He wondered if any man could fail to fall in love with a girl who came, or merely thought she came, from another era of time—always the ultimate in feminine strangeness and attraction.

He thought of Martin Kesserich's nearly incredible scientific triumph, now forever hidden.

Scientific?—that wasn't the greatest part. . . .

He thought of death, and of time, and of love that defies them both.

He stepped, limping, into the *Annie O.*

Then he saw the square of paper tied around the tiller.

He untied and unrolled it and read:

Dear Jack,

Martin and I thank you. We both love you. And now we say goodbye. We're going to a farther island.

Mrs. Mary Alice Pope Kesserich
July 22, 1933

After a long space, he nodded.

He waved once—toward the open Atlantic.

He pushed off and set sail for the mainland.

THE SNOWBALL EFFECT

by Katherine MacLean (1925–)

Katherine MacLean worked as an office manager and as a food manufacturing and medical technician and these experiences find clear expression in her always interesting and well-crafted stories. And although she has had a couple of collections, most recently *The Trouble With You People* (1980) and has also published four novels, I still feel that she is rather underevaluated and underappreciated. Her short stories were one of the best things about the science fiction of the 1950s, when she was a relative rarity—a writer who used social science concepts and at the same time obviously had a good working knowledge of the "hard" sciences. She won a Nebula Award in 1971 for "The Missing Man."

"The Snowball Effect" remains wonderful social satire. (MHG)

The story you are about to read is a satire. That is, it takes a situation and deliberately exaggerates it to an extreme. The effect is that you look at something under a magnifying glass and see it in detail. It is very useful if it is well done.

Of course, you can smile and dismiss it as an exaggeration that need not really frighten you. Under the proper magnification, a fly might look the size of a horse, but it is *really* the size of a fly.

But then how much of an exaggeration is the magnification? Is the "snowball effect" truly exaggerated?

When Jesus was crucified, he left behind him twelve poor and largely ineffective disciples. The movement might have come to nothing but for the conversion of the charismatic Saul of Tarsus (who became the Apostle Paul). He started a movement that snowballed to such an extent that Christians are for the most part rather sure that it succeeded only through divine will. Nothing less would account for it.

Or, if you want to go to the other extreme, Adolf Hitler joined a tiny National Socialist party in 1919, and in a quarter-century had snowballed it to the point where it took the whole world's extremest efforts and some 40,000,000 dead to stop him.

You want to smile at the "snowball effect." Well, smile, if you can. (IA)

"All right," I said, "what is sociology good for?"

Wilton Caswell, Ph.D., was head of my Sociology Department, and right then he was mad enough to chew nails. On the office wall behind him were three or four framed documents in Latin, but I didn't care at that moment if he papered the walls with his degrees. I had been appointed Dean and President to see to it that the University made money. I had a job to do, and I meant to do it.

He bit off each word with great restraint: "Sociology is the study of social institutions, Mr. Halloway."

I tried to make him understand my position. "Look, it's the big-money men who are supposed to be contributing to the support of this college. To them, sociology sounds like socialism— nothing can sound worse than that—and an institution is where they put Aunt Maggy when she began collecting Wheaties in a stamp album. We can't appeal to them that way. Come on now," I smiled condescendingly, knowing it would irritate him. "What are you doing that's worth anything?"

He glared at me, his white hair bristling and his nostrils dilated like a war horse about to whinny. I can say one thing for them—these scientists and professors always keep themselves well under control. He had a book in his hand and I was expecting him to throw it, but he spoke instead:

"This department's analysis of institutional accretion, by the use of open-system mathematics, has been recognized as an outstanding and valuable contribution to—"

The words were impressive, whatever they meant, but this still didn't sound like anything that would pull in money. I interrupted, "Valuable in what way?"

He sat down on the edge of his desk thoughtfully, apparently recovering from the shock of being asked to produce something solid for his position, and ran his eyes over the titles of the books that lined his office walls.

"Well, sociology has been valuable to business in initiating worker efficiency and group motivation studies, which they now use in management decisions. And, of course, since the Depression, Washington has been using sociological studies of employment, labor, and standards of living as a basis for its general policies of—"

I stopped him with both hands raised. "Please, Professor Caswell! That would hardly be a recommendation. Washington, the New Deal and the present Administration are somewhat touchy subjects to the men I have to deal with. They consider its value debatable, if you know what I mean. If they got the idea that sociology professors are giving advice and guidance— No, we have to stick to brass tacks and leave Washington out of this. What, specifically, has the work of this specific department done that would make it as worthy to receive money as—say, a heart-disease research fund?"

He began to tap the corner of his book absently on the desk, watching me. "Fundamental research doesn't show immediate effects, Mr. Halloway, but its value is recognized."

I smiled and took out my pipe. "All right, tell me about it. Maybe I'll recognize its value."

Professor Caswell smiled back tightly. He knew his department was at stake. The other departments were popular with donors and pulled in gift money by scholarships and fellowships, and supported their professors and graduate students by research contracts with the Government and industry. Caswell had to show a way to make his own department popular—or else.

He laid down his book and ran a hand over his ruffled hair. "Institutions—organizations, that is"—his voice became more resonant; like most professors, when he had to explain something he instinctively slipped into his platform lecture mannerisms, and began to deliver an essay—"have certain tendencies built into the way they happen to have been organized, which cause them to expand or contract without reference to the needs they were founded to serve."

He was becoming flushed with the pleasure of explaining his subject. "All through the ages, it has been a matter of wonder and dismay to men that a simple organization—such as a church to worship in, or a delegation of weapons to a warrior class merely for defense against an outside enemy—will either grow insensately and extend its control until it is a tyranny over their whole lives, or, like other organizations set up to serve a vital need, will tend to dwindle repeatedly and vanish, and have to be painfully rebuilt.

"The reason can be traced to little quirks in the way they were organized, a matter of positive and negative power feedbacks. Such simple questions as 'Is there a way a holder of authority in this organization can use the power available to him to increase his power?' provide the key. But it still could not be handled until the complex questions of interacting motives and long-range accumulations of minor effects could somehow be simplified and formulated. In working on the problem, I found that the mathematics of open system, as introduced to biology by Ludwig von Bertalanffy and George Kreezer, could be used as a base that would enable me to develop a specifically social mathematics, expressing the human factors of intermeshing authority and motives in simple formulas.

"By these formulations, it is possible to determine automatically the amount of growth and period of life of any organization. The U.N., to choose an unfortunate example, is a shrinker-type organization. Its monetary support is not in the hands of those who personally benefit by its governmental activities, but, instead, in the hands of those who would personally lose by any extension and encroachment of its authority on their own. Yet by the use of formula analysis—"

"That's theory," I said. "How about proof?"

"My equations are already being used in the study of limited-size Federal corporations. Washington—"

I held up my palm again. "Please, not that nasty word again. I mean, where else has it been put into operation? Just a simple demonstration, something to show that it works, that's all."

He looked away from me thoughtfully, picked up the book and began to tap it on the desk again. It had some unreadable title and his name on it in gold letters. I got the distinct impression again that he was repressing an urge to hit me with it.

He spoke quietly. "All right. I'll give you a demonstration. Are you willing to wait six months?"

"Certainly, if you can show me something at the end of that time."

Reminded of time, I glanced at my watch and stood up.

"Could we discuss this over lunch?" he asked.

"I wouldn't mind hearing more, but I'm having lunch with some executors of a millionaire's will. They have to be convinced that by "furtherance of research into human ills" he meant that the money should go to research fellowships for postgraduate biologists at the University, rather than to a medical foundation."

"I see you have your problems, too," Caswell said, conceding me nothing. He extended his hand with a chilly smile. "Well, good afternoon, Mr. Halloway. I'm glad we had this talk."

I shook hands and left him standing there, sure of his place in the progress of science and the respect of his colleagues, yet seething inside because I, the President and Dean, had boorishly demanded that he produce something tangible.

My job isn't easy. For a crumb of favorable publicity and respect in the newspapers and an annual ceremony in a silly costume, I spend the rest of the year going hat in hand, asking politely for money at everyone's door, like a well-dressed panhandler, and trying to manage the University on the dribble I get. As far as I was concerned, a department had to support itself or be cut down to what student tuition pays for, which is a handful of overcrowded courses taught by an assistant lecturer. Caswell had to make it work or get out.

But, the more I thought about it, the more I wanted to hear what he was going to do for a demonstration.

At lunch, three days later, while we were waiting for our order, he opened a small notebook. "Ever hear of feedback effects?"

"Not enough to have it clear."

"You know the snowball effect, though."

"Sure, start a snowball rolling downhill and it grows."

"Well, now—" He wrote a short line of symbols on a blank page and turned the notebook around for me to inspect it. "Here's the formula for the snowball process. It's the basic general growth formula—covers everything."

It was a row of little symbols arranged like an algebra equation. One was a concentric spiral going up, like a cross-section of a snowball rolling in snow. That was a growth sign.

I hadn't expected to understand the equation, but it was almost as clear as a sentence. I was impressed and slightly intimidated by it. He had already explained enough so that I knew that, if he was right, here was the growth of the Catholic Church and the Roman Empire, the conquests of Alexander and the spread of the smoking habit and the change and rigidity of the unwritten law of styles.

"Is it really as simple as that?" I asked.

"You notice," he said, 'that when it becomes too heavy for the cohesion strength of snow it breaks apart. Now, in human terms—"

The chops and mashed potatoes and peas arrived.

"Go on," I urged.

He was deep in the symbology of human motives and the equations of human behavior in groups. After running through a few different types of grower- and shrinker-type organizations, we came back to the snowball, and decided to run the test by making something grow.

"You add the motives," he said, "and the equation will translate them into organization."

"How about a good selfish reason for the ins to drag others into the group—some sort of bounty on new members, a cut of their membership fee?" I suggested uncertainly, feeling slightly foolish. "And maybe a reason why the members would lose if any of them resigned, and some indirect way they could use to force each other to stay in."

"The first is the chain-letter principle." He nodded. "I've got that. The other . . ." He put the symbols through some mathematical manipulation so that a special grouping appeared in the middle of the equation. "That's it."

Since I seemed to have the right idea, I suggested some more, and he added some, and juggled them around in different patterns. We threw out a few that would have made the organization too complicated, and finally worked out an idyllically simple and deadly little organization set-up where joining had all the temptation of buying a sweepstakes ticket, going in deeper was as easy as hanging around a race track, and getting out was like trying to pull free from a Malayan thumb-trap. We put our heads closer together and talked lower, picking the best place for the demonstration.

"Abington?"

"How about Watashaw? I have some student sociological surveys of it already. We can pick a suitable group from that."

"This demonstration has got to be convincing. We'd better pick a little group that no one in his right mind would expect to grow."

"There should be a suitable club—"

"Ladies," said the skinny female chairman of the Watashaw Sewing Circle. "Today we have guests." She signaled for us to rise, and we stood up, bowing to polite applause and smiles. "Professor Caswell, and Professor Smith." (My alias.) "They are making a survey of the methods and duties of the clubs of Watashaw."

We sat down to another ripple of applause and slightly wider smiles, and then the meeting of the Watashaw Sewing Circle began. In five minutes I began to feel sleepy.

There were only about thirty people there, and it was a small room, not the halls of Congress, but they discussed their business of collecting and repairing second-hand clothing for charity with the same endless boring parliamentary formality.

I pointed out to Caswell the member I thought would be the natural leader, a tall, well-built woman in a green suit, with conscious gestures and a resonant, penetrating voice, and then went into a half-doze while Caswell stayed awake beside me and wrote in his notebook. After a while the resonant voice roused me to attention for a moment. It was the tall woman holding the floor over some collective dereliction of the club. She was being scathing.

I nudged Caswell and murmured, "Did you fix it so that a shover has a better chance of getting into office than a non-shover?"

"I think there's a way they could find for it," Caswell whispered back, and went to work on his equation again. "Yes, several ways to bias the elections."

"Good. Point them out tactfully to the one you select. Not as if she'd use such methods, but just as an example of the reason why only *she* can be trusted with initiating the change. Just mention all the personal advantages an unscrupulous person could have."

He nodded, keeping a straight and sober face as if we were exchanging admiring remarks about the techniques of clothes repairing, instead of conspiring.

After the meeting, Caswell drew the tall woman in the green suit aside and spoke to her confidentially, showing her the diagram of organization we had drawn up. I saw the responsive glitter in the woman's eyes and knew she was hooked.

We left the diagram of organization and our typed copy of the new by-laws with her and went off soberly, as befitted two social-science experimenters. We didn't start laughing until our car passed the town limits and began the climb for University Heights.

If Caswell's equations meant anything at all, we had given that sewing circle more growth drives than the Roman Empire.

Four months later I had time out from a very busy schedule to wonder how the test was coming along. Passing Caswell's office, I put my head in. He looked up from a student research paper he was correcting.

"Caswell, about that sewing club business—I'm beginning to feel the suspense. Could I get an advance report on how it's coming?"

"I'm not following it. We're supposed to let it run the full six months."

"But I'm curious. Could I get in touch with that woman—what's her name?"

"Searles. Mrs. George Searles."

"Would that change the results?"

"Not in the slightest. If you want to graph the membership rise, it should be going up in a log curve, probably doubling every so often."

I grinned. "If it's not rising, you're fired."

He grinned back. "If it's not rising, you won't have to fire me—I'll burn my books and shoot myself."

I returned to my office and put in a call to Watashaw.

While I was waiting for the phone to be answered, I took a piece of graph paper and ruled it off into six sections, one for each month. After the phone had rung in the distance for a long time, a servant answered with a bored drawl:

"Mrs. Searles' residence."

I picked up a red gummed star and licked it.

"Mrs. Searles, please."

"She's not in just now. Could I take a message?"

I placed the star at the thirty line in the beginning of the first section. Thirty members they'd started with.

"No, thanks. Could you tell me when she'll be back?"

"Not until dinner. She's at the meetin'."

"The sewing club?" I asked.

"No, *sir*, not that thing. There isn't any sewing club anymore, not for a long time. She's at the Civic Welfare meeting."

Somehow I hadn't expected anything like that.

"Thank you," I said and hung up, and after a moment noticed I was holding a box of red gummed stars in my hand. I closed it and put it down on top of the graph of membership in the sewing circle. No more members. . . .

Poor Caswell. The bet between us was ironclad. He wouldn't let me back down on it even if I wanted to. He'd probably quit before I put through the first slow move to fire him. His professional pride would be shattered, sunk without a trace. I remembered what he said about shooting himself. It had seemed funny to both of us at the time, but. . . . What a mess that would make for the University.

I had to talk to Mrs. Searles. Perhaps there was some outside reason why the club had disbanded. Perhaps it had not just died.

I called back. "This is Professor Smith," I said, giving the alias I had used before. "I called a few minutes ago. When did you say Mrs. Searles will return?"

"About six-thirty or seven o'clock."

Five hours to wait.

And what if Caswell asked me what I had found out in the meantime? I didn't want to tell him anything until I had talked it over with that woman Searles first.

"Where is this Civic Welfare meeting?"

She told me.

Five minutes later, I was in my car, heading for Watashaw, driving considerably faster than usual and keeping a careful watch for highway-patrol cars as the speedometer climbed.

The town meeting-hall and theatre was a big place, probably with lots of small rooms for different clubs. I went in through the center door and found myself in the huge central hall where some sort of rally was being held. A political-type rally—you know, cheers and chants, with bunting already down on the floor, people holding banners, and plenty of enthusiasm and excitement in the air. Someone was making a speech up on the platform. Most of the people there were women.

I wondered how the Civic Welfare League could dare hold its meeting at the same time as a political rally that could pull its members away. The group with Mrs. Searles was probably holding a shrunken and almost memberless meeting somewhere in an upper room.

There probably was a side door that would lead upstairs.

While I glanced around, a pretty girl usher put a printed bulletin in my hand, whispering, "Here's one of the new copies." As I attempted to hand it back, she retreated. "Oh, you can keep it. It's the new one. Everyone's supposed to have it. We've just printed up six thousand copies to make sure there'll be enough to last."

The tall woman on the platform had been making a driving, forceful speech about some plans for rebuilding Watashaw's slum section. It began to penetrate my mind dimly as I glanced down at the bulletin in my hands.

"Civic Welfare League of Watashaw. The United Organization of Church and Secular Charities." That's what it said. Below began the rules of membership.

I looked up. The speaker, with a clear, determined voice and conscious, forceful gestures, had entered the home stretch of her speech, an appeal to the civic pride of all citizens of Watashaw.

"With a bright and glorious future—potentially without poor and without uncared-for ill—potentially with no ugliness, no vistas which are not beautiful—the best people in the best-planned town in the country—jewel of the United States."

She paused and then leaned forward intensely, striking her clenched hand on the speaker's stand with each word for emphasis.

"*All we need is more members. Now, get out there and recruit!*"

I finally recognized Mrs. Searles, as an answering sudden blast of sound half deafened me. The crowd was chanting at the top of its lungs: "Recruit! Recruit!"

Mrs. Searles stood still at the speaker's table and behind her, seated in a row of chairs, was a group that was probably the board of directors. It was mostly women, and the women began to look vaguely familiar, as if they could be members of the sewing circle.

I put my lips close to the ear of the pretty usher while I turned over the stiff printed bulletin on a hunch. "How long has the

League been organized?'' On the back of the bulletin was a constitution.

She was cheering with the crowd, her eyes sparkling. ''I don't know,'' she answered between cheers. ''I only joined two days ago. Isn't it wonderful?''

I went into the quiet outer air and got into my car with my skin prickling. Even as I drove away, I could hear them. They were singing some kind of organization song with the tune of ''Marching through Georgia.''

Even at the single glance I had given it, the constitution looked exactly like the one we had given the Watashaw Sewing Circle.

All I told Caswell when I got back was that the sewing circle had changed its name and the membership seemed to be rising.

Next day, after calling Mrs. Searles, I placed some red stars on my graph for the first three months. They made a nice curve, rising steeply as it reached the fourth month. They had picked up their first increase in membership simply by amalgamating with all the other types of charity organizations in Watashaw, changing the club name with each fusion, but keeping the same constitution—the constitution with the bright promise of advantages as long as there were always new members being brought in.

By the fifth month, the League had added a mutual baby-sitting service and had induced the local school board to add a nursery school to the town service, so as to free more women for League activity. But charity must have been completely organized by then, and expansion had to be in other directions.

Some real-estate agents evidently had been drawn into the whirlpool early, along with their ideas. The slum improvement plans began to blossom and take on a tinge of real-estate planning later in the month.

The first day of the sixth month, a big two-page spread appeared in the local paper of a mass meeting which had approved a full-fledged scheme for slum clearance of Watashaw's shack-town section, plus plans for rehousing, civic building, and re-zoning. And good prospects for attracting some new industries to the town, industries which had already been contacted and seemed interested by the privileges offered.

And, with all this, an arrangement for securing and distributing to the club members *alone* most of the profit that would come to the town in the form of a rise in the price of building sites and a boom in the building industry. The profit-distributing arrangement was the same one that had been built into the organization plan for the distribution of the small profits of membership fees and honorary promotions. It was becoming an openly profitable business. Membership was rising more rapidly now.

By the second week of the sixth month, news appeared in the local paper that the club had filed an application to incorporate itself as the Watashaw Mutual Trade and Civic Development Corporation, and all the local real-estate promoters had finished joining *en masse*. The Mutual Trade part sounded to me as if the Chamber of Commerce was on the point of being pulled in with them, ideas, ambitions and all.

I chuckled while reading the next page of the paper, on which a local politician was reported as having addressed the club with long flowery oration on their enterprise, charity and civic spirit. He had been made an honorary member. If he allowed himself to be made a *full member* with its contractual obligations and its lures, if the politicians went into this, too. . . .

I laughed, filing the newspaper with the other documents on the Watashaw test. These proofs would fascinate any businessman with the sense to see where his bread was buttered. A businessman is constantly dealing with organizations, including his own, and finding them either inert, cantankerous, or both. Caswell's formula could be a handle to grasp them with. Gratitude alone would bring money into the University in car-load lots.

The end of the sixth month came. The test was over and the end reports were spectacular. Caswell's formulas were proven to the hilt.

After reading the last newspaper reports, I called him up.

"Perfect, Wilt, *perfect*! I can use this Watashaw thing to get you so many fellowships and scholarships and grants for your department that you'll think it's snowing money!"

He answered somewhat uninterestedly, "I've been busy working with students on their research papers and marking tests—not following the Watashaw business at all, I'm afraid. You say the demonstration went well and you're satisfied?"

He was definitely putting on a chill. We were friends now, but obviously he was still peeved whenever he was reminded that I had doubted that his theory could work. And he was using its success to rub my nose in the realization that I had been wrong. A man with a string of degrees after his name is just as human as anyone else. I had needled him pretty hard that first time.

"I'm satisfied," I acknowledged. "I was wrong. The formulas work beautifully. Come over and see my file of documents on it if you want a boost for your ego. Now let's see the formula for stopping it."

He sounded cheerful again. "I didn't complicate that organization with negatives. I wanted it to *grow*. It falls apart naturally when it stops growing for more than two months. It's like the great stock boom before an economic crash. Everyone in it is prosperous as long as the prices must keep going up and new buyers come into the market, but they all know what would happen if it stopped growing. You remember, we built in as one of the incentives that the members know they are going to lose if membership stops growing. Why, if I tried to stop it now, they'd cut my throat."

I remembered the drive and frenzy of the crowd in the one early meeting I had seen. They probably would.

"No," he continued. "We'll just let it play out to the end of its tether and die of old age."

"When will that be?"

"It can't grow past the female population of the town. There are only so many women in Watashaw, and some of them don't like sewing."

The graph on the desk before me began to look sinister. Surely Caswell must have made some provision for—

"You underestimate their ingenuity," I said into the phone. "Since they wanted to expand, they didn't stick to sewing. They went from general charity to social welfare schemes to something that's pretty close to an incorporated government. The name is now the Watashaw Mutual Trade and Civic Development Corporation, and they're filing an application to change it to Civic Property Pool and Social Dividend, membership contractual, open to all. That social dividend sounds like a Technocrat climbed on the bandwagon, eh?"

While I spoke, I carefully added another red star to the curve above the thousand-member level, checking with the newspaper that still lay open on my desk. The curve was definitely some sort of log curve now, growing more rapidly with each increase.

"Leaving out practical limitations for a moment, where does the formula say it will stop." I asked.

"When you run out of people to join it. But, after all, there are only so many peple in Watashaw. It's a pretty small town."

"They've opened a branch office in New York," I said carefully into the phone, a few weeks later.

With my pencil, very carefully, I extended the membership curve from where it was then.

After the next doubling, the curve went almost straight up and off the page.

Allowing for a lag of contagion from one nation to another, depending on how much their citizens intermingled, I'd give the rest of the world about twelve years.

There was a long silence while Caswell probably drew the same graph in his own mind. Then he laughed weakly. "Well, you asked me for a demonstration."

That was as good an answer as any. We got together and had lunch in a bar, if you can call it lunch. The movement we started will expand by hook or by crook, by seduction or by bribery or by propaganda or by conquest, but it will expand. And maybe a total world government will be a fine thing—until it hits the end of its rope in twelve years or so.

What happens then, I don't know.

But I don't want anyone to pin that on me. From now on, if anyone asks me, I've never heard of Watashaw.

DELAY IN TRANSIT

by F(loyd) L. Wallace

Floyd Wallace is a writer of great accomplishment and even greater potential who published roughly two dozen stories and one novel—*Address: Centauri,* (1955) itself expanded from one of the shorter works—most of which appeared in *Galaxy,* and then disappeared from science fiction. There also exist two mystery novels, *Three Times a Victim* (1957) and *Wired for Scandal* (1959) which I have never been able to locate.

His legacy to us (and there may be more; he has told me that he is again writing sf) is nevertheless substantial and noteworthy, especially "Accidental Flight," "Big Ancestor," "Student Body," "Bolden's Pets," and "Mezzerow Loves Company." He excelled in the depiction of alien life forms, and there is a powerful and subtle ecological theme in much of his work.

"Delay in Transit" shows him at the top of his form. (MHG)

I have always been interested in what it is that causes a writer to turn out a great many stories over a restricted period—successful stories of quality, often—and then, quite suddenly, stop writing.

One can make up reasons: the writer gets tired of the hard work involved; he's used up the ideas that till then came flooding into his mind; he's found a good job that pays more than writing. (Or, if the writer is a woman, "she" in all these cases.) Weighing against all these reasons is my personal knowledge to the effect that once the writing bug has bitten you, you *can't* quit.

Yet F. L. Wallace, as Marty points out, was strictly a writer of the 1950's.

Can it be, it suddenly occurs to me, that some writers are so symbiotically bound to a particular editor, that the passing of the editor means the passing of the writer as well? Thus, toward the end of the 1940's, I began to fear that I could write only for Campbell and that if anything happened to him, I would be through. That didn't happen because as the 1950's opened, I discovered that I could write just as easily for H. L. Gold, Tony Boucher, and Walter Bradbury.

But what if alternate outlets *aren't* found? I wonder if Wallace might not have been so entirely an H. L. Gold editor, that when Horace passed from the scene, Wallace found he could no longer write (or no longer wanted to write). (IA)

"Muscles tense," said Dimanche. "Neural index 1.76, unusually high. Adrenalin squirting through his system. In effect, he's stalking you. Intent: probably assault with a deadly weapon."

"Not interested," said Cassal firmly, his subvocalization inaudible to anyone but Dimanche. "I'm not the victim type. He was standing on the walkway near the brink of the thoroughfare. I'm going back to the habitat hotel and sit tight."

"First you have to get there," Dimanche pointed out. "I mean, is it safe for a stranger to walk through the city?"

"Now that you mention it, no," answered Cassal. He looked around apprehensively. "Where is he?"

"Behind you. At the moment he's pretending interest in a merchandise display."

A native stamped by, eyes brown and incurious. Apparently he was accustomed to the sight of an Earthman standing alone, Adam's apple bobbing up and down silently. It was a Godolphian axiom that all travelers were crazy.

Cassal looked up. Not an air taxi in sight; Godolph shut down at dusk. It would be pure luck if he found a taxi before morning. Of course he *could* walk back to the hotel, but was that such a good idea?

A Godolphian city was peculiar. And, though not intended, it was peculiarly suited to certain kinds of violence. A human pedestrian was at a definite disadvantage.

"Correction," said Dimanche. "Not simple assault. He has murder in mind."

"It still doesn't appeal to me," said Cassal. Striving to look unconcerned, he strolled toward the building side of the walkway and stared into the interior of a small cafe. Warm, bright and dry. Inside, he might find safety for a time.

Damn the man who was following him! It would be easy enough to elude him in a normal city. On Godolph, nothing was normal. In an hour the streets would be brightly lighted—for native eyes. A human would consider it dim.

"Why did he choose me?" asked Cassal plaintively. "There must be something he hopes to gain."

"I'm working on it," said Dimanche. "But remember, I have limitations. At short distances I can scan nervous systems, collect and interpret physiological data. I can't read minds. The best I can do is report what a person says or subvocalizes. If you're really interested in finding out why he wants to kill you, I suggest you turn the problem over to the godawful police."

"Godolph, not godawful," corrected Cassal absently.

That was advice he couldn't follow, good as it seemed. He could give the police no evidence save through Dimanche. There were various reasons, many of them involving the law, for leaving the device called Dimanche out of it. The police would act if they found a body. His own, say, floating face-down on some quiet street. That didn't seem the proper approach, either.

"Weapons?"

"The first thing I searched him for. Nothing very dangerous. A long knife, a hard striking object. Both concealed on his person."

Cassal strangled slightly. Dimanche needed a good stiff course in semantics. A knife was still the most silent of weapons. A man could die from it. His hand strayed toward his pocket. He had a measure of protection himself.

"Report," said Dimanche. "Not necessarily final. Based, perhaps, on tenuous evidence."

"Let's have it anyway."

"His motivation is connected somehow with your being marooned here. For some reason you can't get off this planet."

That was startling information, though not strictly true. A

thousand star systems were waiting for him, and a ship to take him to each one.

Of course, the one ship he wanted hadn't come in. Godolph was a transfer point for stars nearer the center of the Galaxy. When he had left the Earth, he had known he would have to wait a few days here. He hadn't expected a delay of nearly three weeks. Still, it wasn't unusual. Interstellar schedules over great distances were not as reliable as they might be.

Was this man, whoever and whatever he might be, connected with that delay? According to Dimanche, the man thought he was. He was self-deluded or did he have access to information that Cassal didn't?

Denton Cassal, sales engineer, paused for a mental survey of himself. He was a good engineer and, because he was exceptionally well matched to his instrument, the best salesman that Neuronics, Inc., had. On the basis of these qualifications, he had been selected to make a long journey, the first part of which already lay behind him. He had to go to Tunney 21 to see a man. That man wasn't important to anyone save the company that employed him, and possibly not even to them.

The thug trailing him wouldn't be interested in Cassal himself, his mission, which was a commercial one, nor the man on Tunney. And money wasn't the objective, if Dimanche's analysis was right. What *did* the thug want?

Secrets? Cassal had none, except, in a sense, Dimanche. And that was too well kept on Earth, where the instrument was invented and made, for anyone this far away to have learned about it.

And yet the thug wanted to kill him. Wanted to? Regarded him as good as dead. It might pay him to investigate the matter further, if it didn't involve too much risk.

"Better start moving." That was Dimanche. "He's getting suspicious."

Cassal went slowly along the narrow walkway that bordered each side of that boulevard, the transport tide. It was raining again. It usually was on Godolph, which was a weather-controlled planet where the natives like rain.

He adjusted the controls of the weak force field that repelled the rain. He widened the angle of the field until water slanted through it unhindered. He narrowed it around him until it approached visibility and the drops bounced away. He swore at the miserable climate and the near amphibians who created it.

A few hundred feet away, a Godolphian girl waded out of the transport tide and climbed to the walkway. It was this sort of thing that made life dangerous for a human—Venice revised, brought up to date in a faster-than-light age.

Water. It was a perfect engineering material. Simple, cheap, infinitely flexible. With a minimum of mechanism and at break-neck speed, the ribbon of the transport tide flowed at different levels throughout the city. The Godolphian merely plunged in and was carried swiftly and noiselessly to his destination. Whereas a human—Cassal shivered. If he were found drowned, it would be considered an accident. No investigation would be made. The thug who was trailing him had certainly picked the right place.

The Godolphian girl passed. She wore a sleek brown fur, her own. Cassal was almost positive she muttered a polite "Arf?" as she sloshed by. What she meant by that, he didn't know and didn't intend to find out.

"Follow her," instructed Dimanche. "We've got to investigate our man at closer range."

Obediently, Cassal turned and began walking after the girl. Atrractive in an anthropomorphic, seal-like way, even from behind. Not graceful out of her element, though.

The would-be assassin was still looking at merchandise as Cassal retraced his steps. A man, or at least man type. A big fellow, physically quite capable of violence, if size had anything to do with it. The face, though, was out of character. Mild, almost meek. A scientist or scholar. It didn't fit with murder.

"Nothing," said Dimanche disgustedly. "His mind froze when we got close. I could feel his shoulderblades twitching as we passed. Anticipated guilt, of course. Projecting to you the action he plans. That makes the knife definite."

Well beyond the window at which the thug watched and waited, Cassal stopped. Shakily he produced a cigarette and fumbled for a lighter.

"Excellent thinking," commended Dimanche. "He won't attempt anything on this street. Too dangerous. Turn aside at the next deserted intersection and let him follow the glow of your cigarette."

The lighter flared in his hand. "That's one way of finding out," said Cassal. "But wouldn't I be a lot safer if I just concentrated on getting back to the hotel?"

"I'm curious. Turn here."

"Go to hell," said Cassal nervously. Nevertheless, when he came to that intersection, he turned there.

It was a Godolphian equivalent of an alley, narrow and dark, oily slow-moving water gurgling at one side, high cavernous walls looming on the other.

He would have to adjust the curiosity factor of Dimanche. It was all very well to be interested in the man who trailed him, but there was also the problem of coming out of this adventure alive. Dimanche, an electronic instrument, naturally wouldn't consider that.

"Easy," warned Dimanche. "He's at the entrance to the alley, walking fast. He's surprised and pleased that you took this route."

"I'm surprised, too," remarked Cassal. "But I wouldn't say I'm pleased. Not just now."

"Careful. Even subvocalized conversation is distracting." The mechanism concealed within his body was silent for an instant and then continued: "His blood pressure is rising, breathing is faster. At a time like this, he may be ready to verbalize why he wants to murder you. This is critical."

"That's no lie," agreed Cassal bitterly. The lighter was in his hand. He clutched it grimly. It was difficult not to look back. The darkness assumed an even more sinister quality.

"Quiet," said Dimanche. "He's verbalizing about you."

"He's decided I'm a nice fellow after all. He's going to stop and ask me for a light."

"I don't think so," answered Dimanche. "He's whispering: 'Poor devil. I hate to do it. But it's really his life or mine.' "

"He's more right than he knows. Why all this violence, though? Isn't there any clue?"

"None at all," admitted Dimanche. "He's very close. You'd better turn around."

Cassal turned, pressed the stud on the lighter. It should have made him feel more secure, but it didn't. He could see very little.

A dim shadow rushed at him. He jumped away from the water side of the alley, barely in time. He could feel the rush of air as the assailant shot by.

"Hey!" shouted Cassal.

Echoes answered; nothing else did. He had the uncomfortable feeling that no one was going to come to his assistance.

"He wasn't expecting that reaction," explained Dimanche.

"That's why he missed. He's turned around and is coming back."

"I'm armed!" shouted Cassal

"That won't stop him. He doesn't believe you."

Cassal grasped the lighter. That is, it had been a lighter a few seconds before. Now a needle-thin blade had snapped out and projected stiffly. Originally it had been designed as an emergency surgical instrument. A little imagination and a few changes had altered its function, converting it into a compact, efficient stiletto.

"Twenty feet away," advised Dimanche. "He knows you can't see him, but he can see your silhouette by the light from the main thoroughfare. What he doesn't know is that I can detect every move he makes and keep you posted below the level of his hearing."

"Stay on him," growled Cassal nervously. He flattened himself against the wall.

"To the right," whispered Dimanche. "Lunge forward. About five feet. Low."

Sickly, he did so. He didn't care to consider the possible effects of a miscalculation. In the darkness, how far was five feet? Fortunately, his estimate was correct. The rapier encountered yielding resistance, the soggy kind: flesh. The tough blade bent, but did not break. His opponent gasped and broke away.

"Attack!" howled Dimanche against the bone behind his ear. "You've got him. He can't imagine how you know where he is in the darkness. He's afraid."

Attack he did, slicing about wildly. Some of the thrusts landed; some didn't. The percentage was low, the total amount high. His opponent fell to the ground, gasped and was silent.

Cassal fumbled in his pockets and flipped on a light. The man lay near the water side of the alley. One leg was crumpled under him. He didn't move.

"Heartbeat slow," said Dimanche solemnly. "Breathing barely perceptible."

"Then he's not dead," said Cassal in relief.

Foam flecked from the still lips and ran down the chin. Blood oozed from cuts on the face.

"Respiration none, heartbeat absent," stated Dimanche.

Horrified, Cassal gazed at the body. Self-defense, of course, but would the police believe it? Assuming they did, they'd still have to investigate. The rapier was an illegal concealed weapon.

And they would question him until they discovered Dimanche. Regrettable, but what could he do about it?

Suppose he were detained long enough to miss the ship bound for Tunney 21?

Grimly, he laid down the rapier. He might as well get to the bottom of this. Why had the man attacked? What did he want?

"I don't know," replied Dimanche irritably. "I can interpret body data—a live body. I can't work on a piece of meat."

Cassal searched the body thoroughly. Miscellaneous personal articles of no value in identifying the man. A clip with a startling amount of money in it. A small white card with something scribbled on it. A picture of a woman and a small child posed against a background which resembled no world Cassal had ever seen. That was all.

Cassal stood up in bewilderment. Dimanche to the contrary, there seemed to be no connection between this dead man and his own problem of getting to Tunney 21.

Right now, though, he had to dispose of the body. He glanced toward the boulevard. So far no one had been attracted by the violence.

He bent down to retrieve the lighter-rapier. Dimanche shouted at him. Before he could react, someone landed on him. He fell forward, vainly trying to grasp the weapon. Strong fingers felt for his throat as he was forced to the ground.

He threw the attacker off and staggered to his feet. He heard footsteps rushing away. A slight splash followed. Whoever it was, he was escaping by way of water.

Whoever it was. The man he had thought he had slain was no longer in sight.

"Interpret body data, do you?" muttered Cassal. "Liveliest dead man I've ever been strangled by."

"It's just possible there are some breeds of men who can control the basic functions of their body," said Dimanche defensively. "When I checked him, he had no hearbeat."

"Remind me not to accept your next evaluation so completely," grunted Cassal. Nevertheless, he was relieved, in a fashion. He hadn't *wanted* to kill the man. And now there was nothing he'd have to explain to the police.

He needed the cigarette he stuck between his lips. For the second time he attempted to pick up the rapier-lighter. This time he was successful. Smoke swirled into his lungs and quieted his nerves. He squeezed the weapon into the shape of a lighter and put it away.

Something, however, was missing—his wallet.

The thug had relieved him of it in the second round of the scuffle. Persistent fellow. Damned persistent.

It really didn't matter. He fingered the clip he had taken from the supposedly dead body. He had intended to turn it over to the police. Now he might as well keep it to reimburse him for his loss. It contained more money than his wallet had.

Except for the identification tab he always carried in his wallet, it was more than a fair exchange. The identification, a rectangular piece of plastic, was useful in establishing credit, but with the money he now had, he wouldn't need credit. If he did, he could always send for another tab.

A white card fluttered from the clip. He caught it as it fell. Curiously he examined it. Blank except for one crudely printed word, STAB. His unknown assailant certainly had tried.

The old man stared at the door, an obsolete visual projector wobbling precariously on his head. He closed his eyes and the lettering on the door disappeared. Cassal was too far away to see what it had been. The technician opened his eyes and concentrated. Slowly a new sign formed on the door.

TRAVELERS AID BUREAU
Murra Foray, First Counselor

It was a drab sign, but, then, it was a dismal, backward planet. The old technician passed on to the next door and closed his eyes again.

With a sinking feeling, Cassal walked toward the entrance. He needed help and he had to find it in this dingy rathole.

Inside, though, it wasn't dingy and it wasn't a rathole. More like a maze, an approved scientific one. Efficient, though not comfortable. Travelers Aid was busier than he thought it would be. Eventually he managed to squeeze into one of the many small counseling rooms.

A woman appeared on the screen, crisp and cool. "Please answer everything the machine asks. When the tape is complete, I'll be available for consultation."

Cassal wasn't sure he was going to like her. "Is this necessary?" he asked. "It's merely a matter of information."

"We have certain regulations we abide by." The woman smiled frostily. "I can't give you any information until you comply with them."

"Sometimes regulations are silly," said Cassal firmly. "Let me speak to the first counselor."

"You are speaking to her," she said. Her face disappeared from the screen.

Cassal sighed. So far he hadn't made a good impression.

Travelers Aid Bureau, in addition to regulations, was abundantly supplied with official curiosity. When the machine finished with him, Cassal had the feeling he could be recreated from the record it had of him. His individuality had been capsuled into a series of questions and answers. One thing he drew the line at—why he wanted to go to Tunney 21 was his own business.

The first counselor reappeared. Age, indeterminate. Not, he supposed, that anyone would be curious about it. Slightly taller than average, rather on the slender side. Face was broad at the brow, narrow at the chin and her eyes were enigmatic. A dangerous woman.

She glanced down at the data. "Denton Cassal, native of Earth. Destination, Tunney 21." She looked up at him. "Occupation, sales engineer. Isn't that an odd combination?" Her smile was quite superior.

"Not at all. Scientific training as an engineer. Special knowledge of customer relations."

"Special knowledge of a thousand races? How convenient." Her eyebrows arched.

"I think so," he agreed blandly. "Anything else you'd like to know?"

"Sorry. I didn't mean to offend you."

He could believe that or not as he wished. He didn't.

"You refused to answer why you were going to Tunney 21. Perhaps I can guess. They're the best scientists in the Galaxy. You wish to study under them."

Close—but wrong on two counts. They were good scientists, though not necessarily the best. For instance, it was doubtful that they could build Dimanche, even if they had ever thought of it, which was even less likely.

There was, however, one relatively obscure research worker on Tunney 21 that Neuronics wanted on their staff. If the fragments of his studies that had reached Earth across the vast distance meant anything, he could help Neuronics perfect instantaneous radio. The company that could build a radio to span the reaches of the Galaxy with no time lag could set its own price, which could be control of all communications, transport, trade—a galactic monopoly. Cassal's share would be a cut of all that.

His part was simple, on the surface. He was to persuade that researcher to come to Earth, *if he could*. Literally, he had to guess the Tunnesian's price before the Tunnesian himself knew it. In addition, the reputation of Tunnesian scientists being exceeded only by their arrogance, Cassal had to convince him that he wouldn't be working for ignorant Earth savages. The existence of such an instrument as Dimanche was a key factor.

Her voice broke through his thoughts. "Now, then, what's your problem?"

"I was told on Earth I might have to wait a few days on Godolph. I've been here three weeks. I want information on the ship bound for Tunney 21."

"Just a moment." She glanced at something below the angle of the screen. She looked up and her eyes were grave. "*Rickrock C* arrived yesterday. Departed for Tunney early this morning."

"Departed?" He got up and sat down again, swallowing hard. "When will the next ship arrive?"

"Do you know how many stars there are in the Galaxy?" she asked.

He didn't answer.

"That's right," she said. "Billions. Tunney, according to the notation, is near the center of the Galaxy, inside the third ring. You've covered about a third of the distance to it. Local traffic, anything within a thousand light-years, is relatively easy to manage. At longer distances, you take a chance. You've had yours and missed it. Frankly, Cassal, I don't know when another ship bound for Tunney will show up on or near Godolph. Within the next five years—maybe."

He blanched. "How long would it take to get there using local transportation, star-hopping?"

"Take my advice: don't try it. Five years, if you're lucky."

"I don't need that kind of luck."

"I suppose not." She hesitated. "You're determined to go on?" At the emphatic nod, she sighed. "If that's your decision, we'll try to help you. To start things moving, we'll need a print of your identification tab."

"There's something funny about her," Dimanche decided. It

was the usual speaking voice of the instrument, no louder than the noise the blood made in coursing through arteries and veins. Cassal could hear it plainly, because it was virtually inside his ear.

Cassal ignored his private voice. "Identification tab? I don't have it with me. In fact, I may have lost it."

She smiled in instant disbelief. "We're not trying to pry into any part of your past you may wish concealed. However, it's much easier for us to help you if you have your identification. Now if you can't *remember* your real name and where you put your identification—" She arose and left the screen. "Just a moment."

He glared uneasily at the spot where the first counselor wasn't. His *real* name!

"Relax," Dimanche suggested. "She didn't mean it as a personal insult."

Presently she returned.

"I have news for you, whoever you are."

"Cassal," he said firmly. "Denton Cassal, sales engineer, Earth. If you don't believe it, send back to—" He stopped. It had taken him four months to get to Godolph, non-stop, plus a six-month wait on Earth for a ship to show up that was bound in the right direction. Over distances such as these, it just wasn't practical to send back to Earth for anything.

"I see you understand." She glanced at the card in her hand. "The spaceport records indicate that when *Rickrock C* took off this morning, there was a Denton Cassal on board, bound for Tunney 21."

"It wasn't I," he said dazedly. He knew who it was, though. The man who had tried to kill him last night. The reason for the attack now became clear. The thug had wanted his identification tab. Worse, he had gotten it.

"No doubt it wasn't," she said wearily. "Outsiders don't seem to understand what galactic travel entails."

Outsiders? Evidently what she called those who lived beyond the second transfer ring. Were those who lived at the edge of the Galaxy, beyond the first ring, called Rimmers? Probably.

She was still speaking: "Ten years to cross the Galaxy, without stopping. At present, no ship is capable of that. Real scheduling is impossible. Populations shift and have to be supplied. A ship is taken off a run for repairs and is never put back on. It's more urgently needed elsewhere. The man who depended on it is left waiting; years pass before he learns it's never coming.

"If we had instantaneous radio, that would help. Confusion wouldn't vanish overnight, but it would diminish. We wouldn't have to depend on ships for all the news. Reservations could be made ahead of time, credit established, lost identification replaced—"

"I've traveled before," he interrupted stiffly. "I've never had any trouble."

She seemed to be exaggerating the difficulties. True, the center was more congested. Taking each star as the starting point for a limited number of ships and using statistical probability as a guide—why, no man would arrive at his predetermined destination.

But that wasn't the way it worked. Manifestly, you couldn't compare galactic transportation to the erratic paths of air molecules in a giant room. Or could you?

For the average man, anyone who didn't have his own interstellar ship, was the comparison too apt? It might be.

"You've traveled outside, where there are still free planets waiting to be settled. Where a man is welcome, if he's able to work." She paused. "The center is different. Populations are excessive. Inside the third ring, no man is allowed off a ship without an identification tab. They don't encourage immigration."

In effect, that meant no ship bound for the center would take a passenger without identification. No ship owner would run the risk of having a permanent guest on board, someone who couldn't be rid of when his money was gone.

Cassal held his head in his hands. Tunney 21 was inside the third ring.

"Next time," she said, "don't let anyone take your identification."

"I won't," he promised grimly.

The woman looked directly at him. Her eyes were bright. He revised his estimate of her age drastically downward. She couldn't be as old as he. Nothing outward had happened, but she no longer seemed dowdy. Not that he was interested. Still, it might pay him to be friendly to the first counselor.

"We're a philanthropic agency," said Murra Foray. "Your case is special, though—"

"I understand," he said gruffly. "You accept contributions."

She nodded. "If the donor is able to give. We don't ask so much that you'll have to compromise your standard of living."

But she named a sum that would force him to do just that if getting to Tunney 21 took any appreciable time.

He stared at her unhappily. "I suppose it's worth it. I can always work, if I have to."

"As a salesman?" she asked. "I'm afraid you'll find it difficult to do business with Godolphians."

Irony wasn't called for at a time like this, he thought reproachfully.

"Not just another salesman," he answered definitely. "I have special knowledge of customer reactions. I can tell exactly—"

He stopped abruptly. Was she baiting him? For what reason? The instrument he called Dimanche was not known to the Galaxy at large. From the business angle, it would be poor policy to hand out that information at random. Aside from that, he needed every advantage he could get. Dimanche was his special advantage.

"Anyway," he finished lamely, "I'm a first-class engineer. I can always find something in that line."

"A scientist, maybe," murmured Murra Foray. "But in this part of the Milky Way, an engineer is regarded as merely a technician who hasn't yet gained practical experience." She shook her head. "You'll do better as a salesman."

He got up, glowering. "If that's all—"

"It is. We'll keep you informed. Drop your contribution in the slot provided for that purpose as you leave."

A door, which he hadn't noticed in entering the counseling cubicle, swung open. The agency was efficient.

"Remember," the counselor called out as he left, "identification is hard to work with. Don't accept a crude forgery."

He didn't answer, but it was an idea worth considering. The agency was also eminently practical.

The exit path guided him firmly to an inconspicuous and yet inescapable contribution station. He began to doubt the philanthropic aspect of the bureau.

"I've got it," said Dimanche as Cassal gloomily counted out the sum the first counselor had named.

"Got what?" asked Cassal. He rolled the currency into a neat bundle, attached his name, and dropped it into the chute.

"The woman, Murra Foray, the first counselor. She's a Huntner."

"What's a Huntner?"

"A sub-race of men on the other side of the Galaxy. She was

vocalizing about her home planet when I managed to locate her.''

''Any other information?''

''None. Electronic guards were sliding into place as soon as I reached her. I got out as fast as I could.''

''I see.'' The significance of that, if any, escaped him. Nevertheless, it sounded depressing.

''What I want to know is,'' said Dimanche, ''why such precautions as electronic guards? What does Travelers Aid have that's so secret?''

Cassal grunted and didn't answer. Dimanche could be annoyingly inquisitive at times.

Cassal had entered one side of a block-square building. He came out on the other side. The agency was larger than he had thought. The old man was staring at a door as Cassal came out. He had apparently changed every sign in the building. His work finished, the technician was removing the visual projector from his head as Cassal came up to him. He turned and peered.

''You stuck here, too?'' he asked in the uneven voice of the aged.

''Stuck?'' repeated Cassal. ''I suppose you can call it that. I'm waiting for my ship.'' He frowned. He was the one who wanted to ask questions. ''Why all the redecoration? I thought Travelers Aid was an old agency. Why did you change so many signs? I could understand it if the agency were new.''

''The previous counselor resigned suddenly, in the middle of the night, they say. The new one didn't like the name of the agency, so she ordered it changed.''

She would do just that, thought Cassal. ''What about this Murra Foray?''

The old man winked mysteriously. He opened his mouth and then seemed overcome with senile fright. Hurriedly he shuffled away.

Cassal gazed after him, baffled. The old man was afraid for his job, afraid of the first counselor. Why he should be, Cassal didn't know. He shrugged and went on. The agency was now in motion in his behalf, but he didn't intend to depend on that alone.

''The girl ahead of you is making unnecessary wriggling motions as she walks,'' observed Dimanche. ''Several men are looking on with approval. I don't understand.''

Cassal glanced up. They walked that way back in good old L.A. A pang of homesickness swept through him.

"Shut up," he growled plaintively. "Attend to the business at hand."

"Business? Very well," said Dimanche. "Watch out for the transport tide."

Cassal swerved back from the edge of the water. Murra Foray had been right. Godolphians didn't want or need his skills, at least not on terms that were acceptable to him. The natives didn't have to exert themselves. They lived off the income provided by travelers, with which the planet was abundantly supplied by ship after ship.

Still, that didn't alter his need for money. He walked the streets at random while Dimanche probed.

"Ah!"

"What is it?"

"That man. He crinkles something in his hands. Not enough, he is subvocalizing."

"I know how he feels," commented Cassal.

"Now his throat tightens. He bunches his muscles. 'I know where I can get more,' he tells himself. He is going there."

"A sensible man," declared Cassal. "Follow him."

Boldly the man headed toward a section of the city which Cassal had not previously entered. He believed opportunity lay there. Not for everyone. The shrewd, observant, and the courageous could succeed if— The word that the quarry used was a slang term, unfamiliar to either Cassal or Dimanche. It didn't matter as long as it led to money.

Cassal stretched his stride and managed to keep the man in sight. He skipped nimbly over the narrow walkways that curved through the great buildings. The section grew dingier as they proceeded. Not slums; not the showplace city frequented by travelers, either.

Abruptly the man turned into a building. He was out of sight when Cassal reached the structure.

He stood at the entrance and stared in disappointment. "Opportunities Inc.," Dimanche quoted softly in his ear. "Science, thrills, chance. What does that mean?"

"It means that we followed a gravity ghost!"

"What's a gravity ghost?"

"An unexplained phenomenon," said Cassal nastily. "It affects the instruments of spaceships, giving the illusion of a massive dark body that isn't there.''

"But you're not a pilot. I don't understand."

"You're not a very good pilot yourself. We followed the man to a gambling joint."

"Gambling," mused Dimanche. "Well, isn't it an opportunity of a sort? Someone inside is thinking of the money he's winning."

"The owner, no doubt."

Dimanche was silent, investigating. "It is the owner," he confirmed finally. "Why not go in, anyway. It's raining. And they serve drinks." Left unstated was the admission that Dimanche was curious, as usual.

Cassal went in and ordered a drink. It was a variable place, depending on the spectator—bright, cheerful, and harmonious if he was winning, garish and depressingly vulgar if he was not. At the moment Cassal belonged to neither group. He reserved judgment.

An assortment of gaming devices were in operation. One in particular seemed interesting. It involved the counting of electrons passing through an aperture, based on probability.

"Not that," whispered Dimanche. "It's rigged."

"But it's not necessary," Cassal murmured. "Pure chance alone is good enough."

"They don't take chances, pure or adulterated. Look around. How many Godolphians do you see?"

Cassal looked. Natives were not even there as servants. Strictly a clip joint, working travelers.

Unconsciously, he nodded. "That does it. It's not the kind of opportunity I had in mind."

"Don't be hasty," objected Dimanche. "Certain devices I can't control. There may be others in which my knowledge will help you. Stroll around and sample some games."

Cassal equipped himself with a supply of coins and sauntered through the establishment, disbursing them so as to give himself the widest possible acquaintance with the layout.

"That one," instructed Dimanche.

It received a coin. In return, it rewarded him with a large shower of change. The money spilled to the floor with a satisfying clatter. An audience gathered rapidly, ostensibly to help him pick up the coins.

"There was a circuit in it," explained Dimanche. "I gave it a shot of electrons and it paid out."

"Let's try it again," suggested Cassal.

"Let's not," Dimanche said regretfully. "Look at the man on your right."

Cassal did so. He jammed the money back in his pocket and stood up. Hastily, he began thrusting the money back into the machine. A large and very unconcerned man watched him.

"You get the idea," said Dimanche. "It paid off two months ago. It wasn't scheduled for another this year." Dimanche scrutinized the man in a multitude of ways while Cassal continued play. "He's satisfied," was the report at last. "He doesn't detect any sign of crookedness."

"Crookedness?"

"On your part, that is. In the ethics of a gambling house, what's done to insure profit is merely prudence."

They moved on to other games, though Cassal lost his briefly acquired enthusiasm. The possibility of winning seemed to grow more remote.

"Hold it," said Dimanche. "Let's look into this."

"Let me give *you* some advice," said Cassal. "This is one thing we can't win at. Every race in the Galaxy has a game like this. Pieces of plastic with values printed on them are distributed. The trick is to get certain arbitrarily selected sets of values in the plastics dealt to you. It seems simple, but against a skilled player a beginner can't win."

"Every race in the Galaxy," mused Dimanche. "What do men call it?"

"Cards," said Cassal, "though there are many varieties within that general classification." He launched into a detailed exposition of the subject. If it were something he was familiar with, all right, but a foreign deck and strange rules—

Nevertheless, Dimanche was interested. They stayed and observed.

The dealer was clumsy. His great hands enfolded the cards. Not a Godolphian nor quite human, he was an odd type, difficult to place. Physically burly, he wore a garment chiefly remarkable for its ill-fitting appearance. A hard round hat jammed closely over his skull completed the outfit. He was dressed in a manner that somewhere in the Universe was evidently considered the height of fashion.

"It doesn't seem bad," commented Cassal. "There might be a chance."

"Look around," said Dimanche. "Everyone thinks that. It's the classic struggle, person against person and everyone against the house. Naturally, the house doesn't lose."

"Then why are we wasting our time?"

"Because I've got an idea," said Dimanche. "Sit down and take a hand."

"Make up your mind. You said the house doesn't lose."

"The house hasn't played against us. Sit down. You get eight cards, with the option of two more. I'll tell you what to do."

Cassal waited until a disconsolate player relinquished his seat and stalked moodily away. He played a few hands and bet small sums in accordance with Dimanche's instructions. He held his own and won insignificant amounts while learning.

It was simple. Nine orders, or suits, of twenty-seven cards each. Each suit would build a different equation. The lowest hand was a quadratic. A cubic would beat it. All he had to do was remember his math, guess at what he didn't remember, and draw the right cards.

"What's the highest possible hand?" asked Dimanche. There was a note of abstraction in his voice, as if he were paying more attention to something else.

Cassal peeked at the cards that were face-down on the table. He shoved some money into the betting square in front of him and didn't answer.

"You had it last time," said Dimanche. "A three dimensional encephalocurve. A time modulated brainwave. If you had bet right, you could have owned the house by now."

"I did? Why didn't you tell me?"

"Because you had it three successive times. The probabilities against that are astronomical. I've got to find out what's happening before you start betting recklessly."

"It's not the dealer," declared Cassal. "Look at those hands."

They were huge hands, more suitable, seemingly, for crushing the life from some alien beast than the delicate manipulation of cards. Cassal continued to play, betting brilliantly by the only standard that mattered: he won.

One player dropped out and was replaced by a recruit from the surrounding crowd. Cassal ordered a drink. The waiter was placing it in his hand when Dimanche made a discovery.

"I've got it!"

A shout from Dimanche was roughly equivalent to a noiseless kick in the head. Cassal dropped the drink. The player next to him scowled but said nothing. The dealer blinked and went on dealing.

"What have you got?" asked Cassal, wiping up the mess and trying to keep track of the cards.

"How he fixes the deck," explained Dimanche in a lower and less painful tone. "Clever."

Muttering, Cassal shoved a bet in front of him.

"Look at that hat," said Dimanche.

"Ridiculous, isn't it? But I see no reason to gloat because I have better taste."

"That's not what I meant. It's pulled down low over his knobby ears and touches his jacket. His jacket rubs against his trousers, which in turn come in contact with the stool on which he sits."

"True," agreed Cassal, increasing his wager. "But except for his physique, I don't see anything unusual."

"It's a circuit, a visual projector broken down into components. The hat is a command circuit which makes contact, via his clothing, with the broadcasting unit built into the chair. The existence of a visual projector is completely concealed."

Cassal bit his lip and squinted at his cards. "Interesting. What does it have to do with anything?"

"The deck," exclaimed Dimanche excitedly. "The backs are regular, printed with an intricate design. The front is a special plastic, susceptible to the influence of the visual projector. He doesn't need manual dexterity. He can make any value appear on any card he wants. It will stay there until he changes it."

Cassal picked up the cards. "I've got a Loreenaroo equation. Can he change that to anything else?"

"He can, but he doesn't work that way. He decides before he deals who's going to get what. He concentrates on each card as he deals it. He can change a hand after a player gets it, but it wouldn't look good."

"It wouldn't." Cassal wistfully watched the dealer rake in his wager. His winnings were gone, plus. The newcomer to the game won.

He started to get up. "Sit down," whispered Dimanche. "We're just beginning. Now that we know what he does and how he does it, we're going to take him."

*   *   *

The next hand started in the familiar pattern, two cards of
fairly good possibilities, a bet, and then another card. Cassal
watched the dealer closely. His clumsiness was only superficial.
At no time were the faces of the cards visible. The real skill was
unobservable, of course—the swift bookkeeping that went on in
his mind. A duplication in the hands of the players, for instance,
would be ruinous.

Cassal received the last card. "Bet high," said Dimanche. With
trepidation, Cassal shoved the money into the betting area.

The dealer glanced at his hand and started to sit down. Abruptly
he stood up again. He scratched his cheek and stared puzzledly
at the players around him. Gently he lowered himself onto the
stool. The contact was even briefer. He stood up in indecision.
An impatient murmur arose. He dealt himself a card, looked at
it, and paid off all the way around. The players buzzed with
curiosity.

"What happened?" asked Cassal as the next hand started.

"I induced a short in the circuit," said Dimanche. "He
couldn't sit down to change the last card he got. He took a
chance, as he had to, and dealt himself a card, anyway."

"But he paid off without asking to see what we had."

"It was the only thing he could do," explained Dimanche.
"He had duplicate cards."

The dealer was scowling. He didn't seem quite so much at
ease. The cards were dealt and the betting proceeded almost as
usual. True, the dealer was nervous. He couldn't sit down and
stay down. He was sweating. Again he paid off. Cassal won
heavily and he was not the only one.

The crowd around them grew almost in a rush. There is an
indefinable sense that tells one gambler when another is winning.

This time the dealer stood up. His leg contacted the stool
occasionally. He jerked it away each time he dealt to himself. At
the last card he hesitated. It was amazing how much he could
sweat. He lifted a corner of the cards. Without indicating what he
had drawn, determinedly and deliberately he sat down. The chair
broke. The dealer grinned weakly as a waiter brought him another stool.

"They still think it may be a defective circuit," whispered
Dimanche.

The dealer sat down and sprang up from the new chair in one
motion. He gazed bitterly at the players and paid them.

"He had a blank hand," explained Dimanche. "He made contact with the broadcasting circuit long enough to erase, but not long enough to put anything in its place."

The dealer adjusted his coat. "I have a nervous disability," he declared thickly. "If you'll pardon me for a few minutes while I take a treatment—"

"Probably going to consult with the manager," observed Cassal.

"He is the manager. He's talking with the owner."

"Keep track of him."

A blonde, pretty, perhaps even Earth-type human, smiled and wriggled closer to Cassal. He smiled back.

"Don't fall for it," warned Dimanche. "She's an undercover agent for the house."

Cassal looked her over carefully. "Not much under cover."

"But if she should discover—"

"Don't be stupid. She'll never guess you exist. There's a small lump behind my ear and a small round tube cleverly concealed elsewhere."

"All right," sighed Dimanche resignedly. "I suppose people will always be a mystery to me."

The dealer reappeared, followed by an unobtrusive man who carried a new stool. The dealer looked subtly different, though he was the same person. It took a close inspection to determine what the difference was. His clothing was new, unrumpled, unmarked by perspiration. During his brief absence, he had been furnished with new visual projector equipment, and it had been thoroughly checked out. The house intended to locate the source of the disturbance.

Mentally, Cassal counted his assets. He was solvent again, but in other ways his position was not so good.

"Maybe," he suggested, "we should leave. With no further interference from us, they might believe defective equipment is the cause of their losses."

"Maybe," replied Dimanche, "you think the crowd around us is composed solely of patrons?"

"I see," said Cassal soberly.

He stretched his legs. The crowd pressed closer, uncommonly aggressive and ill-tempered for mere spectators. He decided against leaving.

"Let's resume play." The dealer-manager smiled blandly at each player. He didn't suspect any one person—yet.

"He might be using an honest deck," said Cassal hopefully.

"They don't have that kind," answered Dimanche. He added absently: "During his conference with the owner, he was given authority to handle the situation in any way he sees fit."

Bad, but not too bad. At least Cassal was opposing someone who had authority to let him keep his winnings, *if he could be convinced*.

The dealer deliberately sat down on the stool. Testing. He could endure the charge that trickled through him. The bland smile spread into a triumphant one.

"While he was gone, he took a sedative," analyzed Dimanche. "He also had the strength of the broadcasting circuit reduced. He thinks that will do it."

"Sedatives wear off," said Cassal. "By the time he knows it's me, see that it has worn off. Mess him up."

The game went on. The situation was too much for the others. They played poorly and bet atrociously, on purpose. One by one they lost and dropped out. They wanted badly to win, but they wanted to live even more.

The joint was jumping, and so was the dealer again. Sweat rolled down his face and there were tears in his eyes. So much liquid began to erode his fixed smile. He kept replenishing it from some inner source of determination.

Cassal looked up. The crowd had drawn back, or had been forced back by hirelings who mingled with them. He was alone with the dealer at the table. Money was piled high around him. It was more than he needed, more than he wanted.

"I suggest one last hand," said the dealer-manager, grimacing. It sounded a little stronger than a suggestion.

Cassal nodded.

"For a substantial sum," said the dealer, naming it.

Miraculously, it was an amount that equaled everything Cassal had. Again Cassal nodded.

"Pressure," muttered Cassal to Dimanche. "The sedative has worn off. He's back at the level at which he started. Fry him if you have to."

The cards came out slowly. The dealer was jittering as he dealt. Soft music was lacking, but not the motions that normally accompanied it. Cassal couldn't believe that cards could be so bad. Somehow the dealer was rising to the occasion. Rising and sitting.

"There's a nerve in your body," Cassal began conversationally, "which, if it were overloaded, would cause you to drop dead."

The dealer didn't examine his cards. He didn't have to. "In that event, someone would be arrested for murder," he said. "You."

That was the wrong tack; the humanoid had too much courage. Cassal passed his hand over his eyes. "You can't do this to men, but, strictly speaking, the dealer's not human. Try suggestion on him. Make him change the cards. Play him like a piano. Pizzicato on the nerve strings."

Dimanche didn't answer; presumably he was busy scrambling the circuits.

The dealer stretched out his hand. It never reached the cards. Danger: Dimanche at work. The smile dropped from his face. What remained was pure anguish. He was too dry for tears. Smoke curled up faintly from his jacket.

"Hot, isn't it?" asked Cassal. "It might be cooler if you took off your cap."

The cap tinkled to the floor. The mechanism in it was destroyed. What the cards were, they were. Now they couldn't be changed.

"That's better," said Cassal.

He glanced at his hand. In the interim, it had changed slightly. Dimanche had got there.

The dealer examined his cards one by one. His face changed color. He sat utterly still on a cool stool.

"You win," he said hopelessly.

"Let's see what you have."

The dealer-manager roused himself. "You won. That's good enough for you, isn't it?"

Cassal shrugged. "You have Bank of the Galaxy service here. I'll deposit my money with them *before* you pick up your cards."

The dealer nodded unhappily and summoned an assistant. The crowd, which had anticipated violence, slowly began to drift away.

"What did you do?" asked Cassal silently.

"Men have no shame," sighed Dimanche. "Some humanoids

do. The dealer was one who did. I forced him to project onto his cards something that wasn't a suit at all."

"Embarrassing if that got out," agreed Cassal. "What did you project?"

Dimanche told him. Cassal blushed, which was unusual for a man.

The dealer-manager returned and the transaction was completed. His money was safe in the Bank of the Galaxy.

"Hereafter, you're not welcome," said the dealer morosely. "Don't come back."

Cassal picked up the cards without looking at them. "And no accidents after I leave," he said, extending the cards face-down. The manager took them and trembled.

"He's an honorable humanoid, in his own way," whispered Dimanche. "I think you're safe."

It was time to leave. "One question," Cassal called back. "What do you call this game?"

Automatically the dealer started to answer. "Why everyone knows . . ." He sat down, his mouth open.

It was more than time to leave.

Outside, he hailed an air taxi. No point in tempting the management.

"Look," said Dimanche as the cab rose from the surface of the transport tide.

A technician with a visual projector was at work on the sign in front of the gaming house. Huge words took shape: WARNING—NO TELEPATHS ALLOWED.

There were no such things anywhere, but now there were rumors of them.

Arriving at the habitat wing of the hotel, Cassal went directly to his room. He awaited the delivery of the equipment he had ordered and checked through it thoroughly. Satisfied that everything was there, he estimated the size of the room. Too small for his purpose.

He picked up the intercom and dialed Services. "Put a Life Stage Cordon around my suite," he said briskly.

The face opposite his went blank. "But you're an Earthman. I thought—"

"I know more about my own requirements than your Life Stage Bureau. Earthmen do have life stages. You know the penalty if you refuse that service."

There were some races who went without sleep for five months and then had to make up for it. Others grew vestigial wings for brief periods and had to fly with them or die; reduced gravity would suffice for that. Still others—

But the one common feature was always a critical time in which certain conditions were necessary. Insofar as there was a universal law, from one end of the Galaxy to the other, this was it: The habitat hotel had to furnish appropriate conditions for the maintenance of any life-form that requested it.

The Godolphian disappeared from the screen. When he came back, he seemed disturbed.

"You spoke of a suite. I find that you're listed as occupying one room."

"I am. It's too small. Convert the rooms around me into a suite."

"That's very expensive."

"I'm aware of that. Check the Bank of the Galaxy for my credit rating."

He watched the process take place. Service would be amazingly good from now on.

"Your suite will be converted in about two hours. The Life Stage Cordon will begin as soon after that as you want. If you tell me how long you'll need it, I can make arrangements now."

"About ten hours is all I'll need." Cassal rubbed his jaw reflectively. "One more thing. Put a perpetual service at the spaceport. If a ship comes in bound for Tunney 21 or the vicinity of it, get accommodations on it for me. And hold it until I get ready, no matter what it costs."

He flipped off the intercom and promptly went to sleep. Hours later, he was awakened by a faint hum. The Life Stage Cordon had just been snapped safely around his newly created suite.

"Now what?" asked Dimanche.

"I need an identification tab."

"You do. And forgeries are expensive and generally crude, as that Huntner woman, Murra Foray, observed."

Cassal glanced at the equipment. "Expensive, yes. Not crude when we do it."

"*We* forge it?" Dimanche was incredulous.

"That's what I said. Consider it this way. I've seen my tab a countless number of times. If I tried to draw it as I remember it, it would be inept and wouldn't pass. Nevertheless, that memory is in my mind, recorded in neuronic chains, exact and accurate." He paused significantly. "You have access to that memory."

"At least partially. But what good does that do?"

"Visual projector and plastic which will take the imprint. I think hard about the identification as I remember it. You record and feed it back to me while I concentrate on projecting it on the plastic. After we get it down, we change the chemical composition of the plastic. It will then pass everything except destructive analysis, and they don't often do that."

Dimanche was silent. "Ingenious," was its comment. "Part of that we can manage, the official engraving, even the electron stamp. That, however, is gross detail. The print of the brain area is beyond our capacity. We can put down what you remember, and you remember what you saw. You didn't see fine enough, though. The general area will be recognizable, but not the fine structure, nor the charges stored there nor their interrelationship."

"But we've got to do it," Cassal insisted, pacing about nervously.

"With more equipment to probe—"

"Not a chance. I got one Life Stage Cordon on a bluff. If I ask for another, they'll look it up and refuse."

"All right," said Dimanche, humming. The mechanical attempt at music made Cassal's head ache. "I've got an idea. Think about the identification tab."

Cassal thought.

"Enough," said Dimanche. "Now poke yourself."

"Where?"

"Everywhere," replied Dimanche irritably. "One place at a time."

Cassal did so, though it soon became monotonous.

Dimanche stopped him. "Just above your right knee."

"What above my right knee?"

"The principal access to that part of your brain we're concerned with," said Dimanche. "We can't photomeasure your brain the way it was originally done, but we can investigate it remotely. The results will be simplified, naturally. Something like a scale model as compared to the original. A more apt comparison might be that of a relief map to an actual locality."

"Investigate it remotely?" muttered Cassal. A horrible suspicion touched his consciousness. He jerked away from that touch. "What does that mean?"

"What it sounds like. Stimulus and response. From that I can construct an accurate chart of the proper portion of your brain. Our probing instruments will be crude out of necessity, but effective.''

"I've already visualized those probing instruments," said Cassal worriedly. "Maybe we'd better work first on the official engraving and the electron stamp, while I'm still fresh. I have a feeling . . ."

"Excellent suggestion," said Dimanche.

Cassal gathered the articles slowly. His lighter would burn and it would also cut. He needed a heavy object to pound with. A violent irritant for the nerve endings. Something to freeze his flesh . . .

Dimanche interrupted: "There are also a few glands we've got to pick up. See if there's a stimi in the room."

"Stimi? Oh yes, a stimulator. Never use the damned things." But he was going to. The next few hours weren't going to be pleasant. Nor dull, either.

Life could be difficult in Godolph.

As soon as the Life Stage Cordon came down, Cassal called for a doctor. The native looked at him professionally.

"Is this a part of the Earth life process?" he asked incredulously. Gingerly, he touched the swollen and lacerated leg.

Cassel nodded wearily. "A matter of life and death," he croaked.

"If it is, then it is," said the doctor, shaking his head. "I, for one, am glad to be a Godolphian."

"To each his own habitat," Cassal quoted the motto of the hotel.

Godolphians were clumsy, good-natured caricatures of seals. There was nothing wrong with their medicine, however. In a matter of minutes he was feeling better. By the time the doctor left, the swelling had subsided and the open wounds were fast closing.

Eagerly, he examined the identification tab. As far as he could tell, it was perfect. What the scanner would reveal was, of course, another matter. He had to check that as best he could without exposing himself.

Services came up to the suite right after he laid the intercom down. A machine was placed over his head and the identification slipped into the slot. The code on the tab was noted; the machine hunted and found the corresponding brain area. Structure was mapped, impulses recorded, scrambled, converted into a ray of light which danced over a film.

The identification tab was similarly recorded. There was now a means of comparison.

Fingerprints could be duplicated—that is, if the race in question had fingers. Every intelligence, however much it differed from its neighbors, had a brain, and tampering with that brain was easily detected. Each identification tab carried a psychometric number which corresponded to the total personality. Alteration of any part of the brain could only subtract from personality index.

The technician removed the identification and gave it to Cassal. "Where shall I send the strips?"

"You don't," said Cassal. "I have a private message to go with them."

"But that will invalidate the process."

"I know. This isn't a formal contract."

Removing the two strips and handing them to Cassal, the technician wheeled the machine away. After due thought, Cassal composed the message:

Travelers Aid Bureau
Murra Foray, first counselor:
    If you were considering another identification tab for me, don't. As you can see, I've located the missing item.

He attached the message to the strips and dropped them into the communication chute.

He was wiping his whiskers away when the answer came. Hastily he finished and wrapped himself, noting but not approving the amused glint in her eyes as she watched. His morals were his own, wherever he went.

"Denton Cassal," she said. "A wonderful job. The two strips were in register within one per cent. The best previous forgery I've seen was six per cent, and that was merely a lucky accident. It couldn't be duplicated. Let me congratulate you."

His dignity was professional. "I wish you weren't so fond of that word 'forgery.' I told you I mislaid the tab. As soon as I found it, I sent you proof. I want to get to Tunney 21. I'm willing to do anything I can to speed up the process."

Her laughter tinkled. "You don't *have* to tell me how you did it or where you got it. I'm inclined to think you made it. You understand that I'm not concerned with legality as such. From time to time the agency has to furnish missing documents. If there's a better way than we have, I'd like to know it."

He sighed and shook his head. For some reason, his heart was beating fast. He wanted to say more, but there was nothing to say.

When he failed to respond, she leaned toward him. "Perhaps you'll discuss this with me. At greater length."

"At the agency?"

She looked at him in surprise. "Have you been sleeping? The agency is closed for the day. The first counselor can't work all the time, you know."

Sleeping? He grimaced at the remembrance of the self-administered beating. No, he hadn't been sleeping. He brushed the thought aside and boldly named a place. Dinner was acceptable.

Dimanche waited until the screen was dark. The words were carefully chosen.

"Did you notice," he asked, "that there was no apparent change in clothing and makeup, yet she seemed younger, more attractive?"

"I didn't think you could trace her that far."

"I can't. I looked at her through your eyes."

"Don't trust my reaction," advised Cassal. "It's likely to be subjective."

"I don't," answered Dimanche. "It is."

Cassal hummed thoughtfully. Dimanche was a business neurological instrument. It didn't follow that it was an expert in human psychology.

Cassal stared at the woman coming toward him. Center-of-the-Galaxy fashion. Decadent, of course, or maybe ultra-civlized. As an Outsider, he wasn't sure which. Whatever it was, it did to the human body what should have been done long ago.

And this body wasn't exactly human. The subtle skirt of proportions betrayed it as an offshoot or deviation from the human race. Some of the new subraces stacked up against the original stock much in the same way Cro-Magnons did against Neanderthals, in beauty, at least.

Dimanche spoke a single syllable and subsided, an event Cassal didn't notice. His consciousness was focused on another discovery: the woman was Murra Foray.

He knew vaguely that the first counselor was not necessarily what she had seemed that first time at the agency. That she was capable of such a metamorphosis was hard to believe, though pleasant to accept. His attitude must have shown on his face.

"Please," said Murra Foray. "I'm a Huntner. We're adept at camouflage."

"Huntner," he repeated blankly. "I knew that. But what's Huntner?"

She wrinkled her lovely nose at the question. "I didn't expect you to ask that. I won't answer it now." She came closer. "I thought you'd ask which was the camouflage—the person you see here, or the one at the Bureau?"

He never remembered the reply he made. It must have been satisfactory, for she smiled and drew her fragile wrap closer. The reservations were waiting.

Dimanche seized the opportunity to speak. "There's something phony about her. I don't understand it and I don't like it."

"You," said Cassal, "are a machine. You don't have to like it."

"That's what I mean. You *have* to like it. You have no choice."

Murra Foray looked back questioningly. Cassal hurried to her side.

The evening passed swiftly. Food that he ate and didn't taste. Music he heard and didn't listen to. Geometric light fugues that were seen and not observed. Liquor that he drank—and here the sequence ended, in the complicated chemistry of Godolphian stimulants.

Cassal reacted to that smooth liquid, though his physical reactions were not slowed. Certain mental centers were depressed, others left wide open, subject to acceleration at whatever speed he demanded.

Murra Foray, in his eyes at least, might look like a dream, the kind men have and never talk about. She was, however, interested solely in her work, or so it seemed.

"Godolph is a nice place," she said, toying with a drink, "if you like rain. The natives seem happy enough. But the Galaxy is big and there are lots of strange planets in it, each of which seems ideal to those who are adapted to it. I don't have to tell you what happens when people travel. They get stranded. It's not the time spent in actual flight that's important; it's waiting for the right ship to show up and then having all the necessary documents. Believe me, that can be important, as you found out."

He nodded. He had.

"That's the origin of Travelers Aid Bureau," she continued. "A loose organization, propagated mainly by example. Sometimes it's called Star Travelers Aid. It may have other names. The aim, however, is always the same: to see that stranded persons get where they want to go."

She looked at him wistfully, appealingly. "That's why I'm interested in your method of creating identification tabs. It's the thing most commonly lost. Stolen, if you prefer the truth."

She seemed to anticipate his question. "How can anyone use another's identification? It can be done under certain circumstances. By neural lobotomy, a portion of one brain may be made to match, more or less exactly, the code area of another brain. The person operated on suffers a certain loss of function, of course. How great that loss is depends on the degree of similarity between the two brain areas before the operation took place."

She ought to know, and he was inclined to believe her. Still, it didn't sound feasible.

"You haven't accounted for the psychometric index," he said.

"I thought you'd see it. That's diminished, too."

Logical enough, though not a pretty picture. A genius could always be made into an average man or lowered to the level of an idiot. There was no operation, however, that could raise an idiot to the level of a genius.

The scramble for the precious identification tabs went on, from the higher to the lower, a game of musical chairs with grim overtones.

She smiled gravely. "You haven't answered my implied question."

The company that employed him wasn't anxious to let the secret of Dimanche get out. They didn't sell the instrument; they made it for their own use. It was an advantage over their competitors they intended to keep. Even on his recommendation, they wouldn't sell to the agency.

Moreover, it wouldn't help Travelers Aid Bureau if they did.

Since she was first counselor, it was probably that she'd be the one to use it. She couldn't make identification for anyone except herself, and then only if she developed exceptional skill.

The alternative was to surgery it in and out of whoever needed it. When that happened, secrecy was gone. Travelers couldn't be trusted.

He shook his head. "It's an appealing idea, but I'm afraid I can't help you."

"Meaning you won't."

This was intriguing. Now it was the agency, not he, who wanted help.

"Don't overplay it," cautioned Dimanche, who had been consistently silent.

She leaned forward attentively. He experienced an uneasy moment. Was it possible she had noticed his private conversation? Of course not. Yet—

"Please," she said, and the tone allayed his fears. "There's an emergency situation and I've got to attend to it. Will you go with me?"

She smiled understandingly at his quizzical expression. "Travelers Aid is always having emergencies."

She was rising. "It's too late to go to the Bureau. My place has a number of machines with which I keep in touch with the spaceport."

"I wonder," said Dimanche puzzledly. "She doesn't subvocalize at all. I haven't been able to get a line on her. I'm certain she didn't receive any sort of call. Be careful.

"This might be a trick."

"Interesting," said Cassal. He wasn't in the mood to discuss it.

Her habitation was luxurious, though Cassal wasn't impressed. Luxury was found everywhere in the Universe. Huntner women weren't. He watched as she adjusted the machines grouped at one side of the room. She spoke in a low voice; he couldn't distinguish words. She actuated levers, pressed buttons: impedimenta of communication.

At last she finished. "I'm tired. Will you wait till I change?"

Inarticulately, he nodded.

"I think her 'emergency' was a fake," said Dimanche flatly

as soon as she left. "I'm positive she wasn't operating the communicator. She merely went through the motions."

"Motions," murmured Cassal dreamily, leaning back. "And what motions."

"I've been watching her," said Dimanche. "She frightens me."

"I've been watching her, too. Maybe in a different way."

"Get out of here while you can," warned Dimanche. "She's dangerous."

Momentarily, Cassal considered it. Dimanche had never failed him. He ought to follow that advice. And yet there was another explanation.

"Look," said Cassal. "A machine is a machine. But among humans there are men and women. What seems dangerous to you may be merely a pattern of normal behavior . . ." He broke off. Murra Foray had entered.

Strictly from the other side of the Galaxy, which she was. A woman can be slender and still be womanly beautiful, without being obvious about it. Not that Murra disdained the obvious, technically. But he could see through technicalities.

The tendons in his hands ached and his mouth was dry, though not with fear. An urgent ringing pounded in his ears. He shook it out of his head and got up.

She came to him.

The ringing was still in his ears. It wasn't a figment of imagination; it was a real voice—that of Dimanche, howling:

"Huntner! It's a word variant. In their language it means Hunter. *She can hear me!*"

"Hear you?" repeated Cassal vacantly.

She was kissing him.

"A descendant of carnivores. An audiosensitive. She's been listening to you and me all the time."

"Of course I have, ever since the first interview at the bureau," said Murra. "In the beginning I couldn't see what value it was, but you convinced me." She laid her hand gently over his eyes. "I hate to do this to you, dear, but I've got to have Dimanche."

She had been smothering him with caresses. Now, deliberately, she began smothering him in actuality.

Cassal had thought he was an athlete. For an Earthman, he was. Murra Foray, however, was a Huntner, which meant hunter—a descendant of incredibly strong carnivores.

He didn't have a chance. He knew that when he couldn't budge her hands and he fell into the airless blackness of space.

Alone and naked, Cassal awakened. He wished he hadn't. He turned over and, though he tried hard not to, promptly woke up again. His body was willing to sleep, but his mind was panicked and disturbed. About what, he wasn't sure.

He sat up shakily and held his roaring head in his hands. He ran aching fingers through his hair. He stopped. The lump behind his ear was gone.

"Dimanche!" he called, and looked at his abdomen.

There was a thin scar, healing visibly before his eyes.

"Dimanche!" he cried again. "Dimanche!"

There was no answer. Dimanche was no longer with him.

He staggered to his feet and stared at the wall. She'd been kind enough to return him to his own rooms. At length he gathered enough strength to rummage through his belongings. Nothing was missing. Money, identification—all were there.

He could go to the police. He grimaced as he thought of it. The neighborly Godolphian police were hardly a match for the Huntner; she'd fake them out of their skins.

He couldn't prove she'd taken Dimanche. Nothing else normally considered valuable was missing. Besides, there might even be a local prohibition against Dimanche. Not by name, of course; but they could dig up an ancient ordinance—invasion of privacy or something like that. Anything would do if it gave them an opportunity to confiscate the device for intensive study.

For the police to believe his story was the worst that could happen. They might locate Dimanche, but he'd never get it.

He smiled bitterly and the effort hurt. "Dear," she had called him as she had strangled and beaten him into unconsciousness. Afterward singing, very likely, as she had sliced the little instrument out of him.

He could picture her not very remote ancestors springing from cover and overtaking a fleeing herd—

No use pursuing that line of thought.

Why did she want Dimanche? She had hinted that the agency wasn't always concerned with legality as such. He could believe her. If she wanted it for making identification tabs, she'd soon find that it was useless. Not that that was much comfort—she wasn't likely to return Dimanche after she'd made that discovery.

For that matter, what was the purpose of Travelers Aid Bureau? It was a front for another kind of activity. Philanthropy had nothing to do with it.

If he still had possession of Dimanche, he'd be able to find out. Everything seemed to hinge on that. With it, he was nearly a superman, able to hold his own in practically all situations—anything that didn't involve a Huntner woman, that is.

Without it—well, Tunney 21 was still far away. Even if he should manage to get there without it, his mission on the planet was certain to fail.

He dismissed the idea of trying to recover it immediately from Murra Foray. She was an audio-sensitive. At twenty feet, unaided, she could hear a heartbeat, the internal noise muscles made in sliding over each other. With Dimanche, she could hear electrons rustling. As an antagonist she was altogether too formidable.

He began pulling on his clothing, wincing as he did so. The alternative was to make another Dimanche. *If* he could. It would be a tough job even for a neuronic expert familiar with the process. He wasn't that expert, but it still had to be done.

The new instrument would have to be better than the original. Maybe not such a slick machine, but more comprehensive. More wallop. He grinned as he thought hopefully about giving Murra Foray a surprise.

Ignoring his aches and pains, he went right to work. With money not a factor, it was an easy matter to line up the best electronic and neuron concerns on Godolph. Two were put on a standby basis. When he gave them plans, they were to rush construction at all possible speed.

Each concern was to build a part of the new instrument. Neither part was of value without the other. The slow-thinking Godolphians weren't likely to make the necessary mental connection between the seemingly unrelated projects.

He retired to his suite and began to draw diagrams. It was harder than he thought. He knew the principles, but the actual details were far more complicated than he remembered.

Functionally, the Dimanche instrument was divided into three main phases. There was a brain and memory unit that operated much as the human counterpart did. Unlike the human brain, however, it had no body to control, hence more of it was available for thought processes. Entirely neuronic in construction, it was far smaller than an electronic brain of the same capacity.

The second function was electronic, akin to radar. Instead of material objects, it traced and recorded distant nerve impulses. It could count the heartbeat, measure the rate of respiration, was even capable of approximate analysis of the contents of the bloodstream. Properly focused on the nerves of tongue, lips or larynx, it transmitted that data back to the neuronic brain, which then reconstructed it into speech. Lip reading, after a fashion, carried to the ultimate.

Finally, there was the voice of Dimanche, a speaker under the control of the neuronic brain.

For convenience of installation in the body, Dimanche was packaged in two units. The larger package was usually surgeried into the abdomen. The small one, containing the speaker, was attached to the skull just behind the ear. It worked by bone conduction, allowing silent communication between operator and instrument. A real convenience.

It wasn't enough to know this, as Cassal did. He'd talked to the company experts, had seen the symbolical drawings, the plans for an improved version. He needed something better than the best though, that had been planned.

The drawback was this: *Dimanche was powered directly by the nervous system of the body in which it was housed*. Against Murra Foray, he'd be overmatched. She was stronger than he physically, probably also in the production of nervous energy.

One solution was to make available to the new instrument a larger fraction of the neural currents of the body. That was dangerous—a slight miscalculation and the user was dead. Yet he had to have an instrument that would overpower her.

Cassal rubbed his eyes wearily. How could he find some way of supplying additional power?

Abruptly, Cassal sat up. That was the way, of course—an auxiliary power pack that need not be surgeried into his body, extra power that he would use only in emergencies.

Neuronics. Inc., had never done this, had never thought that such an instrument would ever be necessary. They didn't need to overpower their customers. They merely wanted advance information via subvocalized thoughts.

It was easier for Cassal to conceive this idea than to engineer it. At the end of the first day, he knew it would be a slow process.

Twice he postponed deadlines to the manufacturing concerns he'd engaged. He locked himself in his rooms and took Anti-Sleep against the doctor's vigorous protests. In one week he had the necessary drawings, crude but legible. An expert would have to make innumerable corrections, but the intent was plain.

One week. During that time Murra Foray would be growing hourly more proficient in the use of Dimanche.

Cassal followed the neuronics expert groggily, seventy-two hours' sleep still clogging his reactions. Not that he hadn't needed sleep after that week. The Godolphian showed him proudly through the shops, though he wasn't at all interested in their achievements. The only noteworthy aspect was the grand scale of their architecture.

"We did it, though I don't think we'd have the job if we'd known how hard it was going to be," the neuronics expert chattered. "It works exactly as you specified. We had to make substitutions, of course, but you understand that was inevitable."

He glanced anxiously at Cassal, who nodded. That was to be expected. Components that were common on Earth wouldn't necessarily be available here. Still, any expert worth his pay could always make the proper combinations and achieve the same results.

Inside the lab, Cassal frowned. "I thought you were keeping my work separate. What is the planetary drive doing here?"

The Godolphian spread his broad hands and looked hurt. "Planetary drive?" He tried to laugh. "This is the instrument you ordered!"

Cassal started. It was supposed to fit under a flap of skin behind his ear. A Three World saurian couldn't carry it.

He turned savagely on the expert. "I told you it had to be small."

"But it is. I quote your orders exactly: 'I'm not familiar with your system of measurement, but make it tiny, very tiny. Figure the size you think it will have to be and cut it in half. And then cut *that* in half.' This is the fraction remaining."

It certainly was. Cassal glanced at the Godolphian's hands. Excellent for swimming. No wonder they built on a grand scale. Broad, blunt, webbed hands weren't exactly suited for precision work.

Valueless. Completely valueless. He knew now what he would find at the other lab. He shook his head in dismay, personally saw to it that the instrument was destroyed. He paid for the work and retrieved the plans.

Back in his rooms again, he sat and thought. It was still the only solution. If the Godolphians couldn't do it, he'd have to find some race that could. He grabbed the intercom and jangled it savagely. In half an hour he had a dozen leads.

The best seemed to be the Spirella. A small, insectlike race, about three feet tall, they were supposed to have excellent manual dexterity, and were technically advanced. They sounded as if they were acquainted with the necessary fields. Three light-years away, they could be reached by readily available local transportation within the day. Their idea of what was small was likely to coincide with his.

He didn't bother to pack. The suite would remain his headquarters. Home was where his enemies were.

He made a mental correction—enemy.

He rubbed his sensitive ear, grateful for the discomfort. His stomach was sore, but it wouldn't be for long. The Spirella had made the new instrument just as he had wanted it. They had built an even better auxiliary power unit than he had specified. He fingered the flat cases in his pocket. In an emergency, he could draw on these, whereas Murra Foray would be limited to the energy in her nervous system.

What he had now was hardly the same instrument. A military version of it, perhaps. It didn't seem right to use the same name. Call it something staunch and crisp, suggestive of raw power. Manche. As good a name as any. Manche against Dimanche. Cassal against a queen.

He swung confidently along the walkway beside the transport tide. It was raining. He decided to test the new instrument. The Godolphian across the way bent double and wondered why his knees wouldn't work. They had suddenly became swollen and painful to move. Maybe it was the climate.

And maybe it wasn't, thought Cassal. Eventually the pain would leave, but he hadn't meant to be so rough on the native. He'd have to watch how he used Manche.

He scouted the vicinity of Travelers Aid Bureau, keeping at least one building between him and possible detection. Purely precautionary. There was no indication that Murra Foray had spotted him. For a Huntner, she wasn't very alert, apparently.

He sent Manche out on exploration at minimum strength. The electronic guards which Dimanche had spoken of were still in place. Manche went through easily and didn't disturb an electron. Behind the guards there was no trace of the first counselor.

He went closer. Still no warning of danger. The same old technician shuffled in front of the entrance. A horrible thought hit him. It was easy enough to verify. Another "reorganization" *had* taken place. The new sign read:

STAR TRAVELERS AID BUREAU
STAB *Your Hour*
of Need
Delly Mortinbras, first counselor

Cassal leaned against the building, unable to understand what it was that frightened and bewildered him. Then it gradually became, if not clear, at least not quite so muddy.

STAB was the word that had been printed on the card in the money clip that his assailant in the alley had left behind. Cassal had naturally interpreted it as an order to the thug. It wasn't, of course.

The first time Cassal had visited the Travelers Aid Bureau, it had been in the process of reorganization. The only purpose of the reorganization, he realized now, had been to change the name so he wouldn't translate the word on the slip into the original initials of the Bureau.

Now it probably didn't matter any more whether or not he knew so the name had been changed back to Star Travelers Aid Bureau—STAB.

That, he saw bitterly, was why Murra Foray had been so positive that the identification tab he'd made with the aid of Dimanche had been a forgery.

She had known the man who robbed Cassal of the original one, perhaps had even helped him plan the theft.

That didn't make sense to Cassal. Yet it had to. He'd suspected the organization of being a racket, but it obviously wasn't. By whatever name it was called, it actually was dedicated to helping the stranded traveler. The question was—which travelers?

There must be agency operatives at the spaceport, checking every likely prospect who arrived, finding out where they were going, whether their papers were in order. Then, just as had happened to Cassal, the prospect was robbed of his papers so somebody stranded here could go on to that destination!

The shabby, aging technician finished changing the last door sign and hobbled over to Cassal. He peered through the rain and darkness.

"You stuck here, too?" he quavered.

"No," said Cassal with dignity, shaky dignity. "I'm not stuck. I'm here because I want to be."

"You're crazy," declared the old man. "I remember—"

Cassal didn't wait to find out what it was he remembered. An impossible land, perhaps, a planet which swings in perfect orbit around an ideal sun. A continent which reared a purple mountain range to hold up a honey sky. People with whom anyone could relax easily and without worry or anxiety. In short, his own native world from which, at night, all the constellations were familiar.

Somehow, Cassal managed to get back to his suite, tumbled wearily onto his bed. The showdown wasn't going to take place.

Everyone connected with the agency—including Murra Foray—had been "stuck here" for one reason or another: no identification tab, no money, whatever it was. That was the staff of the Bureau, a pack of desperate castaways. The "philanthropy" extended to them and nobody else. They grabbed their tabs and money from the likeliest travelers, leaving them marooned here—and they in turn had to join the Bureau and use the same methods to continue their journeys through the Galaxy.

It was an endless belt of stranded travelers robbing and stranding other travelers, who then had to rob and strand still others, and so on and on . . .

Cassal didn't have a chance of catching up with Murra Foray. She had used the time—and Dimanche—to create her own identification tab and escape. She was going back to Kettikat, home of the Huntners, must already be light-years away.

Or was she? The signs on the Bureau had just been changed. Perhaps the ship was still in the spaceport, or cruising along below the speed of light. He shrugged defeatedly. It would do him no good; he could never get on board.

He got up suddenly on one elbow. He couldn't, but Manche could! Unlike his old instrument, it could operate at tremendous distances, its power no longer dependent only on his limited nervous energy.

With calculated fury, he let Manche strike out into space.

"There you are!" exclaimed Murra Foray. "I thought you could do it."

"Did you?" he asked coldly. "Where are you now?"

"Leaving the atmosphere, if you can call the stuff around this planet an atmosphere."

"It's not the atmosphere that's bad," he said as nastily as he could. "It's the philanthropy."

"Please don't feel that way," she appealed. "Huntners are rather unusual people, I admit, but sometimes even we need help. I had to have Dimanche and I took it."

"At the risk of killing me."

Her amusement was strange; it held a sort of sadness. "I didn't hurt you. I couldn't. You were too cute, like a—well, the animal native to Kettikat that would be called a teddy bear on Earth. A cute, lovable teddy bear."

"Teddy bear," he repeated, really stung now. "Careful. This one may have claws."

"Long claws? Long enough to reach from here to Kettikat?" She was laughing, but it sounded thin and wistful.

Manche struck out at Cassal's unspoken command. The laughter was canceled.

"Now you've done it," said Dimanche. "She's out cold."

There was no reason for remorse; it was strange that he felt it. His throat was dry.

"So you, too, can communicate with me. Through Manche, of course. I built a wonderful instrument, didn't I?"

"A fearful one," said Dimanche sternly. "She's unconscious."

"I heard you the first time." Cassal hesitated. "Is she dead?"

Dimanche investigated. "Of course not. A little thing like that wouldn't hurt her. Her nerve system is marvelous. I think it could carry current for a city. Beautiful!"

"I'm aware of the beauty," said Cassal.

An awkward silence followed. Dimanche broke it. "Now that I know the facts, I'm proud to be her chosen instrument. Her need was greater than yours."

Cassal growled, "As first counselor, she had access to every—"

"Don't interrupt with your half truths," said Dimanche. "Huntners *are* special; their brain structure, too. Not necessarily better, just different. Only the auditory and visual centers of their brains resemble that of man. You can guess the results of even superficial tampering with those parts of her mind. And stolen identification would involve lobotomy."

He could imagine? Cassal shook his head. No, he couldn't. A blinded and deaf Murra Foray would not go back to the home of the Huntners. According to her racial conditioning, a sightless young tiger should creep away and die.

Again there was silence. "No, she's not pretending unconsciousness," announced Dimanche. "For a moment I thought—but never mind."

The conversation was lasting longer than he expected. The ship must be obsolete and slow. There were still a few things he wanted to find out, if there was time.

"When are you going on Drive?" he asked.

"We've been on it for some time," answered Dimanche.

"Repeat that!" said Cassal, stunned.

"I said that we've been on faster-than-light drive for some time. Is there anything wrong with that?"

Nothing wrong with that at all. Theoretically, there was only one means of communicating with a ship hurtling along faster than light, and that way hadn't been invented.

Hadn't been until he had put together the instrument he called Manche.

Unwittingly, he had created far more than he intended. He ought to have felt elated.

Dimanche interrupted his thoughts. "I suppose you know what she thinks of you."

"She made it plain enough," said Cassal wearily. "A teddy bear. A brainless, childish toy."

"Among the Huntners, women are vigorous and aggressive," said Dimanche. The voice grew weaker as the ship, already light-years away, slid into unfathomable distances. "Where words are concerned, morals are very strict. For instance, 'dear' is never used unless the person means it. Huntner men are weak and not overburdened with intelligence."

The voice was barely audible, but it continued: "The principal romantic figure in the dreams of women . . ." Dimanche failed altogether.

"Manche!" cried Cassal.

Manche responded with everything it had. ". . . is the teddy bear."

The elation that had been missing, and the triumph, came now. It was no time for hesitation, and Cassal didn't hesitate. Their actions had been directed against each other, but their emotions, which each had tried to ignore, were real and strong.

The gravitor dropped him to the ground floor. In a few minutes, Cassal was at the Travelers Aid Bureau.

Correction. Now it was Star Travelers Aid Bureau.

And, though no one but himself knew it, even that was wrong. Quickly he found the old technician.

"There's been a reorganization," said Cassal bluntly. "I want the signs changed."

The old man drew himself up. "Who are you?"

"I've just elected myself," said Cassal. "I'm the new first counselor."

He hoped no one would be foolish enough to challenge him. He wanted an organization that could function immediately, not a hospital full of cripples.

The old man thought about it. He was merely a menial, but he had been with the bureau for a long time. He was nobody, nothing, but he could recognize power when it was near him. He wiped his eyes and shambled out into the fine cold rain. Swiftly the new signs went up.

STAR TRAVELERS AID BUREAU
S.T.A. WITH US
DENTON CASSAL, FIRST COUNSELOR

Cassal sat at the control center. Every question cubicle was visible at a glance. In addition there was a special panel, direct from the spaceport, which recorded essential data about every newly arrived traveler. He could think of a few minor improvements, but he wouldn't have time to put them into effect. He'd mention them to his assistant, a man with a fine, logical mind. Not really first-rate, of course, but well suited to his secondary position. Every member quickly rose or sank to his proper level in this organization, and this one had, without a struggle.

Business was dull. The last few ships had brought travelers who were bound for unimaginably dreary destinations, nothing he need be concerned with.

He thought about the instrument. It was the addition of power that made the difference. Dimanche plus power equaled Manche, and Manche raised the user far above the level of other men. There was little to fear.

But essentially the real value of Manche lay in this—it was a beginning. Through it, he had communicated with a ship traveling far faster than light. The only one instrument capable of that was instantaneous radio. Actually it wasn't radio, but the old name had stuck to it.

Manche was really a very primitive model of instantaneous radio. It was crude; all first steps were. Limited in range, it was practically valueless for that purpose now. Eventually the range would be extended. Hitch a neuronic manufactured brain to a human one, add the power of a tiny atomic battery, and Manche was created.

The last step was his share of the invention. Or maybe the credit belonged to Murra Foray. If she hadn't stolen Dimanche, it never would have been necessary to put together the new instrument.

The stern lines on his face relaxed. Murra Foray. He wondered about the marriage customs of the Huntners. He hoped marriage was a custom on Kettikat.

Cassal leaned back; officially, his mission was complete. There was no longer any need to go to Tunney 21. The scientist he was sent to bring back might as well remain there in obscure arrogance. Cassal knew he should return to Earth immediately. But the Galaxy was wide and there were lots of places to go.

Only one he was interested in, though—Kettikat, as far from the center of the Galaxy as Earth, but in the opposite direction, incredibly far away in terms of trouble and transportation. It would be difficult even for a man who had the services of Manche.

Cassal glanced at the board. Someone wanted to go to Zombo.

"Delly," he called to his assistant. "Try 13. This may be what you want to get back to your own planet."

Delly Mortinbras nodded gratefully and cut in.

Cassal continued scanning. There was more to it than he imagined, though he was learning fast. It wasn't enough to have identification, money, and a destination. The right ship might come in with standing room only. Someone had to be "persuaded" that Godolph was a cozy little place, as good as any for an unscheduled stopover.

It wouldn't change appreciably during his lifetime. There were too many billions of stars. First he had to perfect it, isolate from dependence on the human element, and then there would come the installation. A slow process, even with Murra to help him.

Someday he would go back to Earth. He should be welcome. The information he was sending back to his former employers, Neuronics, Inc., would more than compensate them for the loss of Dimanche.

Suddenly he was alert. A report had just come in.

Once upon a time, he thought tenderly, scanning the report, there was a teddy bear that could reach to Kettikat. With claws— but he didn't think they would be needed.

GAME FOR BLONDES

by John D. MacDonald (1916–)

John D. MacDonald is one of America's best-selling authors, the creator of Travis McGee, with seventy novels and more than 500 short stories to his credit, and a man who has never forgotten his roots in the pulp magazines of the late 1940s. In 1952 he published a very good suspense novel, *The Damned*, and an excellent science fiction novel, *Ballroom in the Skies,* a good example of the "test" story so popular in the 1950s. It is a pleasure to welcome him back to the pages of this series (see "Spectator Sport" in Volume 12) with one of his best stories.

"Game for Blondes" reflects the hard-boiled tradition out of which the author emerged, and is additional evidence of his unique feel for the sf field, and the loss we all suffered when he left it for other pastures. (MHG)

"Oh, if I only had it to do over again!" How many times have you heard that?

Well, is there any moment in your life so fraught with consequences of an evil kind that you wish you could go back and do it over again?

The trouble is, what would be the new consequences? You don't really know. In this connection, there is O. Henry's classic "The Roads of Destiny," in which our hero comes to a crossroads, and chooses to go to the right—or to the left—or go home. And in each case he ends up dead with a bullet from the same pistol.

Of course, I'm not quite that much of a fatalist, but then, in real life, you don't know what the consequences might be. I agreed to take a job in Boston back in 1949, and only a few months later I sold my first book. Had the book sale come

206

earlier I might have decided not to take the job but to stick it out in New York where I wanted desperately to remain.

Suppose I had done that. What would have been the effect on my subsequent writing career? I haven't the faintest idea.—And therefore I have no choice but to accept what *is*. It's my Hobson's choice, to repeat a notion from an earlier story.

Except that after you read "Game for Blondes" you might decide to look a little harder for that key moment. It's a game with no answer, but it might be interesting. (IA)

Martin Greynor was very very drunk, not gaily drunk, not freshly six-quick-ones drunk, but drunk in varying degrees since December tenth at ten P.M. Two big red 10s in his mind, always with him—zeroes like a pair of headlights. Ruth beside him, sweet-scented, fur-clad. And one of his fits of stupid, vicious, reckless anger. December 10. 10 P.M. Hitting the slick black curves hard, motor droning, forcing her to tell him he was going too fast. Once she said it, he could slow down and that would be a little victory.

"Too fast, Marty!" she said. They were the last words she ever spoke.

Fat headlights and the long whining skid, and the crash, and the jangle that went on forever. Ripped fur and blood and gone the sweet scent.

Now it was New Year's Eve. Ruth was gone. His job was gone, the car gone. Money was left, though, money a-plenty. Funny about drinking. The wobbling, falling-down, sick stage lasts about twelve days, he discovered. Important discovery. Boon to science. Then you're armor-plated. Liquor drops into a pit, *clunk*. Walk steady, talk steady. But in come the illusions on little soft pink feet.

Ruth ahead of you, hurrying down a dark street. "Ruth! Wait!"

Hurriedly she puts on a wattled mask, turns and grimaces at you, rasps in a mocking gin-husky voice. "Ya wan' something, sweetie?"

She has slipped around the next corner. Run, now, and see her in the next block. Cake the wet December slush on the shrinking, stiffening leather of the shoes that came out of that store window.

"Marty, let's buy you a pair of those. I like those shoes."

Suit she liked. Now a bit dribbled, a shade rancid. Apartment the way they had left it that night. Never gone back. Beds not made, no doubt.

Walk through the night streets, looking for punishment. Looking for a way to release the load of guilt. Now the old places don't want you. "Sorry, Mr. Greynor. You've begun to stink." The little bars don't care.

"*HAP-PEEE* NEW YEAR!"

The bar mirrors are enchanted. Ruth stands behind you. She said, "Never run away from me, darling. You'd be too easy to find. Wanted—a red-headed man with one blue eye and one brown eye. See? You couldn't get away with it."

The face that looks back has become gaunt, because you stopped eating.

He bent low over the bar until his lips almost touched the shot glass, then lifted it in a hard arc, tossing his head back. It burned its way down into the nothingness. The bartender slapped the change down. Martin Greynor fumbled with it, pushed a quarter over to the far edge. The bartender slipped it off the bar with a surly grunt and clinked it into a glass on the back bar.

Martin turned around and saw the three girls again. He wondered if it was again, or if he was seeing them for the first time. The mind performs such odd little hop, skip, jumps. He debated it solemnly, got nowhere.

They were at a table. They were all looking at him with an air of watchfulness. That could be imagined, too. Three lovelies like that are not going to make the weary ginmill rounds with you and keep watching you. You ain't that purty, Martin.

When in doubt, you write it down on top of your mind and underline it very firmly and hope that when the situation occurs again, you can find the place where you wrote it down.

He walked out steadily and stood on the sidewalk. He had the strong impression that Ruth was stretched flat on the roof, her head over the edge of the building, grinning down at him. He turned sharply and looked up. The moon hung misty over Manhattan, debauched by neon.

Next block. Don't turn right. That will take you toward midtown, toward the higher prices, toward the places where they let you get three steps inside the door, then turn you firmly and walk you back out. Stay over here, buster.

They'd rolled him a few times that first week. Made a nuisance to go to the bank and get more cash each time. Now they'd stopped bothering. One of the times they'd left him sitting, spitting out a tooth. His tongue kept finding the hole.

Neon in the middle of the next block. Two couples sitting on the curb.

"Down by-ee the old mill streeeeeeem . . ."

Spotted by the prowl car.

"Break it up! Move along there!"

He looked back. Three female silhouettes, arm in arm, step in step, tick-tock-tick of the pretty stilt heels avoiding the gray smears of slush.

He ducked into the door under the neon. This was a dark one. Dancing was going on back there somewhere to the cat-fence yowl of a clarinet and pulse-thump of piano. He edged in at the bar. The bartender came over fast, with that trouble-look on his face. Martin shoved the five out fast.

"Rye straight," he said.

The bartender paused for a count of three, then turned back to the rye department.

Martin looked over and saw them come in. He hunted on top of his mind and found the heavily underlined place. He read it off. Three blondes. Three arrogant, damp-mouthed, hot-eyed, overdressed blondes—sugary in the gloom. Same ones.

It brought him up out of himself, hand clutching the rim of his soul, for a quick look over the edge. One lone blonde in this place would have pivoted heads in tennis-match style. Two would bring hot and heart-felt exhalations. Three, he saw, seemed to stun the joint. It put a crimp in the rumble of bar-talk. It ran furry fingers down male spines.

They were watching him. He stared back until he was certain. Okay. Fact confirmed. Three blondes following him from joint to joint. Watching him. Next step—watch real close, see if anybody walks through them.

They got a table along the wall. He watched. A hefty young man strutted over to their table, hiking up his pants, making with the bold smile. He bent over the table. They all gave him cold looks. One shook her shining head. He persisted.

The young man turned fast and hard and went high and rigid into the air. Martin saw him go up in that jet-leap of spasmed muscles, head thrown back, agony-masked face. He fell like something pushed out of a window. People gathered around him. They blocked Martin's view.

He looked at the blondes. They were watching him. In an empty lot in the back of his mind, a rabbit bounded for cover, where there was no cover, and the dogs sat watching, tongues lolling. Cold started at a spot at the base of his spine. It crept nuzzling into his armpits.

He drank and scooped up his change and left.

He ran to the corner and stood, and the trembling went away. The slush was beginning to freeze. It crunched a bit under his shoes. That was another thing. You didn't have to eat, and you didn't get cold. Ergo, one should be beyond fear. Go around being afraid of blondes and people will begin to point at you.

He snickered. The sound was as rigid as the rind of freeze atop the sidewalk slush. We have nothing to fear but fear itself.

Problem for the class: You got a guy, see. He's dying of cancer or something, see. He's in agony and somebody comes into his room and stands by his bed and lifts a big club to hammer him one. Is the guy afraid? If so, why? If he is, it means that fear is something divorced from an objective and intellectual appraisal of the total situation. It means fear is spawned in the guts, down there where the animal lives, down where the rabbit blood is.

A piece of paper scuttered around the corner and embraced his leg. He bent over, picked it loose and sent it on its way.

"Hell of a big hurry, aren't you?" he said.

Tick, tack, tick, tack. By God, perfect marching. Ex-WACs? All blonde and all coming along. So what can blondes do to you? He stood his ground for a slow count of ten.

Tick, tack.

Fear rocketed into his throat and burst out his ears and he ran like hell.

*   *   *

A cruiser nailed him in the spotlight, tracking him like a floor show, making him feel as though he were running, running, running in one spot. He stopped and leaned against a building, panting. The spot still held him. It nailed his eyes to the wall behind him. Big shoulders blocked it. Creak of leather and brass gleam.

"What you running for, chief?"

"It's . . . a cold night. Keeping warm."

The cuff slid him along the wall and the hand on his rancid suit yanked him back upright. "What you running for, I said?"

"Those three blondes coming. They're after me." He could hear them coming. The spot went away. He was blind. But he could hear them.

"After you, you creep?"

"Yes, I . . ."

"Johnny, we better dump the chief here off at the ward. Come on, Mr. Irresistible."

Tick, tack, tock, tick. Silence.

"What do you girls want?"

Brass buttons took a high, hard, stiff-legged, stiff-armed leap. Martin fell into slush and rolled. Inside the cruiser, the driver stiffened, his head going *bong* on the metal roof.

Martin ran, bleating. An empty field and no cover. The wise eyes of the hunting dogs. Wait until he comes around again, fellows.

He turned, skidding in the freezing slush, and ran into an alley, tangling his legs in a bunch of trash, sprawling, clawing his way up again, running into a wall, stinging his hands. He turned. Three female silhouettes in the alley mouth. High-waisted, long-legged, stilt-heeled, cream-headed.

He made little sounds in his throat and pawed his way along the wall. An alley like a shoe box with one end missing—the end they were at.

He sat down and covered his eyes. Count to ten and they'll go away. One-a-larry, two-a-larry, three-a-larry, four.

New spotlight. This was a different one. It came at him from a lot of little directions, like one of those trick showers with a dozen spray heads.

"Got um," a blonde voice said.

"Up to spec, no?"

They stood outside the radiance.

"Color and out," one said.

"Take um."

Something grew in front of him, a red happy-new-year balloon. So it was a gag, maybe. It lobbed through the air toward him, turning in iridescence. He caught it. It was red jelly with a cellophane skin. It kept trying to slide down between his fingers.

"Yah-hah!" one of the blondes said.

It broke in his hands, showered green needles up to his nose to sizzle in his brain fat.

The sky broke in half and he went over backward and down, heels up and over, sizzling.

Martin slid naked across a mirrored floor. He was bug-sized and it was the mirror on his mother's dressing table a million years ago. He stopped sliding and tried to sit up. The bracing hand skidded and he hit his head.

He tried more cautiously. He could sit up by carefully shifting his weight, but he couldn't stand. The surface was frictionless. Compared to it, glare ice was like sandpaper.

He lay down and looked up. Overhead was nothing. He thought about that for quite a while. Nothing. No thing. Nothing with a flaw in it. A little flaw. He peered at it. It was in the shape of a tiny naked man. He moved a leg. The tiny naked man moved a leg. Everything clicked into focus. A mirror under him and, at an incredible height above him, another.

Now, he thought, I am a germ on a big microscope. His body felt odd. He managed to sit up again. He looked at himself. Clean. Impossibly, incredibly clean. His fingernails were snowy. His toenails were like white paper. His skin was clean and pink with a glow of health, but the old heart went thudding slowly and sickly along.

Silence. All he could hear was the roar of his blood in his ears. Like listening to a sea shell. There had been a big pink conch in his grandfather's house.

"Hear the sea, Marty?"

The mirror tilted and he slid into a hole that wasn't there before. He came out into a square blue room.

His three blondes were there, watching him. We don't get pink elephants. We don't get snakes and bugs. We get blondes.

He stood up, too aware of his nudity. They watched him calmly, ignoring it.

"Now, look," he said, "can't we be friends?"

They had changed. Their mouths were different—vivid green paint in a perfect rectangle. They looked at him with that calm pride of ownership. Nice doggy.

"Now, look," he began again, and stopped when he noticed their strange dresses. He looked closer. Ladies, please, you can't dress with a paint spray. But they had.

"This," he said, "is a nightmare by Petty, out of Varga."

The paint job was nicely shaded at the edges, but just a paint job. One of them stepped to him, grabbed him by the hair and tilted his head back. She looked into his eyes and made a little satisfied clucking sound. She turned and pointed to the corner.

"Yup now," she said.

"How does one go about yupping?" he asked vacantly.

She looked at one of the other blondes, who said slowly and precisely, "Hurry—up—now, late."

There was a pile of clothes in the corner. He went over, glad for a chance of regaining pants, even in a dream world. The garments were recognizable, the material wasn't. A sartorial cartoon of the American male, mid-twentieth century. Every incongruity of the clothing exaggerated. Sleeve buttons like saucers. Shoulders padded out a foot on each side. No buttons, no snaps, no zippers. You just got inside them and they were on, somehow. The buttons on the suit were fakes. The suit was bright blue with a harsh red stripe.

Dressed, he felt like a straight man in a burlesque.

From a distance he heard a great shout. It sounded like "Yah-hah!" from ten thousand throats. He suddenly had the strong hunch that he was going on display.

The nearest blonde confirmed that hunch. She stepped over and clamped a metal circlet around his forehead.

Three golden chains dangled from his headpiece. Each blonde took one chain. The nearest one to one of the blue walls touched it. A slit appeared and folded back. They went through. The blondes began to strut. A midway strut. A stripper stomp.

"Here comes Martin," he said feebly.

He was in the middle of a garden. The clipped turf underfoot was springy. Tailored terraces rose on three sides. A fat sun and a billion flowers and several thousand exceptionally handsome people wearing paint jobs and nothing else.

The center arena had some people in it, people fastened to

chains as he was, each one held by three blondes. The spectators were all on the terraces. There was a picnic atmosphere.

They went into the middle of the arena. The other captives were being led in an endless circle.

"Yah-hah!" the multitude yelled. "Yah-hah-hah!"

They posed in the center and then began the circling. Martin stared at his fellow captives. Some were men and some were women. One wore animal skins; another wore armor. One was dressed like the pictures of George Washington. Some wore clothing he'd never seen before.

He was led around and around. More performers took their center ring bow. Something was bothering him, some silly small thing. He couldn't fit his mind over it. Too much was going on in this delirium.

Then he got it—all the captives had red hair.

He turned and looked at the scared woman who walked behind him. She had red hair, one blue eye and one brown eye. She wore gingham and a sunbonnet.

He sneaked looks at the others. One blue eye. One brown eye. Red hair.

Everyone stopped walking. There was a great and final, 'Yah-hah." Three sets of blondes stood in the center ring without captives. Their heads were bowed.

His blondes trotted him over, took off the circlet and flipped him back into the blue room. The slit was closed. He pinched his leg.

"Hell," he said softly.

The slit opened after what he imagined to be an hour had passed. One of his blondes came back. She had a man with her, a chesty citizen dressed in cerise paint.

"Talkit ya tempo," she said, pointing at the chesty man.

He beamed at Martin. "Blessings," he said.

"Blessings yourself."

"Indebted. Thanking very much."

"Your welcoming very much, bud."

"Knowing all?" the man asked with a wide arm sweep.

"Knowing nothing. Not a damned thing! What's this all about?"

The chesty man beamed some more. He scratched his paint job lightly. He frowned. "Hard to say. You past. I future. Is party. My party. My house. My garden. Having game. Sending ladies our tempo, lot of tempos. All same thing. Bringing only with red on hair, eye brown, eye blue. Hard to find. For game."

Martin goggled at him. "You mean a scavenger hunt through time?"

"Not knowing. Is only game. Some ladies failing. Too bad."

"What happens to them?"

The man grinned. "No present for them. Now, present for you. Returning. Any place in tempo yours. To place taken. To other place. Sooner, later. Your choice."

"Return me to any . . . moment in my life?"

"All tempo function. You say—how?—resonance."

"Send me to December 10th, eight P.M."

Martin Greynor was sitting on the edge of his bed. He had just yanked his shoelaces tight in the left shoe. The tipped laces were still in his hands. He let go of them. He heard a shower pouring. The sound stopped suddenly.

His throat was full of rusty wire. "Ruth?"

She opened the bathroom door. She was wrapped in a big yellow towel.

"What is it now, Marty? My goodness, you've been needling me all evening. You're in a perfectly foul humor. I'm hurrying just as fast as I can."

"Ruth, I . . ." He tried to smile. His lips felt split.

She came to him, quick with concern. "Marty! Are you all right, darling? You look so odd."

"Me? I've never been more all right." He pulled her down beside him.

· "Hey, you! I'm soaking wet."

"Baby, do we have to drive way out there tonight? Do we?"

She stared at him. "Good Lord, it was *your* idea. I detest both of them. You know that."

"Let's stay home. Just the two of us. Bust open that brandy, maybe. Use up some of those birch logs."

"But we accepted and . . ."

He held her tightly. He would never let her go.

She whispered, "I like you better this way, instead of all snarly and grouchy." She giggled. "I think we could phone and tell them you have a fever, darling. It wouldn't *really* be a lie."

She made the call, winking at him as she gave worried noises about his symptoms. She hung up and said, "She was huffy and painfully sweet. Tonight the Greynors are at home. Darling, it would have been a crummy evening."

"A . . . disastrous evening."

"They play kid games all the time. That's what irks me. Remember in the summer? They had a scavenger hunt. If that isn't the height of silliness!"

He looked at the fire glow reflected in her hair.

"It isn't a bad game, baby."

"What do you mean?"

He shrugged. "Guess it depends on who's playing it and what the prize is."

THE ALTAR AT MIDNIGHT

by C.M. Kornbluth (1923–1958)

1952 was a very productive year for twenty-nine-year-old Cyril Kornbluth, which saw the publication of three novels: *Outpost Mars* and *Gunner Cade,* both published in collaboration with Judith Merrill as "Cyril M. Judd," and the rather minor *Takeoff.* When he worked alone he was much better at the shorter lengths (1953's *The Syndic* is a notable exception), where his sardonic elitism brought a great deal of pleasure to this then-insecure adolescent.

"The Altar at Midnight" has a protaganist that reminds me quite a bit of those that would "star" in some of Barry Malzberg's stories two decades or so later. (MHG)

I love to seek out cases, however trivial, where I disagree with Marty.

What do you mean "the rather minor *Takeoff*"? I think it was a very good novel. I know, because I have the best evidence you can imagine. When I read it I decided that I was, comparatively, a rotten writer, and it isn't easy to make me think that, let me tell you.

Cyril, it seemed to me, always had a hard and glossy sense of realism that was very much like that, later on, of Harlan Ellison, but with less exuberance and greater economy of expression. It seemed to me that Cyril, like Harlan later on, was acquainted with the dregs of society and knew just how they talked and acted, and I ground my teeth at the misfortune that had led my steps among the educated and civilized exclusively. It seemed an unfair handicap to wish on a writer, but perhaps (I consoled myself) there were advantages to it, also.

At any rate, there was no question in my mind that Cyril would continue to improve and perhaps leave science fiction for the mainstream, *if* he lived long enough. —But that proved to be an unsurmountable if. (IA)

He had quite a rum blossom on him for a kid, I thought at first. But when he moved closer to the light by the cash register to ask the bartender for a match or something, I saw it wasn't that. Not just the nose. Broken veins on his cheeks, too, and the funny eyes. He must have seen me look, because he slid back away from the light.

The bartender shook my bottle of ale in front of me like a Swiss bell ringer so it foamed inside the green glass.

"You ready for another, sir?" he asked.

I shook my head. Down the bar, he tried it on the kid—he was drinking scotch and water or something like that—and found out he could push him around. He sold him three scotch and waters in ten minutes.

When he tried for number four, the kid had his courage up and said, "I'll tell *you* when I'm ready for another, Jack." But there wasn't any trouble.

It was almost nine and the place began to fill up. The manager, a real hood type, stationed himself by the door to screen out the high school kids and give the big hello to conventioneers. The girls came hurrying in, too, with their little makeup cases and their fancy hair piled up and their frozen faces with the perfect mouths drawn on them. One of them stopped to say something to the manager, some excuse about something, and he said: "That's aw ri'; get inna dressing room."

A three-piece band behind the drapes at the back of the stage began to make warm-up noises and there were two bartenders keeping busy. Mostly it was beer—a midweek crowd. I finished my ale and had to wait a couple of minutes before I could get another bottle. The bar filled up from the end near the stage because all the customers wanted a good, close look at the strippers for their fifty-cent bottles of beer. But I noticed that nobody sat down next to the kid, or, if anybody did, he didn't stay long—you go out for some fun and the bartender pushes you around and nobody wants to sit next to you. I picked up my bottle and glass and went down on the stool to his left.

He turned to me right away and said: "What kind of a place is this, anyway?" The broken veins were all over his face, little ones, but so many, so close, that they made his face look something like marbled rubber. The funny look in his eyes was it—the trick contact lenses. But I tried not to stare and not to look away.

"It's okay," I said. "It's a good show if you don't mind a lot of noise from—"

He stuck a cigarette into his mouth and poked the pack at me. "I'm a spacer," he said, interrupting.

I took one of his cigarettes and said, "Oh."

He snapped a lighter for the cigarettes and said, "Venus."

I was noticing that his pack of cigarettes on the bar had some kind of yellow sticker instead of the blue tax stamp.

"Ain't that a crock?" he asked. "You can't smoke and they give you lighters for a souvenir. But it's a good lighter. On Mars last week, they gave us all some cheap pen-and-pencil sets."

"You get something every trip, hah?" I took a good, long drink of ale and he finished his scotch and water.

"Shoot. You call a trip a 'shoot.' "

One of the girls was working her way down the bar. She was going to slide onto the empty stool at his right and give him the business, but she looked at him first and decided not to. She curled around me and asked if I'd buy her a li'l ole drink. I said no and she moved on to the next. I could kind of feel the young fellow quivering. When I looked at him, he stood up. I followed him out of the dump. The manager grinned without thinking and said, "G'night, boys," to us.

The kid stopped in the street and said to me: "You don't have to follow me around, Pappy." He sounded like one wrong word and I would get socked in the teeth.

"Take it easy. I know a place where they won't spit in your eye."

He pulled himself together and made a joke of it. "This I have to see," he said. "Near here?"

"A few blocks."

We started walking. It was a nice night.

"I don't know this city at all," he said. "I'm from Covington, Kentucky. You do your drinking at home there. We don't have places like this." He meant the whole Skid Row area.

"It's not so bad," I said. "I spend a lot of time here."

"Is that a fact? I mean, down home a man your age would likely have a wife and children."

"I do. The hell with them."

He laughed like a real youngster and I figured he couldn't even be twenty-five. He didn't have any trouble with the broken curbstones in spite of his scotch and waters. I asked him about it.

"Sense of balance," he said. "You have to be tops for balance to be a spacer—you spend so much time outside in a suit. People don't know how much. Punctures. And you aren't worth a damn if you lose your point."

"What's that mean?"

"Oh. Well, it's hard to describe. When you're outside and you lose your point, it means you're all mixed up, you don't know which way the can—that's the ship—which way the can is. It's having all that room around you. But if you have a good balance, you feel a little tugging to the ship, or maybe you just *know* which way the ship is without feeling it. Then you have your point and you can get the work done."

"There must be a lot that's hard to describe."

He thought that might be a crack and he clammed up on me.

"You call this Gandytown," I said after a while. "It's where the stove-up old railroad men hang out. This is the place."

It was the second week of the month, before everybody's pension check was all gone. Oswiak's was jumping. The Grandsons of the Pioneers were on the juke singing the *Man from Mars Yodel* and old Paddy Shea was jigging in the middle of the floor. He had a full seidel of beer in his right hand and his empty left sleeve was flapping.

The kid balked at the screen door. "Too damn bright," he said.

I shrugged and went on in and he followed. We sat down at a table. At Oswiak's you can drink at the bar if you want to, but none of the regulars do.

Paddy jigged over and said: "Welcome home, Doc." He's a Liverpool Irishman; they talk like Scots, some say, but they sound almost like Brooklyn to me.

"Hello, Paddy. I brought somebody uglier than you. Now what do you say?"

Paddy jigged around the kid in a half-circle with his sleeve flapping and then flopped into a chair when the record stopped. He took a big drink from the seidel and said: "Can he do this?" Paddy stretched his face into an awful grin that showed his teeth. He had three of them. The kid laughed and asked me: "What the hell did you drag me into here for?"

"Paddy says he'll buy drinks for the house the day anybody uglier than he is comes in."

Oswiak's wife waddled over for the order and the kid asked us what we'd have. I figured I could start drinking, so it was three double scotches.

After the second round, Paddy started blowing about how they took his arm off without any anesthetics except a bottle of gin because the red-ball freight he was tangled up in couldn't wait.

That brought some of the other old gimps over to the table with their stories.

Blackie Bauer had been sitting in a boxcar with his legs sticking through the door when the train started with a jerk. Wham, the door closed. Everybody laughed at Blackie for being that dumb in the first place, and he got mad.

Sam Fireman has palsy. This week he was claiming he used to be a watchmaker before he began to shake. The week before, he'd said he was a brain surgeon. A woman I didn't know, a real old Boxcar Bertha, dragged herself over and began some kind of story about how her sister married a Greek, but she passed out before we found out what happened.

Somebody wanted to know what was wrong with the kid's face—Bauer, I think it was, after he came back to the table.

"Compression and decompression," the kid said. "You're all the time climbing into your suit and out of your suit. Inboard air's thin to start with. You get a few red lines—that's these ruptured blood vessels—and you say the hell with the money; all you'll make is just one more trip. But, God, it's a lot of money for anybody my age! You keep saying that until you can't be anything but a spacer. The eyes are hard-radiation scars."

"You like dot all ofer?" asked Oswiak's wife politely.

"All over, ma'am," the kid told her in a miserable voice. "But I'm going to quit before I get a Bowman head."

"I don't care," said Maggie Rorty. "I think he's cute."

"Compared with—" Paddy began, but I kicked him under the table.

We sang for a while, and then we told gags and recited limericks for a while, and I noticed that the kid and Maggie had wandered into the back room—the one with the latch on the door.

Oswiak's wife asked me, very puzzled: "Doc, w'y dey do dot flyink by planyets?"

"It's the damn govermint," Sam Fireman said.

"Why not?" I said. "They got the Bowman Drive, why the hell shouldn't they use it? Serves 'em right." I had a double scotch and added, "Twenty years of it and they found out a few things they didn't know. Red lines are only one of them. Twenty years more, maybe they'll find out a few more things they didn't know. Maybe by the time there's a bathtub in every American home and an alcoholism clinic in every American town, they'll find out a whole *lot* of things they didn't know. And every American boy will be a pop-eyed, blood-raddled wreck, like our friend here, from riding the Bowman Drive."

"It's the damn govermint," Sam Fireman repeated.

"And what the hell did you mean by that remark about alcoholism?" Paddy said, real sore. "Personally, I can take it or leave it alone."

So we got to talking about that and everybody there turned out to be people who could take it or leave it alone.

It was maybe midnight when the kid showed at the table again, looking kind of dazed. I was drunker than I ought to have been by midnight, so I said I was going for a walk. He tagged along and we wound up on a bench at Screwball Square. The soapboxers were still going strong. As I said, it was a nice night. After a while, a pot-bellied old auntie who didn't give a damn about the face sat down and tried to talk the kid into going to see some etchings. The kid didn't get it and I led him over to hear the soapboxers before there was trouble.

One of the orators was a mush-mouthed evangelist. "And oh, my friends," he said, "When I looked through the porthole of the space ship and beheld the wonder of the firmament—"

"You're a stinkin' Yankee liar!" the kid yelled at him. "You say one damn more word about can shootin' and I'll ram your space ship down your lyin' throat! Wheah's your red lines if you're such a hot spacer?"

The crowd didn't know what he was talking about, but "wheah's your red lines" sounded good to them, so they heckled mush-mouth off his box with it.

I got the kid to a bench. The liquor was working in him all of a sudden. He simmered down after a while and asked: "Doc, should I've given Miz Rorty some money? I asked her afterward and she said she'd admire to have something to remember me by, so I gave her my lighter. She seem' to be real pleased with it. But I was wondering if maybe I embarrassed her by asking her right out. Like I tol' you, back in Covington, Kentucky, we don't have places like that. Or maybe we did and I just didn't know about them. But what do you think I should've done about Miz Rorty?"

"Just what you did," I told him. "If they want money, they ask you for it first. Where you staying?"

"YMCA," he said, almost asleep. "Back in Covington, Kentucky, I was a member of the Y and I kept up my membership. They have to let me in because I'm a member. Spacers have all kinds of trouble, Doc. Woman trouble. Hotel trouble. Fam'ly trouble. Religious trouble. I was raised a Southern Baptist, but wheah's Heaven, anyway? I ask' Doctor Chitwood las' time home before the red lines got so thick—Doc, you aren't a minister of the Gospel, are you? I hope I di'n' say anything to offend you."

"No offense, son," I said. "No offense."

I walked him to the avenue and waited for a fleet cab. It was almost five minutes. The independents that roll drunks dent the fenders of fleet cabs if they show up in Skid Row and then the fleet drivers have to make reports on their own time to the company. It keeps them away. But I got one and dumped the kid in.

"The Y hotel," I told the driver. "Here's five. Help him in when you get there."

When I walked through Screwball Square again, some college kids were yelling "wheah's your red lines" at old Charlie, the last of the Wobblies.

Old Charlie kept roaring, "The hell with your bread lines! I'm talking about atomic bombs. *Right—up—there!*" And he pointed at the Moon.

It was a nice night, but the liquor was dying in me.

There was a joint around the corner, so I went in and had a drink to carry me to the club; I had a bottle there. I got into the first cab that came.

"Athletic Club," I said.

"Inna dawghouse, harh?" the driver said, and he gave me a big personality smile.

I didn't say anything and he started the car.

He was right, of course. I was in everybody's doghouse. Some day I'd scare hell out of Tom and Lise by going home and showing them what their daddy looked like.

Down at the Institute, I was in the doghouse.

"Oh, dear," everybody at the Institute said to everybody, "I'm sure I don't know what ails the man. A lovely wife and two lovely grown children and she had to tell him 'either you go or I go.' And *drinking!* And this is rather subtle, but it's a well-known fact that neurotics seek out low company to compensate for their guilt feelings. The *places* he frequents. Doctor Francis Bowman, the man who made space flight a reality. The man who put the Bomb Base on the Moon! Really, I'm sure I don't know what ails him."

The hell with them all.

COMMAND PERFORMANCE

by Walter M. Miller, Jr. (1922–

Walter Miller's output (what a terrible word) in science fiction consists of about forty stories and one novel, not terribly impressive for a man who began publishing in 1951. But what a group—the novel is the now-classic *A Canticle for Leibowitz* (1960), the prototypical and still unsurpassed masterwork of modern post-holocaust fiction, and the stories include such stunning conceptions as the Hugo Award winning "The Darfsteller," "Conditionally Human," "Crucifixus Etiam," and "The Hoofer." Tragically for all who love his work, the short stories stopped in 1957 and *Canticle* is his last published work of fiction to date. Twenty-five empty years; a quarter of a century. However, he did publish a very interesting review in *The New York Times Book Review* in 1984, so hope springs eternal.

"Command Performance" is simply one of the best stories about telepathy that you will ever read. (MHG)

Walter Miller is another writer of the 1950's who was very highly regarded and who then stopped without warning and at the height of his science fiction career.

In this case, I can't speculate that it was too close a symbiosis with a particular editor, because Miller wrote for every important magazine in his time.

But then, Miller tended to write complex stories and while this (when well done) gives great pleasure to the readers, it also has its penalties. I suspect that anyone who writes complex stories feels that each story must break new ground and surpass those that preceded it.

Heaven knows I experienced that with the Foundation series and after writing enough to fill three volumes, I quit. I just didn't feel I could undertake the superhuman effort required to get more complex still. So I turned to my robot novels and after the second, quit again, and turned to non-fiction (and occasional sf interspersed with mysteries).

Perhaps Miller stopped after the magnificent *A Canticle for Leibowitz* for the same reason.

To be sure, I could write to Miller and ask him but 1) he might not answer, 2) he might not know himself why he stopped, and 3) it's more fun to speculate, and gives one much needed mental exercise. (IA)

Quiet misery in a darkened room. The clock spoke nine times with a cold brass voice. She stood motionless, leaning against the drapes by the window, alone. The night was black, the house empty and silent.

"Come, Lisa!" she told herself. *"You're not dying!"*

She was thirty-four, still lovely, with a slender white body and a short, rich thatch of warm red hair. She had a good dependable husband, three children, and security. She had friends, hobbies, social activities. She painted mediocre pictures for her own amusement, played the piano rather well, and wrote fair poetry for the University's literary quarterly. She was well-read, well-rounded, well-informed. She loved and was loved.

Then why this quiet misery?

Wanting something, expecting nothing, she stared out into the darkness of the stone-walled garden. The night was too quiet. A distant street lamp played in the branches of the elm, and the elm threw its shadow across another wing of the house. She watched the shadow's wandering for a time. A lone car purred past in the street and was gone. A horn sounded raucously in the distance.

What was wrong? A thousand times since childhood she had felt this uneasy stirring, this crawling of the mind that called out for some unfound expression. It had been particularly strong in recent weeks.

She tried to analyze. What was different about recent weeks? Events: Frank's job had sent him on the road for a month; the children were at Mother's; the city council had recommended a bond issue; she had fired her maid; a drunk had strangled his wife; the University had opened its new psychophysics lab; her art class had adjourned for the summer.

Nothing there. No clue to the unreasoning, goalless urge that called like a voice crying in mental wilderness: "*come, share, satisfy, express it to the fullest!*"

Express what? Satisfy what? How?

A baby, deserted at birth and dying of starvation, would feel terrible hunger. But if it had never tasted milk, it could not know the meaning of the hunger nor how to ease it.

"*I need to relate this thing to something else, to something in my own experience or in the experience of others.*" She had tried to satisfy the urge with the goals of other hungers: her children, her husband's lovemaking, food, drink, art, friendship. But the craving was something else, crying for its pound of unknown flesh, and there was no fulfillment.

"*How am I different from others?*" she asked herself. But she was different only in the normal ways that every human being is different from the exact Average. Her intelligence was high, short of genius, but superior. To a limited extent, she felt the call of creativity. Physically, she was delicately beautiful. The only peculiarities that she knew about seemed ridiculously irrelevant: a dark birthmark on her thigh, a soft fontanel in the top of her long narrow head, like the soft spot in an infant's cranium. Silly little differences!

One big difference: the quiet misery of the unfed hunger.

A scattering of big raindrops suddenly whispered on the walk and in the grass and through the foliage of the elm. A few drops splattered on the screen, spraying her face and arms with faint points of coolness. It had been oppressively hot. Now there was a chill breath in the night.

Reluctantly she closed the window. The oppression of the warm and empty house increased. She walked to the door opening into the walled garden.

Ready for a lonely bed, she was wearing a negligee over nothing. Vaguely, idly, her hand fumbled at the waist-knot, loosened it. The robe parted, and the fine spray of rain was delightfully cool on her skin.

The garden was dark, the shadows inky, the nearest neighbor a block away. The wall screened it from prying eyes. She brushed her hands over her shoulders; the sleeves slipped down her arms. Peeled clean, feeling like a freed animal, she pressed open the screen and stepped out under the eaves to stand on the warm stone walk.

The rain was rattling in the hedge and roaring softly all about her, splashing coldness about her slender calves. She hugged herself and stepped into it. The drench of icy fingers stroked her pleasantly; she laughed and ran along the walk toward the elm. The drops stung her breasts, rivered her face, and coursed coldly down her sides and legs.

She exulted in the rain, tried to dance and laughed at herself. She ran. Then, tired, she threw herself down on the crisp wet lawn, stretching her arms and legs and rolling slowly on the grass. Eyes closed, drenched and languorous, she laughed softly and played imagining games with the rain.

The drops were steel-jacketed wasps, zipping down out of the blackness, but she melted them with her mind, made them soft and cool and caressing. The drops took impersonal liberties with her body, and she rolled demurely to lie face down in the rainsoft gras.

"*I am still a pale beast,*" she thought happily, "*still kin of my grandmother the ape who danced in the tree and chattered when it rained. How utterly barren life would be, if I were not a pale beast!*"

She dug her fingers into the sodden turf, bared her teeth, pressed her forehead against the ground, and growled a little animal growl. It amused her, and she laughed again. Crouching, she came up on her hands and knees, hunching low, teeth still bared. Like a cat, she hissed—and pounced upon a sleeping bird, caught it and shook it to death.

Again she lay laughing in the grass.

"*If Frank were to see me like this,*" she thought, "*he would put me to bed with a couple of sleeping pills, and call that smug Dr. Mensley to have a look at my mind. And Dr. Mensley would check my ambivalences and my repressions and my narcissistic, voyeuristic, masochistic impulses. He would tighten my screws and readjust me to reality, fit me into a comfortable groove, and take the pale beast out of me to make me a talking doll.*"

He had done it several times before. Thinking of Dr. Mensley, Lisa searched her vocabulary for the most savage word she could remember. She growled it aloud and felt better.

The rain was slowly subsiding. A siren was wailing in the distance. The police. She giggled and imagined a headline in

tomorrow's paper: PROMINENT SOCIALITE JAILED FOR INDECENT
EXPOSURE. And the story would go on: "Mrs. Lisa Waverly was
taken into custody by the police after neighbors reported that she
was running around stark naked in her back yard. Said Mrs.
Heinehoffer who called the law: 'It was just terrible. Looked to
me like she was having fits.' Mr. Heinehoffer, when asked for
comment, simply closed his eyes and smiled ecstatically."

Lisa sighed wearily. The siren had gone away. The rain had
stopped, except for drippings out of the elm. She was tired,
emotionally spent, yet strangely melancholy. She sat up slowly
in the grass and hugged her shins.

The feeling came over her gradually.

"Someone has been watching me!"

She stiffened slowly, but remained in place, letting her eyes
probe about her in the shadows. If only the drippings would stop
so she could listen! She peered along the hedge, and along the
shadows by the garden wall, toward the dark windows of the
house, up toward the low-hanging mist faintly illuminated from
below by street lights. She saw nothing, heard nothing. There
was no movement in the night. Yet the feeling lingered, even
though she scoffed.

"If anyone is here," she thought, *"I'll call them gently, and
if anyone appears, I'll scream so loud that Mrs. Heinehoffer will
hear me."*

"Hey!" she said in a low voice, but loud enough to penetrate
any of the nearby shadows.

There was no answer. She folded her arms behind her head
and spoke again, quietly, sensually.

"Come and get me."

No black monster slithered from behind the hedge to devour
her. No panther sprang from the elm. No succubus congealed out
of wet darkness. She giggled.

"Come have a bite."

No bull-ape came to crush her in ravenous jaws.

She had only imagined the eyes upon her. She stretched lazily
and picked herself up, pausing to brush off the leaves of grass
pasted to her wet skin. It was over, the strange worship in the
rain, and she was weary. She walked slowly toward the house.

Then she heard it—a faint crackling sound, intermittent, distant. She stood poised in the black shadow of the house, listening. The crackle of paper . . . then a small pop . . . then crisp
fragments dropped in the street. It was repeated at short intervals.

Taking nervous, shallow breaths, she tiptoed quietly toward the stone wall of the garden. It was six feet high, but there was a concrete bench under the trellis. The sound was coming from over the wall. She stood crouching on the bench; then, hiding her face behind the vines, she lifted her head to peer.

The street lamp was half a block away, but she could see dimly. A man was standing across the street in the shadows, apparently waiting for a bus. He was eating peanuts out of a paper bag, tossing the shells in the street. That explained the crackling sound.

She glared at him balefully from behind the trellis.

"*I'd claw your eyes out,*" she thought, "*if you came and peeped over my wall.*"

"Hi!" the man said.

Lisa stiffened and remained motionless. It was impossible that he could see her. She was in shadow, against a dark background. Had he heard her foolish babbling a moment ago?

More likely, he had only cleared his throat.

"Hi!" he said again.

Her face was hidden in the dripping vines, and she could not move without rustling. She froze in place, staring. She could see little of him. Dark raincoat, dark hat, slender shadow. Was he looking toward her? She was desperately frightened.

Suddenly the man chucked the paper bag in the gutter, stepped off the curb, and came sauntering across the street toward the wall. He removed his hat, and crisp blond hair glinted in the distant streetlight. He stopped three yards away, smiling uncertainly at the vines.

Lisa stood trembling and frozen, staring at him in horror. Strange sensations, utterly alien, passed over her in waves. There was no describing them, no understanding them.

"I—I found you," he stammered sheepishly. "Do you know what it is?"

"*I know you,*" she thought. "*You have a small scar on the back of your neck, and a mole between your toes. Your eyes are blue, and you have an impacted wisdom tooth, and your feet are hurting you because you walked all the way out here from the University, and I'm almost old enough to be your mother. But I can't know you, because I've never seen you before!*"

"Strange, isn't it?" he said uncertainly. He was holding his hat in his hand and cocking his head politely.

"What?" she whispered.

He shuffled his feet and stared at them. "It must be some sort of palpable biophysical energy-form, analytically definable—if we had enough data. Lord knows, I'm no mystic. If it exists, it's got to be mathematically definable. But why us?"

Horrified curiosity made her step aside and lean her arms on the wall to stare down at him. He looked up bashfully, and his eyes widened slightly.

"Oh!"

"Oh what?" she demanded, putting on a terrible frown.

"You're beautiful!"

"What do you want?" she asked icily. "Go away!"

"I—" He paused and closed his mouth slowly. He stared at her with narrowed eyes, and touched one hand to his temple as if concentrating.

For an instant, she was no longer herself. She was looking up at her own shadowy face from down in the street, looking through the eyes of a stranger who was not a stranger. She was feeling the fatigue in the weary ankles, and the nasal ache of a slight head cold, and the strange sadness in a curious heart—a sadness too akin to her own.

She rocked dizzily. It was like being in two places at once, like wearing someone else's body for a moment.

The feeling passed. "*It didn't happen!*" she told herself.

"No use denying it," he said quietly. "I tried to make it go away, too, but apparently we've got something unique. It would be interesting to study. Do you suppose we're related?"

"Who are you?" she choked, only half-hearing his question.

"You know my name," he said, "if you'll just take the trouble to think about it. Yours is Lisa—Lisa O'Brien, or Lisa Waverly—I'm never sure which. Sometimes it comes to me one way, sometimes the other."

She swallowed hard. Her maiden name had been O'Brien.

"I don't know you," she snapped.

His name was trying to form in her mind. She refused to allow it. The young man sighed.

"I'm Kenneth Grearly, if you really don't know." He stepped back a pace and lifted his hat toward his head. "I—I guess I better go. I see this disturbs you. I had hoped we could talk about it, but—well, good night, Mrs. Waverly."

He turned and started away.

"Wait!" she called out against her will.

He stopped again. "Yes?"

"Were—were you watching me—while it was raining?"

He opened his mouth and stared thoughtfully down the street toward the light. "You mean watching visually? You really are repressing this thing, aren't you? I thought you understood." He looked at her sharply, forlornly. "They say the failure to communicate is the basis of all tragedy. Do you suppose in our case . . .?"

"What?"

"Nothing." He shifted restlessly for a moment. "Good night."

"Good night," she whispered many seconds after he was gone.

Her bedroom was hot and lonely, and she tossed in growing restlessness. If only Frank were home! But he would be gone for two more weeks. The children would be back on Monday, but that was three whole days away. Crazy! It was just stark raving crazy!

Had the man really existed—what was his name?—Kenneth Grearly? Or was he only a phantasm invented by a mind that was failing—her mind? Dancing naked in the rain! Calling out to shadow shapes in the brush! Talking to a specter in the street! Schizophrenic syndrome—dream-world stuff. It could not be otherwise, for unless she had invented Kenneth Grearly, how could she know he had sore feet, an impacted wisdom tooth, and a head cold. Not only did she know about those things, but she felt them!

She buried her face in the dusty pillow and sobbed. Tomorrow she would have to call Dr. Mensley.

But fearing the specter's return, she arose a few minutes later and locked all the doors in the house. When she returned to bed, she tried to pray but it was as if the prayer were being watched. Someone was listening, eavesdropping from outside.

Kenneth Grearly appeared in her dreams, stood half-shrouded in a slowly swirling fog. He stared at her with his head cocked aside, smiling slightly, holding his hat respectfully in his hands.

"Don't you realize, Mrs. Waverly, that we are mutants perhaps," he asked politely.

"No!" she screamed. "I'm happily married and I have three children and a place in society! Don't come near me!"

He melted slowly into the fog. But echoes came monotonously from invisible cliffs: *mutant mutant mutant mutant mutant* . . .

Dawn came, splashing pink paint across the eastern sky. The light woke her to a dry and empty consciousness, to a headachy awareness full of dull anxiety. She arose wearily and trudged to the kitchen for a pot of coffee.

Lord! Couldn't it all be only a bad dream?

In the cold light of early morning, the things of the past night looked somehow detached, unreal. She tried to analyze objectively.

That sense of sharing a mind, a consciousness, with the stranger who came out of the shadows—what crazy thing had he called it?—*"some sort of palpable biophysical energy-form, analytically definable."*

"If I invented the stranger," she thought, *"I must have also invented the words."*

But where had she heard such words before?

Lisa went to the telephone and thumbed through the directory. No Grearly was listed. If he existed at all, he probably lived in a rooming house. The University—last night she had thought that he had something to do with the University. She lifted the phone and dialed.

"University Station; number please," the operator said.

"I—uh—don't know the extension number. Could you tell me if there is a Kenneth Grearly connected with the school?"

"Student or faculty, Madam?"

"I don't know."

"Give me your number, please, and I'll call you back."

"Lawrence 4750. Thanks, Operator."

She sat down to wait. Almost immediately it rang again.

"Hello?"

"Mrs. Waverly, you were calling me?" A man's voice. His voice!

"The operator found you rather quickly." It was the only thing she could think of saying.

"No, no. I knew you were calling. In fact, I hoped you into it."

"Hoped me? Now look here, Mr. Grearly, I—"

"You were trying to explain our phenomenon in terms of insanity rather than telepathy. I didn't want you to do that, and so I hoped you into calling me."

Lisa was coldly speechless. "What phenomenon are you talking about?" she asked after a few dazed seconds.

"Still repressing it? Listen, I can share your mind any time I want to, now that I understand where and who you are. You might as well face the fact. And it can work both ways, if you let it. Up to now, you've been—well, keeping your mind's eye closed, so to speak.''

Her scalp was crawling. The whole thing had become intensely disgusting to her.

''I don't know what you're up to, Mr. Grearly, but I wish you'd stop it. I admit something strange is going on, but your explanation is ridiculous—offensive, even.''

He was silent for a long time, then: ''I wonder if the first man-ape found his prehensile thumb ridiculous. I wonder if he thought using his hands for grasping was offensive.''

''What are you trying to say?''

''That I think we're mutants. We're not the first ones. I had this same experience when I was in Boston once. There must be one of us there, too, but suddenly I got the feeling that he had committed suicide. I never saw him. We're probably the first ones to discover each other.''

''Boston? If what you say is true, what would distance have to do with it?''

''Well, if telepathy exists, it certainly involves tranfer of energy from one point to another. What *kind* of energy, I don't know. Possibly electromagnetic in character. But it seems likely that it would obey the inverse square law, like radiant energy forms. I came to town about three weeks ago. I didn't feel you until I got close.''

''*There is a connection,*'' she thought. She had been wondering about the increased anxiety of the past three weeks.

''I don't know what you're talking about,'' she evaded icily, though. ''I'm no mutant. I don't believe in telepathy. I'm not insane. Now let me alone.''

She slammed the telephone in its cradle and started to walk away.

Evidently he was angry, for she was suddenly communicating with him again.

She reeled dizzily and clutched at the wall, because she was in two places at once, and the two settings merged in her mind to become a blur, like a double exposure. She was in her own hallway, and she was also in an office, looking at a calculator keyboard, hearing glassware rattling from across a corridor, aware of the smell of formaldehyde. There was a chart on the wall behind the desk and it was covered with strange tracery—schematics of some neural arcs. The office of the psychophysics lab. She closed her eyes, and her own hallway disappeared.

She felt anger—his anger.

"*We've got to face this thing. If this is a new direction for human evolution, then we'd better study it and see what to do about it. I knew I was different and I became a psychophysicist to find out why. I haven't been able to measure much, but now with Lisa's help . . .*"

She tried to shut him out. She opened her eyes and summoned her strength and tried to force him away. She stared at the bright doorway, but the tracery of neural arcs still remained. She fought him, but his mind lingered in hers.

"*. . . perhaps we can get to the bottom of it. I know my encephalograph recordings are abnormal, and now I can check them against hers. A few correlations will help. I'm glad to know about her soft fontanel. I wondered about mine. Now I think that underneath that fontanel lies a pattern of specialized neural—*"

She sagged to the floor of the hall and babbled aloud: "Hickory Dickory Dock the mouse ran up the clock. The clock struck one—"

Slowly he withdrew. The laboratory office faded from her vision. His thoughts left her. She lay there panting for a time.

Had she won?

No, there was no sense in claiming victory. She had not driven him away. He had withdrawn of his own volition when he felt her babbling. She knew his withdrawal was free, because she had felt his parting state of mind: sadness. He had stopped the forced contact because he pitied her, and there was a trace of contempt in the pity.

She climbed slowly to her feet, looking around wildly, touching the walls and the door-frame to reassure herself that she was still in her own home. She staggered into the parlor and sat shivering on the sofa.

Last night! That crazy running around in the rain! He was responsible for that. He had hoped her into doing it, or maybe he had just wondered what she looked like undressed, and she had subconsciously satisfied his curiosity. He had planted the suggestion—innocently, perhaps—and she had unknowingly taken the cue.

He could be with her whenever he wanted to! He had been with her while she frollicked insanely in the rain-sodden grass! Perhaps he was with her now.

Whom could she talk to? Where could she seek help? Dr. Mensley? He would immediately chalk it up as a delusion, and probably call for a sanity hearing if she wouldn't voluntarily enter a psycho-ward for observation.

The police? "Sergeant, I want to report a telepathic prowler. A man is burglarizing my mind."

A clergyman? He would shudder and refer her to a psychiatrist.

All roads led to the booby-hatch, it seemed. Frank wouldn't believe her. No one would believe her.

Lisa wandered through the day like a caged animal. She put on her brightest summer frock and a pert straw hat and went downtown. She wandered through the crowds in the business district, window-shopping. But she was alone. The herds of people about her brushed past and wandered on. A man whistled at her in front of a cigar store. A policeman waved her back to the curb when she started across an intersection.

"Wake up, lady!" he called irritably.

People all about her, but she could not tell them, explain to them, and so she was alone. She caught a taxi and went to visit a friend, the wife of an English teacher, and drank a glass of iced tea in the friend's parlor, and talked of small things, and admitted that she was tired when the friend suggested that she looked that way. When she went back home, the sun was sinking in the west.

She called long distance and talked to her mother, then spoke to her children, asked them if they were ready to come home, but they wanted to stay another week. They begged, and her mother begged, and she reluctantly consented. It had been a mistake to call. Now the kids would be gone even longer.

She tried to call Frank in St. Louis, but the hotel clerk reported that he had just checked out. Lisa knew this meant he was on the road again.

"*Maybe I ought to go join the kids at Mother's,*" she thought. But Frank had wanted her to stay home. He was expecting a registered letter from Chicago, and it was apparently important, and she had to take care of it.

"*I'll invite somebody over,*" she thought. But the wives were home with their husbands, and it was a social mistake to invite a couple when her husband was gone. It always wound up with two women yammering at each other while the lone male sat and glowered in uneasy isolation, occasionally disagreeing with his wife, just to let her know he was there and he was annoyed and bored and why didn't they go home? It was different if the business-widow called on a couple. Then the lone male could retire to some other part of the house to escape the yammering.

But she decided it wasn't company she wanted; she wanted help. And there was no place to get it.

When she allowed her thoughts to drift toward Kenneth Grearly, it was almost like tuning in a radio station. He was eating early dinner in the University cafeteria with a bedraggled, bespectacled brunette from the laboratory. Lisa closed her eyes and let herself sift gingerly into his thoughs. His attention was on the conversation and on the food, and he failed to realize Lisa's presence. That knowledge gave her courage.

He was eating Swiss steak and hashed brown potatoes, and the flavors formed perceptions in her mind. She heard the rattle of silverware, the low murmur of voices, and smelled the food. She marveled at it. The strange ability had apparently been brought into focus by learning what it was and how to use it.

"Our work has been too empirical," he was saying. "We've studied phenomena, gathered data, looked for correlations. But that method has limitations. We should try to find a way to approach psychology from below. Like the invariantive approach to physics."

The girl shook her head. "The nervous system is too complicated for writing theoretical equations about it. Empirical equations are the best we can do."

"They aren't good enough, Sarah. You can predict results with them, inside the limits of their accuracy. But you can't extrapolate them very well, and they won't stack up together into a single integrated structure. And when you're investigating a new field, they no longer apply. We need a broad mathematical theory, covering all hypothetically possible neural arrangements. It would let us predict not only results, but also predict patterns of possible order."

"Seems to me the possible patterns are infinite."

"No, Sarah. They're limited by the nature of the building blocks—neurons, synaptic connections, and so forth. With limited materials, you have structural limitations. You don't build skyscrapers out of modeling clay. And there is only a finite number of ways you can build atoms out of electrons, protons and neutrons. Similarly, brains are confined to the limitations of the things they're made of. We need a broad theory for defining the limits."

"Why?"

"Because . . ." He paused. Lisa felt his urge to explain his urgency, felt him suppress it, felt for a moment his loneliness in the awareness of his uniqueness and the way it isolated him from humanity.

"You must be doing new work," the girl offered, "If you feel the lack of such a theoretical approach. I just can't imagine an invariantive approach to psychology—or an all-defining set of laws for it, either. Why do you need such a psychological 'Relativity'?"

He hesitated, frowning down at his plate, watching a fly crawl around its rim. "I'm interested in—in the quantitative aspects of nerve impulses. I—I suspect that there can be such a thing as neural resonance."

She laughed politely and shook her head. "I'll stick to my empirical data-gathering, thank you."

Lisa felt him thinking:

"She could understand, if I could show her data. But my data is all subjective, experimental, personal. I share it with that Waverly woman, but she is only a social thinker, analytically shallow, refusing even to recognize facts. Why did it have to be her? She's flighty, emotional, and in a cultural rut. If she doesn't conform, she thinks she's nuts. But then at least she's a woman—and if this is really a mutation, we'll have to arrange for some children . . ."

Lisa gasped and sat bolt upright. Her shock revealed her presence to him, and he dropped his fork with a clatter.

"Lisa!"

She wrenched herself free of him abruptly. She angrily stalked about the house, slamming doors and muttering her rage. The nerve! The maddening, presumptuous, ill-mannered, self-centered, over-educated boor!

Arrange for some children indeed! An impossible situation!

As her anger gathered momentum, she contacted him again— like a snake striking. Thought was thunder out of a dark cloud.

"I'm decent and I'm respectable, Mr. Grearly! I have a husband and three fine children and I love them, and you can go to hell! I never want to see you again or have you prowling around my mind. Get out and STAY out. And if you ever bother me again—I'll—I'll kill you."

He was outdoors, striding across the campus alone. She saw the gray buildings, immersed in twilight, felt the wind on his face, hated him. He was thinking nothing, letting himself follow her angry flow of thought. When she finished, his thoughts began like the passionate pleading of a poem.

He was imagining a human race with telepathic abilities, in near-perfect communication with one another. So many of the world's troubles could be traced to imperfect communication of ideas, to misunderstandings.

Then he thought briefly of Sarah—the nondescript laboratory girl he had taken to dinner—and Lisa realized he was in love with Sarah. There were sadness and resentment here. He couldn't have Sarah now, not if he were to be certain of perpetuating the mutant characteristic. The Waverly woman ought to be good for three or four children yet, before she reached middle age.

Lisa stood transfixed by shock. Then he was thinking directly to her.

"I'm sorry. You're a beautiful, intelligent woman—but I don't love you. We're not alike. But I'm stuck with you and you're stuck with me, because I've decided it's going to be that way. I can't convince you since your thinking habits are already fixed, so I won't even try. I'm sorry it has to be against your will, but in any event it has to be. And now that I know what you're like, I don't dare wait—for fear you'll do something to mess things up."

"No!" she screamed, watching the scenery that moved past his field of vision.

He had left the campus and was walking up the street—toward her neighborhood. He was walking with the briskness of purpose. He was coming to her house.

"Call the police!" she thought, and tried to dissolve him out of her mind.

But this time he followed, clung to her thoughts, would not let her go. It was like two flashlight beams playing over a wall, one trying to escape, the other following its frantic circle of brightness.

She staggered, groped her way toward the hall, which was confused with a superimposed image of a sidewalk and a street. A phanton automobile came out of the hall wall, drove through her and vanished. Double exposures. He stared at a street light and it blinded her. At last she found the phone, but he was laughing at her.

"Eight seven six five twenty-one Mary had a little lamb seven seven sixty-seven yesterday was May March April . . ."

He was deliberately filling her mind with confusion. She fumbled at the directory, trying to find the police, but he thought a confused jumble of numbers and symbols, and they scampered across the page, blurring the letters.

She whimpered and groped at the phone-dial, trying to get the operator, but he was doing something with his fingertips, and she couldn't get the feel of the dial.

On her third try, it finally worked.

"Information," said a pleasant impersonal voice.

She had to get the police! She had to say—

"*Pease porridge hot, pease porridge cold, pease porridge in the pot, nine days pretty polly parrot played peacefully plentiwise pease porridge . . .*"

He was jamming her speech centers with gibberish, and she blurted nonsense syllables into the mouthpiece.

"You'll have to speak more distinctly, madam. I can't understand you."

"Poress, Policer . . ."

"The police? Just a moment."

A series of jumbled sounds and visions clouded her mind. Then a masculine voice rumbled, "Desk, Sergeant Harris."

She found a clear path through the confusion and gasped, "Three-oh-oh-three Willow Drive—'mergency—come quick—man going to—"

"Three-oh-oh-three Willow. Check. We'll have a car right over there."

She hung up quickly—or tried to—but she couldn't find the cradle. Then her vision cleared and she screamed. She wasn't in the hall at all!

The telephone was an eggbeater!

His voice came through her trapped panic.

"*You might as well give in,*" he told her with a note of sadness. "*I know how to mess you up like that, you see. And you haven't learned to retaliate yet. We're going to cooperate with this evolutionary trend, whether you like it or not—but it would be more pleasant if you agree to it.*"

"*No!*"

"*All right, but I'm coming anyway. I hoped it wouldn't be like this. I wanted to convince you gradually. Now I know that it's impossible.*"

He was still ten blocks away. She had a few minutes in which to escape. She bolted for the door. A black shadow-shape loomed up in the twilight, flung its arms wide, and emitted an apelike roar.

She yelped and darted back, fleeing frantically for the front. A boa constrictor lay coiled in the hall; it slithered toward her. She screamed again and raced toward the stairway.

She made it to the top and looked back. The living room was filling slowly with murky water. She rushed shrieking into the bedroom and bolted the door.

She smelled smoke. Her dress was on fire! The flames licked up, searing her skin.

She tore at it madly, and got it off, but her slip was afire. She ripped it away, scooped up the flaming clothing on a transom hook, opened the screen, and dropped them out the window. Flames still licked about her, and she rolled up in the bed-clothing to snuff them out.

Quiet laughter.

"*New syndrome,*" he called to her pleasantly. "*The patient confuses someone else's fantasy with her own reality. Not schizophrenia—duophrenia, maybe?*"

She lay sobbing in hysterical desperation. He was just down the street now, coming rapidly up the walk. A car whisked slowly past. He felt her terrified despair and pitied her. The torment ceased.

She stayed there, panting for a moment, summoning spirit. He was nearing the intersection just two blocks south, and she could hear the rapid traffic with his ears.

Suddenly she clenched her eyes closed and gritted her teeth. He was stepping off the curb, walking across—

She imagined a fire engine thundering toward her like a juggernaut, rumbling and wailing. She imagined another car racing out into the intersection, with herself caught in the cross-fire. She imagined a woman screaming, "Look out, Mister!"

And then she was caught in his own responding fright, and it was easier to imagine. He was bolting for the other corner. She conjured a third car from another direction, brought it lunging at him to avoid the impending wreck. He staggered away from the phantom cars and screamed.

A real car confused the scene.

She echoed his scream. There was a moment of rending pain, and then the vision was gone. Brakes were still yowling two blocks away. Someone was running down the sidewalk. A part of her mind had heard the crashing thud. She was desperately sick.

And a sudden sense of complete aloneness told her that Grearly was dead. A siren was approaching out of the distance.

Voices from the sidewalk: ". . . just threw a fit in the middle of the street . . . running around like crazy and hollering . . . it was a delivery truck . . . crushed his skull . . . nobody else hurt . . ."

After the street returned to normal, she arose and went to get a drink of water. But she stood staring at her sick white face in the mirror. There were crow's feet forming at the corners of her eyes, and her skin was growing tired, almost middle-aged.

It was funny that she should notice that now, at this strange moment. She had just killed a man in self-defense. And no one would believe it if she told the truth. There was no cause for guilt.

Was there?

Frank would be back soon, and everything would be the same again: peace, security, nice kids, nice home, nice husband. Just the way it always had been.

But something was already different. An emptiness. A loneliness of the mind that she had never before felt. She kept looking around to see if the lights hadn't gone dim, or the clock stopped ticking, or the faucet stopped dripping.

It was none of those things. The awful silence was within her.

Gingerly, she touched the soft spot at the top of her head and felt an utter aloneness. She closed her eyes and thought a hopeless plea to the Universe:

"Is there anybody else like me? Can anybody hear me?"

There was only complete silence, the silence of the voiceless void.

And for the first time in her life she felt the confinement of total isolation and knew it for what it was.

THE MARTIAN WAY

by Isaac Asimov (1920–)

Aha! My own story of the year, at last.

Damon Knight, who could be a caustic and articulate flayer of stories, when he was wearing his critic hat, *liked* this story and said so very eloquently in a review, and, for the first time, I said to myself what I have since said to myself many a time and oft. "The old man still has it," I said.

Of course, I wasn't old at the time. I was only thirty-two, but I had never been that old before and besides I had been publishing for thirteen years by then and in the fast-turnover world of science fiction writing, I felt superannuated, and very much a veteran waiting to be replaced. Fortunately that still hasn't happened now, a third of a century later, but only because I'm incredibly stubborn.

This story was originally written without any female characters. Horace Gold wanted a female character and wouldn't listen to my insistence that there was no need for a female character and I wanted no unneeded character, no unneeded event, no unneeded anything in the story. He said, "One female, any kind of female, and I'll take the story."

So if you'll read the story you'll find one female and I *know* that was *not* the kind Horace wanted, but he kept his word and took the story. He even put it on the cover of the issue in which it appeared—but on that cover my name was badly misspelled. I don't suppose he did it on purpose, but at the time, I was pretty suspicious.

One more point. This story was written at the height of the infamous power of Joseph McCarthy. I wrote it with him in mind and expected (even hoped) that I would get in trouble as a result. I didn't. Not a word. I must have been too subtle.(1A)

From the doorway of the short corridor between the only two rooms in the travel-head of the spaceship. Mario Esteban Rioz watched sourly as Ted Long adjusted the video dials painstakingly. Long tried a touch clockwise, then a touch counter. The picture was lousy.

Rioz knew it would stay lousy. They were too far from Earth and at a bad position facing the Sun. But then Long would not be expected to know that. Rioz remained standing in the doorway for an additional moment, head bent to clear the upper lintel, body turned half sidewise to fit the narrow opening. Then he jerked into the galley like a cork popping out of a bottle.

"What are you after?" he asked.

"I thought I'd get Hilder," said Long.

Rioz propped his rump on the corner of a table shelf. He lifted a conical can of milk from the companion shelf just above his head. Its point popped under pressure. He swirled it gently as he waited for it to warm.

"What for?" he said. He upended the cone and sucked noisily.

"Thought I'd listen."

"I think it's a waste of power."

Long looked up, frowning. "It's customary to allow free use of personal video sets."

"Within reason," retorted Rioz.

Their eyes met challengingly. Rioz had the rangy body, the gaunt, cheek-sunken face that was almost the hallmark of the Martian Scavenger, those Spacers who patiently haunted the space routes between Earth and Mars. Pale blue eyes were set keenly in the brown, lined face which, in turn, stood darkly out against the white surrounding syntho-fur that lined the up-turned collar of his leathtic space jacket.

Long was altogether paler and softer. He bore some of the marks of the Grounder, although no second-generation Martian could be a Grounder in the sense that Earthmen were. His own collar was thrown back and his dark brown hair freely exposed.

"What do you call within reason?" demanded Long.

Rioz's thin lips grew thinner. He said, "Considering that we're not even going to make expenses this trip, the way it looks, any power drain at all is outside reason."

Long said, "If we're losing money, hadn't you better get back to your post? It's your watch."

Rioz grunted and ran a thumb and forefinger over the stubble on his chin. He got up and trudged to the door, his soft, heavy boots muting the sound of his steps. He paused to look at the thermostat, then turned with a flare of fury.

"I *thought* it was hot. Where do you think you are?"

Long said, "Forty degrees isn't excessive."

"For you it isn't, maybe. But this is space, not a heated office at the iron mines." Rioz swung the thermostat control down to minimum with a quick thumb movement. "Sun's warm enough."

"The galley isn't on Sunside."

"It'll percolate through, damn it."

Rioz stepped through the door and Long stared after him for a long moment, then turned back to the video. He did not turn up the thermostat.

The picture was still flickering badly, but it would have to do. Long folded a chair down out of the wall. He leaned forward waiting through the formal announcement, the momentary pause before the slow dissolution of the curtain, the spotlight picking out the well-known bearded figure which grew as it was brought forward until it filled the screen.

The voice, impressive even through the flutings and croakings induced by the electron storms of twenty millions of miles, began:

"Friends! My fellow citizens of Earth . . ."

2

Rioz's eye caught the flash of the radio signal as he stepped into the pilot room. For one moment, the palms of his hands grew clammy when it seemed to him that it was a radar pip; but that was only his guilt speaking. He should not have left the pilot room while on duty theoretically, though all Scavengers did it. Still, it was the standard nightmare, this business of a strike turning up during just those five minutes when one knocked off for a quick coffee because it seemed certain that space was clear. And the nightmare had been known to happen, too.

Rioz threw in the multi-scanner. It was a waste of power, but while he was thinking about it, he might as well make sure.

Space was clear except for the far-distant echoes from the neighboring ships on the scavenging line.

He hooked up the radio circuit, and the blond, long-nosed

head of Richard Swenson, co-pilot of the next ship on the Marsward side, filled it.

"Hey, Mario," said Swenson.

"Hi. What's new?"

There was a second and a fraction of pause between that and Swenson's next comment, since the speed of electromagnetic radiation is not infinite.

"What a day I've *had*."

"Something happened?" Rioz asked.

"I had a strike."

"Well, good."

"Sure, if I'd roped it in," said Swenson morosely.

"What happened?"

"Damn it, I headed in the wrong direction."

Rioz knew better than to laugh. He said, "How did you do that?"

"It wasn't my fault. The trouble was the shell was moving way out of the ecliptic. Can you imagine the stupidity of a pilot that can't work the release maneuver decently? How was I to know? I got the distance of the shell and let it go at that. I just assumed its orbit was in the usual trajectory family. Wouldn't you? I started along what I thought was a good line of intersection and it was five minutes before I noticed the distance was still going up. The pips were taking their sweet time returning. So then I took the angular projections of the thing, and it was too late to catch up with it."

"Any of the other boys getting it?"

"No. It's 'way out of the ecliptic and'll keep on going forever. That's not what bothers me so much. It was only an inner shell. But I hate to tell you how many tons of propulsion I wasted getting up speed and then getting back to station. You should have heard Canute."

Canute was Richard Swenson's brother and partner.

"Mad, huh?" said Rioz.

"Mad? Like to have killed me! But then we've been out five months now and it's getting kind of sticky. You know."

"I know."

"How are you doing, Mario?"

Rioz made a spitting gesture. "About that much this trip. Two shells in the last two weeks and I had to chase each one for six hours."

"Big ones?"

"Are you kidding? I could have scaled them down to Phobos by hand. This is the worst trip I've ever had."

"How much longer are you staying?"

"For my part, we can quit tomorrow. We've only been out two months and it's got so I'm chewing Long out all the time."

There was a pause over and above the electromagnetic lag.

Swenson said, "What's he like, anyway? Long, I mean."

Rioz looked over his shoulder. He could hear the soft, crackly mutter of the video in the galley. "I can't make him out. He says to me about a week after the start of the trip, 'Mario, why are you a Scavenger?' I just look at him and say, 'To make a living. Why do you suppose?' I mean, what the hell kind of a question is that? Why is anyone a Scavenger?

"Anyway, he says, 'That's not it, Mario.' *He's* telling *me*, you see. He says, 'You're a Scavenger because this is part of the Martian way.' "

Swenson said, "And what did he mean by that?"

Rioz shrugged. "I never asked him. Right now he's sitting in there listening to the ultra-microwave from Earth. He's listening to some Grounder called Hilder."

"Hilder? A Grounder politician, an Assemblyman or something, isn't he?"

"That's right. At least, I think that's right. Long is always doing things like that. He brought about fifteen pounds of books with him, all about Earth. Just plain dead weight, you know."

"Well, he's your partner. And talking about partners, I think I'll get back on the job. If I miss another strike, there'll be murder around here."

He was gone and Rioz leaned back. He watched the even green line that was the pulse scanner. He tried the multi-scanner a moment. Space was still clear.

He felt a little better. A bad spell is always worse if the Scavengers all about you are pulling in shell after shell; if the shells go spiraling down to the Phobos scrap forges with everyone's brand welded on except your own. Then, too, he had managed to work off some of his resentment toward Long.

It was a mistake teaming up with Long. It was always a mistake to team up with a tenderfoot. They thought what you wanted was conversation, especially Long, with his eternal theories about Mars and its great new role in human progress. That was the way he said it—Human Progress: the Martian Way; the

New Creative Minority. And all the time what Rioz wanted wasn't talk, but a strike, a few shells to call their own.

At that, he hadn't any choice, really. Long was pretty well known down on Mars and made good pay as a mining engineer. He was a friend of Commissioner Sankov and he'd been out on one or two short scavenging missions before. You can't turn a fellow down flat before a tryout, even though it did look funny. Why should a mining engineer with a comfortable job and good money want to muck around in space?

Rioz never asked Long that question. Scavenger partners are forced too close together to make curiosity desirable, or sometimes even safe. But Long talked so much that he answered the question.

"I had to come out here, Mario," he said. "The future of Mars isn't in the mines; it's in space."

Rioz wondered how it would be to try a trip alone. Everyone said it was impossible. Even discounting lost opportunities when one man had to go off watch to sleep or attend to other things, it was well known that one man alone in space would become intolerably depressed in a relatively short while.

Taking a partner along made a six-month trip possible. A regular crew would be better, but no Scavenger could make money on a ship large enough to carry one. The capital it would take in propulsion alone!

Even two didn't find it exactly fun in space. Usually you had to change partners each trip and you could stay out longer with some than with others. Look at Richard and Canute Swenson. They teamed up every five or six trips because they were brothers. And yet whenever they did, it was a case of constantly mounting tension and antagonism after the first week.

Oh well. Space was clear. Rioz would feel a little better if he went back in the galley and smoothed down some of the bickering with Long. He might as well show he was an old spacehand who took the irritations of space as they came.

He stood up, walked the three steps necessary to reach the short, narrow corridor that tied together the two rooms of the spaceship.

3

Once again Rioz stood in the doorway for a moment, watching. Long was intent on the flickering screen.

Rioz said gruffly, "I'm shoving up the thermostat. It's all right—we can spare the power."

Long nodded. "If you like."

Rioz took a hesitant step forward. Space was clear, so to hell with sitting and looking at a blank, green, pipless line. He said, "What's the Grounder been talking about?"

"History of space travel mostly. Old stuff, but he's doing it well. He's giving the whole works—color cartoons, trick photography, stills from old films, everything."

As if to illustrate Long's remarks, the bearded figure faded out of view, and a cross-sectional view of a spaceship flitted onto the screen. Hilder's voice continued, pointing out features of interest that appeared in schematic color. The communications system of the ship outlined itself in red as he talked about it, the storerooms, the proton micropile drive, the cybernetic circuits . . .

Then Hilder was back on the screen. "But this is only the travel-head of the ship. What moves it? What gets it off the Earth?"

Everyone knew what moved a spaceship, but Hilder's voice was like a drug. He made spaceship propulsion sound like the secret of the ages, like an ultimate revelation. Even Rioz felt a slight tingling of suspense, though he had spent the greater part of his life aboard ship.

Hilder went on. "Scientists call it different names. They call it the Law of Action and Reaction. Sometimes they call it Newton's Third Law. Sometimes they call it Conservation of Momentum. But we don't have to call it any name. We can just use our common sense. When we swim, we push water backward and move forward ourselves. When we walk, we push back against the ground and move forward. When we fly a gyroflivver, we push air backward and move forward.

"Nothing can move forward unless something else moves backward. It's the old principle of 'You can't get something for nothing.'

"Now imagine a spaceship that weighs a hundred thousand tons lifting off Earth. To do that, something else must be moved downward. Since a spaceship is extremely heavy, a great deal of material must be moved downward. So much material, in fact, that there is no place to keep it all aboard ship. A special compartment must be built behind the ship to hold it.''

Again Hilder faded out and the ship returned. It shrank and a truncated cone appeared behind it. In bright yellow, words appeared within it: MATERIAL TO BE THROWN AWAY.

''But now,'' said Hilder, ''the total weight of the ship is much greater. You need still more propulsion and still more.''

The ship shrank enormously to add on another larger shell and still another immense one. The ship proper, the travelhead, was a little dot on the screen, a glowing red dot.

Rioz said, ''Hell, this is kindergarten stuff.''

''Not to the people he's speaking to, Mario,'' replied Long. ''Earth isn't Mars. There must be billions of Earth people who've never even seen a spaceship; don't know the first thing about it.''

Hilder was saying, ''When the material inside the biggest shell is used up, the shell is detached. It's thrown away, too.''

The outermost shell came loose, wobbled about the screen.

''Then the second one goes,'' said Hilder, ''and then, if the trip is a long one, the last is ejected.''

The ship was just a red dot now, with three shells shifting and moving, lost in space.

Hilder said, ''These shells represent a hundred thousand tons of tungsten, magnesium, aluminum, and steel. They are gone forever from Earth. Mars is ringed by Scavengers, waiting along the routes of space travel, waiting for the cast-off shells, netting and branding them, saving them for Mars. Not one cent of payment reaches Earth for them. They are salvage. They belong to the ship that finds them.''

Rioz said, ''We risk our investment and our lives. If we don't pick them up, no one gets them. What loss is that to Earth?''

''Look,'' said Long, ''he's been talking about nothing but the drain that Mars, Venus, and the Moon put on Earth. This is just another item of loss.''

''They'll get their return. We're mining more iron every year.''

''And most of it goes right back into Mars. If you can believe his figures, Earth has invested two hundred billion dollars in Mars and received back about five billion dollars' worth of iron. It's put five hundred billion dollars into the Moon and gotten back a little over twenty-five billion dollars of magnesium, titanium, and assorted light metals. It's put fifty billion dollars into Venus and gotten back nothing. And that's what the taxpayers of Earth are really interested in—tax money out; nothing in.''

The screen was filled, as he spoke, with diagrams of the Scavengers on the route to Mars; little, grinning caricatures of ships, reaching out wiry, tenuous arms that groped for the tumbling, empty shells, seizing and snaking them in, branding them MARS PROPERTY in glowing letters, then scaling them down to Phobos.

Then it was Hilder again. "They tell us eventually they will return it all to us. Eventually! Once they are a going concern! We don't know when that will be. A century from now? A thousand years? A million? 'Eventually.' Let's take them at their word. Someday they will give us back all our metals. Someday they will grow their own food, use their own power, live their own lives.

"But one thing they can never return. Not in a hundred million years. *Water!*

"Mars has only a trickle of water because it is too small. Venus has no water at all because it is too hot. The Moon has none because it is too hot and too small. So Earth must supply not only drinking water and washing water for the Spacers, water to run their industries, water for the hydroponic factories they claim to be setting up—but even water to throw away by the millions of tons.

"What is the propulsive force that spaceships use? What is it they throw out behind so that they can accelerate forward? Once it was the gases generated from explosives. That was very expensive. Then the proton micropile was invented—a cheap power source that could heat up any liquid until it was a gas under tremendous pressure. What is the cheapest and most plentiful liquid available? Why, water, of course.

"Each spaceship leaves Earth carrying nearly a million tons—not pounds, *tons*—of water, for the sole purpose of driving it into space so that it may speed up or slow down.

"Our ancestors burned the oil of Earth madly and wilfully. They destroyed its coal recklessly. We despise and condemn them for that, but at least they had this excuse—they thought that when the need arose, substitutes would be found. And they were right. We have our plankton farms and our proton micropiles.

"But there is no substitute for water. None! There never can be. And when our descendants view the desert we will have made of Earth, what excuse will they find for us? When the droughts come and grow—''

Long leaned forward and turned off the set. He said, ''That bothers me. The damn fool is deliberately— What's the matter?''

Rioz had risen uneasily to his feet. ''I ought to be watching the pips.''

''The hell with the pips.'' Long got up likewise, followed Rioz through the narrow corridor, and stood just inside the pilot room. ''If Hilder carries this through, if he's got the guts to make a real issue out of it— *Wow!*''

He had seen it too. The pip was a Class A, racing after the outgoing signal like a greyhound after a mechanical rabbit.

Rioz was babbling, ''Space was clear, I tell you, *clear*. For Mars' sake, Ted, don't just freeze on me. See if you can spot it visually.''

Rioz was working speedily and with an efficiency that was the result of nearly twenty years of scavenging. He had the distance in two minutes. Then, remembering Swenson's experience, he measured the angle of declination and the radial velocity as well.

He yelled at Long, ''One point seven six radians. You can't miss it, man.''

Long held his breath as he adjusted the vernier. ''It's only half a radian off the Sun. It'll only be crescent-lit.''

He increased magnification as rapidly as he dared, watching for the one ''star'' that changed position and grew to have a form, revealing itself to be no star.

''I'm starting, anyway,'' said Rioz. ''We can't wait.''

''I've got it. I've got it.'' Magnification was still too small to give it a definite shape, but the dot Long watched was brightening and dimming rhythmically as the shell rotated and caught sunlight on cross sections of different sizes.

''Hold on.''

The first of many fine spurts of steam squirted out of the proper vents, leaving long trails of micro-crystals of ice gleaming mistily in the pale beams of the distant Sun. They thinned out for a hundred miles or more. One spurt, then another, then another, as the Scavenger ship moved out of its stable trajectory and took up a course tangential to that of the shell.

''It's moving like a comet at perihelion!'' yelled Rioz. ''Those damned Grounder pilots knock the shells off that way on purpose. I'd like to—''

He swore his anger in a frustrated frenzy as he kicked steam backward and backward recklessly, till the hydraulic cusioning of his chair had soughed back a full foot and Long had found himself all but unable to maintain his grip on the guard rail.

"Have a heart," he begged.

But Rioz had his eye on the pips. "If you can't take it, man, stay on Mars!" The steam spurts continued to boom distantly.

The radio came to life. Long managed to lean forward through what seemed like molasses and closed contact. It was Swenson, eyes glaring.

Swenson yelled, "Where the hell are you guys going? You'll be in my sector in ten seconds."

Rioz said, "I'm chasing a shell."

"In *my* sector?"

"It started in mine and you're not in position to get it. Shut off that radio, Ted."

The ship thundered through space, a thunder that could be heard only within the hull. And then Rioz cut the engines in stages large enough to make Long flail forward. The sudden silence was more ear-shattering than the noise that had preceded it.

Rioz said, "All right. Let me have the 'scope."

They both watched. The shell was a definite truncated cone now, tumbling with slow solemnity as it passed along among the stars.

"It's a Class A shell, all right," said Rioz with satisfaction. A giant among shells, he thought. It would put them into the black.

Long said, "We've got another pip on the scanner. I think it's Swenson taking after us."

Rioz scarcely gave it a glance. "He won't catch us."

The shell grew larger still, filling the visiplate.

Rioz's hands were on the harpoon lever. He waited, adjusted the angle microscopically twice, played out the length allotment. Then he yanked, tripping the release.

For a moment, nothing happened. Then a metal mesh cable snaked out onto the visiplate, moving toward the shell like a striking cobra. It made contact, but it did not hold. If it had, it would have snapped instantly like a cobweb strand. The shell was turning with a rotational momentum amounting to thousands of tons. What the cable did do was to set up a powerful magnetic field that acted as a brake on the shell.

Another cable and another lashed out. Rioz sent them out in an almost heedless expenditure of energy.

"I'll get this one! By Mars, I'll get this one!"

With some two dozen cables stretching between ship and shell, he desisted. The shell's rotational energy, converted by breaking into heat, had raised its temperature to a point where its radiation could be picked up by the ship's meters.

Long said, "Do you want me to put our brand on?"

"Suits me. But you don't have to if you don't want to. It's my watch."

"I don't mind."

Long clambered into his suit and went out the lock. It was the surest sign of his newness to the game that he could count the number of times he had been out in space in a suit. This was the fifth time.

He went out along the nearest cable, hand over hand, feeling the vibration of the mesh against the metal of his mitten.

He burned their serial number in the smooth metal of the shell. There was nothing to oxidize the steel in the emptiness of space. It simply melted and vaporized, condensing some feet away from the energy beam, turning the surface it touched into a gray, powdery dullness.

Long swung back toward the ship.

Inside again, he took off his helmet, white and thick with frost that collected as soon as he had entered.

The first thing he heard was Swenson's voice coming over the radio in an almost unrecognizable rage: ". . . straight to the Commissioner. Damn it, there are rules to this game!"

Rioz sat back, unbothered. "Look, it hit my sector. I was late spotting it and I chased it into yours. You couldn't have gotten it with Mars for a backstop. That's all there is to it—You back, Long?"

He cut contact.

The signal button raged at him, but he paid no attention.

"He's going to the Commissioner?" Long asked.

"Not a chance. He just goes on like that because it breaks the monotony. He doesn't mean anything by it. He knows it's our shell. And how do you like that hunk of stuff, Ted?"

"Pretty good."

"Pretty good? It's terrific! Hold on. I'm setting it swinging."

The side jets spat steam and the ship started a slow rotation about the shell. The shell followed it. In thirty minutes, they were a gigantic bolo spinning in emptiness. Long checked the *Ephemeris* for the position of Deimos.

At a precisely calculated moment, the cables released their magnetic field and the shell went streaking off tangentially in a trajectory that would, in a day or so, bring it within pronging distance of the shell stores on the Martian satellite.

Rioz watched it go. He felt good. He turned to Long. "This is one fine day for us."

"What about Hilder's speech?" asked Long.

"What? Who? Oh, that. Listen, if I had to worry about every thing some damned Grounder said, I'd never get any sleep. Forget it."

"I don't think we should forget it."

"You're nuts. Don't bother me about it, will you? Get some sleep instead."

4

Ted Long found the breadth and height of the city's main thoroughfare exhilarating. It had been two months since the Commissioner had declared a moratorium on scavenging and had pulled all ships out of space, but this feeling of a stretched-out vista had not stopped thrilling Long. Even the thought that the moratorium was called pending a decision on the part of Earth to enforce its new insistence on water economy, by deciding upon a ration limit for scavenging, did not cast him entirely down.

The roof of the avenue was painted a luminous light blue, perhaps as an old-fashioned imitation of Earth's sky. Ted wasn't sure. The walls were lit with the store windows that pierced it.

Off in the distance, over the hum of traffic and the sloughing noise of people's feet passing him, he could hear the intermittent blasting as new channels were being bored into Mars' crust. All his life he remembered such blastings. The ground he walked on had been part of solid, unbroken rock when he was born. The city was growing and would keep on growing—if Earth would only let it.

He turned off at a cross street, narrower, not quite as brilliantly lit, shop windows giving way to apartment houses, each with its row of lights along the front façade. Shoppers and traffic gave way to slower-paced individuals and to squawling young-sters who had as yet evaded the maternal summons to the evening meal.

At the last minute, Long remembered the social amenities and stopped off at a corner water store.

He passed over his canteen. "Fill 'er up."

The plump storekeeper unscrewed the cap, cocked an eye into the opening. He shook it a little and let it gurgle. "Not much left," he said cheerfully.

"No," agreed Long.

The storekeeper trickled water in, holding the neck of the canteen close to the hose tip to avoid spillage. The volume gauge whirred. He screwed the cap back on.

Long passed over the coins and took his canteen. It clanked against his hip now with a pleasing heaviness. It would never do to visit a family without a full canteen. Among the boys, it didn't matter. Not as much, anyway.

He entered the hallway of No. 27, climbed a short flight of stairs, and paused with his thumb on the signal.

The sound of voices could be heard quite plainly.

One was a woman's voice, somewhat shrill. "It's all right for you to have your Scavenger friends here, isn't it? I'm supposed to be thankful you manage to get home two months a year. Oh, it's quite enough that you spend a day or two with me. After that, it's the Scavengers again."

"I've been home for a long time now," said a male voice, "and this is business. For Mars' sake, let up, Dora. They'll be here soon."

Long decided to wait a moment before signaling. It might give them a chance to hit a more neutral topic.

"What do I care if they come?" retorted Dora. "Let them hear me. And I'd just as soon the Commissioner kept the moratorium on permanently. You hear me?"

"And what would we live on?" came the male voice hotly. "You tell me that."

"I'll tell you. You can make a decent, honorable living right here on Mars, just like everybody else. I'm the only one in this apartment house that's a Scavenger widow. That's what I am—a widow. I'm worse than a widow, because if I were a widow, I'd at least have a chance to marry someone else— What did you say?"

"Nothing. Nothing at all."

"Oh, I know what you said. Now listen here, Dick Swenson—"

"I only said," cried Swenson, "that now I know why Scavengers usually don't marry."

"You shouldn't have either. I'm tired of having every person in the neighborhood pity me and smirk and ask when you're coming home. Other people can be mining engineers and administrators and even tunnel borers. At least tunnel borers' wives have a decent home life and their children don't grow up like vagabonds. Peter might as well not have a father—"

A thin boy-soprano voice made its way through the door. It was somewhat more distant, as though it were in another room. "Hey, Mom, what's a vagabond?"

Dora's voice rose a notch. "Peter! You keep your mind on your homework."

Swenson said in a low voice, "It's not right to talk this way in front of the kid. What kind of notions will he get about me?"

"Stay home then and teach him better notions."

Peter's voice called out again. "Hey, Mom, I'm going to be a Scavenger when I grow up."

Footsteps sounded rapidly. There was a momentary hiatus in the sounds, then a piercing, "Mom! Hey, Mom! Leggo my ear! What did I do?" and a snuffling silence.

Long seized the chance. He worked the signal vigorously.

Swenson opened the door, brushing down his hair with both hands.

"Hello, Ted," he said in a subdued voice. Then loudly, "Ted's here, Dora. Where's Mario, Ted?"

Long said, "He'll be here in a while."

Dora came bustling out of the next room, a small, dark woman with a pinched nose, and hair, just beginning to show touches of gray, combed off the forehead.

"Hello, Ted. Have you eaten?"

"Quite well, thanks. I haven't interrupted you, have I?"

"Not at all. We finished ages ago. Would you like some coffee?"

"I think so." Ted unslung his canteen and offered it.

"Oh, goodness, that's all right. We've plenty of water."

"I insist."

"Well, then—"

Back into the kitchen she went. Through the swinging door, Long caught a glimpse of dishes sitting in Secoterg, the "waterless cleaner that soaks up and absorbs grease and dirt in a twinkling. On ounce of water will rinse eight square feet of dish surface clean as clean. Buy Secoterg. Secoterg just cleans it

right, makes your dishes shiny bright, does away with water
waste—''

The tune started whining through his mind and Long crushed
it with speech. He said, ''How's Pete?''

''Fine, fine. The kid's in the fourth grade now. You know I
don't get to see him much. Well, sir, when I came back last
time, he looked at me and said . . .''

It went on for a while and wasn't too bad as bright sayings of
bright children as told by dull parents go.

The door signal burped and Mario Rioz came in, frowning and
red.

Swenson stepped to him quickly. ''Listen, don't say anything
about shell-snaring. Dora still remembers the time you fingered a
Class A shell out of my territory and she's in one of her moods
now.''

''Who the hell wants to talk about shells?'' Rioz slung off a
fur-lined jacket, threw it over the back of the chair, and sat
down.

Dora came through the swinging door, viewed the newcomer
with a synthetic smile, and said, ''Hello, Mario. Coffee for you,
too?''

''Yeah,'' he said, reaching automatically for his canteen.

''Just use some more of my water, Dora,'' said Long quickly.
''He'll owe it to me.''

''Yeah,'' said Rioz.

''What's wrong, Mario?'' asked Long.

Rioz said heavily, ''Go on. Say you told me so. A year ago
when Hilder made that speech, you told me so. Say it.''

Long shrugged.

Rioz said, ''They've set up the quota. Fifteen minutes ago the
news came out.''

''Well?''

''Fifty thousand tons of water per trip.''

''What?'' yelled Swenson, burning. ''You can't get off Mars
with fifty thousand!''

''That's the figure. It's a deliberate piece of gutting. No more
scavenging.''

Dora came out with the coffee and set it down all around.

'What's all this about no more scavenging?'' She sat down
very firmly and Swenson looked helpless.

''It seems,'' said Long, ''that they're rationing us at fifty
thousand tons and that means we can't make any more trips.''

"Well, what of it?" Dora sipped her coffee and smiled gaily. "If you want my opinion, it's a good thing. It's time all you Scavengers found yourselves a nice, steady job here on Mars. I mean it. It's no life to be running all over space—"

"Please, Dora," said Swenson.

Rioz came close to a snort.

Dora raised her eyebrows. "I'm just giving my opinions."

Long said, "Please feel free to do so. But I would like to say something. Fifty thousand is just a detail. We know that Earth—or at least Hilder's party—wants to make political capital out of a campaign for water economy, so we're in a bad hole. We've got to get water somehow or they'll shut us down altogether, right?"

"Well, sure," said Swenson.

"But the question is how, right?"

"If it's only getting water," said Rioz in a sudden gush of words, "there's only one thing to do and you know it. If the Grounders won't give us water, we'll take it. The water doesn't belong to them just because their fathers and grandfathers were too damned sick-yellow ever to leave their fat planet. Water belongs to people wherever they are. We're people and the water's ours, too. We have a right to it."

"How do you propose taking it?" asked Long.

"Easy! They've got oceans of water on Earth. They can't post a guard over every square mile. We can sink down on the night side of the planet any time we want, fill our shells, then get away. How can they stop us?"

"In half a dozen ways, Mario. How do you spot shells in space up to distances of a hundred thousand miles? One thin metal shell in all that space. How? By radar. Do you think there's no radar on Earth? Do you think that if Earth ever gets the notion we're engaged in waterlegging, it won't be simple for them to set up a radar network to spot ships coming in from space?"

Dora broke in indignantly. "I'll tell you one thing, Mario Rioz. My husband isn't going to be part of any raid to get water to keep up his scavenging with."

"It isn't just scavenging," said Mario. "Next they'll be cutting down on everything else. We've got to stop them now."

"But we don't need their water, anyway," said Dora. "We're not the Moon or Venus. We pipe enough water down from the polar caps for all we need. We have a water tap right in this apartment. There's one in every apartment on this block."

Long said, "Home use is the smallest part of it. The mines use water. And what do we do about the hydroponic tanks?"

"That's right," said Swenson. "What about the hydroponic tanks, Dora? They've got to have water and it's about time we arranged to grow our own fresh food instead of having to live on the condensed crud they ship us from Earth."

"Listen to him," said Dora scornfully. "What do you know about fresh food? You've never eaten any."

"I've eaten more than you think. Do you remember those carrots I picked up once?"

"Well, what was so wonderful about them? If you ask me, good baked protomeal is much better. And healthier, too. It just seems to be the fashion now to be talking fresh vegetables because they're increasing taxes for these hydroponics. Besides, all this will blow over."

Long said, "I don't think so. Not by itself, anyway. Hilder will probably be the next Co-ordinator, and then things may really get bad. If they cut down on food shipments, too—"

"Well, then," shouted Rioz, "what do we do? I still say take it! Take the water!"

"And I say we can't do that, Mario. Don't you see that what you're suggesting is the Earth way, the Grounder way? You're trying to hold on to the umbilical cord that ties Mars to Earth. Can't you get away from that? Can't you see the Martian way?"

"No, I can't. Suppose you tell me."

"I will, if you'll listen. When we think about the Solar System, what do we think about? Mercury, Venus, Earth, Moon, Mars, Phobos, and Deimos. There you are—seven bodies, that's all. But that doesn't represent 1 per cent of the Solar System. We Martians are right at the edge of the other 99 per cent. Out there, farther from the Sun, there's unbelievable amounts of water!"

The others stared.

Swenson said uncertainly, "You mean the layers of ice on Jupiter and Saturn?"

"Not that specifically, but it *is* water, you'll admit. A thousand-mile-thick layer of water is a lot of water."

"But it's all covered up with layers of amomonia or—or something, isn't it?" asked Swenson. "Besides, we can't land on the major planets."

"I know that," said Long, "but I haven't said that was the answer. The major planets aren't the only objects out there.

What about the asteroids and the satellites? Vesta is a two-hundred-mile-diameter asteroid that's hardly more than a chunk of ice. One of the moons of Saturn is mostly ice. How about that?''

Rioz said, ''Haven't you ever been in space, Ted?''

''You know I have. Why do you ask?''

''Sure, I know you have, but you still talk like a Grounder. Have you thought of the distances involved? The average asteroid is a hundred twenty million miles from Mars at the closest. That's twice the Venus-Mars hop and you know that hardly any liners do even that in one jump. They usually stop off at Earth or the Moon. After all, how long do you expect anyone to stay in space, man?''

''I don't know. What's your limit?''

''You know the limit. You don't have to ask me. It's six months. That's handbook data. After six months, if you're still in space, you're psychotherapy meat. Right, Dick?''

Swenson nodded.

''And that's just the asteroids,'' Rioz went on. ''From Mars to Jupiter is three hundred thirty million miles, and to Saturn it's seven hundred million. How can anyone handle that kind of distance? Suppose you hit standard velocity or, to make it even, say you get up to a good two hundred kilomiles an hour. It would take you—let's see, allowing time for acceleration and deceleration—about six or seven months to get to Jupiter and nearly a year to get to Saturn. Of course, you could hike the speed to a million miles an hour, theoretically, but where would you get the water to do that?''

''Gee,'' said a small voice attached to a smutty nose and round eyes. ''Saturn!''

Dora whirled in her chair. ''Peter, march right back into your room!''

''Aw, Ma.''

''Don't 'Aw, Ma' me.'' She began to get out of the chair, and Peter scuttled away.

Swenson said, ''Say, Dora, why don't you keep him company for a while? It's hard to keep his mind on homework if we're all out here talking.''

Dora sniffed obstinately and stayed put. ''I'll sit right here until I find out what Ted Long is thinking of. I tell you right now I don't like the sound of it.''

Swenson said nervously, ''Well, never mind Jupiter and Saturn.

I'm sure Ted isn't figuring on that. But what about Vesta? We could make it in ten or twelve weeks there and the same back. And two hundred miles in diameter. That's four million cubic miles of ice!''

"So what?" said Rioz. "What do we do on Vesta? Quarry the ice? Set up mining machinery? Say, do you know how long that would take?"

Long said, "I'm talking about Saturn, not Vesta."

Rioz addressed an unseen audience. "I tell him seven hundred million miles—and he keeps on talking."

"All right," said Long, "suppose you tell me how you know we can only stay in space six months, Mario?"

"It's common knowledge, damn it."

"Because it's in the *Handbook of Space Flight*. It's data compiled by Earth scientists from experience with Earth pilots and spacemen. You're still thinking Grounder style. You won't think the Martian way."

"A Martian may be a Martian, but he's still a man."

"But how can you be so blind? How many times have you fellows been out for over six months without a break?"

Rioz said, "That's different."

"Because you're Martians? Because you're professional Scavengers?"

"No. Because we're not on a flight. We can put back for Mars any time we want to."

"But you *don't* want to. That's my point. Earthmen have tremendous ships with libraries of films, with a crew of fifteen plus passengers. Still, they can only stay out six months maximum. Martian Scavengers have a two-room ship with only one partner. But we can stick it out more than six months."

Dora said, "I suppose you want to stay in a ship for a year and go to Saturn."

"Why not, Dora?" said Long. "We can do it. Don't you see we can? Earthmen can't. They've got a real world. They've got open sky and fresh food, all the air and water they want. Getting into a ship is a terrible change for them. More than six months is too much for them for that very reason. Martians are different. We've been living on a ship our entire lives.

"That's all Mars is—a ship. It's just a big ship forty-five hundred miles across with one tiny room in it occupied by fifty thousand people. It's closed in like a ship. We breathe packaged air and drink packaged water, which we repurify over and over.

We eat the same food rations we eat aboard ship. When we get into a ship, it's the same thing we've known all our lives. We can stand it for a lot more than a year if we have to."

Dora said, "Dick, too?"

"We all can."

"Well, Dick can't. It's all very well for you, Ted Long, and this shell stealer here, this Mario, to talk about jaunting off for a year. You're not married. Dick is. He has a wife and he has a child and that's enough for him. He can just get a regular job right here on Mars. Why, my goodness, suppose you go to Saturn and find there's no water there. How'll you get back? Even if you had water left, you'd be out of food. It's the most ridiculous thing I ever heard of."

"No. Now listen," said Long tightly. "I've thought this thing out. I've talked to Commissioner Sankov and he'll help. But we've got to have ships and men. I can't get them, The men won't listen to me. I'm green. You two are known and respected. You're veterans. If you back me, even if you don't go yourselves, if you'll just help me sell this thing to the rest, get volunteers—"

"First," said Rioz grumpily, "you'll have to do a lot more explaining. Once we get to Saturn, where's the water?"

"That's the beauty of it," said Long. "That's why it's got to be Saturn. The water there is just floating around in space for the taking."

5

When Hamish Sankov had come to Mars, there was no such thing as a native Martian. Now there were two-hundred-odd babies whose grandfathers had been born on Mars—native in the third generation.

When he had come as a boy in his teens, Mars had been scarcely more than a huddle of grounded spaceships connected by sealed underground tunnels. Through the years, he had seen buildings grow and burrow widely, thrusting blunt snouts up into the thin, unbreathable atmosphere. He had seen huge storage depots spring up into which spaceships and their loads could be swallowed whole. He had seen the mines grow from nothing to a huge gouge in the Martian crust, while the population of Mars grew from fifty to fifty thousand.

It made him feel old, these long memories—they and the even dimmer memories induced by the presence of this Earthman before him. His visitor brought up those long-forgotten scraps of thought about a soft-warm world that was as kind and gentle to mankind as the mother's womb.

The Earthman seemed fresh from that womb. Not very tall, not very lean; in fact, distinctly plump. Dark hair with a neat little wave in it, a neat little mustache, and neatly scrubbed skin. His clothing was right in style and as fresh and neatly turned as plastek could be.

Sankov's own clothes were of Martian manufacture, serviceable and clean, but many years behind the times. His face was craggy and lined; his hair was pure white; and his Adam's apple wobbled when he talked.

The Earthman was Myron Digby, member of Earth's General Assembly. Sankov was Martian Commissioner.

Sankov said, "This all hits us hard, Assemblyman."

"It's hit most of us hard, too, Commissioner."

"Uh-huh. Can't honestly say then that I can make it out. Of course, you understand, I don't make out that I can understand Earth ways, for all that I was born there. Mars is a hard place to live, Assemblyman, and you have to understand that. It takes a lot of shipping space just to bring us food, water, and raw materials so we can live. There's not much room left for books and news films. Even video programs can't reach Mars, except for about a month when Earth is in conjunction, and even then nobody has much time to listen.

"My office gets a weekly summary film from Planetary Press. Generally, I don't have time to pay attention to it. Maybe you'd call us provincial, and you'd be right. When something like this happens, all we can do is kind of helplessly look at each other."

Digby said slowly, "You can't mean that your people on Mars haven't heard of Hilder's anti-Waster campaign."

"No, can't exactly say that. There's a young Scavenger, son of a good friend of mine who died in space"—Sankov scratched the side of his neck doubtfully—"who makes a hobby out of reading up on Earth history and things like that. He catches video broadcasts when he's out in space and he listened to this man Hilder. Near as I can make out, that was the first talk Hilder made about Wasters.

"The young fellow came to me with that. Naturally, I didn't take him very serious. I kept an eye on the Planetary Press films for a while after that, but there wasn't much mention of Hilder and what there was made him out to look pretty funny.''

"Yes, Commissioner," said Digby, "it all seemed quite a joke when it started."

Sankov stretched out a pair of long legs to one side of his desk and crossed them at the ankles. "Seems to me it's still pretty much of a joke. What's his argument? We're using up water. Has he tried looking at some figures? I got them all here. Had them brought to me when this committee arrived.

"Seems that Earth has four hundred million cubic miles of water in its oceans and each cubic mile weighs four and a half billion tons. That's a lot of water. Now we use some of that heap in space flight. Most of the thrust is inside Earth's gravitational field, and that means the water thrown out finds its way back to the oceans. Hilder doesn't figure that in. When he says a million tons of water is used up per flight, he's a liar. It's less than a hundred thousand tons.

"Suppose, now, we have fifty thousand flights a year. We don't, of course; not even fifteen hundred. But let's say there are fifty thousand. I figure there's going to be considerable expansion as time goes on. With fifty thousand flights, one cubic mile of water would be lost to space each year. That means that in a million years, Earth would lose *one quarter of 1 per cent* of its total water supply!"

Digby spread his hands, palms upward, and let them drop. "Commissioner, Interplanetary Alloys has used figures like that in their campaign against Hilder, but you can't fight a tremendous, emotion-filled drive with cold mathematics. This man Hilder has invented a name, 'Wasters.' Slowly he has built this name up into a gigantic conspiracy; a gang of brutal, profit-seeking wretches raping Earth for their own immediate benefit.

"He has accused the government of being riddled with them, the Assembly of being dominated by them, the press of being owned by them. None of this, unfortunately, seems ridiculous to the average man. He knows all too well what selfish men can do to Earth's resources. He knows what happened to Earth's oil during the Time of Trouble, for instance, and the way topsoil was ruined.

"When a farmer experiences a drought, he doesn't care that the amount of water lost in space flight isn't a droplet in a fog as far as Earth's over-all water supply is concerned. Hilder has given him something to blame and that's the strongest possible consolation for disaster. He isn't going to give that up for a diet of figures.''

Sankov said, "That's where I get puzzled. Maybe it's because I don't know how things work on Earth, but it seems to me that there aren't just droughty farmers there. As near as I could make out from the news summaries, these Hilder people are a minority. Why is it Earth goes along with a few farmers and some crackpots that egg them on?''

"Because, Commissioner, there are such things as worried human beings. The steel industry sees that an era of space flight will stress increasingly the light, nonferrous alloys. The various miners' unions worry about extraterrestrial competition. Any Earthman who can't get aluminum to build a prefab is certain that it is because the aluminum is going to Mars. I know a professor of archaeology who's an anti-Waster because he can't get a government grant to cover his excavations. He's convinced that all government money is going into rocketry research and space medicine and he resents it.''

Sankov said, "That doesn't sound like Earth people are much different from us here on Mars. But what about the General Assembly? Why do they have to go along with Hilder?''

Digby smiled sourly. "Politics isn't pleasant to explain. Hilder introduced this bill to set up a committee to investigate waste in space flight. Maybe three fourths or more of the General Assembly was against such an investigation as an intolerable and useless extension of bureaucracy—which it is. But then how could any legislator be against a mere investigation of waste? It would sound as though he had something to fear or to conceal. It would sound as though he were himself profiting from waste. Hilder is not in the least afraid of making such accusations, and whether true or not, they would be a powerful factor with the voters in the next election. The bill passed.

"And then there came the question of appointing the members of the committee. Those who were against Hilder shied away from membership, which would have meant decisions that would be continually embarrassing. Remaining on the side lines would make that one that much less a target for Hilder. The result is that I am the only member of the committee who is outspokenly anti-Hilder and it may cost me re-election.''

Sankov said, "I'd be sorry to hear that, Assemblyman. It looks as though Mars didn't have as many friends as we thought we had. We wouldn't like to lose one. But if Hilder wins out, what's he after, anyway?''

"I should think," said Digby, "that that is obvious. He wants to be the next Global Co-ordinator."

"Think he'll make it?"

"If nothing happens to stop him, he will."

"And then what? Will he drop this Waster campaign then?"

"I can't say. I don't know if he's laid his plans past the Co-ordinacy. Still, if you want my guess, he couldn't abandon the campaign and maintain his popularity. It's gotten out of hand."

Sankov scratched the side of his neck. "All right. In that case, I'll ask you for some advice. What can we folks on Mars do? You know Earth. You know the situation. We don't. Tell us what to do."

Digby rose and stepped to the window. He looked out upon the low domes of other buildings; red, rocky, completely desolate plain in between; a purple sky and a shrunken sun.

He said, without turning, "Do you people really like it on Mars?"

Sankov smiled. "Most of us don't exactly know any other world, Assemblyman. Seems to me Earth would be something queer and uncomfortable to them."

"But wouldn't Martians get used to it? Earth isn't hard to take after this. Wouldn't your people learn to enjoy the privilege of breathing air under an open sky? You once lived on Earth. You remember what it was like."

"I sort of remember. Still, it doesn't seem to be easy to explain. Earth is just there. It fits people and people fit it. People take Earth the way they find it. Mars is different. It's sort of raw and doesn't fit people. People got to make something out of it. They got to *build* a world, and not take what they find. Mars isn't much yet, but we're building, and when we're finished, we're going to have just what we like. It's sort of a great feeling to know you're building a world. Earth would be kind of unexciting after that."

The Assemblyman said, "Surely the ordinary Martian isn't such a philosopher that he's content to live this terribly hard life for the sake of a future that must be hundreds of generations away."

"No-o, not just like that." Sankov put his right ankle on his left knee and cradled it as he spoke. "Like I said, Martians are a lot like Earthmen, which means they're sort of human beings, and human beings don't go in for philosophy much. Just the same, there's something to living in a growing world, whether you think about it much or not.

"My father used to send me letters when I first came to Mars. He was an accountant and he just sort of stayed an accountant. Earth wasn't much different when he died from what it was when he was born. He didn't see anything happen. Every day was like every other day, and living was just a way of passing time until he died.

"On Mars, it's different. Every day there's something new— the city's bigger, the ventilation system gets another kick, the water lines from the poles get slicked up. Right now, we're planning to set up a news-film association of our own. We're going to call it Mars Press. If you haven't lived when things are growing all about you, you'll never understand how wonderful it feels.

"No, Assemblyman, Mars is hard and tough and Earth is a lot more comfortable, but seems to me if you take our boys to Earth, they'll be unhappy. They probably wouldn't be able to figure out why, most of them, but they'd feel lost; lost and useless. Seems to me lots of them would never make the adjustment."

Digby turned away from the window and the smooth, pink skin of his forehead was creased into a frown. "In that case, Commissioner, I am sorry for you. For all of you."

"Why?"

"Because I don't think there's anything your people on Mars can do. Or the people on the Moon or Venus. It won't happen now; maybe it won't happen for a year or two, or even for five years. But pretty soon you'll all have to come back to Earth, unless—"

Sankov's white eyebrows bent low over his eyes. "Well?"

"Unless you can find another source of water besides the planet Earth."

Sankov shook his head. "Don't seem likely, does it?"

"Not very."

"And except for that, seems to you there's no chance?"

"None at all."

Digby said that and left, and Sankov stared for a long time at nothing before he punched a combination of the local communiline.

After a while, Ted Long looked out at him.

Sankov said, "You were right, son. There's nothing they can do. Even the ones that mean well see no way out. How did you know?"

"Commissioner," said Long, "when you've read all you can about the Time of Troubles, particularly about the twentieth century, nothing political can come as a real surprise."

"Well, maybe. Anyway, son, Assemblyman Digby is sorry for us, quite a piece sorry, you might say, but that's all. He says we'll have to leave Mars—or else get water somewhere else. Only he thinks that we can't get water somewhere else."

"You know we can, don't you, Commissioner?"

"I know we *might*, son. It's a terrible risk."

"If I find enough volunteers, the risk is our business."

"How is it going?"

"Not bad. Some of the boys are on my side right now. I talked Mario Rioz into it, for instance, and you know he's one of the best."

"That's just it—the volunteers will be the best men we have. I hate to allow it."

"If we get back, it will be worth it."

"If! It's a big word, son."

"And a big thing we're trying to do."

"Well, I gave my word that if there was no help on Earth, I'll see that the Phobos water hole lets you have all the water you'll need. Good luck."

6

Half a million miles above Saturn, Mario Rioz was cradled on nothing and sleep was delicious. He came out of it slowly and for a while, alone in his suit, he counted the stars and traced lines from one to another.

At first, as the weeks flew past, it was scavenging all over again, except for the gnawing feeling that every minute meant an additional number of thousands of miles away from all humanity. That made it worse.

They had aimed high to pass out of the ecliptic while moving through the Asteroid Belt. That had used up water and had probably been unnecessary. Although tens of thousands of worldlets look as thick as vermin in two-dimensional projection upon a photographic plate, they are nevertheless scattered so thinly through the quadrillions of cubic miles that make up their conglomerate orbit that only the most ridiculous of coincidences would have brought about a collision.

Still, they passed over the Belt and someone calculated the chances of collision with a fragment of matter large enough to do damage. The value was so low, so impossibly low, that it was perhaps inevitable that the notion of the "space-float" should occur to someone.

The days were long and many, space was empty, only one man was needed at the controls at any one time. The thought was a natural.

First, it was a particularly daring one who ventured out for fifteen minutes or so. Then another who tried half an hour. Eventually, before the asteroids were entirely behind, each ship regularly had its off-watch member suspended in space at the end of a cable.

It was easy enough. The cable, one of those intended for operations at the conclusion of their journey, was magnetically attached at both ends, one to the space suit to start with. Then you clambered out the lock onto the ship's hull and attached the other end there. You paused awhile, clinging to the metal skin by the electromagnets in your boots. Then you neutralized those and made the slightest muscular effort.

Slowly, ever so slowly, you lifted from the ship and even more slowly the ship's larger mass moved an equivalently shorter distance downward. You floated incredibly, weightlessly, in solid, speckled black. When the ship had moved far enough away from you, your gauntleted hand, which kept touch upon the cable, tightened its grip slightly. Too tightly, and you would begin moving back toward the ship and it toward you. Just tightly enough, and friction would halt you. Because your motion was equivalent to that of the ship, it seemed as motionless below you as though it had been painted against an impossible background while the cable between you hung in coils that had no reason to straighten out.

It was a half-ship to your eye. One half was lit by the light of the feeble Sun, which was still too bright to look at directly without the heavy protection of the polarized space-suit visor. The other half was black on black, invisible.

Space closed in and it was like sleep. Your suit was warm, it renewed its air automatically, it had food and drink in special containers from which it could be sucked with a minimal motion of the head, it took care of wastes appropriately. Most of all, more than anything else, there was the delightful euphoria of weightlessness.

You never felt so well in your life. The days stopped being too long, they weren't long enough, and there weren't enough of them.

They had passed Jupiter's orbit at a spot some 30 degrees from its then position. For months, it was the brightest object in the sky, always excepting the glowing white pea that was the Sun. At its brightest, some of the Scavengers insisted they could make out Jupiter as a tiny sphere, one side squashed out of true by the night shadow.

Then over a period of additional months it faded, while another dot of light grew until it was brighter than Jupiter. It was Saturn, first as a dot of brilliance, then as an oval, glowing splotch.

("Why oval?" someone asked, and after a while, someone else said, "The rings, of course," and it was obvious.)

Everyone space-floated at all possible times toward the end, watching Saturn incessantly.

("Hey, you jerk, come on back in, damn it. You're on duty." "Who's on duty? I've got fifteen minutes more by my watch." "You set your watch back. Besides, I gave you twenty minutes yesterday." "You wouldn't give two minutes to your grandmother." "Come on in, damn it, or I'm coming out anyway." "All right, I'm coming. Holy howlers, what a racket over a lousy minute." But no quarrel could possibly be serious, not in space. It felt too good.)

Saturn grew until at last it rivaled and then surpassed the Sun. The rings, set at a broad angle to their trajectory of approach, swept grandly about the planet, only a small portion being eclipsed. Then, as they approached, the span of the rings grew still wider, yet narrower as the angle of approach constantly decreased.

The larger moons showed up in the surrounding sky like serene fireflies.

Mario Rioz was glad he was awake so that he could watch again.

Saturn filled half the sky, streaked with orange, the night

shadow cutting it fuzzily nearly one quarter of the way in from the right. Two round little dots in the brightness were shadows of two of the moons. To the left and behind him (he could look over his left shoulder to see, and as he did so, the rest of his body inched slightly to the right to conserve angular momentum) was the white diamond of the Sun.

Most of all he liked to watch the rings. At the left, they emerged from behind Saturn, a tight, bright triple band of orange light. At the right, their beginnings were hidden in the night shadow, but showed up closer and broader. They widened as they came, like the flare of a horn, growing hazier as they approached, until, while the eye followed them, they seemed to fill the sky and lose themselves.

From the position of the Scavenger fleet just inside the outer rim of the outermost ring, the rings broke up and assumed their true identity as a phenomenal cluster of solid fragments rather than the tight, solid band of light they seemed.

Below him, or rather in the direction his feet pointed, some twenty miles away, was one of the ring fragments. It looked like a large, irregular splotch, marring the symmetry of space, three quarters in brightness and the night shadow cutting it like a knife. Other fragments were farther off, sparkling like stardust, dimmer and thicker, until, as you followed them down, they became rings once more.

The fragments were motionless, but that was only because the ships had taken up an orbit about Saturn equivalent to that of the outer edge of the rings.

The day before, Rioz reflected, he had been on that nearest fragment, working along with more than a score of others to mold it into the desired shape. Tomorrow he would be at it again.

Today—today he was space-floating.

"Mario?" The voice that broke upon his earphones was questioning.

Momentarily Rioz was flooded with annoyance. Damn it, he wasn't in the mood for company.

"Speaking," he said.

"I thought I had your ship spotted. How are you?"

"Fine. That you, Ted?"

"That's right," said Long.

"Anything wrong on the fragment?"

"Nothing. I'm out here floating."

"You?"

"It gets me, too, occasionally. Beautiful, isn't it?"

"Nice," agreed Rioz.

"You know, I've read Earth books—"

"Grounder books, you mean." Rioz yawned and found it difficult under the circumstances to use the expression with the proper amount of resentment.

"—and sometimes I read descriptions of people lying on grass," continued Long. "You know that green stuff like thin, long pieces of paper they have all over the ground down there, and they look up at the blue sky with clouds in it. Did you ever see any films of that?"

"Sure. It didn't attract me. It looked cold."

"I suppose it isn't, though. After all, Earth is quite close to the Sun, and they say their atmosphere is thick enough to hold the heat. I must admit that personally I would hate to be caught under open sky with nothing on but clothes. Still, I imagine they like it."

"Grounders are nuts!"

"They talk about the trees, big brown stalks, and the winds, air movements, you know."

"You mean drafts. They can keep that, too."

"It doesn't matter. The point is they describe it beautifully, almost passionately. Many times I've wondered, 'What's it really like? Will I ever feel it or is this something only Earthmen can possibly feel?' I've felt so often that I was missing something vital. Now I know what it must be like. It's this. Complete peace in the middle of a beauty-drenched universe."

Rioz said, "They wouldn't like it. The Grounders, I mean. They're so used to their own lousy little world they wouldn't appreciate what it's like to float and look down on Saturn." He flipped his body slightly and began swaying back and forth about his center of mass, slowly, soothingly.

Long said, "Yes, I think so too. They're slaves to their planet. Even if they come to Mars, it will only be their children that are free. There'll be starships someday; great, huge things that can carry thousands of people and maintain their self-contained equilibrium for decades, maybe centuries. Mankind will spread through the whole Galaxy. But people will have to live their lives out on shipboard until new methods of interstellar travel are developed, so it will be Martians, not planet-bound Earthmen, who will colonize the Universe. That's inevitable. It's got to be. It's the Martian way.''

But Rioz made no answer. He had dropped off to sleep again, rocking and swaying gently, half a million miles above Saturn.

7

The work shift of the ring fragment was the tail of the coin. The weightlessness, peace, and privacy of the space-float gave place to something that had neither peace nor privacy. Even the weightlessness, which continued, became more a purgatory than a paradise under the new conditions.

Try to manipulate an ordinarily non-portable heat projector. It could be lifted despite the fact that it was six feet high and wide and almost solid metal, since it weighed only a fraction of an ounce. But its inertia was exactly what it had always been, which meant that if it wasn't moved into position very slowly, it would just keep on going, taking you with it. Then you would have to hike the pseudo-grav field of your suit and come down with a jar.

Keralski had hiked the field a little too high and he came down a little too roughly, with the projector coming down with him at a dangerous angle. His crushed ankle had been the first casualty of the expedition.

Rioz was swearing fluently and nearly continuously. He continued to have the impulse to drag the back of his hand across his forehead in order to wipe away the accumulating sweat. The few times that he had succumbed to the impulse, metal had met silicone with a clash that rang loudly inside his suit, but served no useful purpose. The desiccators within the suit were sucking at maximum and, of course, recovering the water and restoring ion-exchanged liquid, containing a careful proportion of salt, into the appropriate receptacle.

Rioz yelled, "Damn it, Dick, wait till I give the word, will you?"

And Swenson's voice rang in his ears, "Well, how long am I supposed to sit here?"

"Till I say," replied Rioz.

He strengthened pseudo-grav and lifted the projector a bit. He released pseudo-grav, insuring that the projector would stay in place for minutes even if he withdrew support altogether. He kicked the cable out of the way (it stretched beyond the close "horizon" to a power source that was out of sight) and touched the release.

The material of which the fragment was composed bubbled and vanished under its touch. A section of the lip of the tremendous cavity he had already carved into its substance melted away and a roughness in its contour had disappeared.

"Try it now," called Rioz.

Swenson was in the ship that was hovering nearly over Rioz's head.

Swenson called, "All clear?"

"I told you to go ahead."

It was a feeble flicker of steam that issued from one of the ship's forward vents. The ship drifted down toward the ring fragment. Another flicker adjusted a tendency to drift sidewise. It came down straight.

A third flicker to the rear slowed it to a feather rate.

Rioz watched tensely. "Keep her coming. You'll make it. You'll make it."

The rear of the ship entered the hole, nearly filling it. The bellying walls came closer and closer to its rim. There was a grinding vibration as the ship's motion halted.

It was Swenson's turn to curse. "It doesn't fit," he said.

Rioz threw the projector groundward in a passion and went flailing up into space. The projector kicked up a white crystalline dust all about it, and when Rioz came down under pseudo-grav, he did the same.

He said, "You went in on the bias, you dumb Grounder."

"I hit it level, you dirt-eating farmer."

Backward-pointing side jets of the ship were blasting more strongly than before, and Rioz hopped to get out of the way.

The ship scraped up from the pit, then shot into space half a mile before forward jets could bring it to a halt.

Swenson said tensely, "We'll spring half a dozen plates if we do this once again. Get it right, will you?"

"I'll get it right. Don't worry about it. Just you come in right."

Rioz jumped upward and allowed himself to climb three hundred yards to get an over-all look at the cavity. The gouge marks of the ship were plain enough. They were concentrated at one point halfway down the pit. He would get that.

It began to melt outward under the blaze of the projector.

Half an hour later the ship snuggled neatly into its cavity, and Swenson, wearing his spacesuit, emerged to join Rioz.

Swenson said, "If you want to step in and climb out of the suit, I'll take care of the icing."

"It's all right," said Rioz. "I'd just as soon sit here and watch Saturn."

He sat down at the lip of the pit. There was a six-foot gap between it and the ship. In some places about the circle, it was two feet; in a few places, even merely a matter of inches. You couldn't expect a better fit out of handwork. The final adjustment would be made by steaming ice gently and letting it freeze into the cavity between the lip and the ship.

Saturn moved visibly across the sky, its vast bulk inching below the horizon.

Rioz said, "How many ships are left to put in place?"

Swenson said, "Last I heard, it was eleven. We're in now, so that means only ten. Seven of the ones that are placed are iced in. Two or three are dismantled."

"We're coming along fine."

"There's plenty to do yet. Don't forget the main jets at the other end. And the cables and the power lines. Sometimes I wonder if we'll make it. On the way out, it didn't bother me so much, but just now I was sitting at the controls and I was saying, 'We won't make it. We'll sit out here and starve and die with nothing but Saturn over us.' It makes me feel—"

He didn't explain how it made him feel. He just sat there.

Rioz said, "You think too damn much."

"It's different with you," said Swenson. "I keep thinking of Pete—and Dora."

"What for? She said you could go, didn't she? The Commissioner gave her that talk on patriotism and how you'd be a hero and set for life once you got back, and she said you could go. You didn't sneak out the way Adams did."

"Adams is different. That wife of his should have been shot when she was born. Some women can make hell for a guy, can't they? She didn't want him to go—but she'd probably rather he didn't come back if she can get his settlement pay."

"What's your kick, then? Dora wants you back, doesn't she?"

Swenson sighed. "I never treated her right."

"You turned over your pay, it seems to me. I wouldn't do that for any woman. Money for value received, not a cent more."

"Money isn't it. I get to thinking out here. A woman likes company. A kid needs his father. What am I doing 'way out here?''

"Getting set to go home.''

"Ah-h, you don't understand.''

8

Ted Long wandered over the ridged surface of the ring fragment with his spirits as icy as the ground he walked on. It had all seemed perfectly logical back on Mars, but that was Mars. He had worked it out carefully in his mind in perfectly reasonable steps. He could still remember exactly how it went.

It didn't take a ton of water to move a ton of ship. It was not mass equals mass, but mass times velocity equals mass times velocity. It didn't matter, in other words, whether you shot out a ton of water at a mile a second or a hundred pounds of water at twenty miles a second. You got the same final velocity out of the ship.

That meant the jet nozzles had to be made narrower and the steam hotter. But then drawbacks appeared. The narrower the nozzle, the more energy was lost in friction and turbulence. The hotter the steam, the more refractory the nozzle had to be and the shorter its life. The limit in that direction was quickly reached.

Then, since a given weight of water could move considerably more than its own weight under the narrow-nozzle conditions, it paid to be big. The bigger the water-storage space, the larger the size of the actual travel-head, even in proportion. So they started to make liners heavier and bigger. But then the larger the shell, the heavier the bracings, the more difficult the weldings, the more exacting the engineering requirements. At the moment, the limit in that direction had been reached also.

And then he had put his finger on what had seemed to him to be the basic flaw—the original unswervable conception that the fuel had to be placed *inside* the ship; the metal had to be built to encircle a million tons of water.

Why? Water did not have to be water. It could be ice, and ice could be shaped. Holes could be melted into it. Travel-heads and jets could be fitted into it. Cables could hold travel-heads and jets stiffly together under the influence of magnetic field-force grips.

Long felt the trembling of the ground he walked on. He was at the head of the fragment. A dozen ships were blasting in and out of sheaths carved in its substance, and the fragment shuddered under the continuing impact.

The ice didn't have to be quarried. It existed in proper chunks in the rings of Saturn. That's all the rings were—pieces of nearly pure ice, circling Saturn. So spectroscopy stated and so it had turned out to be. He was standing on one such piece now, over two miles long, nearly one mile thick. It was almost half a billion tons of water, all in one piece, and he was standing on it.

But now he was face to face with the realities of life. He had never told the men just how quickly he had expected to set up the fragment as a ship, but in his heart, he had imagined it would be two days. It was a week now and he didn't dare to estimate the remaining time. He no longer even had any confidence that the task was a possible one. Would they be able to control jets with enough delicacy through leads slung across two miles of ice to manipulate out of Saturn's dragging gravity?

Drinking water was low, though they could always distill more out of the ice. Still, the food stores were not in a good way either.

He paused, looked up into the sky, eyes straining. *Was* the object growing larger? He ought to measure its distance. Actually, he lacked the spirit to add that trouble to the others. His mind slid back to greater immediacies.

Morale, at least, was high. The men seemed to enjoy being out Saturn way. They were the first humans to penetrate this far, the first to pass the asteroids, the first to see Jupiter like a glowing pebble to the naked eye, the first to see Saturn—like that.

He didn't think fifty practical, case-hardened, shell-snatching Scavengers would take time to feel that sort of emotion. But they did. And they were proud.

Two men and a half-buried ship slid up the moving horizon as he walked.

He called crisply, "Hello, there!"

Rioz answered, "That you, Ted?"

"You bet. Is that Dick with you?"

"Sure. Come on, sit down. We were just getting ready to ice in and we were looking for an excuse to delay."

"I'm not," said Swenson promptly. "When will we be leaving, Ted?"

"As soon as we get through. That's no answer, is it?"

Swenson said dispiritedly, "I suppose there isn't any other answer."

Long looked up, staring at the irregular bright splotch in the sky.

Rioz followed his glance. "What's the matter?"

For a moment, Long did not reply. The sky was black otherwise and the ring fragments were an orange dust against it. Saturn was more than three fourths below the horizon and the rings were going with it. Half a mile away a ship bounded past the icy rim of the planetoid into the sky, was orange-lit by Saturn-light, and sank down again.

The ground trembled gently.

Rioz said, "Something bothering you about the Shadow?"

They called it that. It was the nearest fragment of the rings, quite close considering that they were at the outer rim of the rings, where the pieces spread themselves relatively thin. It was perhaps twenty miles off, a jagged mountain, its shape clearly visible.

"How does it look to you?" asked Long.

Rioz shrugged. "Okay, I guess. I don't see anything wrong."

"Doesn't it seem to be getting larger?"

"Why should it?"

"Well, doesn't it?" Long insisted.

Rioz and Swenson stared at it thoughtfully.

"It does look bigger," said Swenson.

"You're just putting the notion into our minds," Rioz argued. "If it were getting bigger, it would be coming closer."

"What's impossible about that?"

"These things are on stable orbits."

"They were when we came here," said Long. "There, did you feel that?"

The ground had trembled again.

Long said, "We've been blasting this thing for a week now. First, twenty-five ships landed on it, which changed its momentum right there. Not much, of course. Then we've been melting parts of it away and our ships have been blasting in and out of it—all at one end, too. In a week, we may have changed its orbit just a bit. The two fragments, this one and the Shadow, might be converging."

"It's got plenty of room to miss us in." Rioz watched it thoughtfully. "Besides, if we can't even tell for sure that it's getting bigger, how quickly can it be moving? Relative to us, I mean."

"It doesn't have to be moving quickly. Its momentum is as large as ours, so that, however gently it hits, we'll be nudged completely out of our orbit, maybe in toward Saturn, where we don't want to go. As a matter of fact, ice has a very low tensile strength, so that both planetoids might break up into gravel."

Swenson rose to his feet. "Damn it, if I can tell how a shell is moving a thousand miles away, I can tell what a mountain is doing twenty miles away." He turned toward the ship.

Long didn't stop him.

Rioz said, "There's a nervous guy."

The neighboring planetoid rose to zenith, passed overhead, began sinking. Twenty minutes later, the horizon opposite that portion behind which Saturn had disappeared burst into orange flame as its bulk began lifting again.

Rioz called into his radio, "Hey, Dick, are you dead in there?"

"I'm checking," came the muffled response.

"Is it moving?" asked Long.

"Yes."

"Toward us?"

There was a pause. Swenson's voice was a sick one. "On the nose, Ted. Intersection of orbits will take place in three days."

"You're crazy!" yelled Rioz.

"I checked four times," said Swenson.

Long thought blankly, What do we do now?

9

Some of the men were having trouble with the cables. They had to be laid precisely; their geometry had to be very nearly perfect for the magnetic field to attain maximum strength. In space, or even in air, it wouldn't have mattered. The cables would have lined up automatically once the juice went on.

Here it was different. A gouge had to be plowed along the planetoid's surface and into it the cable had to be laid. If it was not lined up within a few minutes of arc of the calculated direction, a torque would be applied to the entire planetoid, with consequent loss of energy, none of which could be spared. The gouges then had to be redriven, the cables shifted and iced into the new positions.

The men plodded wearily through the routine.

And then the word reached them:

"All hands to the jets!"

Scavengers could not be said to be the type that took kindly to discipline. It was a grumbling, growling, muttering group that set about disassembling the jets of the ships that yet remained intact, carrying them to the tail end of the planetoid, grubbing them into position, and stringing the leads along the surface.

It was almost twenty-four hours before one of them looked into the sky and said, "Holy jeepers!" followed by something less printable.

His neighbor looked and said, "I'll be damned!"

Once they noticed, all did. It became the most astonishing fact in the Universe.

"Look at the Shadow!"

It was spreading across the sky like an infected wound. Men looked at it, found it had doubled its size, wondered why they hadn't noticed that sooner.

Work came to a virtual halt. They besieged Ted Long.

He said, "We can't leave. We don't have the fuel to see us back to Mars and we don't have the equipment to capture another planetoid. So we've got to stay. Now the Shadow is creeping in on us because our blasting has thrown us out of orbit. We've got to change that by continuing the blasting. Since we can't blast the front end any more without endangering the ship we're building, let's try another way."

They went back to work on the jets with a furious energy that received impetus every half hour when the Shadow rose again over the horizon, bigger and more menacing than before.

Long had no assurance that it would work. Even if the jets would respond to the distant controls, even if the supply of water, which depended upon a storage chamber opening directly into the icy body of the planetoid, with built-in heat projectors steaming the propulsive fluid directly into the driving cells, were adequate, there was still no certainty that the body of the planetoid without a magnetic cable sheathing would hold together under the enormously disruptive stresses.

"Ready!" came the signal in Long's receiver.

Long called, "Ready!" and depressed the contact.

The vibration grew about him. The star field in the visiplate trembled.

In the rearview, there was a distant gleaming spume of swiftly moving ice crystals.

"It's blowing!" was the cry.

It kept on blowing. Long dared not stop. For six hours, it blew, hissing, bubbling, steaming into space; the body of the planetoid converted to vapor and hurled away.

The Shadow came closer until men did nothing but stare at the mountain in the sky, surpassing Saturn itself in spectacularity. Its every groove and valley was a plain scar upon its face. But when it passed through the planetoid's orbit, it crossed more than half a mile behind its then position.

The steam jet ceased.

Long bent in his seat and covered his eyes. He hadn't eaten in two days. He could eat now, though. Not another planetoid was close enough to interrupt them, even if it began an approach that very moment.

Back on the planetoid's surface, Swenson said, "All the time I watched that damned rock coming down, I kept saying to myself, 'This can't happen. We can't let it happen.' ".

"Hell," said Rioz, "we were all nervous. Did you see Jim Davis? He was green. I was a little jumpy myself."

"That's not it. It wasn't just—dying, you know. I was thinking—I know it's funny, but I can't help it—I was thinking that Dora warned me I'd get myself killed. She'll never let me hear the last of it. Isn't that a crummy sort of attitude at a time like that?"

"Listen," said Rioz, "you wanted to get married, so you got married. Why come to me with your troubles?"

10

The flotilla, welded into a single unit, was returning over its mighty course from Saturn to Mars. Each day it flashed over a length of space it had taken nine days outward.

Ted Long had put the entire crew on emergency. With twenty-five ships embedded in the planetoid taken out of Saturn's rings and unable to move or maneuver independently, the co-ordination of their power sources into unified blasts was a ticklish problem.

The jarring that took place on the first day of travel nearly shook them out from under their hair.

That, at least, smoothed itself out as the velocity raced upward under the steady thrust from behind. They passed the one-hundred-thousand-mile-an-hour mark late on the second day, and climbed steadily toward the million-mile mark and beyond.

Long's ship, which formed the needle point of the frozen fleet, was the only one which possessed a five-way view of space. It was an uncomfortable position under the circumstances. Long found himself watching tensely, imagining somehow that the stars would slowly begin to slip backward, to whizz past them, under the influence of the multi-ship's tremendous rate of travel.

They didn't, of course. They remained nailed to the black backdrop, their distance scorning with patient immobility any speed mere man could achieve.

The men complained bitterly after the first few days. It was not only that they were deprived of the space-float. They were burdened by much more than the ordinary psuedo-gravity field of the ships, by the effects of the fierce acceleration under which they were living. Long himself was weary to death of the relentless pressure against hydraulic cushions.

They took to shutting off the jet thrusts one hour out of every four and Long fretted.

It had been just over a year that he had last seen Mars shrinking in an observation window from this ship, which had then been an independent entity. What had happened since then? Was the colony still there?

In something like a growing panic, Long sent out radio pulses toward Mars daily, with the combined power of twenty-five ships behind it. There was no answer. He expected none. Mars and Saturn were on opposite sides of the Sun now, and until he mounted high enough above the ecliptic to get the Sun well beyond the line connecting himself and Mars, solar interference would prevent any signal from getting through.

High above the outer rim of the Asteroid Belt, they reached maximum velocity. With short spurts of power from first one side jet, then another, the huge vessel reversed itself. The composite jet in the rear began its mighty roaring once again, but now the result was deceleration.

They passed a hundred million miles over the Sun, curving down to intersect the orbit of Mars.

*   *   *

A week out of Mars, answering signals were heard for the first time, fragmentary, ether-torn, and incomprehensible, but they were coming from Mars. Earth and Venus were at angles sufficiently different to leave no doubt of that.

Long relaxed. There were still humans on Mars, at any rate.

Two days out of Mars, the signal was strong and clear and Sankov was at the other end.

Sankov said, "Hello, son. It's three in the morning here. Seems like people have no consideration for an old man. Dragged me right out of bed."

"I'm sorry, sir."

"Don't be. They were following orders. I'm afraid to ask, son. Anyone hurt? Maybe dead?"

"No deaths, sir. Not one."

"And—and the water? Any left?"

Long said, with an effort at nonchalance, "Enough."

"In that case, get home as fast as you can. Don't take any chances, of course."

"There's trouble, then."

"Fair to middling. When will you come down?"

"Two days. Can you hold out that long?"

"I'll hold out."

Forty hours later Mars had grown to a ruddy-orange ball that filled the ports and they were in the final planet-landing spiral.

"Slowly," Long said to himself, "slowly." Under these conditions, even the thin atmosphere of Mars could do dreadful damage if they moved through it too quickly.

Since they came in from well above the ecliptic, their spiral passed from north to south. A polar cap shot whitely below them, then the much smaller one of the summer hemisphere, the large one again, the small one, at longer and longer intervals. The planet approached closer, the landscape began to show features.

"Prepare for landing!" called Long.

11

Sankov did his best to look placid, which was difficult considering how closely the boys had shaved their return. But it had worked out well enough.

Until a few days ago, he had no sure knowledge that they had survived. It seemed more likely—inevitable, almost—that they were nothing but frozen corpses somewhere in the trackless stretches from Mars to Saturn, new planetoids that had once been alive.

The Committee had been dickering with him for weeks before the news had come. They had insisted on his signature to the paper for the sake of appearances. It would look like an agreement, voluntarily and mutually arrived at. But Sankov knew well that, given complete obstinacy on his part, they would act unilaterally and be damned with appearances. It seemed fairly certain that Hilder's election was secure now and they would take the chance of arousing a reaction of sympathy for Mars.

So he dragged out the negotiations, dangling before them always the possibility of surrender.

And then he heard from Long and concluded the deal quickly.

The papers had lain before him and he had made a last statement for the benefit of the reporters who were present.

He said, "Total imports of water from Earth are twenty million tons a year. This is declining as we develop our own piping system. If I sign this paper agreeing to an embargo, our industry will be paralyzed, any possibilities of expansion will halt. It looks to me as if that can't be what's in Earth's mind, can it?"

Their eyes met his and held only a hard glitter. Assemblyman Digby had already been replaced and they were unanimous against him.

The Committee Chairman impatiently pointed out, "You have said all this before."

"I know, but right now I'm kind of getting ready to sign and I want it clear in my head. Is Earth set and determined to bring us to an end here?"

"Of course not. Earth is interested in conserving its irreplaceable water supply, nothing else."

"You have one and a half quintillion tons of water on Earth."

The Committee Chairman said, "We cannot spare water."

And Sankov had signed.

That had been the final note he wanted. Earth had one and a half quintillion tons of water and could spare none of it.

Now, a day and a half later, the Committee and the reporters waited in the spaceport dome. Through thick, curving windows, they could see the bare and empty grounds of Mars Spaceport.

The Committee Chairman asked with annoyance, "How much longer do we have to wait? And, if you don't mind, what are we waiting for?"

Sankov said, "Some of our boys have been out in space, out past the asteroids."

The Committee Chairman removed a pair of spectacles and cleaned them with a snowy-white handkerchief. "And they're returning?"

"They are."

The Chairman shrugged, lifted his eyebrows in the direction of the reporters.

In the smaller room adjoining, a knot of women and children clustered about another window. Sankov stepped back a bit to cast a glance toward them. He would much rather have been with them, been part of their excitement and tension. He, like them, had waited over a year now. He, like them, had thought, over and over again, that the men must be dead.

"You see that?" said Sankov, pointing.

"Hey!" cried a reporter. "It's a ship!"

A confused shouting came from the adjoining room.

It wasn't a ship so much as a bright dot obscured by a drifting white cloud. The cloud grew larger and began to have form. It was a double streak against the sky, the lower ends billowing out and upward again. As it dropped still closer, the bright dot at the upper end took on a crudely cylindrical form.

It was rough and craggy, but where the sunlight hit, brilliant highlights bounced back.

The cylinder dropped toward the ground with the ponderous slowness characteristic of space vessels. It hung suspended on those blasting jets and settled down upon the recoil of tons of matter hurling downward like a tired man dropping into his easy chair.

And as it did so, a silence fell upon all within the dome. The women and children in one room, the politicians and reporters in the other remained frozen, heads craned incredulously upward.

The cylinder's landing flanges, extending far below the two rear jets, touched ground and sank into the pebbly morass. And then the ship was motionless and the jet action ceased.

But the silence continued in the dome. It continued for a long time.

Men came clambering down the sides of the immense vessel, inching down, down the two-mile trek to the ground, with spikes on their shoes and ice axes in their hands. They were gnats against the blinding surface.

One of the reporters croaked, "What is it?"

"That," said Sankov calmly, "happens to be a chunk of matter that spent its time scooting around Saturn as part of its rings. Our boys fitted it out with travel-head and jets and ferried it home. It just turns out the fragments in Saturn's rings are made out of ice."

He spoke into a continuing deathlike silence. "That thing that looks like a spaceship is just a mountain of hard water. If it were standing like that on Earth, it would be melting into a puddle and maybe it would break under its own weight. Mars is colder and has less gravity, so there's no such danger.

"Of course, once we get this thing really organized, we can have water stations on the moons of Saturn and Jupiter and on the asteroids. We can scale in chunks of Saturn's rings and pick them up and send them on at the various stations. Our Scavengers are good at that sort of thing.

"We'll have all the water we need. That one chunk you see is just under a cubic mile—or about what Earth would send us in two hundred years. The boys used quite a bit of it coming back from Saturn. They made it in five weeks, they tell me, and used up about a hundred million tons. But, Lord, that didn't make any dent at all in that mountain. Are you getting all this, boys?"

He turned to the reporters. There was no doubt they were getting it.

He said, "Then get this, too. Earth is worried about its water supply. It only has one and a half quintillion tons. It can't spare us a single ton out of it. Write down that we folks on Mars are worried about Earth and don't want anything to happen to Earth people. Write down that we'll sell water to Earth. Write down that we'll let them have million-ton lots for a reasonable fee. Write down that in ten years, we figure we can sell it in cubic-mile lots. Write down that Earth can quit worrying because Mars can sell it all the water it needs and wants."

The Committee Chairman was past hearing. He was feeling the future rushing in. Dimly he could see the reporters grinning as they wrote furiously.

Grinning.

He could hear the grin become laughter on Earth as Mars turned the tables so neatly on the anti-Wasters. He could hear the laughter thunder from every continent when word of the fiasco spread. And he could see the abyss, deep and black as space, into which would drop forever the political hopes of John Hilder and of every opponent of space flight left on Earth—his own included, of course.

In the adjoining room, Dora Swenson screamed with joy, and Peter, grown two inches, jumped up and down, calling, "Daddy! Daddy!"

Richard Swenson had just stepped off the extremity of the flange and, face showing clearly through the clear silicone of the headpiece, marched toward the dome.

"Did you ever see a guy look so happy?" asked Ted Long. "Maybe there's something in this marriage business."

"Ah, you've just been out in space too long," Rioz said.

THE IMPACTED MAN

by Robert Sheckley (1928–)

One of the nice things about reaching 1952 is that we can
now begin to include stories by Robert Sheckley. He is a man
and a writer who elicits adjectives—witty, clever, urbane, cyni-
cal, intelligent, and absurdist all have used and come to mind—
but most of all he is *good,* and at the shorter lengths, amazingly
and consistently so. Although "The Impacted Man" appeared
in *Astounding,* Sheckley quickly became the quintessential
Galaxy author, at least under the editorship of Horace Gold.
The stories poured from his typewriter in breathtaking numbers
from 1952 into the early sixties, so much so that he had to use
several pen names, the best known of which is "Fin O'Donnevan."

He would later publish fifteen or more novels both inside
and outside of science fiction, but these have so far not equalled
the impact of quality of his shorter works. Fortunately, his stories
were early and continuously collected in book form, beginning in
1954 with *Untouched by Human Hands.* His central theme is that
"things are not what they appear to be," that reality is in the eye
of the beholder. He is one of the very few writers who can be profoundly funny and humorously profound at the same time. (MHG)

I suppose that I'm as good as the next man at recognizing
talent at once. According to Alexei Panshin, I was the first
person to write letters to *Astounding* praising Robert Heinlein to
the skies. I didn't remember myself as being the first, but Alexei
is a meticulous researcher, and if he says so, it must be so.

I do know that I must have been among the very first to
notice how good Bob Sheckley was. I met him first when I
walked into Fred Pohl's office and found him there. Fred was
an agent in those days and, for a period of three years, he was

my agent (the only literary agent I ever had—and a good one, just as he was a good editor when he was an editor, a good writer when he is a writer, and a good human being all the time except for being a chain smoker)—

Where was I—Oh, yes, I walked into Fred's office and there was the young Bob Sheckley, still in his early twenties and there was Fred soothing and reassuring him. Naturally, that marked Bob off in my mind and I watched for his stories and liked them.

As a matter of fact, there were lots of his stories I particularly liked and I'll see how many of them I can get past Marty in future volumes. —But that shouldn't be hard. He likes him, too. (IA)

TO: CENTER
  Office 41
ATTN: Controller Miglese
FROM: Contractor Carienomen
SUBJ: ATTALA Metagalaxy
Dear Controller Miglese:
  This is to inform you that I have completed contract 13371A. In the region of space coded ATTALA I have constructed one metagalaxy, incorporating 549 billion galaxies, with the normal distribution of star clusters, variables, novae, et cetera. See attached data sheet.
  The outer limits of ATTALA metagalaxy are defined in the accompanying map.
  Speaking for myself, as chief designer, and for my company, I am confident that we have done a sound construction job, as well as a work of great artistic merit.
  We welcome your inspection.
  Having fulfilled the terms of our contract, the agreed-upon fee is payable at any time.

  Respectfully,
  Carienomen

Enclosed:
1 data sheet, installations
1 map of metagalaxy ATTALA

TO: Construction Headquarters
   334132, Extension 12
ATTN: Chief Designer, Carienomen
FROM: Asst. Controller Miglese
SUBJ: ATTALA Metagalaxy
Dear Carienomen:

   We have inspected your construction, and have held up your fee accordingly. Artistic! I suppose it's artistic. But haven't you forgotten our prime concern in construction work?

   Consistency, just to remind you.

   Our inspectors discovered large amounts of unexplained data occurring even around the metagalactic center, a region one would think you would build with care. That can't go on. Luckily, the region is unpopulated.

   And that's not all. Would you care to explain your spatial phenomena? What in chaos is this red shift you've built in? I've read your explanation of it, and it doesn't make any sense to me. How will planetary observers take it?

   Artistry is no excuse.

   Furthermore, what kinds of atoms are you using? Carienomen, are you trying to save money with shoddy materials? A good percentage of those atoms were unstable! They break down at the touch of a finger, or even without the touch of a finger. Couldn't you figure out any other way of lighting your suns?

   Enclosed is a data sheet, outlining the findings of our inspectors. No payment until they're cleared up.

   And there is another serious matter, just brought to my attention. Evidently you weren't watching too closely for stresses and strains in your spatial fabric. We have detected a time-flaw near the periphery of one of your galaxies. It is small, at present, but it could grow. I suggest that you take care of it at once, before you have to rebuild a galaxy or two.

   One of the inhabitants of a planet inpinging on the flaw is impacted already; wedged into the flaw, due entirely to your carelessness. I suggest that you correct this before he moves out of his normal time-sequence, creating paradoxes right and left.

   Get in touch with him, if need be.

   Also, I have word of unexplained phenomena on some of your planets; items such as flying pigs, moving mountains, ghosts, and others, all enumerated in the complaint sheet.

*We won't have this sort of thing, Carienomen. A paradox is
strictly forbidden in the created galaxies, since a paradox is the
inevitable forerunner of chaos.*

*Take care of that impaction at once. I don't know whether the
impacted individual realizes it yet.*

Miglese

*Enclosed:
1 complaint sheet*

Kay Masrin folded the last blouse into the suitcase and, with
her husband's assistance, closed it.

"That's that," Jack Masrin said, hefting the bulging case.
"Say good-bye to the old homestead." They looked around at
the furnished room where they had spent their last year.

"Good-bye, homestead," Kay said. "Let's not miss the
train."

"Plenty of time." Masrin started to the door. "Shall we say
good-bye to Happy Boy?" They had given Mr. Harf, their
landlord, that nickname because he smiled, once a month, when
they handed him the rent. Of course, he immediately reshaped
his mouth to its usual prim line.

"Let's not," Kay said, smoothing out her tailored suit. "He
just might wish us luck, and what would happen then?"

"You're perfectly right," Masrin said. "No use starting a
new life with Happy Boy's blessings. I'd rather have the Witch of
Endor curse me."

With Kay following him, Masrin walked to the head of the
stairs. He looked down at the first floor landing, started to take
the first step, and stopped abruptly.

"What's wrong?" Kay asked.

"Have we forgotten anything?" Masrin asked, frowning.

"I checked all the drawers and under the bed. Come on, we'll
be late."

Masrin looked down the stairs again. Something was bothering him. He searched quickly for the source of the trouble. Of
course, they had practically no money. But that had never
worried him in the past. He *did* have a teaching job, finally,
even if it was in Iowa. That was the important thing, after a year
of working in a bookstore. Everything was going right. Why
should he be worried?

He took a step down, and stopped again. The feeling was

stronger. There was something he shouldn't do. He glanced back at Kay.

"Do you hate leaving that much?" Kay asked. "Let's go, or Happy Boy'll charge us another month's rent. Which, for some strange reason, we haven't got."

Still Masrin hesitated. Kay pushed past him and trotted downstairs.

"See?" she said from the first-floor landing. "It's easy. Come on. Walk to Mummy."

Masrin mumbled a few subdued curses and started down the stairs. The feeling became stronger.

He reached the eighth step, and—

He was standing on a grassy plain. The transition was as sudden as that.

He gasped and blinked. The suitcase was still in his hand. But where was the brownstone? Where was Kay? Where, for that matter, was New York?

In the distance was a small blue mountain. There was a clump of trees nearby. In front of the clump were a dozen or so men.

Masrin was in a dreamlike state of shock. He observed, almost idly, that the men were short, swarthy, thickly muscled. They wore loincloths, and carried beautifully carved and polished clubs.

They were watching him, and Masrin decided it was a tossup, who was the most surprised.

Then one of them grunted something, and they started moving toward him.

A club bounced off his suitcase.

The shock dissolved. Masrin turned, dropped the suitcase and ran like a greyhound. A club whacked his spine, nearly knocking him over. He was facing a little hill, and he bounded up it, arrows showering around him.

A few feet up, he realized that he was back in New York.

He was at the top of the stairs, still in full stride, and before he could stop himself he had run into the wall. Kay was on the first-floor landing, looking up. She gasped when she saw him, but didn't say anything.

Masrin looked at the familiar murky mauve walls of the brownstone, and at his wife.

No savages.

"What happened?" Kay whispered, white-faced, coming up the stairs.

"What did you see?" Masrin asked. He didn't have a chance to feel the full impact of what had happened. Ideas were pouring into his head, theories, conclusions.

Key hesitated, gnawing at her lower lip. "You walked down a couple of steps and then you were gone. I couldn't see you any more. I just stood there and looked and looked. And then I heard a noise, and you were back on the stairs. Running."

They walked back to their room and opened the door. Kay sat down at once on the bed. Masrin walked around, catching his breath. Ideas were still pouring in, and he was having trouble sifting them.

"You won't believe me," he said.

"Oh won't I? Try me!"

He told her about the savages.

"You could tell me you were on Mars," Kay said. "I'd believe you. I saw you disappear!"

"My suitcase!" Masrin said suddenly, remembering that he had dropped it.

"Forget the suitcase," Kay said.

"I have to go back for it," Masrin said.

"No!"

"I must. Look, dear, it's pretty obvious what happened. I walked through some sort of time-flaw, which sent me back to the past. I must have landed in prehistoric times, to judge by the welcoming committee I met. I have to go back for that suitcase."

"Why?" Kay asked.

"Because I can't allow a paradox to occur." Masrin didn't even wonder how he knew this. His normal egotism saved him from wondering how the idea had originated in his mind.

"Look," he said, "my suitcase lands in the past. In it I've got an electric shaver, some pants with zippers, a plastic hairbrush, a nylon shirt, and a dozen or so books—some of them published as late as 1951. I've even got Ettison's *Western Ways* in there, a text on Western civilization from 1490 to the present day.

"The contents of that case could give these savages the impetus to change their own history. And suppose some of that stuff got into the hands of Europeans, after they discovered America? How would that affect the present?"

"I don't know," Kay said. "And you don't either."

"Of course I know," Masrin said. It was all crystal-clear. He was amazed that she wasn't able to follow it logically.

"Look at it this way," Masrin said. "Minutiae makes history. The present is made up of a tremendous number of infinitesimal factors, which shaped and molded the past. If you add another factor to the past, you're bound get another result in the present. But the present is as it is, unchangeable. So we have a paradox. And there can't be any paradox!"

"Why can't there?" Kay asked.

Masrin frowned. For a bright girl, she was following him very poorly. "Just believe me," he said. "Paradox isn't allowed in a logical universe." Allowed by whom? He had the answer.

"The way I see it," Masrin said, "there must be a regulating principle in the universe. All our natural laws are expressions of it. This principle can't stand paradox, because . . . because—" He knew that the answer had to do with suppressing the fundamental chaos, but he didn't know why.

"Anyhow, this principle can't stand paradox."

"Where did you get that idea?" Kay asked. She had never heard Jack talk that way before.

"I've had these ideas for a long time," Masrin said, and believed it. "There was just never any reason to talk about it. Anyhow, I'm going back for my suitcase."

He walked out to the landing, followed by Kay. "Sorry I can't bring you any souvenirs," Masrin said cheerfully. "Unfortunately, that would result in a paradox also. Everything in the past has had a part in shaping the present. Remove something, and it's like removing one unknown from an equation. You wouldn't get the same result." He started down the stairs.

On the eighth step, he disappeared again.

He was back in prehistoric America. The savages were gathered around the suitcase, only a few feet from him. They hadn't opened it yet, Masrin noticed thankfully. Of course, the suitcase itself was a pretty paradoxical article. But its appearance—and his—would probably be swallowed up in myth and legend. Time had a certain amount of flexibility.

Looking at them, Masrin couldn't decide if they were forerunners of Indians, or a separate sub-race which didn't survive. He wondered if they thought he was an enemy, or a garden-variety evil spirit.

Masrin darted forward, shoved two of them aside, and grabbed his suitcase. He ran back, circling the little hill, and stopped.

He was still in the past.

Where in chaos was that hole in time, Masrin wondered, not noticing the strangeness of his oath. The savages were coming after him now, starting around the little hill. Masrin almost had the answer, then lost it as an arrow sped past him. He sprinted, trying to keep the hill between himself and the Indians. His long legs pumped, and a club bounced behind him.

Where was that hole in time? What if it had moved? Perspiration poured from his face as he ran. A club grazed his arm, and he twisted around the side of the hill, looking wildly for shelter.

He met three squat savages, coming after him.

Masrin fell to the ground as they swung their clubs, and they tripped over his body. Others were coming now, and he jumped to his feet.

Up! The thought struck him suddenly, cutting through his fear. Up!

He charged the hill, certain that he would never reach the top alive.

And he was back in the boarding house, still holding the suitcase.

"Are you hurt, darling?" Kay put her arms around him. "What happened?"

Masrin had only one rational thought. He couldn't remember any prehistoric tribe that carved their clubs as elaborately as these savages. It was almost a unique art form, and he wished he could get one of the clubs to a museum.

Then he looked at the mauve walls wildly, expecting to see the savages come bounding out of them. Or perhaps there were little men in his suitcase. He fought for control. The thinking portion of his mind told him not to be alarmed; flaws in time were possible, and he had become wedged, impacted in one. Everything else followed logically. All he had to do—

But another part of his mind wasn't interested in logic. It had been staring blankly at the impossibility of the whole thing, uninfluenced by any rational arguments. That part knew an impossibility when it saw one, and said so.

Masrin screamed and fainted.

TO: CENTER
  Office 41
ATTN: Asst. Controller Miglese
FROM: Contractor Carienomen
SUBJ: ATTALA Metagalaxy
Dear Sir:

I consider your attitude unfair. True, I have utilized some new ideas in my approach to this particular metagalaxy. I have allowed myself the latitude of artistry, never thinking I would be beset by the howls of a static, reactionary CENTER.

Believe me, I am as interested as you in our great job— that of suppressing the fundamental chaos. But in doing this, we must not sacrifice our values.

Enclosed is a statement of defense concerning my use of the red shift, and another statement of the advantages gained by using a small percentage of unstable atoms for lighting and energy purposes.

As to the time-flaw, that was merely a small error in duration-flow, and has nothing to do with the fabric of space, which is, I assure you, of first-rate quality.

There is, as you pointed out, an individual impacted in the flaw, which makes the job of repair slightly more difficult. I have been in contact with him, indirectly of course, and have succeeded in giving him a limited understanding of his rôle.

If he doesn't disturb the flaw too much by time-traveling, I should be able to sew it up with little difficulty. I don't know if this procedure is possible, though. My rapport with him is quite shaky, and he seems to have a number of strong influences around him, counseling him to move.

I could perform an extraction of course, and ultimately I may have to do just that. For that matter, if the thing gets out of hand I may be forced to extract the entire planet. I hope not, since that would necessitate clearing that entire portion of space, where there are also local observers. This, in turn, might necessitate rebuilding an entire galaxy.

However, I hope to have the problem settled by the time I next communicate with you.

The warp in the metagalactic center was caused by some workmen leaving a disposal unit open. It has been closed.

The phenomena such as walking mountains, et cetera, are being handled in the usual way.

Payment is still due on my work.

Respectfully,
Carienomen

Enclosed:
1 statement 5541 pages, Red Shift
1 statement, 7689 pages, Unstable Atoms

TO: *Construction Headquarters*
334132, Extension 12
ATTN: *Contractor Carienomen*
FROM: *Asst. Controller Miglese*
SUBJ: *ATTALA Metagalaxy*
Carienomen:

You will be paid after *you can show me a logical, decently constructed job. I'll read your statements when and if I have time. Take care of the flaw-impaction before it tears a hole in the fabric of space.*

Miglese

Masrin recovered his nerve in half an hour. Kay put a compress on a purple bruise on his arm. Masrin started pacing the room. Once again, he was in complete possession of his faculties. Ideas started to come.

"The past is down," he said, half to Kay, half to himself.

"I don't mean really 'down'; but when I move in that apparent direction, I step through the hole in time. It's a case of shifted conjoined dimensionality."

"What does that mean?" Kay asked, staring wide-eyed at her husband.

"Just take my word for it," Masrin said, "I can't go down." He couldn't explain it to her any better. There weren't words to fit the concepts.

"Can you go up?" Kay asked, completely confused.

"I don't know. I suppose, if I went up, I'd go into the future."

"Oh, I can't stand it," Kay said. "What's wrong with you? How will you get out of here? How will you get down that haunted staircase?"

"Are you people still there?" Mr. Harf's voice croaked from outside. Masrin walked over and opened the door.

"I think we're going to stay for a while," he said to the landlord.

"You're not," Harf said. "I've already rented this room again." Happy Boy Harf was small and bony, with a narrow skull and lips as thin as a spider's thread. He stalked into the room, looking around for signs of damage to his property. One of Mr. Harf's little idiosyncrasies was his belief that the nicest people were capable of the worst crimes.

"When are the people coming?" Masrin asked.

"This afternoon. And I want you out before they get here."

"Couldn't we make some arrangement?" Masrin asked. The impossibility of the situation struck him. He couldn't go downstairs. If Harf forced him out, he would have to go to prehistoric New York, where he was sure his return was eagerly awaited.

And there was the over-all problem of paradox!

"I'm sick," Kay said in a stifled little voice. "I can't leave yet."

"What are you sick from? I'll call an ambulance if you're sick," Harf said, looking suspiciously around the room for any signs of bubonic plague.

"I'd gladly pay you double the rent if you'd let us stay a little longer," Masrin said.

Harf scratched his head, and stared at Masrin. He wiped his nose on the back of his hand, and said, "Where's the money?"

Masrin realized that he had about ten dollars left, and his train tickets. He and Kay were going to ask for an advance as soon as they reached the college.

"Broke," Harf said. "I thought you had a job at some school?"

"He does," Kay said staunchly.

"Then why don't you go there and get out of my place?" Harf asked.

The Masrins were silent. Harf glared at them.

"Very suspicious. Get out before noon, or I'll call a cop."

"Hold it," Masrin said. "We've paid the rent for today. The room's ours until twelve midnight."

Harf stared at them. He wiped his nose again, thoughtfully.

"Don't try staying one minute over," he said, stamping out of the room.

As soon as Harf was gone, Kay hurried over and closed the door. "Honey," she said, "why don't you call up some scientists here in New York and tell them what's happened? I'm sure they'd arrange something, until . . . how long will we have to stay here?''

''Until the flaw's repaired,'' Masrin said. ''But we can't tell anyone; especially, we can't tell any scientists.''

''Why not?'' Kay asked.

''Look, the important thing, as I told you, is to avoid a paradox. That means I have to keep my hands off the past, and the future. Right?''

''If you say so,'' Kay said.

''We call in a team of scientists, and what happens? Naturally, they're skeptical. They want to *see* me do it. So I do it. Immediately, they bring in a few of their colleagues. *They* watch me disappear. Understand, all this time there's no proof that I've gone into the past. All they know is, if I walk downstairs, I disappear.

''Photographers are called in, to make sure I'm not hypnotizing the scientists. Then they demand proof. They want me to bring back a scalp, or one of those carved clubs. The newspapers get hold of it. It's inevitable that somewhere along the line I produce a paradox. And do you know what happens then?''

''No, and you don't either.''

''I do,'' Masrin said firmly. ''Once a paradox is caused, the agent—the man who caused it—me—disappears. For good. And it goes down in the books as another unsolved mystery. That way, the paradox is resolved in its easiest way—by getting rid of the paradoxical element.''

''If you think you're in danger, then of course we won't call in any scientists,'' Kay said. ''Although I wish I knew what you were driving at. I don't understand anything you've said.'' She went to the window and looked out. There was New York, and beyond it, somewhere, was Iowa, where they should be going. She looked at her watch. They had already missed the train.

''Phone the college,'' Masrin said. ''Tell them I'll be delayed a few days.''

''Will it be a few days?'' Kay asked. ''How will you ever get out?''

''Oh, the hole in time isn't permanent,'' Masrin said confidently. ''It'll heal—if I don't go sticking myself in it.''

''But we can only stay here until midnight. What happens then?''

"I don't know," Masrin said. "We can only hope it'll be fixed by then."

TO: CENTER
  Office 41
ATTN: Asst. Controller Miglese
FROM: Contractor Carienomen
SUBJ: MORSTT Metagalaxy
Dear Sir:

  Herein, enclosed, is my bid for work on the new metagalaxy in the region coded MORSTT. If you have heard any discussions in art circles recently, I think that you will see that my use of unstable atoms in ATTALA Metagalaxy has been proclaimed "the first great advance in creative engineering since the invention of variable time-flow." See the enclosed reviews.

  My artistry has stirred many favorable comments.

  Most of the inconsistencies—natural inconsistencies, let me remind you—in ATTALA Metagalaxy have been corrected. I am still working with the man impacted in the time flaw. He is proving quite co-operative; at least, as co-operative as he can be, with the various influences around him.

  To date, I have coalesced the edges of the flaw, and am allowing them to harden. I hope the individual remains immobile, since I don't like to extract anyone or anything. After all, each person, each planet, each star system, no matter how minute, has an integral part in my metagalactic scheme.

  Artistically, at any rate.

  Your inspection welcomed again. Please note the galactic configurations around the metagalactic center. They are a dream of beauty you will wish to carry with you always.

  Please consider this for the MORSTT Metagalaxy project in light of my past achievements.

  Payment is still due on ATTALA Metagalaxy.

Respectfully,
Carienomen

Enclosed:
1 bid, for MORSTT Metagalaxy project
3 critical reviews, ATTALA Metagalaxy

"It's eleven forty-five, honey," Kay said nervously. "Do you think we could go now?"

"Let's wait a few minutes longer," Masrin said. He could hear Harf prowling around on the landing, waiting eagerly for the dot of twelve.

Masrin watched the seconds tick by on his watch.

At five minutes to twelve, he decided that he might as well find out. If the hole wasn't fixed by now, another five minutes wouldn't do it.

He placed the suitcase on the dresser, and moved a chair next to it.

"What are you doing?" Kay asked.

"I don't feel like trying those stairs at night," Masrin said. "It's bad enough playing with those pre-Indians in the daylight. I'm going to try going up, instead." His wife gave him an under-the-eyelids now-I-know-you're-cracking look.

"It's not the stairs that does it," Masrin told her again. "It's the act of going up or down. The critical distance seems to be about five feet. This will do just as well."

Kay stood nervously, clenching and unclenching both hands, as Masrin climbed on the chair and put one foot on the dresser. Then the other, and he stood up.

"I think it's all right," he said, teetering a little. "I'm going to try it a little higher."

He climbed on the suitcase.

And disappeared.

It was day, and he was in a city. But the city didn't look like New York. It was breathtakingly beautiful—so beautiful that Masrin didn't dare breathe, for fear of disturbing its fragile loveliness.

It was a place of delicate, wispy towers and buildings. And people. But what people, Masrin thought, letting out his breath with a sigh.

The people were blue-skinned. The light was green, coming from a green-tinged sun.

Masrin drew in a breath of air, and strangled. He gasped again, and started to lose his balance. There was no air in the place! At least, no air he could breathe. He felt for a step behind him, and then tumbled down—

To land, choking and writhing, on the floor of his room.

After a few moments he could breathe again. He heard Harf pounding on the door. Masrin staggered to his feet, and tried to think of something. He knew Harf; the man was probably certain by now that Masrin headed the Mafia. He would call a cop if they didn't leave. And that would ultimately result in—

"Listen," he said to Kay, "I've got another idea." His throat was burning from the atmosphere of the future. However, he told himself, there was no reason why he should be surprised. He had made quite a jump forward. The composition of the Earth's atmosphere must have changed, gradually, and the people had adapted to it. But it was a poison for him.

"There are two possibilities now," he said to Kay. "One, that under the prehistoric layer is another, earlier layer. Two, that the prehistoric layer is only a temporary discontinuity. That under it, is present New York again. Follow me?"

"No."

"I'm going to try going under the prehistoric layer. It might get me down to the ground floor. Certainly, it can't be any worse." Kay considered the logic of going some thousands of years into the past in order to walk ten feet, but didn't say anything.

Masrin opened the door and went out to the stairs, followed by Kay. "Wish me luck," he said.

"Luck, nothing," Mr. Harf said, on the landing. "Just get out of here."

Masrin plunged down the stairs.

It was still morning in prehistoric New York, and the savages were still waiting for him. Masrin estimated that only about half an hour had gone by here. He didn't have time to wonder why.

He had caught them by surprise, and was twenty yards away before they saw him. They followed, and Masrin looked for a depression. He had to go down five feet, in order to get out.

He found a shelving of the land, and jumped down.

He was in water. Not just on the surface, but *under*. The pressure was tremendous, and Masrin could not see sunlight above him.

He must have gone through to a time when this section was under the Atlantic.

Masrin kicked furiously, eardrums bursting. He started to rise toward the surface, and—

He was back on the plain, dripping wet.

This time, the savages had had enough. They looked at him,

materialized in front of them, gave a shriek of horror, and bolted.

This water sprite was too strong for them.

Wearily, Masrin walked back to the hill, climbed it, and was back in the brownstone.

Kay was staring at him, and Harf's jaw was hanging slack. Masrin grinned weakly.

"Mr. Harf," he said, "will you come into my room? There's something I want to tell you."

TO: CENTER
  Office 41
ATTN: Asst. Controller Miglese
FROM: Contractor Carienomen
SUBJ: MORSTT Metagalaxy

My dear Sir:
  I cannot understand your reply to my bid for the job of constructing MORSTT Metagalaxy. Moreover, I do not think that obscenity has any place in a business letter.
  If you have taken the trouble to inspect my latest work in ATTALA, you will see that it is, take it all for all, a beautiful job, and one that will go a long way toward holding back the fundamental chaos.
  The only detail left to attend to is the matter of the impacted man. I fear I shall have to extract.
  The flaw was hardening nicely, when he blundered into it again, tearing it worse than ever. No paradox as yet, but I can see one coming.
  Unless he can control his immediate environment, and do it at once, I shall take the necessary step. Paradox is not allowed.
  I consider it my duty to ask you to reconsider my bid for the MORSTT Metagalaxy project.
  And I trust you will excuse me for bringing this oversight to your attention, but payment is still due.

Respectfully,
Carienomen

"So that's the story, Mr. Harf," Masrin said, an hour later. "I know how weird it sounds; but you saw me disappear yourself."

"That I did," Harf said. Masrin went into the bathroom to hang up his wet clothes.

"Yes," Harf said, "I guess you disappeared at that."

"I certainly did."

"And you don't want the scientists to know about your deal with the devil?" Harf asked slyly.

"No! I explained about paradox, and—"

"Let me see," Harf said. He wiped his nose vigorously. "Those carved clubs you said they had. Wouldn't one of those be valuable to a museum? You said there was nothing like it."

"What?" Masrin asked, coming out of the bathroom. "Listen, I can't touch any of that stuff. It'll result in—"

"Of course," Harf said, "I could call in some newspaper boys instead. And some scientists. I could probably make me a nice little pile out of this devil-worship."

"You wouldn't!" Kay said, remembering only that her husband had said something bad would happen.

"Be reasonable," Harf said. "All I want is one or two of those clubs. That won't cause any trouble. You can just ask your devil—"

"There's no devil involved," Masrin said. "You have no idea what part one of those clubs might have played in history. The club I take might have killed the man who would have united these people, and the North American Indians might have met the Europeans as a single nation. Think how that would change—"

"Don't hand me that stuff," Harf said. "Are you getting me a club or aren't you?"

"I've explained it to you," Masrin said wearily.

"And don't tell me any more about this paradox business. I don't understand it, anyhow. But I'll split fifty-fifty with you on what I get for the club."

"No."

"O.K. I'll be seeing you." Harf started for the door.

"Wait."

"Yes?" Harf's thin, spidery mouth was smiling now.

Masrin examined his choice of evils. If he brought back a club there was a good chance of starting a paradox, by removing all that the club had done in the past. But if he didn't, Harf would call in the newspapers and scientists. They could find out if Harf was speaking the truth by simply carrying him downstairs; something the police would do anyhow. He would disappear, and then—"

With more people in on it, a paradox would be inevitable. And all Earth might, very possibly, be removed. Although he didn't know why, Masrin knew this for a certainty.

He was lost either way, but getting the club seemed the simpler alternative.

"I'll get it," Masrin said. He walked to the staircase, followed by Kay and Harf. Kay grabbed his hand.

"Don't do it," she said.

"There's nothing else I can do." He thought for a moment of killing Harf. But that would only result in the electric chair for him. Of course, he could kill Harf and take his body into the past, and bury it.

But the corpse of a twentieth century man in prehistoric America might constitute a paradox anyhow. Suppose it was dug up?

Besides, he didn't have it in him to kill a man.

Masrin kissed his wife, and walked downstairs.

There were no savages in sight on the plain, although Masrin thought he could feel their eyes, watching him. He found two clubs on the ground. The ones that struck him must be taboo, he decided, and picked one up, expecting another to crush his skull any moment. But the plain was silent.

"Good boy!" Harf said. "Hand it here!" Masrin handed him the club. He went over to Kay and put his arm around her. It was a paradox now, as certainly as if he had killed his great-great-grandfather before he was born. "That's a lovely thing," Harf said, admiring the club under the light. "Consider your rent paid for the rest of the month—"

The club disappeared from his hand.

Harf disappeared.

Kay fainted.

Masrin carried her to the bed, and splashed water on her face. "What happened?" she asked.

"I don't know," Masrin said, suddenly very puzzled about everything. "All I know is, we're going to stay here for at least two weeks. Even if we have to eat beans."

TO: CENTER
    Office 41
ATTN: Asst. Controller Miglese
FROM: Contractor Carienomen
SUBJ: MORSTT Metagalaxy

Sir:
    Your offer of a job repairing damaged stars is an insult to my company and myself. We refuse. Let me point out my work in the

past, outlined in the brochure I am enclosing. How can you offer so menial a job to one of CENTER'S greatest companies?

Again, I would like to put in my request for work on the new MORSTT Metagalaxy.

As for ATTALA Metagalaxy—the work is now completed, and a finer job cannot be found anywhere this side of chaos. The place is a wonder.

The impacted man is no longer impacted. I was forced to extract. However, I did not extract the man himself. Instead, I was able to remove one of the external influences on him. Now he can grow out normally.

A nice job, I think you'll admit, and solved with the ingenuity that characterizes all my work.

My decision was: Why extract a good man, when I could save him by pulling the rotten one beside him?

Again, I welcome your inspection. I request reconsideration on MORSTT Metagalaxy.

PAYMENT IS STILL DUE!

Respectfully,
Carienomen

Enclosed:
1 brochure, 9978 pages

WHAT'S IT LIKE OUT THERE?

by Edmond Hamilton (1904–1977)

Thrilling wonder stories. Stories that thrill and fill the reader with a sense of wonder. That's exactly what Edmond Hamilton did in a career that began in 1926 and lasted almost half a century. They called him "World Wrecker Hamilton" because he could write super science space opera with the best of them, and he published these stories in every sf magazine of the 1930s, later moving on to do the *Captain Future* tales for the magazine of the same name. As he was married to the late Leigh Brackett, a writer who had still more talent than he did, it is easy to dismiss him. Yet he enriched this field, and in between the space combat and the damsels in distress one can find a solid body of work. This has been preserved for us in *The Best of Edmond Hamilton* (1977).

I feel that "What's It Like Out There?" is his best short story, one whose very title sums up much of the appeal of science fiction. Interestingly, it was written in *1933*, could not find a market, and then was rewritten and finally sold two decades later. Its theme of the clash between science and wonder could not be more timely today. (MHG)

Exploring has always been a hard task. However glamorous and exciting we might think it to be as a general sort of thing, we know darned well that the details are difficult and risky. Who on Earth would think that climbing Mt. Everest, or crossing a polar ice cap, or penetrating the African forests in search of the sources of the Nile, or slogging across the Sahara, the Gobi, or the Kalahari can be fun?

So far, though, we haven't had anything but fun in space flight. Three days to the Moon and three days back—or even seven continuous months in space—isn't bad if all the multimillion-dollars' worth of high technology are at the service of astronauts/cosmonauts who are always, or almost always, in contact with home.

I think, though, that we've come to the end of the good times. Any space flight that will take us beyond the Moon is going to be hazardous in the extreme and the chances of rescue in case of need will be negligible.

It is absolutely astonishing to me, then, that Ed Hamilton could have taken so realistic a view of space flight back in 1933. And no wonder it could find no takers then, since space flight was strictly cops-and-robbers before Campbell, and engineers-and-slide rules after Campbell. (IA)

I hadn't wanted to wear my uniform when I left the hospital, but I didn't have any other clothes there and I was too glad to get out to argue about it. But as soon as I got on the local plane I was taking to Los Angeles, I was sorry I had it on.

People gawked at me and began to whisper. The stewardess gave me a special big smile. She must have spoken to the pilot, for he came back and shook hands, and said, "Well, guess a trip like this is sort of a comedown for *you.*"

A little man came in, looked around for a seat, and took the one beside me. He was a fussy, spectacled guy in his fifties, and he took a few minutes to get settled. Then he looked at me, and stared at my uniform and at the little brass button on it that said TWO.

"Why," he said, "you're one of those Expedition Two men!" And then, as though he'd only just figured it out, "Why, you've been to Mars!"

"Yeah," I said. "I was there."

He beamed at me in a kind of wonder. I didn't like it, but his curiosity was so friendly that I couldn't quite resent it.

"Tell me," he said, "what's it like out there?"

The plane was lifting, and I looked out at the Arizona desert sliding by close underneath.

"Different," I said. "It's different."

The answer seemed to satisfy him completely. "I'll just bet it is," he said. "Are you going home, Mr.—"

"Haddon. Sergeant Frank Haddon."

"You going home, Sergeant?"

"My home's back in Ohio," I told him. "I'm going in to L.A. to look up some people before I go home."

"Well, that's fine. I hope you have a good time, Sergeant. You deserve it. You boys did a great job out there. Why, I read in the newspapers that after the U.N. sends out a couple more expeditions, we'll have cities out there, and regular passenger lines, and all that."

"Look," I said, "that stuff is for the birds. You might as well build cities down there in Mojave, and have them a lot closer. There's only one reason for going to Mars now, and that's uranium."

I could see he didn't quite believe me. "Oh, sure," he said, "I know that's important too, the uranium we're all using now for our power-stations—but that isn't all, is it?"

"It'll be all, for a long, long time," I said.

"But look, Sergeant, this newspaper article said—"

I didn't say anything more. By the time he'd finished telling about the newspaper article, we were coming down into L.A. He pumped my hand when we got out of the plane.

"Have yourself a time, Sergeant! You deserve it. . . . I hear a lot of chaps on Two didn't come back."

"Yeah," I said. "I heard that."

I was feeling shaky again by the time I got to downtown L.A. I went to a bar and had a double whisky and it made me feel a little better.

I went out and found a cabby and asked him to drive me out to San Gabriel. He was a fat man with a broad red face.

"Hop right in, buddy," he said. "Say, you're one of those Mars guys, aren't you?"

I said, "That's right."

"Well, well," he said. "Tell me, how was it out there?"

"It was a pretty dull grind, in a way," I told him.

"I'll bet it was!" he said, as we started through traffic. "Me, I was in the army in World War Two, twenty years ago. That's just what it was, a dull grind nine-tenths of the time. I guess it hasn't changed any."

"This wasn't any army expedition," I explained. "It was a

United Nations one, not an army one—but we had officers and rules of discipline like the army.''

''Sure, it's the same thing,'' said the cabby. ''You don't need to tell me what it's like, buddy. Why, back there in '42—or was it '43?—anyway, back there I remember that—''

I leaned back and watched Huntington Boulevard slide past. The sun poured in on me and seemed very hot, and the air seemed very thick and soupy. It hadn't been so bad up on the Arizona plateau, but it was a little hard to breathe down here.

The cabby wanted to know what address in San Gabriel. I got the little packet of letters out of my pocket and found the one that had ''Martin Valinez'' and a street address on the back. I told the cabby, and put the letters back into my pocket.

I wish now that I'd never answered them.

But how could I keep from answering when Joe Valinez' parents wrote to me at the hospital? And it was the same with Jim's girl, and Walter's family. I'd had to write back, and the first thing I knew I'd promised to come and see them, and now if I went back to Ohio without doing it I'd feel like a heel. Right now, I wish I'd decided to be a heel.

The address was on the south side of San Gabriel, in a section that still had a faintly Mexican tinge to it. There was a little grocery store with a small house beside it, and a picket fence around the yard of the house; very neat, but a queerly homely place after all the slick California stucco.

I went into the little grocery, and a tall, dark man with quiet eyes took a look at me and called a woman's name in a low voice, and she came around the counter and took my hand.

''You're Sergeant Haddon,'' he said. ''Yes. Of course. We've been hoping you'd come.''

His wife came in a hurry from the back. She looked a little too old to be Joe's mother, for Joe had been just a kid; but then she didn't look so old either, but just sort of worn.

She said to Valinez, ''Please, a chair. Can't you see he's tired. And just from the hospital—''

I sat down and looked between them at a case of tinned peppers, and they asked me how I felt, and wouldn't I be glad to get home, and they hoped all my family were well.

They were gentlefolk. They hadn't said a word about Joe, just waited for me to say something. And I felt in a spot, for I hadn't known Joe well, not really. He'd been moved into our squad only a couple of weeks before take-off, and since he'd been our first casualty, I'd never got to know him much.

I finally had to get it over with, and all I could think to say was, "They wrote you in detail about Joe, didn't they?"

Valinez nodded gravely. "Yes—that he died from shock within twenty-four hours after take-off. The letter was very nice."

His wife nodded too. "Very nice," she murmured. She looked at me, and I guess she saw that I didn't know quite what to say, for she said, "You can tell us more about it. Yet you must not, if it pains you."

I could tell them more. Oh, yes, I could tell them a lot more, if I wanted to. It was all clear in my mind, like a film you run over and over till you know it by heart.

I could tell them all about the take-off that had killed their son. The long lines of us, uniformed backs going up into Rocket Four and all the other nineteen rockets—the lights flaring up there on the plateau, the grind of machinery and blast of whistles and the inside of the big rocket as we climbed up the ladders of its center well.

The film was running again in my mind, clear as crystal, and I was back in Cell Fourteen of Rocket Four, with the minutes ticking away and the walls quivering every time one of the other rockets blasted off, and we ten men in our hammocks, prisoned inside that odd-shaped windowless metal room, waiting. Waiting, till that big, giant hand came and smacked us down deep into our recoil-springs, crushing the breath out of us, so that you fought to breathe, and the blood roared into your head, and your stomach heaved in spite of all the pills they'd given you, and you heard the giant laughing, *b-r-room! b-r-r-room! b-r-r-oom!*

Smash, smash, again and again, hitting us in the guts and cutting our breath, and someone being sick, and someone else sobbing, and the *b-r-r-oom! b-r-r-oom!* laughing as it killed us; and then the giant quit laughing, and quit slapping us down, and you could feel your sore and shaky body and wonder if it was still all there.

Walter Millis cursing continually in the hammock underneath me, and Breck Jergen, our sergeant then, clambering painfully out of his straps to look us over, and then through the voices a thin, ragged voice saying uncertainly, "Breck, I think I'm hurt—"

Sure, that was their boy Joe, and there was blood on his lips, and he'd had it—we knew when we first looked at him that he'd had it. A handsome kid, turned waxy now as he held his hand on his middle and looked up at us. Expedition One had proved that take-off would hit a certain percentage with internal injuries every time, and in our squad, in our little windowless cell, it was Joe that had been hit.

If only he'd died right off. But he couldn't die right off, he had to lie in the hammock all those hours and hours. The doctors came and put a straitjacket around his body and doped him up, and that was that, and the hours went by. And we were so shaken and deathly sick ourselves that we didn't have the sympathy for him that we should have had—not till he started moaning and begging us to take the jacket off.

Finally Walter Millis wanted to do it, and Breck wouldn't allow it, and they were arguing and we were listening when the moaning stopped, and there was no need to do anything about Joe Valinez any more. Nothing but to call the doctors, who came into our little iron prison and took him away.

Sure, I could tell the Valinezes all about how their Joe died, couldn't I?

"Please," whispered Mrs. Valinez, and her husband looked at me and nodded silently.

So I told them.

I said, "You know Joe died in space. He'd been knocked out by the shock of take-off, and he was unconscious, not feeling a thing. And then he woke up, before he died. He didn't seem to be feeling any pain, not a bit. He lay there, looking out the window at the stars. They're beautiful, the stars out there in space, like angels. He looked, and then he whispered something and lay back and was gone."

Mrs. Valinez began to cry softly. "To die out there, looking at stars like angels—"

I got up to go, and she didn't look up. I went out the door of the little grocery store, and Valinez came with me.

He shook my hand. "Thank you, Sergeant Haddon. Thank you very much."

"Sure," I said.

I got into the cab. I took out my letters and tore that one into bits. I wished to God I'd never got it. I wished I didn't have any of the other letters I still had.

I took the early plane for Omaha. Before we got there I fell asleep in my seat, and then I began to dream, and that wasn't good.

A voice said, "We're coming down."

And we were coming down, Rocket Four was coming down, and there we were in our squad-cell, all of us strapped into our hammocks, waiting and scared, wishing there was a window so we could see out, hoping our rocket wouldn't be the one to crack up, hoping none of the rockets cracked up, but if one does, don't let it be *ours*. . . .

"We're coming down. . . ."

Coming down, with the blasts starting to boom again underneath us, hitting us hard, not steady like at take-off, but blast-blast-blast, and then again, blast-blast.

Breck's voice, calling us from across the cell, but I couldn't hear for the roaring that was in my ears between blasts. No, it was *not* in my ears, that roaring came from the wall beside me: we had hit atmosphere, we were coming in.

The blasts in lightning succession without stopping, crash-crash-crash-crash-crash! Mountains fell on me, and this was it, and don't let it be ours, please, God, don't let it be ours. . . .

Then the bump and the blackness, and finally somebody yelling hoarsely in my ears, and Breck Jergen, his face deathly white, leaning over me.

"Unstrap and get out, Frank! All men out of hammocks—all men out!"

We'd landed, and we hadn't cracked up, but we were half dead and they wanted us to turn out, right this minute, and we couldn't.

Breck yelling at us, "Breathing-masks on! Masks on! We've got to go out!"

"My God, we've just landed, we're torn to bits, we can't!"

"We've got to! Some of the other rockets cracked up in landing and we've got to save whoever's still living in them! Masks on! Hurry!"

We couldn't, but we did. They hadn't given us all those months of discipline for nothing. Jim Clymer was already on his feet, Walter was trying to unstrap underneath me, whistles were blowing like mad somewhere and voices shouted hoarsely.

My knees wobbled under me as I hit the floor. Young Lassen, beside me, tried to say something and then crumpled up. Jim bent over him, but Breck was at the door yelling, "Let him go! Come on!"

The whistles screeching at us all the way down the ladders of the well, and the mask-clip hurting my nose, and down at the bottom a disheveled officer yelling at us to get out and join Squad Five, and the gangway reeling under us.

Cold. Freezing cold, and a wan sunshine from the shrunken little sun up there in the brassy sky, and a rolling plain of ochrous red sand stretching around us, sand that slid away under our feet as our squads followed Captain Wall toward the distant metal bulk that lay oddly canted and broken in a little shallow valley.

"Come on, men—hurry! Hurry!"

Sure, all of it a dream, the dreamlike way we walked with our lead-soled shoes dragging our feet back after each step, and the voices coming through the mask-resonators muffled and distant.

Only not a dream, but a nightmare, when we got up to the canted metal bulk and saw what had happened to Rocket Seven—the metal hull ripped like paper, and a few men crawling out of the wreck with blood on them, and a gurgling sound where shattered tanks were emptying, and voices whimpering, "First aid! First aid!"

Only it hadn't happened, it hadn't happened yet at all, for we were still back in Rocket Four coming in, we hadn't landed yet at all but we were going to any minute—

"We're coming down. . . ."

I couldn't go through it all again. I yelled and fought my hammock-straps and woke up, and I was in my plane seat and a scared hostess was a foot away from me, saying, "This is Omaha, Sergeant! We're coming down."

They were all looking at me, all the other passengers, and I guessed I'd been talking in the dream—I still had the sweat down my back like all those nights in the hospital when I'd keep waking up.

I sat up, and they all looked away from me quick and pretended they hadn't been staring.

We came down to the airport. It was midday, and the hot Nebraska sun felt good on my back when I got out. I was lucky, for when I asked at the bus depôt about going to Cuffington, there was a bus all ready to roll.

A farmer sat down beside me, a big, young fellow who offered me cigarettes and told me it was only a few hours' ride to Cuffington.

"Your home there?" he asked.

"No, my home's back in Ohio," I said. "A friend of mine came from there. Name of Clymer."

He didn't know him, but he remembered that one of the town boys had gone on that Second Expedition, to Mars.

"Yeah," I said. "That was Jim."

He couldn't keep it in any longer. "What's it like out there, anyway?"

I said, "Dry. Terribly dry."

"I'll bet it is," he said. "To tell the truth, it's too dry here, this year, for good wheat weather. Last year, it was fine. Last year—"

Cuffington, Nebraska, was a wide street of stores, and other streets with trees and old houses, and yellow wheatfields all around as far as you could see. It was pretty hot, and I was glad to sit down in the bus depôt while I went through the thin little phone book.

There were three Graham families in the book, but the first one I called was the right one—Miss Ila Graham. She talked fast and excited, and said she'd come right over, and I said I'd wait in the front of the bus depôt.

I stood underneath the awning, looking down the quiet street and thinking that it sort of explained why Jim Clymer had always been such a quiet, slow-moving sort of guy. The place was sort of relaxed, like he'd been.

A coupé pulled up, and Miss Graham opened the door. She was a brown-haired girl, not especially good-looking, but the kind you think of as a nice girl, a very nice girl.

She said, "You look so tired that I feel guilty now about asking you to stop."

"I'm all right," I said. "And it's no trouble stopping over a couple of places on my way back to Ohio."

As we drove across the little town, I asked her if Jim hadn't had any family of his own here.

"His parents were killed in a car crash years ago," Miss Graham said. "He lived with an uncle on a farm outside Grandview, but they didn't get along, and Jim came into town and got a job at the power station."

She added, as we turned a corner, "My mother rented him a room. That's how we got to know each other. That's how we—how we got engaged."

"Yeah, sure," I said.

It was a big square house with a deep front porch, and some trees around it. I sat down in a wicker chair, and Miss Graham brought her mother out. Her mother talked a little about Jim, how they missed him, and how she declared he'd been just like a son.

When her mother went back in, Miss Graham showed me a little bunch of blue envelopes. "These were the letters I got from Jim. There weren't very many of them, and they weren't very long."

"We were only allowed to send one short message every two weeks," I told her. "There were a couple of thousand of us out there, and they couldn't let us jam up the message-transmitter all the time."

"It was wonderful, how much Jim could put into just a few words," she said, and handed me some of them.

I read a couple. One said, "I have to pinch myself to realize that I'm one of the first Earthmen to stand on an alien world. At night, in the cold, I look up at the green star that's Earth and can't quite realize I've helped an age-old dream come true."

Another one said, "This world's grim and lonely, and mysterious. We don't know much about it, yet. So far, nobody's seen anything living but the lichens that Expedition One reported, but there might be anything here."

Miss Graham asked me, "Was that all there was, just lichens?"

"That, and two or three kinds of queer cactus things," I said. "And rock and sand. That's all."

As I read more of those little blue letters, I found that now that Jim was gone, I knew him better than I ever had. There was something about him I'd never suspected. He was romantic, inside. We hadn't suspected it, he was always so quiet and slow; but now I saw that all the time he was more romantic about the thing we were doing than any of us.

He hadn't let on. We'd have kidded him, if he had. Our name for Mars, after we got sick of it, was The Hole. We always talked about it as The Hole. I could see now that Jim had been too shy of our kidding to ever let us know that he glamourized the thing in his mind.

"This was the last one I got from him before his sickness," Miss Graham said.

That one said, "I'm starting north tomorrow with one of the mapping expeditions. We'll travel over country no human has ever seen before."

I nodded. "I was on that party, myself. Jim and I were on the same half-track."

"He was thrilled by it, wasn't he, Sergeant?"

I wondered. I remembered that trip, and it was hell. Our job was simply to run a preliminary topographical survey, checking with Geigers for possible uranium deposits.

It wouldn't have been so bad if the sand hadn't started to blow.

It wasn't sand like Earth sand. It was ground to dust by billions of years of blowing around that dry world. It got inside your breathing-mask, and your goggles, and the engines of the half-tracks, in your food and water and clothes. There was nothing for three days but cold, and wind, and sand.

Thrilled? I'd have laughed at that, before. But now, I didn't know. Maybe Jim had been, at that. He had lots of patience, a lot more than I ever had. Maybe he glamourized that hellish trip into wonderful adventure on a foreign world.

"Sure, he was thrilled," I said. "We all were. Anybody would be."

Miss Graham took the letters back, and then said, "You had Martian sickness too, didn't you?"

I said, Yes, I had, just a touch, and that was why I'd had to spend a stretch in Reconditioning Hospital when I got back.

She waited for me to go on, and I knew I had to. "They don't know yet if it's some sort of virus, or just the effect of Martian conditions on Earthmen's bodies. It hit forty percent of us. It wasn't really so bad—fever and dopiness, mostly."

"When Jim got it, was he well cared for?" she asked. Her lips were quivering a little.

"Sure, he was well cared for. He got the best care there was," I lied.

The best care there was? That was a laugh. The first cases got decent care, maybe. But they'd never figured on so many coming down. There wasn't any room in our little hospital—they just had to stay in their bunks in the aluminium Quonsets when it hit them. All our doctors but one were down, and two of them died.

We'd been on Mars six months when it hit us, and the loneliness had already got us down. All but four of our rockets had gone back to Earth, and we were alone on a dead world, our little town of Quonsets huddled together under that hateful, brassy sky, and beyond it the sand and rocks that went on forever.

You go up to the North Pole and camp there, and find out how lonely that is. It was worse, out there, a lot worse. The first excitement was gone long ago, and we were tired, and homesick in a way nobody was ever homesick before—we wanted to see green grass, and real sunshine, and women's faces, and hear running water; and we wouldn't until Expedition Three came to relieve us. No wonder guys blew their tops out there. And then came Martian sickness, on top of it.

"We did everything for him that we could," I said.

Sure we had. I could still remember Walter and me tramping through the cold night to the hospital to try to get a doctor, while Breck stayed with him, and how we couldn't get one.

I remember how Walter had looked up at the blazing sky as we tramped back, and shaken his fist at the big green star of Earth.

"People up there are going to dances tonight, watching shows, sitting around in warm rooms laughing! Why should good men have to die out here to get them uranium for cheap power?"

"Shut up," I told him tiredly. "Jim's not going to die. A lot of guys got over it."

The best care there was? That was real funny. All we could do was wash his face, and give him the pills the medic left, and watch him get weaker every day till he died.

"Nobody could have done more for him than was done," I told Miss Graham.

"I'm glad," she said. "I guess—it's just one of those things."

When I got up to go she asked me if I didn't want to see Jim's room. They'd kept it for him just the same, she said.

I didn't want to, but how are you going to say so? I went up with her and looked and said it was nice. She opened a big cupboard. It was full of neat rows of old magazines.

"They're all the old science-fiction magazines he read when he was a boy," she said. "He always saved them."

I took one out. It had a bright cover, with a spaceship on it, not like our rockets but a streamlined thing, and the rings of Saturn in the background.

When I laid it down, Miss Graham took it up and put it back carefully into its place in the row, as though somebody was coming back who wouldn't like to find things out of order.

She insisted on driving me back to Omaha, and out to the airport. She seemed sorry to let me go, and I suppose it was because I was the last real tie to Jim, and when I was gone it was all over then for good.

I wondered if she'd get over it in time, and I guessed she would. People do get over things. I suppose she'd marry some other nice guy, and I wondered what they'd do with Jim's things—with all those old magazines nobody was ever coming back to read.

I would never have stopped at Chicago at all if I could have got out of it, for the last person I wanted to talk to anybody about was Walter Millis. It would be too easy for me to make a slip, and let out stuff nobody was supposed to know.

But Walter's father had called me at the hospital, a couple of times. The last time he called, he said he was having Breck's parents come down from Wisconsin so they could see me too, so what could I do then but say, Yes, I'd stop. But I didn't like it at all, and I knew I'd have to be careful.

Mr. Millis was waiting at the airport and shook hands with me and said what a big favor I was doing them all, and how he appreciated my stopping when I must be anxious to get back to my own home and parents.

"That's all right," I said. "My dad and mother came out to the hospital to see me when I first got back."

He was a big, fine-looking important sort of man, with a little bit of the stuffed shirt about him, I thought. He seemed friendly enough, but I got the feeling he was looking at me and wondering why I'd come back and his son Walter hadn't. Well, I couldn't blame him for that.

His car was waiting, a big car with a driver, and we started north through the city. Mr. Millis pointed out a few things to me to make conversation, especially a big atomic power station we passed.

"It's only one of thousands, strung all over the world," he said. "They're going to transform our whole economy. This Martian uranium will be a big thing, Sergeant."

I said, Yes, I guessed it would.

I was sweating blood, waiting for him to start asking about Walter, and I didn't know yet just what I could tell him. I could get myself into plenty of trouble if I opened my mouth too wide, for that one thing that had happened to Expedition Two was supposed to be strictly secret, and we'd all been briefed on why we had to keep our mouths shut.

But he let it go for the time being, and talked about other stuff. I gathered that his wife wasn't too well, and that Walter had been their only child. I also gathered that he was a very big shot in business, and dough-heavy.

I didn't like him. Walter, I'd liked plenty, but his old man seemed a pretty pompous person, with his heavy business talk.

He wanted to know how soon I thought Martian uranium would come through in quantity, and I said I didn't think it'd be very soon.

"Expedition One only located the deposits," I said, "and Two just did mapping and setting up a preliminary base. Of course, the thing keeps expanding, and I hear Four will have a hundred rockets. But Mars is a tough setup."

Mr. Millis said decisively that I was wrong, that the world was power-hungry, that it would be pushed a lot faster than I expected.

He suddenly quit talking business and looked at me and asked, "Who was Walter's best friend, out there?"

He asked it sort of apologetically. He was a stuffed shirt; but all my dislike of him went away, then.

"Breck Jergen," I told him. "Breck was our sergeant . . . he sort of held our squad together, and he and Walter cottoned to each other from the first."

Mr. Millis nodded, but didn't say anything more about it. He pointed out the window at the distant lake, and said we were almost to his home.

It wasn't a home, it was a real mansion. We went in and he introduced me to Mrs. Millis. She was a limp, pale-looking woman, who said she was glad to meet one of Walter's friends. Somehow I got the feeling that even though he was a stuffed shirt, he felt it about Walter a lot more than she did.

He took me up to a bedroom and said that Breck's parents would arrive before dinner, and that I could get a little rest before then.

I sat looking around the room. It was the plushiest one I'd ever been in, and seeing this house and the way these people lived, I began to understand why Walter had blown his top more than the rest of us.

He'd been a good guy, Walter, but hot-tempered, and I could see now he'd been a little spoiled. The discipline at Training Base had been tougher on him than on most of us, and this was why.

I sat and dreaded this dinner that was coming up, and looked out the window at a swimming pool and tennis court, and wondered if anybody ever used them now that Walter was gone.

It seemed a queer thing for a fellow with a set-up like this to go out to Mars and get himself killed.

I took the satin cover off the bed so my shoes wouldn't dirty it, and lay down and closed my eyes, and wondered what I was going to tell them. The trouble was, I didn't know what story the officials had given them.

"The Commanding Officer regrets to inform you that your son was shot down like a dog—"

They'd never got any telegram like that. But just what line *had* been handed them? I wished I'd had a chance to check on that.

Damn it, why didn't all these people let me alone? They started it all going through my mind again, and the doctors had told me I ought to forget it for a while, but how could I?

It might be better just to tell them the truth. After all, Walter wasn't the only one who'd blown his top out there. In that grim last couple of months, plenty of guys had gone around sounding off.

Expedition Three isn't coming!

We're stuck, and they don't care enough about us to send help!

That was the line of talk. You heard it plenty, in those days. You couldn't blame the guys for it, either. A fourth of us down with Martian sickness, the little grave-markers clotting up the valley beyond the ridge, rations getting thin, medicine running low, everything running low, all of us watching the sky for rockets that never came.

There'd been a little hitch back on Earth, Colonel Nichols explained. (He was our CO now that General Rayen had died.) There was a little delay, but the rockets would be on their way soon, we'd get relief, we just had to hold on—

Holding on—that's what we were doing. Nights we'd sit in the Quonset, and listen to Lassen coughing in his bunk, and it seemed like wind-giants, cold-giants, were bawling and laughing around our little huddle of shelters.

"Damn it, if they're not coming, why don't we go home?" Walter said. "We've still got the four rockets—they could take us all back."

Breck's serious face got graver. "Look, Walter, there's too much of that stuff being talked around. Lay off."

"Can you blame the men for talking it? We're not story-book heroes. If they've forgotten about us back on Earth, why do we just sit and take it?"

"We have to," Breck said. "Three will come."

I've always thought that it wouldn't have happened, what did happen, if we hadn't had that false alarm. The one that set the whole camp wild that night, with guys shouting, "Three's here! The rockets landed over west of Rock Ridge!"

Only when they charged out there, they found they hadn't seen rockets landing at all, but a little shower of tiny meteors burning themselves up as they fell.

It was the disappointment that did it, I think. I can't say for sure, because that same day was the day I conked out with Martian sickness, and the floor came up and hit me and I woke up in the bunk, with somebody giving me a hypo, and my head big as a balloon.

I wasn't clear out, it was only a touch of it, but it was enough to make everything foggy, and I didn't know about the mutiny that was boiling up until I woke up once with Breck leaning over me, and saw he wore a gun and an MP brassard now.

When I asked him how come, he said there'd been so much wild talk about grabbing the four rockets and going home, that the MP force had been doubled, and Nichols had issued stern warnings.

"Walter?" I said, and Breck nodded.

"He's a leader and he'll get hit with a court-martial when this is over. The blasted idiot!"

"I don't get it—he's got plenty of guts, you know that," I said.

"Yes, but he can't take discipline, he never did take it very well, and now that the squeeze is on he's blowing up. Well, see you later, Frank."

I saw him later, but not the way I expected. For that was the day we heard the faint echo of shots, and then the alarm-siren screaming, and men running, and half-tracks starting up in a hurry. And when I managed to get out of my bunk and out of the hut, they were all going toward the big rockets, and a corporal yelled to me from a jeep, "That's blown it! The damn fools swiped guns and tried to take over the rockets and make the crews fly 'em home!"

I could still remember the sickening slidings and bouncings of the jeep as it took us out there, the little crowd under the looming rockets, milling around and hiding something on the ground, and Major Weiler yelling himself hoarse giving orders.

When I got to see what was on the ground, it was seven or

eight men and most of them dead. Walter had been shot right through the heart. They told me later it was because he'd been the leader, out in front, that he got it first of the mutineers.

One MP was dead, and one was sitting with red all over the middle of his uniform, and that one was Breck, and they were bringing a stretcher for him now.

The corporal said, "Hey, that's Jergen, your squad-leader!"

And I said, "Yes, that's him." Funny, how you can't talk when something hits you—how you just say words, like "Yes, that's him."

Breck died that night without ever regaining consciousness, and there I was, still half-sick myself, and with Lassen dying in his bunk, and five of us were all that was left of Squad Fourteen, and that was that.

How could HQ let a thing like that get known? A fine advertisement it would be for recruiting more Mars expeditions, if they told how guys on Two cracked up and did a crazy thing like that. I didn't blame them for telling us to keep it top secret. Anyway, it wasn't something we'd want to talk about.

But it sure left me in a fine spot now, a sweet spot. I was going down to talk to Breck's parents and Walter's parents, and they'd want to know how their sons died, and I could tell them, "Your sons probably killed each other, out there."

Sure, I could tell them that, couldn't I? But what *was* I going to tell them? I knew HQ had reported those casualties as "accidental deaths," but what kind of accident?

Well, it got late, and I had to go down, and when I did, Breck's parents were there. Mr. Jergen was a carpenter, a tall, bony man with level blue eyes like Breck's. He didn't say much, but his wife was a little woman who talked enough for both of them.

She told me I looked just like I did in the pictures of us Breck had sent home from Training Base. She said she had three daughters too—two of them married, and one of the married ones living in Milwaukee and one out on the Coast.

She said that she'd named Breck after a character in a book by Robert Louis Stevenson, and I said I'd read the book in high school.

"It's a nice name," I said.

She looked at me with bright eyes and said, "Yes. It was a nice name."

That was a fine dinner. They'd got everything they thought I might like, and all the best, and a maid served it, and I couldn't taste a thing I ate.

Then afterward, in the big living room, they all just sort of sat and waited, and I knew it was up to me.

I asked them if they'd had any details about the accident, and Mr. Millis said, No, just "accidental death" was all they'd been told.

Well, that made it easier. I sat there, with all four of them watching my face, and dreamed it up.

I said, "It was one of those one-in-a-million things. You see, more little meteorites hit the ground on Mars than here, because the air's so much thinner it doesn't burn them up so fast. And one hit the edge of the fuel-dump and a bunch of little tanks started to blow. I was down with the sickness, so I didn't see it, but I heard all about it."

You could hear everybody breathing, it was so quiet as I went on with my yarn.

"A couple of guys were knocked out by the concussion, and would have been burned up if a few fellows hadn't got in there fast with foamite extinguishers. They kept it away from the big tanks, but another little tank let go, and Breck and Walter were two of the fellows who'd gone in, and they were killed instantly."

When I'd got it told, it sounded corny to me and I was afraid they'd never believe it. But nobody said anything, until Mr. Millis let out a sigh and said, "So that was it. Well—well, if it had to be, it was mercifully quick, wasn't it?"

I said, Yes, it was quick.

"Only, I can't see why they couldn't have let us know. It doesn't seem fair—"

I had an answer for that. "It's hush-hush because they don't want people to know about the meteor danger. That's why."

Mrs. Millis got up and said she wasn't feeling so well, and would I excuse her and she'd see me in the morning. The rest of us didn't seem to have much to say to each other, and nobody objected when I went up to my bedroom a little later.

I was getting ready to turn in when there was a knock on the door. It was Breck's father, and he came in and looked at me, steadily.

"It was just a story, wasn't it?" he said.

I said, "Yes. It was just a story."

His eyes bored into me and he said, "I guess you've got your reasons. Just tell me one thing. Whatever it was, did Breck behave right?''

"He behaved like a man, all the way," I said. "He was the best man of us, first to last.''

He looked at me, and I guess something made him believe me. He shook hands and said, ''All right, son. We'll let it go.''

I'd had enough. I wasn't going to face them again in the morning. I wrote a note, thanking them all and making excuses, and then went down and slipped quietly out of the house.

It was late, but a truck coming along picked me up, and the driver said he was going near the airport. He asked me what it was like on Mars and I told him it was lonesome. I slept in a chair at the airport, and I felt better, for next day I'd be home, and it would be over.

That's what I thought.

It was getting toward evening when we reached the village, for my father and mother hadn't known I was coming on an earlier plane, and I'd had to wait for them up at Cleveland airport. When we drove into Market Street, I saw there was a big painted banner stretching across:

''HARMONVILLE WELCOMES HOME ITS SPACEMAN!''

Spaceman—that was me. The newspapers had started calling us that, I guess, because it was a short word good for headlines. Everybody called us that now. We'd sat cooped up in a prison-cell that flew, that was all—but now we were ''spacemen.''

There were bright uniforms clustered under the banner, and I saw that it was the high school band. I didn't say anything, but my father saw my face.

''Now, Frank, I know you're tired, but these people are your friends and they want to show you a real welcome.''

That was fine. Only it was all gone again, the relaxed feeling I'd been beginning to get as we drove down from Cleveland.

This was my home-country, this old Ohio country with its neat little white villages and fat, rolling farms. It looked good, in June. It looked very good, and I'd been feeling better all the time. And now I didn't feel so good, for I saw that I was going to have to talk some more about Mars.

Dad stopped the car under the banner, and the high school band started to play, and Mr. Robinson, who was the local car dealer and also the mayor of Harmonville, got into the car with us.

He shook hands with me and said, 'Welcome home, Frank! What was it like out on Mars?''

I said, "It was cold, Mr. Robinson. Awful cold."

"You should have been here last February!" he said. "Eighteen below—nearly a record."

He leaned out and gave a signal, and Dad started driving again, with the band marching along in front of us and playing. We didn't have far to go, just down Market Street under the big old maples, past the churches and the old white houses to the square white Grange Hall.

There was a little crowd in front of it, and they made a sound like a cheer—not a real loud one, you know how peole can be self-conscious about really cheering—when we drove up. I got out and shook hands with people I didn't really see, and then Mr. Robinson took my elbow and took me on inside.

The seats were all filled and people standing up, and over the little stage at the far end they'd fixed up a big floral decoration— there was a globe all of red roses with a sign above it that said "Mars," and beside it a globe all of white roses that said "Earth," and a little rocketship made out of flowers was hung between them.

"The Garden Club fixed it up," said Mr. Robinson. "Nearly everybody in Harmonville contributed flowers."

"It sure is pretty," I said.

Mr. Robinson took me by the arm, up on the little stage, and everyone clapped. They were all people I knew—people from the farms near ours, my high school teachers, and all that.

I sat down in a chair and Mr. Robinson made a little speech, about how Harmonville boys had always gone out when anything big was doing, how they'd gone to the War of 1812 and the Civil War and the two World Wars, and how now one of them had gone to Mars.

He said, "Folks have always wondered what it's like out there on Mars, and now here's one of our own Harmonville boys come back to tell us all about it."

And he motioned me to get up, and I did, and they clapped some more, and I stood wondering what I could tell them.

And all of a sudden, as I stood there wondering, I got the answer to something that had always puzzled us out there. We'd never been able to understand why the fellows who had come back from Expedition One hadn't tipped us off how tough it was going to be. And now I knew why. They hadn't, because it would have sounded as if they were whining about all they'd been through. And now I couldn't, for the same reason.

I looked down at the bright, interested faces, the faces I'd known almost all my life, and I knew that what I could tell them was no good anyway. For they'd all read those newspaper stories, about "the exotic red planet" and "heroic spacemen," and if anyone tried to give them a different picture now, it would just upset them.

I said, "It was a long way out there. But flying space is a wonderful thing—flying right off the Earth, into the stars—there's nothing quite like it."

Flying space, I called it. It sounded good, and thrilling. How could they know that flying space meant lying strapped in that blind stokehold, listening to Joe Valinez dying, and praying and praying that it wouldn't be our rocket that cracked up?

"And it's a wonderful thrill to come out of a rocket and step on a brand-new world, to look up at a different-looking sun, to look around at a whole new horizon—"

Yes, it was wonderful. Especially for the guys in Rockets Seven and Nine who got squashed like flies and lay around there on the sand, moaning "First aid!" Sure, it was a big thrill, for them and for us who had to try to help them.

"There were hardships out there, but we all knew that a big job had to be done—"

That's a nice word too, "hardships." It's not coarse and ugly like fellows coughing their hearts out from too much dust; it's not like having your best friend die of Martian sickness right in the room you sleep in. It's a nice, cheerful word, "hardships."

"—and the only way we could get the job done, away out there so far from Earth, was by teamwork."

Well, that was true enough in its way, and what was the use of spoiling it by telling them how Walter and Breck had died?

"The job's going on, and Expedition Three is building a bigger base out there right now, and Four will start soon. And it'll mean plenty of uranium, plenty of cheap atomic power, for all Earth."

That's what I said, and I stopped there. But I wanted to go on and add, "And it wasn't worth it! It wasn't worth all those guys, all the hell we went through, just to get cheap atomic power so you people can run more electric washers and television sets and toasters!"

But how are you going to stand up and say things like that to people you know, people who like you? And who was I to decide? Maybe I was wrong, anyway. Maybe lots of things I'd had and never thought about had been squeezed out of other good guys, back in the past.

I wouldn't know.

Anyway, that was all I could tell them, and I sat down, and there was a big lot of applause, and I realized then that I'd done right, I'd told them just what they wanted to hear, and everyone was all happy about it.

Then things broke up, and people came up to me, and I shook a lot more hands. And finally, when I got outside, it was dark—soft, summery dark, the way I hadn't seen it for a long time. And my father said we ought to be getting on home, so I could rest.

I told him, "You folks drive on ahead, and I'll walk. I'll take the short cut. I'd sort of like to walk through town."

Our farm was only a couple of miles out of the village, and the short cut across Heller's farm I'd always taken when I was a kid was only a mile. Dad didn't think maybe I ought to walk so far, but I guess he saw I wanted to, so they went on ahead.

I walked on down Market Street, and around the little square, and the maples and elms were dark over my head, and the flowers on the lawns smelled the way they used to, but it wasn't the same either—I'd thought it would be, but it wasn't.

When I cut off past the Oddfellows' Hall, beyond it I met Hobe Evans, the garage-hand at Robinson's, who was humming along half-tight, the same as always on a Saturday night.

"Hello, Frank, heard you were back," he said. I waited for him to ask the question they all asked, but he didn't. He said: "Boy, you don't look so good! Want a drink?"

He brought out a bottle, and I had one out of it, and he had one, and he said he'd see me around, and went humming on his way. He was feeling too good to care much where I'd been.

I went on, in the dark, across Heller's pasture and then along the creek under the big old willows. I stopped there like I'd always stopped when I was a kid, to hear the frog noises, and there they were, and all the June noises, the night noises, and the night smells.

I did something I hadn't done for a long time. I looked up at the starry sky, and there it was, the same little red dot I'd peered at when I was a kid and read those old stories, the same red dot that Breck and Jim and Walter and I had stared away at on nights at Training Base, wondering if we'd ever really get there.

Well, they'd got there, and weren't ever going to leave it now, and there'd be others to stay with them, more and more of them as time went by.

But it was the ones I knew that made the difference, as I looked up at the red dot.

I wished I could explain to them somehow why I hadn't told the truth, not the whole truth. I tried, sort of, to explain.

"I didn't want to lie," I said. "But I had to—at least, it seemed like I had to—"

I quit it. It was crazy, talking to guys who were dead and forty million miles away. They were dead, and it was over, and that was that. I quit looking up at the red dot in the sky, and started on home again.

But I felt as though something was over for me, too. It was being young. I didn't feel old. But I didn't feel young, either, and I didn't think I ever would, not ever again.

SAIL ON! SAIL ON!

by Philip Jose Farmer (1918–

This now sounds like a cliché, but Philip José Farmer really *did* burst onto the science fiction scene in 1952. His debut was in August with "The Lovers," a stunning treatment of love between a human male and an alien female. It was shocking to some readers and it had a lasting effect—it played a major role in broadening the definition of what was acceptable material in a science fiction magazine. It also won its author a Hugo for Best New Writer. Since that time he has gone on to produce more than forty novels and collections, win several more Hugos, and make the bestseller lists. We will certainly meet him again as this series continues.

"The Lovers," which is too long for inclusion here, was not the only important story that he published in 1952. "Sail on! Sail On!" is almost as remarkable as the former story in its own way, but let's let Phil tell about how he came to write it after experiencing a recurring dream: "I saw the tiny galleon of the Portuguese Prince Henry the Navigator [A.D. 1394–1460]. It was sailing along in a heavy sea and on a dark night. A small building was on the poop deck; in it sat a very fat monk. He had earphones on and was tapping out a coded message, in Latin, on a spark-gap transmitter. . . ."

Phil Farmer has been sharing his dreams with us ever since. (MHG)

Science fiction deals with societies other than our own, and, almost always, the other-society differs from ours in the level of its technology.

Most commonly, such an other-society is in the future and has a level of technology higher than ours in every respect.

Sometimes it is in the past, or in the future after a catastrophe, and is lower than ours in every respect. In time-travel stories, a bit of higher technology is brought into our world, or a bit of our technology into a past world and so on.

Any of this could be treated lightly, but is usually not.

However, it is also possible to have a parallel world, in which the level of technology is jumbled—higher in some respects, but not higher (even lower) in other respects.

The result is almost inevitably humorous to some extent, and it can happen that the humor is made central. The animated cartoon The Flintstones and the comic strip, B.C. deal with jumbled technology.

In dealing with humor and satire, you don't have to worry about self-consistency, so that the Flintstones can take photographs by having a bird peck out the picture inside the stone camera, and B.C. can have a single wheel and protruding axle fulfill all the functions of an automobile.

It's much harder to do it seriously, and labor over consistency. Turn to "Sail On! Sail On!" and read on, read on. (IA)

Friar Sparks sat wedged between the wall and the realizer. He was motionless except for his forefinger and his eyes. From time to time his finger tapped rapidly on the key upon the desk, and now and then his irises, gray-blue as his native Irish sky, swiveled to look through the open door of the *toldilla* in which he crouched, the little shanty on the poop deck. Visibility was low.

Outside was dusk and a lantern by the railing. Two sailors leaned on it. Beyond them bobbed the bright lights and dark shapes of the *Niña* and the *Pinta*. And beyond them was the smooth horizon-brow of the Atlantic, edged in black and blood by the red dome of the rising moon.

The single carbon filament bulb above the monk's tonsure showed a face lost in fat—and in concentration.

The luminiferous ether crackled and hissed tonight, but the

phones clamped over his ears carried, along with them, the steady dots and dashes sent by the operator at the Las Palmas station on the Grand Canary.

"*Zzisss!* So you are out of sherry already. . . . *Pop!* . . . Too bad . . . *Crackle* . . . you hardened old winebutt . . . *Zzz* . . . May God have mercy on your sins. . . .

"Lots of gossip, news, et cetera. . . . *Hisses!* . . . Bend your ear instead of your neck, impious one. . . . The Turks are said to be gathering . . . *crackle* . . . an army to march on Austria. It is rumored that the flying sausages, said by so many to have been seen over the capitals of the Christian world, are of Turkish origin. The rumor goes they have been invented by a renegade Rogerian who was converted to the Muslim religion. . . . I say . . . *zziss* . . . to that. No one of us would do that. It is a falsity spread by our enemies in the Church to discredit us. But many people believe that. . . .

"How close does the Admiral calculate he is to Cipangu now?

"Flash! Savonarola today denounced the Pope, the wealthy of Florence, Greek art and literature, and the experiments of the disciples of Saint Roger Bacon. . . . *Zzz!* . . . The man is sincere but misguided and dangerous. . . . I predict he'll end up at the stake he's always prescribing for us. . . .

"*Pop*. . . . This will kill you. . . . Two Irish mercenaries by the name of Pat and Mike were walking down the street of Granada when a beautiful Saracen lady leaned out of a balcony and emptied a pot of . . . *hiss!* . . . and Pat looked up and . . . *Crackle*. . . . Good, hah? Brother Juan told that last night. . . .

"PV . . . PV . . . Are you coming in? . . . PV . . . PV . . . Yes, I know it's dangerous to bandy such jests about, but nobody is monitoring us tonight. . . . *Zzz*. . . . I think they're not, anyway. . . ."

And so the ether bent and warped with their messages. And presently Friar Sparks tapped out the PV that ended their talk—the "*Pax vobiscum*." Then he pulled the plug out that connected his earphones to the set and, lifting them from his ears, clamped them down forward over his temples in the regulation manner.

After sidling bent-kneed from the *toldilla*, punishing his belly against the desk's hard edge as he did so, he walked over to the railing. De Salcedo and de Torres were leaning there and talking in low tones. The big bulb above gleamed on the page's red-gold hair and on the interpreter's full black beard. It also bounced pinkishly off the priest's smooth-shaven jowls and the light scarlet robe of the Rogerian order. His cowl, thrown back, served as a bag for scratch paper, pens, an ink bottle, tiny wrenches and screwdrivers, a book of cryptography, a slide rule, and a manual of angelic principles.

"Well, old rind," said young de Salcedo familiarly, "what do you hear from Las Palmas?"

"Nothing now. Too much interference from that." He pointed to the moon riding the horizon ahead of them. "What an orb!" bellowed the priest. "It's as big and red as my revered nose!"

The two sailors laughed, and de Salcedo said, "But it will get smaller and paler as the night grows, Father. And your proboscis will, on the contrary, become larger and more sparkling in inverse proportion according to the square of the ascent—"

He stopped and grinned, for the monk had suddenly dipped his nose, like a porpoise diving into the sea, raised it again, like the same animal jumping from a wave, and then once more plunged it into the heavy currents of their breath. Nose to nose, he faced them, his twinkling little eyes seeming to emit sparks like the realizer in his *toldilla*.

Again, porpoiselike, he sniffed and snuffed several times, quite loudly. Then satisfied with what he had gleaned from their breaths, he winked at them. He did not, however, mention his findings at once, preferring to sidle toward the subject.

He said, "This Father Sparks on the Grand Canary is so entertaining. He stimulates me with all sorts of philosophical notions, both valid and fantastic. For instance, tonight, just before we were cut off by that"—he gestured at the huge bloodshot eye in the sky—"he was discussing what he called worlds of parallel time tracks, an idea originated by Dysphagius of Gotham. It's his idea there may be other worlds in coincident but not contacting universes, that God, being infinite and of unlimited creative talent and ability, the Master Alchemist, in other words, has possibly—perhaps necessarily—created a plurality of continua in which every probable event has happened."

"Huh?" grunted de Salcedo.

"Exactly. Thus, Columbus was turned down by Queen Isabella, so this attempt to reach the Indies across the Atlantic was never made. So we could not now be standing here plunging ever deeper into Oceanus in our three cockle-shells, there would be no booster buoys strung out between us and the Canaries, and Father Sparks at Las Palmas and I on the *Santa Maria* would not be carrying on our fascinating conversations across the ether.

"Or, say, Roger Bacon was persecuted by the Church, instead of being encouraged and giving rise to the order whose inventions have done so much to insure the monopoly of the Church on alchemy and its divinely inspired guidance of that formerly pagan and hellish practice."

De Torres opened his mouth, but the priest silenced him with a magnificent and imperious gesture and continued.

"Or, even more ridiculous, but thought-provoking, he speculated just this evening on universes with different physical laws. One, in particular, I thought very droll. As you probably don't know, Angelo Angelei has proved, by dropping objects from the Leaning Tower of Pisa, that different weights fall at different speeds. My delightful colleague on the Grand Canary is writing a satire which takes place in a universe where Aristotle is made out to be a liar, where all things drop with equal velocities, no matter what their size. Silly stuff, but it helps to pass the time. We keep the ether busy with our little angels."

De Salcedo said, "Uh, I don't want to seem too curious about the secrets of your holy and cryptic order, Friar Sparks. But these little angels your machine realizes intrigue me. Is it a sin to presume to ask about them?"

The monk's bull roar slid to a dove cooing. "Whether it's a sin or not depends. Let me illustrate, young fellows. If you were concealing a bottle of, say, very scarce sherry on you, and you did not offer to share it with a very thirsty old gentleman, that would be a sin. A sin of ommission. But if you were to give that desert-dry, that pilgrim-weary, that devout, humble, and decrepit old soul a long, soothing, refreshing, and stimulating draught of life-giving fluid, daughter of the vine, I would find it in my heart to pray for you for that deed of loving kindness, of encompassing charity. And it would please me so much I might tell you a little of our realizer. Not enough to hurt you, just enough so you might gain more respect for the intelligence and glory of my order."

De Salcedo grinned conspiratorially and passed the monk the bottle he'd hidden under his jacket. As the friar tilted it, and the chug-chug-chug of vanishing sherry became louder, the two sailors glanced meaningfully at each other. No wonder the priest, reputed to be so brilliant in his branch of the alchemical mysteries, had yet been sent off on this half-baked voyage to devil-knew-where. The Church had calculated that if he survived, well and good. If he didn't, then he would sin no more.

The monk wiped his lips on his sleeve, belched loudly as a horse, and said, "*Gracias*, boys. From my heart, so deeply buried in this fat, I thank you. An old Irishman, dry as a camel's hoof, choking to death with the dust of abstinence, thanks you. You have saved my life."

"Thank rather that magic nose of yours," replied de Salcedo. "Now, old rind, now that you're well greased again, would you mind explaining as much as you are allowed about that machine of yours?"

Friar Sparks took fifteen minutes. At the end of that time, his listeners asked a few permitted questions.

". . . and you say you broadcast on a frequency of eighteen hundred k.c.?" the page asked. "What does 'k.c.' mean?"

"K stands for the French *kilo*, from a Greek word meaning thousand. And c stands for the Hebrew *cherubim*, the 'little angels.' Angel comes from the Greek *angelos*, meaning messenger. It is our concept that the ether is crammed with these cherubim, these little messengers. Thus, when we Friar Sparkses depress the key of our machine, we are able to realize some of the infinity of 'messengers' waiting for just such a demand for service.

"So, eighteen hundred k.c. means that in a given unit of time one million, eight hundred thousand cherubim line up and hurl themselves across the ether, the nose of one being brushed by the feathertips of the cherub's wings ahead. The height of the wing crests of each little creature is even, so that if you were to draw an outline of the whole train, there would be nothing to distinguish one cherub from the next, the whole column forming that grade of little angels known as C.W."

"C.W.?"

"Continuous wingheight. My machine is a C.W. realizer."

Young de Salcedo said, "My mind reels. Such a concept! Such a revelation! It almost passes comprehension. Imagine, the aerial of your realizer is cut just so long, so that the evil cherubim surging back and forth on it demand a predetermined and equal number of good angels to combat them. And this seduction coil on the realizer crowds 'bad' angels into the left-hand, the sinister, side. And when the bad little cherubim are crowded so closely and numerously that they can't bear each other's evil company, they jump the spark gap and speed around the wire to the 'good' plate. And in this racing back and forth they call themselves to the attention of the 'little messengers,' the yea-saying cherubim. And you, Friar Sparks, by manipulating your machine thus and so, and by lifting and lowering your key, you bring these invisible and friendly lines of carriers, your etheric and winged postmen, into reality. And you are able, thus, to comunicate at great distances with your brothers of the order."

"Great God!" said de Torres.

It was not a vain oath but a pious exclamation of wonder. His eyes bulged; it was evident that he suddenly saw that man was not alone, that on every side, piled on top of each other, flanked on every angle, stood a host. Black and white, they presented a solid chessboard of the seemingly empty cosmos, black for the nay-sayers, white for the yea-sayers, maintained by a Hand in delicate balance and subject as the fowls of the air and the fish of the sea to exploitation by man.

Yet de Torres, having seen such a vision as has made a saint of many a man, could only ask, "Perhaps you could tell me how many angels may stand on the point of a pin?"

Obviously, de Torres would never wear a halo. He was destined, if he lived, to cover his bony head with the mortarboard of a university teacher.

De Salcedo snorted. "I'll tell you. Philosophically speaking, you may put as many angels on a pinhead as you want to. Actually speaking, you may put only as many as there is room for. Enough of that. I'm interested in facts, not fancies. Tell me, how could the moon's rising interrupt your reception of the cherubim sent by the Sparks at Las Palmas?"

"Great Caesar, how would I know? Am I a repository of universal knowledge? No, not I! A humble and ignorant friar, I! All I can tell you is that last night it rose like a bloody tumor on the horizon, and that when it was up I had to quit marshaling my little messengers in their short and long columns. The Canary station was quite overpowered, so that both of us gave up. And the same thing happened tonight."

"The moon sends messages?" asked de Torres.

"Not in a code I can decipher. But it sends, yes."

"Santa Maria!"

"Perhaps," suggested de Salcedo, "there are people on that moon, and they are sending."

Friar Sparks blew derision through his nose. Enormous as were his nostrils, his derision was not smallbore. Artillery of contempt laid down a barrage that would have silenced any but the strongest of souls.

"Maybe"—de Torres spoke in a low tone—"maybe, if the stars are windows in heaven, as I've heard said, the angels of the higher hierarchy, the big ones, are realizing—uh—the smaller? And they only do it when the moon is up so we may know it is a celestial phenomenon?"

He crossed himself and looked around the vessel.

"You need not fear," said the monk gently. "There is no Inquisitor leaning over your shoulder. Remember, I am the only priest on this expedition. Moreover, your conjecture has nothing to do with dogma. However, that's unimportant. Here's what I don't understand: how can a heavenly body broadcast? Why does it have the same frequency as the one I'm restricted to? Why—"

"I could explain," interrupted de Salcedo with all the brashness and impatience of youth. "I could say that the Admiral and the Rogerians are wrong about the earth's shape. I could say the earth is not round but is flat. I could say the horizon exists, not because we live upon a globe, but because the earth is curved only a little ways, like a greatly flattened-out hemisphere. I could also say that the cherubim are coming, not from Luna, but from a ship such as ours, a vessel which is hanging in the void off the edge of the earth."

"What?" gasped the other two.

"Haven't you heard," said de Salcedo, "that the King of Portugal secretly sent out a ship after he turned down Columbus' proposal? How do we know he did not, that the messages are from our predecessor, that he sailed off the world's rim and is now suspended in the air and becomes exposed at night because it follows the moon around Terra—is, in fact, a much smaller and unseen satellite?"

The monk's laughter woke many men on the ship. "I'll have to tell the Las Palmas operator your tale. He can put it in that novel of his. Next you'll be telling me those messages are from one of those fire-shooting sausages so many credulous laymen have been seeing flying around. No, my dear de Salcedo, let's not be ridiculous. Even the ancient Greeks knew the earth was round. Every university in Europe teaches that. And we Rogerians have measured the circumference. We know for sure that the Indies lie just across the Atlantic. Just as we know for sure, through mathematics, that heavier-than-air machines are impossible. Our Friar Ripskulls, our mind doctors, have assured us these flying creations are mass hallucinations or else the tricks of heretics or Turks who want to panic the populace.

"That moon radio is no delusion, I'll grant you. What it is, I don't know. But it's not a Spanish or Portuguese ship. What about its different code? Even if it came from Lisbon, that ship would still have a Rogerian operator. And he would, according to our policy, be of a different nationality from the crew so he might the easier stay out of political embroilments. He wouldn't break our laws by using a different code in order to communicate with Lisbon. We disciples of Saint Roger do not stoop to petty boundary intrigues. Moreover, that realizer would not be powerful enough to reach Europe, and must, therefore, be directed at us."

"How can you be sure?" said de Salcedo. "Distressing though the thought may be to you, a priest could be subverted. Or a layman could learn your secrets and invent a code. I think that a Portuguese ship is sending to another, a ship perhaps not too distant from us."

De Torres shivered and crossed himself again. "Perhaps the angels are warning us of approaching death? Perhaps?"

"Perhaps? Then why don't they use our code? Angels would know it as well as I. No, there is no perhaps. The order does not permit perhaps. It experiments and finds out; nor does it pass judgment until it knows."

"I doubt we'll ever know," said de Salcedo gloomily. "Columbus has promised the crew that if we come across no sign of land by evening tomorrow, we shall turn back. Otherwise"—he drew a finger across his throat—"*kkk!* Another day, and we'll be pointed east and getting away from that evil and bloody-looking moon and its incomprehensible messages."

"It would be a great loss to the order and to the Church," sighed the friar. "But I leave such things in the hands of God and inspect only what He hands me to look at."

With which pious statement Friar Sparks lifted the bottle to ascertain the liquid level. Having determined in a scientific manner its existence, he next measured its quantity and tested its quality by putting all of it in that best of all chemistry tubes, his enormous belly.

Afterward, smacking his lips and ignoring the pained and disappointed looks on the faces of the sailors, he went on to speak enthusiastically of the water screw and the engine which turned it, both of which had been built recently at the St. Jonas

College at Genoa. If Isabella's three ships had been equipped with those, he declared, they would not have to depend upon the wind. However, so far, the fathers had forbidden its extended use because it was feared the engine's fumes might poison the air and the terrible speeds it made possible might be fatal to the human body. After which he plunged into a tedious description of the life of his patron saint, the inventor of the first cherubim realizer and receiver, Jonas of Carcassonne, who had been martyred when he grabbed a wire he thought was insulated.

The two sailors found excuses to walk off. The monk was a good fellow, but hagiography bored them. Besides, they wanted to talk of women. . . .

If Columbus had not succeeded in persuading his crews to sail one more day, events would have been different.

At dawn the sailors were very much cheered by the sight of several large birds circling their ships. Land could not be far off; perhaps these winged creatures came from the coast of fabled Cipangu itself, the country whose houses were roofed with gold.

The birds swooped down. Closer, they were enormous and very strange. Their bodies were flattish and almost saucer-shaped and small in proportion to the wings, which had a spread of at least thirty feet. Nor did they have legs. Only a few sailors saw the significance of that fact. These birds dwelt in the air and never rested upon land or sea.

While they were meditating upon that, they heard a slight sound as of a man clearing his throat. So gentle and far off was the noise that nobody paid any attention to it, for each thought his neighbor had made it.

A few minutes later, the sound had become louder and deeper, like a lute string being twanged.

Everybody looked up. Heads were turned west.

Even yet they did not understand that the noise like a finger plucking a wire came from the line that held the earth together, and that the line was stretched to its utmost, and that the violent finger of the sea was what had plucked the line.

It was some time before they understood. They had run out of horizon.

When they saw that, they were too late.

The dawn had not only come up *like* thunder, it *was* thunder. And though the three ships heeled over at once and tried to sail close-hauled on the port tack, the suddenly speeded-up and relentless current made beating hopeless.

Then it was the Rogerian wished for the Genoese screw and the wood-burning engine that would have made them able to resist the terrible muscles of the charging and bull-like sea. Then it was that some men prayed, some raved, some tried to attack the Admiral, some jumped overboard, and some sank into a stupor.

Only the fearless Columbus and the courageous Friar Sparks stuck to their duties. All that day the fat monk crouched wedged in his little shanty, dot-dashing to his fellow on the Grand Canary. He ceased only when the moon rose like a huge red bubble from the throat of a dying giant. Then he listened intently all night and worked desperately, scribbling and swearing impiously and checking cipher books.

When the dawn came up again in a roar and a rush, he ran from the *toldilla* a piece of paper clutched in his hand. His eyes were wild, and his lips were moving fast, but nobody could understand that he had cracked the code. They could not hear him shouting, "It is the Portuguese! It is the Portuguese!"

Their ears were too overwhelmed to hear a mere human voice. The throat clearing and the twanging of a string had been the noises preliminary to the concert itself. Now came the mighty overture; as compelling as the blast of Gabriel's horn was the topple of Oceanus into space.

COST OF LIVING

COST OF LIVING

by Robert Sheckley

Here's Sheckley again, with what I feel remains one of his very best stories. He has a good handle on the possibilities and limitations of the social sciences, and in the 1950s and 1960s was one of science fiction's premier writers of "soft" sf. The only problem with "Cost of Living" is that thirty-three years later (God, can it be that long?), with an American budget deficit in the hundreds of billions of dollars, it doesn't seem so funny. (MHG)

Well, let's see now. The national debt of the Unied States has doubled in the last four years.

By stringent economies and the evisceration of humane social programs, 76 billion dollars has been saved, but the interest on the debt has increased by 150 billion dollars in the same interval. What's more, the interest is going up as fast as the national debt is going up and further eviscerations must take place just to make the interest go up a little more slowly.

The interest is being paid to rich men who have enough money to spare to lend to the government. The evisceration of services is being done at the expense of poor people who make most use of the services. Taxes which take money from all and don't have to be repaid have been cut, very largely to the benefit of the well off so that the national debt and the interest go up even faster.

We can't stop paying the interest because that's called bankruptcy and we won't be able to borrow any more. Pretty soon, we can't pay the interest because we won't have enough money.

But nobody seems to worry, and President Reagan, who

lowered taxes and raised the amount of money spent on arms (with perhaps a trillion dollars yet to go for his Star Wars programs) smiles and tells us it's all a glad, jolly morning for America, and we re-elect him by a landslide.

You don't understand it, either? Well, read Bob's "Cost of Living," written more than a quarter of a century ago (!!) and see if that helps. (IA)

Carrin decided that he could trace his present mood to Miller's suicide last week. But the knowledge didn't help him get rid of the vague, formless fears in the back of his mind. It was foolish. Miller's suicide didn't concern him.

But why had that fat, jovial man killed himself? Miller had had everything to live for—wife, kids, good job, and all the marvelous luxuries of the age. Why had he done it?

"Good morning, dear," Carrin's wife said as he sat down at the breakfast table.

"Morning, honey. Morning, Billy."

His son grunted something.

You just couldn't tell about people, Carrin decided, and dialed his breakfast. The meal was gracefully prepared and served by the new Avignon Electric Auto-cook.

His mood persisted, annoyingly enough since Carrin wanted to be in top form this morning. It was his day off, and the Avignon Electric finance man was coming. This was an important day.

He walked to the door with his son.

"Have a good day, Billy."

His son nodded, shifted his books and started to school without answering. Carrin wondered if something was bothering him, too. He hoped not. One worrier in the family was plenty.

"See you later, honey." He kissed his wife as she left to go shopping.

At any rate, he thought, watching her go down the walk, she's happy. He wondered how much she'd spend at the A. E. store.

Checking his watch, he found that he had half an hour before the A. E. finance man was due. The best way to get rid of a bad mood was to drown it, he told himself, and headed for the shower.

The shower room was a glittering plastic wonder, and the sheer luxury of it eased Carrin's mind. He threw his clothes into the A. E. automatic Kleen-presser, and adjusted the shower spray to a notch above "brisk." The five-degrees-above-skin-temperature water beat against his thin white body. Delightful! And then a relaxing rub-dry in the A. E. Auto-towel.

Wonderful, he thought, as the towel stretched and kneaded his stringy muscles. And it should be wonderful, he reminded himself. The A. E. Auto-towel with shaving attachments had cost three hundred and thirteen dollars, plus tax.

But worth every penny of it, he decided, as the A. E. shaver came out of a corner and whisked off his rudimentary stubble. After all, what good was life if you couldn't enjoy the luxuries?

His skin tingled when he switched off the Auto-towel. He should have been feeling wonderful, but he wasn't. Miller's suicide kept nagging at his mind, destroying the peace of his day off.

Was there anything else bothering him? Certainly there was nothing wrong with the house. His papers were in order for the finance man.

"Have I forgotten something?" he asked out loud.

"The Avignon Electric finance man will be here in fifteen minutes," his A. E. bathroom Wall-reminder whispered.

"I know that. Is there anything else?"

The Wall-reminder reeled off its memorized data—a vast amount of minutiae about watering the lawn, having the Jet-lash checked, buying lamb chops for Monday, and the like. Things he still hadn't found time for.

"All right, that's enough." He allowed the A. E. Auto-dresser to dress him, skillfully draping a new selection of fabrics over his bony frame. A whiff of fashionable masculine perfume finished him and he went into the living room, threading his way among the appliances that lined the walls.

A quick inspection of the dials on the wall assured him that the house was in order. The breakfast dishes had been sanitized and stacked, the house had been cleaned, dusted, polished, his wife's garments had been hung up; his son's model rocket ships had been put back in the closet.

Stop worrying, you hypochondriac, he told himself angrily.

The door announced, "Mr. Pathis from Avignon Finance is here."

Carrin started to tell the door to open, when he noticed the Automatic Bartender.

Good God, why hadn't he thought of it!

The Automatic Bartender was manufactured by Castile Motors. He had bought it in a weak moment. A. E. wouldn't think very highly of that, since they sold their own brand.

He wheeled the bartender into the kitchen, and told the door to open.

"A very good day to you, sir," Mr. Pathis said.

Pathis was a tall, imposing man, dressed in a conservative tweed drape. His eyes had the crinkled corners of a man who laughs frequently. He beamed broadly and shook Carrin's hand, looking around the crowded living room.

"A beautiful place you have here, sir. Beautiful! As a matter of fact, I don't think I'll be overstepping the company's code to inform you that yours is the nicest interior in this section."

Carrin felt a sudden glow of pride at that, thinking of the rows of identical houses, on this block and the next, and the one after that.

"Now, then, is everything functioning properly?" Mr. Pathis asked, setting his briefcase on a chair. "Everything in order?"

"Oh, yes," Carrin said enthusiastically. "Avignon Electric never goes out of whack."

"The phono all right? Changes records for the full seventeen hours?"

"It certainly does," Carrin said. He hadn't had a chance to try out the phono, but it was a beautiful piece of furniture.

"The Solido-projector all right? Enjoying the programs?"

"Absolutely perfect reception." He had watched a program just last month, and it had been startlingly lifelike.

"How about the kitchen? Auto-cook in order? Recipe-master still knocking 'em out?"

"Marvelous stuff. Simply marvelous."

Mr. Pathis went on to inquire about his refrigerator, his vacuum cleaner, his car, his helicopter, his subterranean swimming pool, and the hundreds of other items Carrin had bought from Avignon Electric.

"Everything is swell," Carrin said, a trifle untruthfully since he hadn't unpacked every item yet. "Just wonderful."

"I'm so glad," Mr. Pathis said, leaning back with a sigh of relief. "You have no idea how hard we try to satisfy our customers. If a product isn't right, back it comes, no questions asked. We believe in pleasing our customers."

"I certainly appreciate it, Mr. Pathis."

Carrin hoped the A. E. man wouldn't ask to see the kitchen. He visualized the Castile Motors Bartender in there, like a porcupine in a dog show.

"I'm proud to say that most of the people in this neighborhood buy from us," Mr. Pathis was saying. "We're a solid firm."

"Was Mr. Miller a customer of yours?" Carrin asked.

"That fellow who killed himself?" Pathis frowned briefly. "He was, as a matter of fact. That amazed me, sir, absolutely amazed me. Why, just last month the fellow bought a brand-new Jet-lash from me, capable of doing three hundred and fifty miles an hour on a straightaway. He was as happy as a kid over it, and then to go and do a thing like that! Of course, the Jet-lash brought up his debt a little."

"Of course."

"But what did that matter? He had hanged every luxury in the world. And then he went and hanged himself."

"Hanged himself?"

"Yes," Pathis said, the frown coming back. "Every modern convenience in his house, and he hanged himself with a piece of rope. Probably unbalanced for a long time."

The frown slid off his face, and the customary smile replaced it. "But enough of that! Let's talk about you."

The smile widened as Pathis opened his briefcase. "Now, then, your account. You owe us two hundred and three thousand dollars and twenty-nine cents, Mr. Carrin, as of your last purchase. Right?"

"Right," Carrin said, remembering the amount from his own papers. "Here's my installment."

He handed Pathis an envelope, which the man checked and put in his pocket.

"Fine. Now you know, Mr. Carrin, that you won't live long enough to pay us the full two hundred thousand, don't you?"

"No, I don't suppose I will," Carrin said soberly.

He was only thirty-nine, with a full hundred years of life before him, thanks to the marvels of medical science. But at a salary of three thousand a year, he still couldn't pay it all off and have enough to support a family at the same time.

"Of course, we would not want to deprive you of necessities. To say nothing of the terrific items that are coming out next year. Things you wouldn't want to miss, sir!"

Mr. Carrin nodded. Certainly he wanted new items.

"Well, suppose we make the customary arrangement. If you will just sign over your son's earnings for the first thirty years of his adult life, we can easily arrange credit for you."

Mr. Pathis whipped the papers out of his briefcase and spread them in front of Carrin.

"If you'll just sign here, sir."

"Well," Carrin said, "I'm not sure. I'd like to give the boy a start in life, not saddle him with—"

"But my dear sir," Pathis interposed, "this is for your son as well. He lives here, doesn't he? He has a right to enjoy the luxuries, the marvels of science."

"Sure," Carrin said. "Only—"

"Why, sir, today the average man is living like a king. A hundred years ago the richest man in the world couldn't buy what any ordinary citizen possesses at present. You mustn't look upon it as a debt. It's an investment."

"That's true," Carrin said dubiously

He thought about his son and his rocket ship models, his star charts, his maps. Would it be right? he asked himself.

"What's wrong?" Pathis asked cheerfully.

"Well, I was just wondering," Carrin said. "Signing over my son's earnings—you don't think I'm getting in a little too deep, do you?"

"Too deep? My dear sir!" Pathis exploded into laughter. "Do you know Mellon down the block? Well, don't say I said it, but he's already mortgaged his grandchildren's salary for their full life-expectancy! And he doesn't have half the goods he's made up his mind to own! We'll work out something for him. Service to the customer is our job and we know it well."

Carrin wavered visibly.

"And after you're gone, sir, they'll all belong to your son."

That was true, Carrin thought. His son would have all the marvelous things that filled the house. And after all, it was only thirty years out of a life expectancy of a hundred and fifty.

He signed with a flourish.

"Excellent!" Pathis said. "And by the way, has your home got an A. E. Master-operator?"

It hadn't. Pathis explained that a Master-operator was new this year, a stupendous advance in scientific engineering. It was designed to take over all the functions of housecleaning and cooking, without its owner having to lift a finger.

"Instead of running around all day, pushing half a dozen different buttons, with the Master-operator all you have to do is push *one!* A remarkable achievement!"

Since it was only five hundred and thirty-five dollars, Carrin signed for one, having it added to his son's debt.

Right's right, he thought, walking Pathis to the door. This house will be Billy's some day. His and his wife's. They certainly will want everything up-to-date.

Just one button, he thought. That *would* be a time-saver!

After Pathis left, Carrin sat back in an adjustable chair and turned on the solido. After twisting the Ezi-dial, he discovered that there was nothing he wanted to see. He tilted back the chair and took a nap.

The something on his mind was still bothering him.

"Hello, darling!" He awoke to find his wife was home. She kissed him on the ear. "Look."

She had bought an A. E. Sexitizer-negligee. He was pleasantly surprised that that was all she had bought. Usually, Leela returned from shopping laden down.

"It's lovely," he said.

She bent over for a kiss, then giggled—a habit he knew she had picked up from the latest popular solido star. He wished she hadn't.

"Going to dial supper," she said, and went to the kitchen. Carrin smiled, thinking that soon she would be able to dial the meals without moving out of the living room. He settled back in his chair, and his son walked in.

"How's it going, Son?" he asked heartily.

"All right," Billy answered listlessly.

"What'sa matter, Son?" The boy stared at his feet, not answering. "Come on, tell Dad what's the trouble."

Billy sat down on a packing case and put his chin in his hands. He looked thoughtfully at his father.

"Dad, could I be a Master Repairman if I wanted to be?"

Mr. Carrin smiled at the question. Billy alternated between

wanting to be a Master Repairman and a rocket pilot. The repairmen were the elite. It was their job to fix the automatic repair machines. The repair machines could fix just about anything, but you couldn't have a machine fix the machine that fixed the machine. That was where the Master Repairmen came in.

But it was a highly competitive field and only a very few of the best brains were able to get their degrees. And, although the boy was bright, he didn't seem to have an engineering bent.

"It's possible, Son. Anything is possible."

"But is it possible for me?"

"I don't know," Carrin answered, as honestly as he could.

"Well, I don't want to be a Master Repairman anyway," the boy said, seeing that the answer was no. "I want to be a space pilot."

"A space pilot, Billy?" Leela asked, coming in to the room. "But there aren't any."

"Yes, there are," Billy argued. "We were told in school that the government is going to send some men to Mars."

"They've been saying that for a hundred years," Carrin said, "and they still haven't gotten around to doing it."

"They will this time."

"Why would you want to go to Mars?" Leela asked, winking at Carrin.

"I'm not interested in girls. I just want to go to Mars."

"There are no pretty girls on Mars."

"You wouldn't like it, honey." Leela said. "It's a nasty old place with no air."

"It's got some air. I'd like to go there," the boy insisted sullenly. "I don't like it here."

"What's that?" Carrin asked, sitting up straight. "Is there anything you haven't got? Anything you want?"

"No, sir. I've got everything I want." Whenever his son called him 'sir,' Carrin knew that something was wrong.

"Look, Son, when I was your age I wanted to go to Mars, too. I wanted to do romantic things. I even wanted to be a Master Repairman."

"Then why didn't you?"

"Well, I grew up. I realized that there were more important things. First I had to pay off the debt my father had left me, and then I met your mother—"

Leela giggled.

"—and I wanted a home of my own. It'll be the same with you. You'll pay off your debt and get married, the same as the rest of us."

Billy was silent for a while. Then he brushed his dark hair—straight, like his father's—back from his forehead and wet his lips.

"How come I have debts, sir?"

Carrin explained carefully. About the things a family needed for civilized living, and the cost of those items. How they had to be paid. How it was customary for a son to take on a part of his parent's debt, when he came of age.

Billy's silence annoyed him. It was almost as if the boy were reproaching him. After he had slaved for years to give the ungrateful whelp every luxury!

"Son," he said harshly, "have you studied history in school? Good. Then you know how it was in the past. Wars. How would you like to get blown up in a war?"

The boy didn't answer.

"Or how would you like to break your back for eight hours a day, doing work a machine should handle? Or be hungry all the time? Or cold, with the rain beating down on you, and no place to sleep?"

He paused for a response, got none and went on. "You live in the most fortunate age mankind has ever known. You are surrounded by every wonder of art and science. The finest music, the greatest books and art, all at your fingertips. All you have to do is push a button." He shifted to a kindlier tone. "Well, what are you thinking?"

"I was just wondering how I could go to Mars," the boy said. "With the debt, I mean. I don't suppose I could get away from that."

"Of course not."

"Unless I stowed away on a rocket."

"But you wouldn't do that."

"No, of course not," the boy said, but his tone lacked conviction.

"You'll stay here and marry a very nice girl," Leela told him.

"Sure I will," Billy said. "Sure." He grinned suddenly. "I didn't mean any of that stuff about going to Mars. I really didn't."

"I'm glad of that," Leela answered.

"Just forget I mentioned it," Billy said, smiling stiffly. He stood up and raced upstairs.

"Probably gone to play with his rockets," Leela said. "He's such a little devil."

The Carrins ate a quiet supper, and then it was time for Mr. Carrin to go to work. He was on night shift this month. He kissed his wife good-bye, climbed into his Jet-lash and roared to the factory. The automatic gates recognized him and opened. He parked and walked in.

Automatic lathes, automatic presses—everything was automatic. The factory was huge and bright, and the machines hummed softly to themselves, doing their job and doing it well.

Carrin walked to the end of the automatic washing machine assembly line, to relieve the man there.

"Everything all right?" he asked.

"Sure," the man said. "Haven't had a bad one all year. These new models here have built-in voices. They don't light up like the old ones."

Carrin sat down where the man had sat and waited for the first washing machine to come through. His job was the soul of simplicity. He just sat there and the machines went by him. He pressed a button on them and found out if they were all right. They always were. After passing him, the washing machines went to the packaging section.

The first one slid by on the long slide of rollers. He pressed the starting button on the side.

"Ready for the wash," the washing machine said.

Carrin pressed the release and let it go by.

That boy of his, Carrin thought. Would he grow up and face his responsibilities? Would he mature and take his place in society? Carrin doubted it. The boy was a born rebel. If anyone got to Mars, it would be his kid.

But the thought didn't especially disturb him.

"Ready for the wash." Another machine went by.

Carrin remembered something about Miller. The jovial man had always been talking about the planets, always kidding about going off somewhere and roughing it. He hadn't, though. He had committed suicide.

"Ready for the wash."

Carrin had eight hours in front of him, and he loosened his belt to prepare for it. Eight hours of pushing buttons and listening to a machine announce its readiness.

"Ready for the wash."

He pressed the release.

"Ready for the wash."

Carrin's mind strayed from the job, which didn't need much attention in any case. He realized now what had been bothering him.

He didn't enjoy pushing buttons.